LIMINAL TIDES

LIMINAL TIDES

Soumitra Banerji

Title: Liminal Tides
Author: Soumitra Banerji

ISBN: 978-93-92210-64-8

Published by:
JGS Enterprises Pvt Ltd
Imprint: The Browser

Publisher's Address:
SCO 14-15, FF, Sector 8-C, Chandigarh 160 009
Website: thebrowser.org
Email: service@thebrowser.in

Printed in India

© Layout and Cover Design by beagles
99beagles.com

To my dear father's divine inspiration...
this book wouldn't have been possible without
the atmosphere of learning and literary pursuits
that he created in the family

Contents

CHAPTER 1

The Bandhopadhyays

Few of the Indian gentry were allowed on Mall Road in Meerut Cantonment—they required special permission to do so. That Sunday, one such Indian dashed across in his buggy, with his coachman urging the handsome horses to top speed.

He was a well-known doctor on his rounds, and one last patient—a Captain, suspected to have influenza—awaited him. The visit over, he sped his way back to his sprawling bungalow about a mile from the Cantonment. It was a crisp December day in 1936, and the doctor was looking forward to becoming a father—to, maybe, his first son. Who knew?

The doctor arrived at the front porch, the carriage and horses spewing dust. It was a huge bungalow, with distinct 'In' and 'Out' gates. The central building was flanked by a left and right wing, enclosing a large, hedged lawn, with a central fountain. There were also some fields growing grains, vegetables, and fruits at the rear. The back of the bungalow had outhouses for the helping hands, stables, cowsheds, a garage for the standard four-door saloon, and sheds that housed horse-drawn carriages.

The house was full of activity, and the midwife was the focus of attention as the doctor's wife was already in labour. The doctor entered the makeshift delivery room in the main building. It was large, with very high ceilings and shining mosaic flooring, which the doctor often declared proudly had been laid by well-known and expensive British contractors. Attached to the ceiling were two huge ornate cloth fans, which, in summer, were pulled by workers through string chains tied to their big toes. They moved them by leveraging their legs, leaving their hands free. The room had an electric ceiling fan as well.

The doctor was not taking any chances. Even though it was winter, the delivery involved a lot of exertion for the mother. The fan was required, so the workers were asked to take their position outside the room, with string chains attached to the manual fans in case the electricity failed. He supervised the required medicines, checked if the tools and surgical gloves were in place, and ordered some of the ladies of the house to assist the midwife while he stood just outside the room to guide and advise.

His daughters Purobee and Surobee played around, running up and down the corridor. Old enough to know that a baby was about to come into their household and would be their brother or sister. They were secretly guessing where it would come from, and whether the new visitor would be adequately clad to face the wintery breeze. Surobee was sure that their mother was hiding the baby in her stomach. She tiptoed to her father and naively asked him whether she was right…and then blushed. The doctor gave a rare loving grin and picked up Surobee, hugging her tight. His younger daughter was his darling and one who could bring a smile to his otherwise stoic countenance.

'Yes, my dear little daughter, Krishna is sending a baby as a gift, through your mother. Even you and Purobee came into this family the same way,' the doctor replied.

The girls were satisfied with the explanation Their faith in him was so strong that they were sure that he could say or do no wrong. Both sisters went straight into the temple room and started a conversation with Krishna about what and how they wanted the baby to be. They wanted a brother, that was for sure. Everyone in the family desired a son. Well, almost everyone.

***

While Urmila, the doctor's wife, was enduring the pains and pleasures of birthing life, the doctor was staring vacantly at the courtyard ahead. As he stood musing, his elder brother, also a doctor, came and stood in front of him, a knowing smile on his handsome and regal face.

Doctor Debendra Nath Bandhopadhyay was tall and robustly built with prominent moustaches groomed to be curled upwards. He had sharp and incisive eyes with bushy eyebrows and wore a dark blue serge suit with a waistcoat, and a watch adorning its lower left pocket, which added to his imposing personality. He put his right hand on his younger sibling's shoulder and squeezed it lovingly—a gesture that said a lot without words.

He was a man of few words anyway, and, unlike his younger brother, far less social. Introspective, simple, and gullible, trust came naturally to him. The world was as it had been left for Adam and Eve, and everyone had impeccable character and no malice. Hence, it was an additional responsibility for the younger brother to safeguard the interest of his elder sibling in a country which was slowly learning the art of deceit and greed.

'Is the clinic going on well, *dada?* enquired the soon-to-be-a-father-again doctor. He had taken paternity leave for the next two days to devote himself to Urmila completely.

'A crowd of native patients because of the fast-spreading influenza, nothing challenging. The same diagnosis and the same medicines.'

'And how many of them got your blessings of not paying your fee or for the medicines?' asked the younger brother, with a knowing grin on his face.

Debendra laughed.

'Not very many today. They all seemed to know that doctors need money too. Another member is coming in, with so much of festivities to follow.'

'I need also to let you know that a British soldier came from the other side of the city. He had a summons for you to meet the Colonel as soon as possible. He said that the issue was of immense importance and prestige for you,' added Debendra.

The younger doctor was too preoccupied with his wife and the prospective new visitor to give more thought to the summons. Debendra sat down beside him and called for some tea. He was equally anxious about siring a nephew. He and his wife, Uma Devi, never had an issue, and such were the vagaries of medical science that both the doctor brothers found it difficult to ascertain the cause.

Babu Lal, the ever so faithful Nepali family retainer, ambled over across the courtyard to the main veranda with a tea tray in hand. The hot and fragrant brew of Darjeeling was loved by them both. Gazing into the horizon, they absent-mindedly stirred the potion making a tinkling noise when the spoon encountered the cup walls. Somehow, the melody was soothing.

Suddenly, the melody was disturbed by a sharp and shrill cry, followed by feminine laughter. The brothers almost spilt the tea on their clothes. The workers handling the manual fans stood up with excitement. Purobee and Surobee rushed ahead as a matter of right, shrieking and shouting with an unknown thrill, joy, and ecstasy. Doctor Narendra Nath Bandhopadhyay and Urmila Bandhopadhyay had become proud parents of Subendhu Nath Bandhopadhyay, the next generation.

***

And we travel an immense distance…rugged terrain…a different clan…with a completely different definition of happiness and life….

CHAPTER 2

The Rawats

It was a small hamlet of not more than twenty big and small dwelling units perched at about seven thousand feet in the mountains, the lush green and dense forests all around peppered with fresh snow in December of 1933. Patches of thin and hard layers of ice had formed on the ground, partially covered with forest debris of mud and dry rotten leaves. The hamlet lay ahead of Rudraprayag and Srinagar in the area of Pauri Garhwal.

Gawana's largest house was that of its headman, built out of stone blocks cemented together with a mixture made of lime and pulses. The roof was made of large square stone slabs cemented on iron girders placed in a crisscross pattern. The building was double-storied with a grey edifice, comprising five rooms and a kitchen on the ground floor and four rooms on the first, joined by a creaky wooden staircase. The front had a large courtyard, to the right corner of which stood two thatched cubicles—one for bathing, the other a dry pit toilet—both conveniences symbols of status, power, and prosperity in the hamlet. Who else other than the village *pradhan* could have them?

There were only two other households that boasted of parallel comforts—the Negis and the Bishts. All the houses shared a common spring at a distance from where the village ladies drew water, met, and gossiped. There was also a stream further ahead for the livestock. Sometimes ladies accompanied the men who took the livestock for grazing to fill water for themselves and wash clothes. The stream flowed through dense forests full of wild animals. For the less fortunate, a call of nature really was a call of nature....

The left-hand corner of the courtyard of the pradhan's house had a small gate that led to the cattle shed with about ten cows, two bullocks, and some goats and sheep. Next to the cattle shed were a series of hutments, where the pradhan's workers and their families stayed.

The medium-sized rooms of the pradhan's house had walls paved bluish-white with lime and floors that were smoothened and cured with baked mud. His room had the luxury of a king-sized bed with seats made of wooden planks, neatly nailed together and covered with a mattress made of beaten cotton sourced from the district headquarters of Pauri. The rest of the rooms had cots with seats sewn out of jute ropes, popularly known as *charpoys*.

The houses were surrounded by large fields, flat and in steps on three sides with a dirt track on the fourth, which was also the high street of the village and connected all the dwelling units and the adjoining fields. The track was bound by mountain ranges on one side, followed by fields, forest, the valley and then the higher Himalayan ranges further ahead, on the other.

The pradhan doubled up as the village moneylender, having a steady interest income apart from his farming and livestock. The other important person in the village was its priest, who boasted of a much smaller single-storied house with four rooms. He also owned an open-air bath which comprised of a cemented platform, a wooden stool, two metal buckets, and a metal tub. His wife would keep these full of water for the priest to wash himself at regular intervals to keep himself clean for the gods. Some villagers respected the priest more than the pradhan.

The pradhan, Thakur Pran Singh Rawat, and his two close friends, Ajay Singh Negi and Bhim Singh Bisht were also partners in farming and livestock rearing. They had formed a cooperative and jointly traded produce at Rudraprayag, Srinagar, and sometimes the Pauri markets. Smaller farmers also traded through this high and mighty village syndicate.

The three powerful friends never minded helping the smaller farmers since they profited out of the procurement and sale and could negotiate better prices on account of the larger quantities. Negi and Bisht also indulged in a bit of moneylending through the influential pradhan, who was more than willing to help his friends, and took that little cut from their interest income for the management services rendered by him.

The three, along with the priest and the pradhan's eldest sons, also formed the quorum for the village *panchayat*—administering equitable justice and taking care of the village affairs. The pradhan's election, appointment and formation of the panchayat were endorsed by the British agent responsible for the region on behalf of the Crown. Hence, the villagers took the pradhan to be the direct link to the ultimate source of world power—the *sarkar*.

Or the sarkar himself....

***

On a crisp, sunny yet windy morning, with fresh snow glistening in the majestic ranges not far away, the pradhan emerged from his room onto the veranda wearing a woollen monkey cap with woollen olive-green army gloves, a thick blanket wrapped around his lean albeit hard body. He sported a pair of rubber slip-ons over army woollen stockings. The monkey cap was a gift from his younger son, who had purchased it from the Chandni Chowk market in Delhi. He stretched himself in the cool, brisk air, admiring the fields and forests around him and the surrounding snow peaks and ranges.

Of late, things had been working out well for him. His produce had done well on his terraced fields. He had grown some *pahadi palak*—nutritious spinach that was good for his family's consumption and readily bartered in Srinagar and Rudraprayag markets. His livestock had some new births, and he had also purchased two healthy cows and a couple of mules for transportation. Moneylending was brisk with few bad debts. The villagers were simple, hardworking, and honest.

His eldest son was helping him with his political ambitions and was already a part of the village panchayat at twenty-three. He was the only son from his first wife, who died when Kadam Singh was still a child. The pradhan's second wife, Vimla, was kind and gentle and had brought up Kadam with utmost care and love. Vimla's son Trilok Singh was the first in the family to venture out to Delhi to study and work at just seventeen making the pradhan proud of him. Vimla was away at her mother's place in a nearby village to give birth to their second child, which the pradhan fervently hoped would again be a son. Three sons would be a great team to have, to take the family forward to new heights and economy. Having two sons had enhanced the pradhan's respect, his neighbours' envy, and his already inflated pride.

He twirled his long moustache and ordered his morning tea excessively sweetened with coarse jaggery, accompanied by his favourite *hukka* (water pipe). His only daughter-in-law knew his routine well, so the pradhan was generally a satisfied man.

Smoke was coming out of the pradhan's kitchen and from all the other nearby hutments, the ladies of the houses already up and about preparing tea and morning meals for their males and then for themselves. It would be followed by planning and preparing lunch—the bread had to be baked fresh in the *chullahs* (earthen ovens) at lunchtime.

Wrapped in a woollen shawl, her head and face covered with the same sari that draped her, Nirmala ambled across with the pradhan's boiling sweet tea in a steel glass. She was closely followed by the family's man Friday, Dhanua, carrying the hukka. The Pradhan looked at his daughter-in-law lovingly and blessed her after she kept the tea on the small table besides his cane chair.

'Namaste, pradhan,' said Dhanua, placing the hukka beside him and touching his feet. This was a daily ritual. The pradhan took a deep drag from it, making a gurgling sound as he puffed out the water-filtered tobacco smoke.

'How are my Bela and Shera, Dhanua?,' asked the pradhan, for his loving Bhutia dog and bitch. Native to the mountains, the large and aggressive canines sported long black and brown hair, which gave them natural heat in the intense cold of the region. They were excellent guard dogs for the house as well as the livestock.

'Pradhan, they will be with you soon, and I am going to fetch you some freshly baked bread for them,' said Dhanua. The pradhan used to feed them every morning, and both Bela and Shera looked forward to it.

'Today, they deserve some butter with their bread, pradhan,' said Dhanua.

'Why, have they hunted down a boar or scared away a leopard?' asked the pradhan.

'Last night, a leopard came down from the forests to pick up one of our sheep. Bela and Shera attacked it with such ferocity that he slipped off and ran away, pradhan,' narrated Dhanua.

'*Shabash*! My brave dogs!' bellowed the pradhan, as he saw them running towards him, their tails wagging swiftly.

Vapours condensed around their mouths as they half barked and whimpered in the excitement of getting their meal and master's love. They came and sat upright by his feet, their tongues hanging out, panting and drooling at the same time, looking longingly at the pradhan for their morning breakfast. They also barked while looking towards Dhanua, who was walking out of the kitchen with their butter-dripping bread in hand.

'Here, Bela, and here, Shera,' exclaimed the pradhan with love and pride for his two brave warriors who jumped up to grab their pieces of freshly baked delights. The morning treat disappeared into the canines' large mouths in a matter of seconds, and they lay down peacefully beside their master, enjoying the bliss of his patronage and the morning sun.

The pradhan sipped his sweet tea and ponderously dragged on his hukka. A packed day lay ahead. The headmaster of the village school would visit him with the school's laundry list of requirements and pain points, followed by the gathering of the panchayat to resolve the issues at hand and hear out the complaints of the people of the village. He, along with Negi and Bisht, had to settle business accounts. They congregated twice a week for this to avoid any gaps in understanding and maintaining cordiality in their relationships.

However, the most important event of the day that the pradhan was looking forward to was the arrival of his younger brother-in-law from his village, Dungari-Pant, about five kilometres from Gawana. His brother-in-law worked in a British trading house in Delhi as an accounts and collection clerk and was a wise man of letters and a respected figure in his village. Craving another son, he was happy to settle down for a healthy child delivered by a healthy mother. The pradhan shut his eyes for a moment and remembered the mighty gods and goddesses of the *devabhumi* (land of gods—Himalayas) whose benevolence had already given him the bounty of two worthy sons.

Finishing his tea and taking the last drags of his morning hukka, he got up to stretch and proceed for his morning ablutions.

***

The pradhan was a meticulous man, shaving and bathing every day, whatever the weather, with fresh hand-pumped cold water. Ready for the day, he came out of the room dressed in a warm, long shirt and pyjamas tied with drawstrings, and a coarse but warm sweater over which he had draped a thick woollen shawl. His feet had leather slip-ons, the tips of which were pointing upwards, with an arrogance parallel to his moustache and bellowing voice. The woollen stockings and the monkey cap were the same as what he had worn early that morning.

As soon as he came out into the veranda, he saw Naresh Bhandari, the village headmaster, walking into his house. Bhandari was a non-descript, middle-aged man, who usually wore an untucked shirt, trousers, a coarse and old sweater, and a short tweed coat over it. Leather shoes, looking tired and worn out, and an equally tired Gurkha cap adorned his knowledgeable head. He was one of the few people in the region who had completed his graduation, that too in History and English. He was also good in Mathematics and Hindi. The government had appointed him as the headmaster of a basic school in the region that had students from neighbouring villages, including Gawana. So, he had his hands full. He also had to visit families and convince them to send their children to get educated. Apart from all his administrative responsibilities, he also taught English, Hindi, Mathematics, and History in the school. Hectic, harrowed, and preoccupied, he had a team of five younger male and female teachers under him who were registered and approved by the district headquarters at Pauri and had passed their Intermediate exams, equivalent to the twelfth grade.

The salaries of the headmaster, as well as the teachers, were paid by the respective village pradhans, who got an education grant from the District Collector's office. However, it was the pradhan of the village where the school was located who was in-charge of the daily management and upkeep of the school, hence his importance for the headmaster. Further, the pradhan had to submit an annual report of the headmaster and the teachers to the respective department at the Collectorate in Pauri. In practice, the teachers' reports were prepared by the headmaster and handed over to the pradhan, and they were on the agenda of the day's meeting since the basic school was in Gawana's jurisdiction.

'Namaste pradhan,' greeted the headmaster, as he took his seat beside the pradhan.

'Namaste master ji,' greeted the pradhan with due reverence and respect. The headmaster had taught both his sons as well as his eldest daughter-in-law and all the educated members of his close and extended family. The pradhan was proud of the fact that most of his village folk were literate, at least till basic school, which was the eighth grade.

'Dhanua, get some tea and the hukka for us,' ordered the pradhan, while he took the teachers' reports from the headmaster and cursorily glanced through them.

'Hope all is in order, master ji?' enquired the pradhan, since his faith in the headmaster was implicit. Having only passed basic school, he could also not grasp details very well. They needed to be vetted by people who were trained for it.

'Yes, the documents are in order for you to submit. However, you can go through the report I have made for you to submit. As a matter of fact, I would request you to,' replied the headmaster.

'Master ji, you are a person whose character I respect equal to God. So please do not insult me by making that request,' retorted the pradhan. The documents were kept aside and the matter was closed.

'Yes, what else master ji?' enquired the pradhan.

'Well, we require more teachers. At least three more since the number of students is swelling, and we need to have two batches in series to run the school,' said the headmaster, sipping his tea and taking a deep drag at the hukka.

'And also, the routine monthly money for salary and other expenses.' Saying this, the headmaster handed the pradhan the accounts book of the school.

The pradhan went through all the entries of the month with a frown on his head, more out of concentration than anything else.

'The repair and maintenance charges are on the higher side. And don't you think that we are paying the chowkidar more than he deserves? Last week, the leopard picked up one of our good guard dogs while the chowkidar slept. The wild boars came and destroyed the vegetable garden behind the school building some ten days back. Please tell him that he can look for some other job in another village in case we have another such incident, and he is caught napping,' spoke the pradhan, trying to play hard.

For the headmaster, this was a routine. The pradhan was very tight-fisted with money and was respected by the district officials for this. Finally, he took out a bundle of notes, counted a part of it and handed it over to the headmaster.

The headmaster counted what was given to him, and as he had expected, it was almost twenty per cent short. Again, as a matter of routine, he sulked, grumbled, wished the pradhan a good day and walked off.

The pradhan got up, grinning to himself, satisfied to have saved some money from the education budget, to be used for the benefit and happiness of the village people. They all loved and respected the pradhan for this.

'Dhanua, tell *bahurani* that I am going to the village panchayat office, and ask her to send Kadam there fast. I would be waiting for him.' Saying this, the pradhan walked off with Bela and Shera trailing behind.

He and the canines got out of the small wicker gate that connected his house to the main village track and turned to move on towards the panchayat office, a reasonable-sized thatched-roof shed with a large courtyard beside a huge and old peepul tree. As soon as he turned towards the panchayat building and started to walk, he heard someone yelling and calling him. The pradhan swung around both with nervousness as well as expectation, since he knew it to be his younger brother-in-law and the reason for his visit. He was accompanied by a mule loaded with goods.

They almost ran towards each other and embraced in a tight and ecstatic hug. Vimla had given birth to Satendra Singh Rawat, the pradhan's third and youngest son, in a small yet comfortable and warm room at the Dungari-Pant village, aided by the experienced village midwife, her mother, and a maid.

The maternal uncle and father celebrated in the centre of the road in Gawana, clapping, dancing, and hugging, then walked to the nearest village liquor vend instead of the house or the village panchayat office. The mule followed with an amusing smirk on its face, loaded with the goods and goodies on its back.

***

The birth of a child...and that too a male...brings similar happiness everywhere else in India....

CHAPTER 3

A Soiree in Town

Uma Devi was the first to come out of the temporary delivery room to announce the new arrival. Narendranath, the proud father, rushed forward and hugged her tightly, and then touched her feet out of traditional respect. He made his way inside the room and gingerly picked up his crying and howling son and hugged him tight. His dreams had come true. Wiping teardrops from the corner of his eyes, he gave the baby to Uma Devi and slowly approached his wife.

Sitting down beside her, he cupped her right hand in both his hands and thanked her tenderly. His expression said it all—his gratitude, happiness, and love for her. Debendranath watched from a distance with a benign smile on his face.

He went out of the room and called out for Babu Lal, who was already by his side, excitement writ large on his face, and a smile that stretched from his crinkled small eyes to his lips.

'Here, take this 100 Rupees and get sweets for everyone in our establishment, and supervise the distribution personally. See to it that none of them are left out,' instructed theelder doctor.

'But doctor sahib, we all want proper festivities,' said Babu Lal, mischievously. For his team, no festivity was complete without liquor and meat, followed by music and merrymaking.

'It is afternoon now, Babu Lal. You cannot start your insanity from this hour. There is a lot of work to do and a lot of guests to handle,' said Debendra in good humour. 'And you should understand that you are the person responsible for managing it all,' reminded the elder doctor. Amongst all the helpers and workers in the Bandhopadhyay establishment, Babu Lal was one of the chosen few who could get his way around both the doctors. After all, he had been with the family for more than two decades.

'You can safely confirm a big feast after we end ours,' said the elder doctor, gently.

He walked away to the ringing telephone while Narendranath got busy with all the visiting friends and relatives, their wishes, and animated enquiries.

The status of the Bandhopadhyay household within the city and in quite a few parts of the country was that of great respect. They were well known in the elite segments of society, and to the masses on account of their profession. God had been kind to them, and they reciprocated by being good and helping others. The Bandhopadhyay bungalow had a well-established guest wing, which housed a regular stream of guests, and those who enjoyed this hospitality became strong friends and acquaintances for life. Narendranath had invited the guests that day for both lunch and dinner in the main building.

The central courtyard, flanked by two long verandas at right angles to each other, was buzzing with activity. There were also two dining rooms attached to both verandas, with the smaller one next to the kitchen and the store used daily by the core family. The larger one was the central dining hall used for more formal meals. At that moment, though, the smaller dining room had been reserved for senior and important ladies who would prefer to sit on chairs and tables for a comfortable tuck-in, while the main dining hall had been allocated to the important and exclusive male guests. For the guests, the choice of dining rooms for sit-in meals was a matter of pride and snobbery.

***

With lunch over, the relatives and guests slowly retired to their respective houses and rooms for an afternoon siesta. Narendra walked down the corridor to retire to his private study, to smoke his pipe and muse over various aspects which required his immediate, and not so immediate, attention. The room had a small fireplace where the ever-so-attentive Babu Lal had kept a few logs and coal simmering for his younger sahib's comfort.

Narendra sucked the smouldering Briar filled with some fine English tobacco, presented by one of his British officer friends. He switched on the radio and tuned it to the national news broadcast as a matter of habit. As an active follower of the Congress, he had close relations with both Nehru and Gandhi, who had been his guests on different occasions. Being near Delhi and a critical cantonment, Meerut was strategically important, and Narendra an important personality of the city. He was also close to Rabindranath Tagore, looking up to him as a guru and mentor.

Sucking on his pipe, Narendra picked up his phone receiver and mouthpiece from his study table and tapped to get the British cantonment exchange. Once through, he asked for Colonel Henry Jones, a good friend and an invitee for the evening soiree.

'Good afternoon, colonel, this is Dr Narendranath Banerji calling,' spoke Narendra softly into the mouthpiece.

The British had coined 'Banerji' instead of the traditional 'Bandhopadhyay' since they found it easier to pronounce. Thereafter, it had become the popular parlance for addressing people with this surname as 'Banerji'.

'Good afternoon, doctor,' replied the Colonel. 'I was about to call you up. What a coincidence and telepathy, my dear friend!

'As a matter of fact, apart from congratulating you, I also have some prestigious news for you. Looking at your position of importance and respect in this region, the Crown is considering conferring on you an honoured title, and I would like to meet you personally in the office to discuss the modalities. When do you think it would be possible?'

Narendra absorbed the news without undue excitement or nervousness. He was too seasoned and mature to throw any such hints. After all, he would have to consider accepting any epithet or title only after conferring with his peers and seniors within his Indian society and his Congress friends.

'We can fix up a time for the day after, Colonel, if not later. Will it suit your convenience?' replied Narendra, in an even baritone.

'That would be fine, doctor. Tomorrow would have been better, but I understand your family and professional commitments,' said the colonel with an adequate dose of reverence. 'By the way, I have ordered the requested liquor and wines to reach your residence within the next couple of hours. Also, the army wants to honour the occasion with the presence of our band today in the evening. Hope you are not going to mind our small participation?'

'Not at all, Colonel, as a matter of fact, I am honoured with this gesture,' assured the doctor, accepting the offer with dignity. He was aware that the British never favoured without reason. For them, India and Indians were all about games and strategies. 'I would be expecting your presence, along with your family, for the soiree today. Hope you have got the invitation which has been sent to you and your colleagues?'

'Oh! Yes, of course, and we would be more than delighted to attend. We are all looking forward to meeting our respected Indian friends of the city there, and bless the child star of the evening,' said the Colonel before hanging up.

There were some letters and telegrams kept on Narendra's study table as a matter of routine, and he perused them. One was important, concerning the title which the Crown wanted to confer on him. Narendra had his decision-making process well cut out—a meeting at the local level, followed by the popular opinion at the national level of the Congress, of which he was a politician in the true sense.

He made a few more calls to important local friends and relatives, to invite them and confirm for the evening. The preparations had been rushed. However, thanks to his large team of cousins and nephews, always willing to oblige him, the progress was immaculate. He was satisfied, despite his fastidious nature. He had a pleasant half grin playing on his face.

Sucking the last bit of juice from his Briar, Narendra got up from his chair, hoping and praying that all would go well in the evening, as well as with the health of his elder sister-in-law. He had to oversee the preparations. But before that, he had to check on the superstar of the celebrations, as well as the health of his dear wife, Urmila.

Narendra walked into his wife's temporary room, as silently as possible, only to find Purobee and Surobee playing with their new kid brother, who looked amusingly at them and their actions. Urmila looked on with love in her eyes. Narendra quietly joined the family, coming and sitting near his wife.

'Hope all of you have had lunch,' he whispered to Urmila.

'Yes, Sharmila and Chameli brought the fare for the three of us, here itself. However, I only had some boiled rice and *daal*, followed by a little sweet rice pudding,' replied Urmila, with a smile on her face. 'Till when will I be given this insipid and uninteresting diet?' she continued, without taking her husband's name, which she was not traditionally allowed to.

'Another week, darling, and then we can put you on more animal protein,' came a typical doctor's reply.

Narendra got up to leave, patting young Subendu. He had a lot of responsibilities to fulfil that day—his hands were full, and his mind was preoccupied. He got to the main veranda, calling out for Babu Lal, Bahadur, Nanu, and some of his responsible cousins and nephews, to take stock of the various preparations. Debendra was in the dispensary for the after-lunch shift with the patients.

***

Like all other towns under the Raj, Meerut had different preoccupations for different segments of society. The club, regimental dinners, soirees, balls, sports, game hunting (*shikar*), plays, mountaineering, and summer and winter vacations were only for British expats and certain elite segments of Indian society. The neighbourhood gatherings, drinking country liquor individually or socially, followed by the likely brawls, street plays, and huddling together to listen to the radio, were for the common man. However, most of the time commoners were occupied with struggling to exist and eking out a living.

The evening of 14 December 1936 was special, with the British officers and Indian gentry all looking forward to getting to the Bandhopadhyay Bungalow in their best outfits. Those left behind were trying to find out if it was by design or only an erratum, in which case they could wiggle their way back into the invitee list through their connections with the family.

Mrs Pandey was talking to Mrs Aggarwal about what she would be wearing for the evening when she came to know that the latter had not been invited. With a superior air of being one up, Mrs Pandey assured Mrs Aggarwal that she would get a call from the Bandhopadhyay household within the hour, which she got. Mrs Aggarwal's husband was also a doctor and reasonably close to both Narendranath and Debendranath. Hence, not getting an invitation was nothing but a slip. Such discussions and gossip for the evening were commonplace that day.

The British side of the city had an air of obliging the good bloke by being present for the occasion. However, each guest was privately excited, though not very British to acknowledge the excitement. The local drycleaners, hairdressers, and all the orderlies had their hands full. The ladies were too busy to even look into their husband's lunch, who in turn had to book tables at the Club.

The common man knew of the occasion, and one could hear various versions of the preparations and anecdotes of the festivity to follow. Some of them were lucky enough to have a connection with workers in the famed household and would be able to get a distant view of the celebrations, as well as enjoy some of the victuals snidely passed on to them. At least it brought them happiness and pride in their otherwise poor and strife-torn life.

For the few Bengali families in the city, it was a matter of honour for the community. They, of course, were all invited and were busy narrating their versions of their intense closeness to the family through some link or the other. One of them boasted of being a regular in Narendranath's team for the monthly shikar, though he only assisted the shikaris in changing their guns and passing on bullets when required.

The city was abuzz with excitement and more preoccupied with the oncoming celebrations than the family themselves.

***

The British military sepoys were at work from about half past four in the evening. A border with white lime was marked on the road on which the Bandhopadhyay bungalow was located to guide the invitees. At the gate, arrows were made from lime powder, directing the guests in. The ramparts of the complete bungalow within the gate were lighted with candles. Once in, the front lawn on the left, outside the main building, was carpeted with a thick red weave. The hedges surrounding it were duly festooned with bright red, pink, blue, and yellow streamers and balloons. The lawn was bounded by gas and electric lanterns on poles. These were permanent fixtures there but were lit up during ceremonies or festivities. The central fountain was also well lit up with candles.

There was a red carpet leading to the main room where the child, the star of the day, rested with his mother. Very few would be allowed to peep in and bless the duo since it was not good for both their health. There would be many functions to follow for taking blessings.

A bar was placed in a corner on the front lawn, and a whole lamb was being barbequed in the opposite corner. At the entrance, the military band had already gathered, and they were getting ready to commence melodies at the stroke of seven.

Babu Lal and his team were all dressed in white liveries, which had been provided to them for such occasions. Bahadur and Nanu were at the cooking area, coordinating the cooks who were hired for the occasion. The fare ranged from North Indian delicacies to English roasts and soups. Hot and cold beverages were there on offer, apart from a range of English liquor. The British establishment had provided specially trained waiters, suitably dressed for the occasion. They did not want any flap or confusion in the presence of all the senior officials who would grace the evening with their presence.

***

The visiting general and his brigade commander, followed by the rest of the brood, were there at the gate, at sharp seven. The military police were doing a good job with the parking of vehicles and horse carriages by the side of the main road outside.

Most of the Indian guests were already there to greet their British friends. Narendranath and Debendranath stood at the gate to greet the distinguished officers of the Raj. The soiree began with the band playing 'God Save the King'.

Beverages, liquor, and wine started to flow, accompanied by all kinds of vegetarian and non-vegetarian snacks—prime cuts of lamb, succulent kebabs, fried fish, marinated and roasted cottage cheese, vegetable and mince cutlets, and salad dips. Narendra was in an animated discussion with the general and his brigadier near the bar. They were fixing up the schedule for the next shikar outing after a fortnight, near the hill station of Nainital, in the Himalayan foothills not very far from Meerut.

While most of the Indian gentry was in attendance to their British guests and the most popular topic doing rounds was that of the upcoming provincial elections, the women went inside the main building in small groups to visit Urmila and the new arrival.

The entrance to the main wing was through a long corridor, and a little further down the entrance was a well-decorated table for leaving gifts before turning into the room where Urmila was present along with the newborn and her two daughters. The baby was in blissful sleep after a stomach full of his mother's milk.

The ladies came into the room in hushed silence, looking at the baby with a silent blessing on their lips and related gestures. They waved and smiled at the mother and then went out to enjoy the banter, giggling and gossiping while devouring delicacies, and sipping wine or soft beverages.

Susan, the general's wife, was the centre of attraction for all the ladies, Indian and British. Every conversation was focused or directed at her. Near the fountain, space had been created for couples to dance in case they wanted. The British always found it to be a very engaging activity in any soiree. The band continued to play some enticing melodies, and the general walked up to his lady asking her hand for a dance, to which she graciously agreed. They were followed by some other English couples, but surprisingly, no Indian participated in it. They were just appreciative, or forcibly appreciative spectators, clapping at the appropriate, and sometimes inappropriate, moments.

The doctors of the city were in one cluster, and one could see the Bengalis in another group with a superior air about themselves. Some lawyers were surrounding the district judge, who was another important dignitary of the evening. A few drinks under their belt had made the lawyers bolder and one could hear many shades of 'Lordships'.

'Lordshhhhip, Lordssssip, Lordsssrrrip, Lorrrdshhhhippp…,' and it carried on.

While all the festivities were on, Uma Devi had shut herself up in a room—she was in acute pain. She howled and cried, biting her lips, and gripping the bed cover on which she lay very tightly. She was having a fit again, but she was alone, with everyone busy for the evening. She needed to survive without any of her vitals damaged.

Debendranath walked over to the dining area to check the arrangements and initiate dinner. The layout had been meticulously completed, and the bell was sounded for the guests to join for dinner while Debendranath went off to call the remaining family in the main living area.

CHAPTER 4

An Offering to the Gods

The country liquor shop owner saw the pradhan and his brother-in-law walking up with a loaded mule following them. The shouting, singing, and clapping made it amply clear that a bottle of the local brew was required. Ram Lal, the shop owner, pulled out a bottle and walked up to the two happy people. The bottle was immediately grabbed without any ceremony, fanfare, or exchange of words; it was uncorked and went straight to the mouth.

'Here Bhuvi, your *jija* will make you drink with his own hands.' Saying this, the pradhan pushed the bottle into his brother-in-law's mouth, who accepted it with thirst, longing and excitement. Taking a few long swigs and with fire in his belly, Bhuvi snatched the bottle from the pradhan and did a repeat with him. Accompanied by Ram Lal, they looked at the mortal remains of the bottle, which was more than three-fourths consumed in the first go in two minutes flat. The remaining portion, too, did not last a minute, in the second go.

Then both caught hold of Ram Lal and burst out crying, thanking God, thanking the pradhan's wife, thanking the pradhan's father-in-law and mother-in-law, the midwife, the Dungari-Pant village, Gawana, Ram Lal, and the list carried on, till Ram Lal asked a basic question.

'Why are you thanking all, including me, pradhan?'

Hearing this, the pradhan disengaged from the embrace with anger and stood apart staring at Ram Lal.

'How dare do you not know?' he bellowed.

'How would he know?' lisped Bhuvi.

'What should I know?' whimpered Ram Lal.

Then the three of them burst into a frenzy of laughter.

'Ram Lal and all of you around, I have become a father to my third son! My family has produced three worthy sons! And if God continues his benevolence on us, we will not stop before replicating the five Pandavas. And then break that record too, thanks to the great Lord Shiva.'

The pradhan's diatribe continued while Bhuvi nodded in affirmative to all that the pradhan had shouted out. A handful of village folk, who had gathered around, agreed with him, shouting out in elation at the end of each proclamation.

While all this commotion was going on, the pradhan's two closest friends, Negi and Bisht, also arrived on the site, wondering about the cause of the commotion. Seeing the pradhan and his brother-in-law dancing and shouting was a blind man's bluff for both. Without any further inquiries, both the friends, Ajay and Bhim, as they were known, grabbed a bottle from the vend, polishing off almost half the bottle in one go, before grabbing hold of the pradhan and Bhuvi and hugging and smooching them. It was taken for granted that the pradhan was blessed with a son since the birth of a daughter would have been a sombre affair, more discretely disseminated.

'Come on, let us go home and have a proper round of drinks with snacks before we walk down to the Devalgarh Temple to thank the great Lord Shiva,' said the pradhan, lisping and halting in his speech on account of the effect of Bacchus.

It would be festival time for the next few days, and the fiery liquid would be the primary entertainer each time. It usually ended with one or more of the ladies in the house putting their foot down with heavy bouts of hysteria, but not this time. The pradhan had to have his way, not only in his house but in the whole village.

Along with his brother-in-law, his two friends, Ajay and Bhim, his eldest son Kadam, and the village schoolmaster, he launched into an extended lunch with bottles of the local brew. Dhanua got a jug of water to dilute the drinks for his master and his friends and then ran off immediately with the pradhan's shoe following him for some distance.

'You bloody fool, are you serving drinks to men or *hijras* (transvestites). We Rajputs do not believe in diluting our drinks. We take it straight from the bottle unless Masterji finds it too hard to gulp and wants water to soften up the punch. After all, he is an intellectual Brahmin and not a warrior like us,' scoffed the pradhan, twirling his moustache with a naughty smile playing provocatively on his lips.

'This weak brew is not capable of dimming my sharp *buddhhee* (brains)...hic! pradhan,' bragged the village schoolmaster, as he stretched to grab the bottle doing the rounds among them, and in the process got dislodged from his chair. He lay there sprawled on the ground with an embarrassed expression while the rest of the gang exercised their lungs to their heart's content.

'Thish chairrr is very unshtable,' lisped the master, and the gang laughed more.

Kadam got up and helped the master back to his chair, trying to look sober in front of his merry, once-upon-a-time teacher.

In the meantime, pradhan turned to the hurt and ignored mule, who continued to stand outside the courtyard door with the payload still on his back, having journeyed from Dungari-Pant to the Gawana Liquor Vend, and now to the pradhan's house.

Pradhan walked up to the door, petted and kissed the embarrassed mule, and dragged it through the door into the courtyard.

'Dhanua, you bloody ass!' shouted the pradhan, in mock temper. 'Where are your etiquettes? Can't you see our revered guest standing at the door with all the gifts it is carrying from my in-law's house? As a matter of fact, he is a very old member of my in-law's family. Another one of my brother-in-laws, you fool.'

To this, Bhuvi, the Pradhan's younger brother-in-law, nodded in agreement. 'Yesshhh,' he said, 'he issh my younger brother, Dhanua, you idiot.'

All this time, the newly crowned brother-in-law stood still, gaping at all of them, confused at this collective show of stupidity, while Kadam and Dhanua unloaded his payload, piece by piece. The master had fallen asleep on his chair. The food lay unfinished, and with the liquor exhausted, the bottles were left rolling around in boredom. Bhuvi sat there looking proud, with a broad smile on his young and pleasant face.

The steel trunk that came was full of clothing for the pradhan, Kadam, his wife, and his younger brother in Delhi; there were packets of jaggery, sweetmeats, dry fruits, bundles of fresh vegetables, and something which made everyone gasp. Bisht and Negi jumped up from their chairs and rushed to it.

'It is a radio! A big radio! The biggest in this whole region!' yelled the pradhan patronizingly, with tears of happiness getting ready to venture out of his eyes. He rushed to Bhuvi and crushed him in an intimate embrace. He knew that it had to be Bhuvi who must have purchased it from one of the big shops in Delhi. It was the pradhan's dream to own such a beauty, that too a Murphy.

Till now, Gawana only had a small Philips radio gifted to the village by one of the wives of a British civil servant, and it was kept in the panchayat office, to be switched on only by one of the office bearers of the village council. It happened at a fixed time, almost every day, with quite a few of the village folk sitting around listening to it, while munching nuts and sipping hot sweet tea. News, music, interviews, and every sound coming out of it was gobbled up. The first cot kept next to the radio was reserved for the pradhan and his coterie.

The pradhan disengaged from Bhuvi, wiped his wet eyes, and pounced on his new possession. Unpacking it, he extended the antenna and felt around the knobs and contours of the large radio. By this time, quite a few people had assembled to look at this object of desire and luxury, including Nirmala, Kadam's wife, and Dhanua, who squatted in front of Marconi's wonder machine, gazing at it as if it was some alien from the outer world. Bela and Shera stood there wagging their tails and barking at all and sundry to maintain discipline in this moment of ecstatic insanity.

The trance was broken by the pradhan himself, who straightened up and, with Dhanua's help, took the radio inside. After coming out of his sitting room, where he placed the new possession, he asked the assembled people to get ready to walk up to the Devalgarh Temple to take blessings of Mother Parvati (Raj Rajeshwari as she was popularly known) and her consort, the great Lord Shiva, for all his boons and bounties on him, his family and the whole village as such.

After coming back, the village would get ready for the evening extravaganza, which would include the opening ceremony of the radio if in case, with Shiva's blessings, the electricity did not play spoilsport. Electricity was generally available for a few hours in the daytime, and then again for a few hours later in the evening, though only a few houses had a rudimentary connection.

The crowd disbursed to prepare for the five-kilometre walk to the Devalgarh temple, washing up and wearing fresh clothes so as not to displease the great Lord Shiva and Mother Rajeshwari.

***

A group of about twenty men, women, and some adolescents, led by the pradhan and Bhuvi, left for the Devalgarh Temple. They began walking down a goat track that cut through some dense forests to a rainwater stream, which was safe to cross at a few points. The track then climbed up to a ridge that had a group of temples on a flat piece of land, at about 6,000 feet with a beautiful sweeping view of the valley below and the great Himalayan peaks above some distance away. This was *Devabhumi*—pristine, beautiful, untouched, and pure, with a naturally perfumed breeze filtered and catalysed through deodars, oaks, and pines. The temples were seventh century in origin as the remembered and scantily recorded history went.

They had started after lunch at about half past one in the afternoon when it was reasonably sunny and comfortable despite it being winter. The jungles, nevertheless, were shady and cold, so they walked fast to keep warm. All of them were hardy mountain people, so walking was never a problem but a part of life. Quite a few of them were walking barefoot comfortably.

The trek was punctuated by a variety of wildlife—from various kinds of birds, hill mynas, pheasants, drongos and the rock thrush, to animals like monkeys, langurs, spotted deer, black bucks, barking deer and blue bulls. Bears and big cats were also common in this part of the countryside and often attacked grazing cattle. But with a group this size, even the two dangerous stalwarts of the jungle were shy of an encounter.

As they approached the riverbed, they observed a herd of elephants drinking water and cleaning themselves while some calves played around their indulgent mothers. The bull was sniffing for potential danger, rotating its trunk and trumpeting at intermittent intervals. The pradhan knew that since the direction of the wind was against them, they were in no danger of being sniffed by the herd unless they were foolish to come close or be heard. They quietly shifted their route to avoid the elephants and decided to cross the rainwater stream further down.

The water there was shallow, till about the shortest boy's knees. Each one of them knew the surrounding terrain like the back of their hands, and after crossing the stream, it was all uphill, the shortcuts treacherously steep. After an hour of walking, panting, and chanting god's name, the group reached the flat platform on which stood the edifice of the revered temple of Devalgarh, overlooking an awesome sight of the valley and lesser Himalayas below.

The chill was accentuated by a strong breeze blowing across. The pines, deodars and silver oaks sang a haunted song with the breeze, while the jungle lore played its own tune. The impact of nature's music conducted by divine intervention was seductive. The environment there was a heaven that could put the cruellest mind into a peaceful trance.

The temple priest knew the pradhan well and knew all the surrounding village folk by name. He was pleased to see the Gawana villagers together and began arranging for a special prayer. The group unloaded the baskets of fruits, nuts, and sweetmeats that had been quickly arranged and decorated by Nirmala, Kadam's wife, supported by other village women and Dhanua. The atmosphere of inebriation rapidly transformed into one of religious fervour, with the chanting of praises for Mother Parvati and Lord Shiva. The last kilometre had been done barefoot, paying reverence to the gods according to prevailing customs. While each member of the group was carrying special offerings for the prayer congregation, it had all been arranged by the pradhan's family, since it was his thanksgiving to Mother Raj Rajeshwari and the great Lord Shiva.

The priest started to chant and sing, followed by the gathering, in chorus. Their eyes closed in deep concentration, while their bodies swayed from side to side. The monkeys and langurs, along with the birds and squirrels, all gathered on the surrounding trees and at the edges of the temple compound, greedily awaiting the fruits, nuts, and sweetmeats that would be consumed after the prayer session for the pradhan's newly born son, Satendra Singh Rawat.

It had been decided earlier by the pradhan and the other elders that Kadam and a band of four youngsters would quickly pray at the temple and then go to the jungle to hunt for a few wild boars or a blue bull. The surrounding jungles were lush with them. The other option would be to sacrifice a goat for the celebrations at night. Some women, along with Nirmala, were waiting behind to do the cooking. Dhanua had to collect all the vegetables, spices, and condiments required. He also had the onerous responsibility of shooting down a few jungle fowl to be curried by the ladies for the community dinner. Dhanua was an expert in shooting down jungle fowls with his catapult in a single shot. The fowl were in abundance around the shrubbery encircling the village, and popular game to freshly hunt and cook on such festive occasions. However, the villagers made sure they did not deplete the fowl population and disturb nature's balance.

Kadam now whispered to his friend, Pochi, Bisht's son, who in turn, nudged Raju, Negi's son, to proceed for the wild boar shoot. They were followed by two other village boys, as helpers, carrying their 12-bore guns and a few rounds of ammunition. The group of five quietly sauntered off into the dense jungles in the direction of their village, climbing down the hill slopes housing the great Devalgarh temple.

In about half an hour they were deep inside the dense oak forests with an equally thick undergrowth of lantana, making the progress painfully slow. At each step, there was a lurking danger of poisonous snakes, porcupines, and the ever so crafty, yet regal king of the jungles and the superhero of Corbett, Kipling, and William Blake—the tiger. However, they could anticipate the presence of the big cats by interpreting the call of jungle mates. Any sense of urgency shown by the monkeys, langurs, and birds, as well as the immediate barking of the muntjac (barking deer), was a sure sign of the nearness of the predator. At that time, all was at peace, and the forest was in tranquil silence and harmony, with an occasional echo of a monkey, peacock or muntjac call. Kadam and his friends knew exactly where the pack of wild boar grazed and could find them nine times out of ten. They were natural hunters, who only hunted for their needs and self-defense, and not for frivolity, which the whites and the native elite called sport. It failed Kadam's understanding why these outlandish game hunters made so much of a fanfare in hunting for boars, antelopes, rabbits, or else the big cats. The same was done without any fuss by his village folk, who had lost count of the number of cats that they had to kill to protect themselves as well as their cattle.

After about half an hour or more of struggling through dense lantana undergrowth, they could see an opening ahead—a decent-sized *bugyal* (meadow) surrounding a waterbody of stale and muddy rainwater, stored in a natural ditch. Such an opening was almost always a home to the various animals making it like a hostel common room. However, before they could get to the opening and take a breather, they saw a large and hairy black Himalayan bear about a hundred yards ahead, looking in their direction.

The group froze in their tracks while the bear stood where it was, sizing what it was seeing. The wait seemed endless before the bear made the first move. Someone passed on the 12-bore to Kadam silently and discretely, loaded and cocked to shoot. Kadam held on to it, without moving to aim, which would have caught the attention of the bear and would have surely ended in a bloody encounter. The wind was still blowing in the same direction, to their advantage. To Kadam's relief, the bear decided to saunter off towards the opening and beyond. However, they waited till the gigantic animal was out of sight.

Breathing a sigh of relief and thanking God that they did not have to kill an animal unnecessarily, Kadam and his group moved on. The meadow was not very populated, with a few shy spotted deer grazing around, accompanied by some monkeys.

The sun was in the process of setting, and the group sat down on the grass to relax and unwind, waiting for the wild boars to arrive. The time was ripe, and if they were lucky, they would find a group near the water body soon indeed.

With a toothy grin, Pochi wiggled out a half bottle of the country brew from his small bag and circulated it around after taking a swig himself, while Kadam circulated a packet of *bidis* (local cigarettes) for everyone to smoke. The liquor vanished in a bit, gurgled down, parching thirsty throats, and warming the cold and tired bodies. The bidis carried on, churning smoke. All this was performed in perfect silence, under the cover of a reasonably wide and old oak tree trunk.

After about an hour's wait, when Kadam and his friends had almost decided to move to another favourable spot, there was a movement in the bushes on the other side of the meadow. It could be a *bagh* (leopard or tiger), or the wild boars, or a bear as well. Kadam and his two friends, Pochi and Raju, were ready with their rifles in position, tense and focused.

The spotted deer kept on grazing after cocking their heads a bit to listen. Monkeys were still playing, and the birds carried on with their animated chirping. The big cat did not seem to be a possibility. A wild boar or a blue bull would be welcome since none of them wanted to kill a deer, which would be the last alternative.

The wait ended with the first of the wild boars appearing in the open. The battle was on. It was a reasonably large group led by the male tusker. The male smelled danger, sighted Kadam and charged at him. Kadam was in position, flanked on the left and right by Pochi and Raju, with the helpers behind the oak tree.

Kadam waited till the tusker was almost a foot away from him, and then pressed the trigger, immediately jumping out of its line of charge. The tusker rushed past him into the thickets and collapsed, wriggled, and then lay still. The bullet had perfectly pierced the boar in its temple. A bull's eye to make any shooter proud, performed without any fanfare or aplomb. Raju and Pochi, too, got their respective kills with equal perfection. Three Boars lay still, with the meadow now deserted after all this activity. The complete drill took much less than a minute.

Two logs were identified, to which two of the kills were tied longitudinally, hanging on their limbs; and each carried by two members of the group. The third boar was carried on the fifth member's shoulders, who also happened to be the area's wrestling champion, tall and well-built.

It was almost eight in the evening when the victorious hunters of Gawana arrived with their prized catch of three wild boars to feed the entire village for the coming two days, apart from the other delicacies being cooked by the village womenfolk, led by Nirmala, Kadam's wife, in the absence of Vimla, the pradhan's wife, who was resting after the recent birth pangs of her second child, Satendra, at her mother's place.

The rest of the villagers, too, were back from Devalgarh, and were freshening up for the long night of celebration and binge ahead. The venue of the gathering was a relatively large flat land surrounding the village council office, fringed by thick bushes on all sides.

The medium-sized hall, which housed the office, as well as its social and official gatherings, was serving as the community kitchen and dining area where the women were cooking the night's feast and singing in chorus while at it. It was a grey stone building, thatched with tin sheets reinforced by thick oak logs. Outside, two fire pits had been prepared to barbeque the skinned and cleaned boars. Chaman Lal, the region's official butcher had cleaned up the hunted game. One of them was preserved for the next day, while the other two were to be the roast for the toast of the day. The flames had already grown to reasonable maturity with fat dripping down into them from the spiced and marinated body of the boars, and a sumptuous aroma was spreading all around.

Kadam and his team of hunter friends had taken ownership of the barbeque. They were already there, freshened up and continuing with their fiery gulps, sprinkling some onto the simmering meat. Dhanua could be seen ambling across with the big new radio carefully perched in his arms, followed closely by the pradhan and Bhuvi.

The late evenings had the fortune of receiving electricity in the villages in that area, and it lasted for a few hours into the night. So, it would be some music, followed by the news, and of course, a nonstop binge of liquor, which had already started. Pradhan and Bhuvi were sharing a bottle of English whisky, a gift from the pradhan's father-in-law on this occasion, while they walked down to the gathering venue. As the music spread from the grand radio, a congregation of more than a dozen village males started to dance and sing along, latching on to their bottles for the energy and zip.

Strips of the boar meat were being taken off fresh from the simmering and roasting bodies and being consumed with speed while still piping hot. The ladies were served separately in a large brass tray. They were perched together on the semi-covered raised platform of the council hall, enjoying the male revelry from a distance.

Kamla Devi, the oldest among the ladies of the village, was above seventy-five, wrinkled but with a very naughty countenance, spiced with an equally naughty half-toothed grin spreading to her eyes, rippling through the two cute dimples in the way. Her husband had been staying with his elder son, daughter-in-law and grandchildren in Lucknow, an important town of the United Provinces. He was very frail and unwell, requiring frequent medical attention. Kamla Devi was enjoying a bidi with some local brew concealed in a steel glass while enjoying the sound coming out of the radio.

'Hey Arjun!' she called out to her son, 'Get me some of that boar meat!' she yelled again over the din, in a rather happy tone, aided more by the liquor than anything else.

Arjun crisscrossed over to her, by now reasonably inebriated with a good tuck-in of the country liquor and boar meat, gave her a plate with meat and collapsed. He got up again, brushed the mud off his clothes and himself, and walked off towards the barbeque pit around which the rest of the village males squatted, stood, or danced while listening to songs from the radio.

Kadam, by now a veteran of a full bottle, sang along, in a voice which would have terrorized a tiger into tame submission.

'My mountains, my forests, my land.... My beautiful land... how I love thee...tra la la...la la....' The croak continued from Kadam's throat, till suddenly Bisht shouted out to all to maintain silence. The night news had begun.

The provincial elections were around the corner, and the pradhan and his friends were eager to know the developments. The Congress was what they wanted since the pradhan was a Congress follower. The news would be lost in liquor and the excitement of celebrations, but the protocol of listening to it followed by some marginal comments was a necessary part of village life.

The electricity helped all those who were not interested in the news. It just pushed off, silencing the radio and putting the revelry on full throttle, with the liquor flowing freely. Nirmala announced dinner and people started trickling into the hall. It would be a sit-in dinner, the perch being on the floor. The males were the first to eat, followed by the women, as was the custom.

Dhanua and some of the farm labour served the steaming hot fare. However, the boar meat and liquor continued to keep company, and so did the animated discussions, a customary consort to inebriation.

'Lllong llllivvve Shatendrrrraaaa!' shouted the village males, shrouded in alcohol vapours, raising a toast to the newly born son of the pradhan with their respective bottles.

***

At another place...another time....

CHAPTER 5

A Bhadralok Affair

Dr Narendra Nath Bandhopadhyay was resting on the veranda, on his favourite Burma Teak armchair, with a vacant look on his face—as if thinking a lot, or maybe nothing. So much had happened in the past six years of his life, which had left sweet and bitter memories within him.

He was now the eldest in his family, with all responsibilities on his singular shoulders. His elder brother and sister-in-law had passed away within six months of each other, as if they had connived to do so, leaving behind no children.

Puffing on his Briar, he gazed through the fragrant smoke. It was a rare moment of solitude for the doctor. His schedule was always packed—clinical work, patient visits, inspecting his estate, meeting his employees, troubleshooting immediate problems, meeting political and other guests, tending to the family problems of his core and distant relatives who all seemed to be depending on him, and above all, taking a call on his investments and accounts. The list just carried on, leaving him just enough time for rushed meals and short appearances at networking parties.

He grinned to himself, recollecting the positive developments in his life amidst the turbulence of deaths and defeats right from his son Subendu's birth in December 1936.

Purobee had married a bright engineer employed with the Indian Railways and belonging to an intellectual and well-to-do family. She was happy with her doting in-laws and an ever-so-tender husband. The doctor looked forward to their visit every vacation.

A brilliant doctor from the British-Indian Army was to visit the Banerji household in a few days, along with his illustrious father, the principal of a well-known college in the eastern part of the country. They were coming to decide about the young doctor's marriage with Surobee. Both acknowledged this alliance to be a dream come true between two great families from two different parts of the country coming together.

For the elder doctor, it would be to ensure the continuity of his robust medical practice in the not-so-distant future, as well as sound guidance and guardianship for his only son, Subendu, who was now six years old.

At the same time, he was also quite amazed that Surobee, the young hot-headed prankster and the apple of his eyes was now to get married and bring up a family of her own. Heart to heart, he also knew that she was reasonably spoilt, emotional, and self-opinionated, for which, he was singularly responsible. His face broke into a grin at the thought of his overindulgence.

Subendu was now going to a local primary school. However, it was the doctor's intention to send him to The Doon School later, when he came of age. The school was not very far from Meerut. He was well-acquainted, impressed, and influenced by the founder of the school, who was a famed Bengali lawyer from

Calcutta. For a person of his eminence, this was an ideal choice for his son, although Urmila, his wife, was not very happy or inclined to send her son away to a boarding school. However, she also knew that she belonged to a traditional patriarchal society, where education only refined thoughts and behaviour but did not change the fact that the last word on such matters was of the male. Young Subendu, too, knew of his father's designs for his future and was reasonably excited.

While Narendra was lost in his thoughts, Babu Lal came and stood next to him, trying to attract his attention. There was an urgent call for the doctor. He looked up and heard the missive from Babu Lal and got up and walked to the telephone kept in the corridor leading to the main entrance.

It was from one of his politically active friends, Ishaq, a wealthy *nawab* of the region, and a close link to the Congress higher-ups. It was a Thursday, and the doctor had a confidential HAM radio session with the Congress freedom fighters' network at Dr Madan's mansion, which was virtually next door.

This broadcasting network was essentially below the British radar, and the doctor was the last person expected to be a part of it. Most of the British officers in the cantonment and Delhi thought of him as having a partial ear for their sensitivities.

The first dent in the doctor's reputation had come when he had refused to accept the British title of an OBE (Order of the British Empire) five to six years previously. He had explained that it was on account of internal pressures of a nationalistic group of native Indians, of which he was a part, and on account of his inheritance and legacy. Nevertheless, his social conduct was impeccable, so the British never had an occasion to doubt his integrity. He was an accepted member of many of their soirees and parties, as well as the elite shikar group. Because of this proximity with the rulers, he was of strategic importance to the nationalist Indians, who were pegging for complete independence —*sampoorn swaraj.*

***

Hectic activities began on Saturday—the sun was yet to show its full prowess at five in the morning. Narendra and his wife Urmila, and sister-in-law, Sharmila, were sitting outside on their front veranda surrounded by nephews and cousins and the core staff. The issue was the preparation to welcome the doctor's prospective son-in-law and his family. Everything, right from music to decoration to food had to be perfect, albeit ethnic Bengali.

Dr Ajit Chatterjee's father, Professor Bijoy Chatterjee, was very much a traditional Bengali from eastern India, which included both his sartorial and gastronomical preferences. The guest list also included the professor's eldest daughter Reba. The reception was to commence at the railway platform when the train arrived at the Meerut Cantonment Station in the morning. Narendra, along with Sharmila and Sujoy, Purobee's husband, were to go to the railway station to receive the guests in their car, followed by Ishaq's car. Nawab sahib was an integral part of the Bandhopadhyay household and, hence, a part of all important functions there.

It was a crisp February morning, with pleasant weather, though on the colder side. The front courtyard of the bungalow was covered with a roofed tent. The food, from breakfast to lunch only had Bengali dishes, and all the ladies of the house were involved in the cooking, with no outside catering. Bahadur oversaw the purchases for the feasts—fish, mutton, vegetables, nuts, milk, curds, and spices. An HMV manual turntable was to provide the choicest Bengali folk and classical music during breakfast and lunch. The Kalibaari's priest was coming all the way from Delhi to conduct a short engagement ceremony.

Sharmila was only slightly older than Surobee and very close to her. So, she, along with Purobee, also had the responsibility of dressing her up for the occasion. Everything settled, Narendra got up to get ready for his day at the clinic and then his other engagements.

Sunday morning was a frenzy of activity at the Bandhopadhyay mansion. People could be seen rushing around the length and breadth of the estate, either carrying various goods or going to fetch them. Nanu had two huge *mahseer* fish occupying both his hands, held by the tail, as Urmila inspected their freshness. Bahadur stood in line with a huge tray of freshly cut goat for Urmila to approve. Babu Lal had rushed to the kitchen with a couple of buckets of milk for the *kheer*, a popular Bengali pudding generally served on such auspicious occasions.

In the dressing room, perched in one corner of the house, stood young Subendu, being fussed over by Chunni Lal, his personal attendant, and Sharmila. Subendu had just come out of the bath, naked and dripping, running around the room with Chunni Lal, trying to grab hold of him to wipe him dry so that he did not catch a cold. He was the star man of the day, being the prospective bride's only brother, as well as the sole successor to the elaborate Bandhopadhyay estate. It had been decided by all the elders that he would accompany his father, elder brother-in-law and aunt to the railway station to receive his prospective younger brother-in-law and the rest.

Subendu was a mixture of a child, brat and snob, albeit a lovable and truthful kid. He would gradually come to know that there were many other qualities and circumstances, which, apart from the unadulterated love of his parents, his near relatives with some exceptions, and true friends, and having nothing to do with his intrinsic nature, were responsible for his overwhelming popularity. Till then, everything would be hunky-dory, and he would have the time of his life. He would enjoy his destiny of being born as Dr Narendra Nath Bandhopadhyay's only son.

Finally, Chunni Lal and Sharmila got Subendu ready in a swanky Bengali attire of *dhoti* and *kurta* of starched white thinly bordered cotton and fine cream-coloured silk. Sharmila also managed to put some *kajal* (black kohl) in his eyes, both for protection as well as to enhance his childlike beauty. It went well with his dusky complexion.

Sharp at six in the morning, Narendra was ready in his dhoti-kurta, joined by Sharmila, Sujoy and Subendu, ready to proceed to the railway station to receive their guest. The cars were waiting at the front porch, sparkling clean with liveried drivers. Narendra noted with pride, for a change, it was as per the doctor's orders.

***

The Banerji representation reached the station well in time and positioned themselves on platform one where the train from Delhi had to arrive. The Kalibaari's priest was also coming on the same train. Narendra had special passes issued for the first-class compartment for his esteemed guests. However, the priest was travelling in a lower class.

After about a fifteen-minute wait, they could see the regal black engine chugging into the station, dragging its load of compartments.

Narendra was fidgety and nervous. After all, he was the girl's father, and that, too, his favourite daughter. While waiting, he was role-playing humility, which, candidly put, was not one of his strong points. Subendu continued to ask him various questions ranging from whether Narendra had ever driven a train to whether he could grow up to be a train driver. Babu Lal had kept the floral garlands ready for Narendra to welcome his guests with. Sharmila would be offering some beetle leaves and very finely sliced areca nuts to them as fresheners. This was also a Bengali custom and a done thing on such occasions.

Hooting, huffing, and puffing the train arrived at the platform, coming to a gentle halt. There was a radical change in the complexion of the platform at that early hour of the morning.

Peace was surgically transplanted with hectic activity of multitudes pouring out of the train, to crowd the city at the next instance. In that great exodus, the priest was catapulted out of his coach, with his dhoti all but left behind. He was well caught by a coolie. Otherwise, he would have landed flat on his stomach along with his divine accompaniments.

Once the crowd had thinned out, Ajit, his father, and his elder sister stepped out of the single first-class compartment. Surprisingly, they had managed to remain quite neatly dressed, despite the crowd and the rigours of the journey. Ajit looked tall, handsome and regal, and so did his father. Narendra was both impressed and proud of his and Urmila's choice.

He had to be pinched out of his gaze by Sharmila, and with an embarrassed expression, he proceeded towards his would-be co-father-in-law. Giving him a customary hug, he garlanded him as was the custom. He repeated the same activity with a shy and circumspect Ajit, while Sharmila greeted Reba with a garland.

Subendu, as programmed and groomed, touched everyone's feet, and was immediately cuddled and kissed by Ajit's father. Thereafter, holding his hand, and peeping shyly at his would-be brother-in-law, he started walking along. While mouthing some of the beetle leaves and areca nuts, the complete group proceeded towards the exit of the station. Ajit, however, kept away from this and was happily sucking on a couple of cardamoms. The priest followed along with Babu Lal. Ajit, Subendu, Sharmila, Reba, and the priest settled down in one of the cars, while Narendra, Professor Bijoy and Babu Lal followed in the other car.

***

After about fifteen minutes, both the cars came to a halt at the porch of the Bandhopadhyay residence, with the Banerji Family members waiting outside with conchs, a plate of sandalwood, vermilion paste and dry rice grains. Urmila, along with Purobee, blew their conch shells. This was a Bengali custom on such occasions. She then moved forward gracefully in her red-bordered cream silk sari, towards Ajit, Bijoy and then Reba, in that order, applying a small dot of the paste on their forehead, blessing them in the process. With the customary welcome over, the group moved inside, along with the esteemed guests, through the corridor, to the front veranda, facing the inner courtyard of the house. The family, along with the guests, sat down for a round of freshly brewed tea, biscuits, and samosas after the Chatterjee family had freshened up.

On their way from the railway station, the two prospective co-fathers-in-law had a brief, albeit important conversation on the way forward to their relationship. Both were in absolute agreement that they should go ahead with the brief engagement ceremony right away since Ajit had to leave for Malaya in a few days in response to an emergency call by the British-Indian Army based there. Hence, there was virtually no time.

Narendra, however, wanted a more elaborate engagement ceremony with some more of his important guests present. Bijoy, on the contrary, was a more simplistic and principled person, with a frugal approach to life, and hence, they settled for a close group ceremony on a far lesser scale. He also insisted on a simple wedding with a small group from their household and no dowry or 'other than customary gifts' from the bride's household, which he thought to be an indirect form of dowry. He was against any extravaganzas or pressures on the bride's family being an ardent follower of the Brahmo Samaj, founded by Raja Ram Mohan Roy.

Narendra agreed on the face of it with mixed feelings of pride and happiness, coupled with some disagreements on the scale of the wedding and the gifts he had thought of giving to his daughter and son-in-law.

Bijoy, Ajit, and Reba settled down, sipping their tea and munching on hot samosas while gazing around appreciatively at the house and the estate, and absorbing the activity going on for the occasion. Even this reduced arrangement and revelry was on a larger-than-expected scale for Bijoy, and that too, at such short notice. Nevertheless, Ajit and Reba were gladly soaking in the atmosphere, liking every bit of the attention and pampering they were receiving.

'Urmila *di*, I have already discussed the critical matters concerning my son Ajit's betrothal, which includes what is very dear to me in terms of my principles. We, including Ajit, have liked your daughter. She is all that any person would like in terms of looks, pedigree, family, and upbringing. Now we would like to interact with her, and so would Ajit, who intends to spend quite a bit of the remainder of his long life along with his new soul mate,' spoke Professor Bijoy Chatterjee with a serious, profound, and even baritone. He was oscillating his right leg, perched over his left, in a crisscross, while he spoke. A sign of control.

'Even I would like to talk to my prospective sister-in-law and put my stamp of approval. Since Ajit *da* is not going to go ahead with the engagement ceremony, pending that,' squeaked the young and sharp Reba, her excitement quite evident in her facial expressions and glinting eyes.

'I would like to compare my brother's height with that of my sister-in-law, to see how it fits,' spoke Reba with a fair amount of excitement and intent. Bijoy kept silent, pursing his lips to suppress his smile at his daughter's banter, looking at the smiling Narendra. Urmila pressed Reba's shoulders affectionately and laughed.

'Urmila di, I have requested Narendra da to scale down the marriage celebrations to more than half of his desires since I am aware of his popularity and means. However, I am an ordinary college professor with limited resources and would like to be comfortable within my pocket,' spoke Bijoy, this time addressing Surobee's mother.

Urmila looked towards Narendra with a smile on her face, evidently pushing him to take charge of the conversation.

'Bijoy da, we are also looking forward to a friend in you, an extended and dear family in your family, and another son in your son,' Narendra put forth, very diplomatically.

Bijoy broke into a smile, got up and embraced Narendra, patting his back in an affectionate and brotherly manner. 'Agreed Narendra da. Now let the priest give us the earliest auspicious day for the marriage. Ideally, I would like to get over with this within the annual vacations of Ajit, when he comes back from Malaya in about two months from now.'

'Let us take that up after the breakfast and the engagement ceremony. We also would be more than happy to have the marriage ceremony as early as possible,' said Narendra, looking forward to one of his primary dreams materializing.

'But first, I and Ajit da should approve of Surobee,' said Reba with an air of fake superiority, customary of a groom's elder sister.

'Yes, of course,' said a smiling Urmila, while she pushed Subendu to hurry up his sister. He rushed inside to drag his elder sister out, as per his mother's missives.

***

A long table with chairs all around was the destination point for the short breakfast and then the elaborate Bengali lunch, spiced with the engagement ceremony and declaration of the wedding date. Breakfast was *luchi* (small round Bengali fried bread) served with cooked vegetables and chutney, followed by some piping hot sweet tea or coffee, served according to taste.

Lunch was more elaborate and in multiple courses, starting with rice and *shukto* (a Bengali dish of boiled mixed vegetable curry with poppy seed and mustard, made slightly bitter by adding bitter gourd to it). This was followed by mahseer fish curry, fried brinjals, potato and cauliflower; and then *kausha mangsho* (a dry meat preparation) along with luchi. To end the meal, there were a variety of sweets—*kheer, gulab jamun*, Lady Kenny, and *sandesh*.

To grace both occasions was the lady of the hour apart from all else. Surobee, in a dazzling *zari* embroidered silk sari, and a diamond necklace set with earrings and bracelets, all shining in the afternoon sun. Surobee and Ajit made a handsome couple, with everyone staring at them. In the background, a soft and lilting Bengali folk song played at the turn table.

Surobee was impish, friendly, and very loving. She had won the hearts of Bijoy and Reba in a split second. It was love at first sight for all of them, including the blushing, quiet, and nervous Ajit. She sat next to her prospective father-in-law, with Reba on the other side and Ajit directly in front of her.

The engagement was a simple exchange of rings and gifts for Surobee and all the close relatives, along with religious chants for the occasion. Ajit and his family were lavished with gifts ranging from exquisite clothing to ornaments and cash. The cash, however, was decently yet sternly returned by Bijoy, true to his words and principles.

The horoscopes had already been mapped and cleared by priests of both families much before the meeting, without which there couldn't have been any movement forward. Now the Bandhopadhyay household priest had to just declare a favourable date to end the proceedings of the day.

After lunch and the ring ceremony, Narendra and Bijoy sat with the priest to look at the auspicious dates according to the Bengali calendar. The most favourable date worked out to 7 May 1942, and that was finalised. Everyone congratulated Ajit and Surobee, as well as Narendra, Urmila, and Bijoy for the forthcoming wedding day.

Ishaq, Dr Singh, Dr Madan, and Sultan Singh were the few friends invited to this otherwise personal ceremony. They blessed the newly engaged couple and pledged all kinds of help and support to Narendra for the oncoming ceremonies.

On the destined day, Mrs Surobee Chatterjee left for Calcutta, along with her husband and his family, after a simple and enjoyable Bengali wedding ceremony. According to Professor Bijoy Chatterjee's wishes, it was a small affair with a few friends of Narendra and some British officers in the station invited. However, the ceremonies and the associated hospitality were near perfection for all those who attended. A time to remember and cherish in retrospect.

***

It was a Thursday evening in April when Narendra, after closing his clinic, went into his house to Urmila, with a large brown envelope in his hand. Subendu's registration application to the Doon School had been finally accepted by their Board of Governors and they had also mailed in further admission process details. They had to apply for admission after a couple of years. Narendra was clear in his mind on Subendu's career roadmap. He wanted a very British finesse in his son, to prepare him for the world, not remaining confined to the perimeter of Meerut. He had visions of an independent India, with its citizens having far more freedom to pursue careers, till then out of bounds or unheard of in the country. He could also venture out abroad, to Oxford or Cambridge to have a more international grooming there. Hence, to be a capable man of the world, in a new and vibrant India, the Doon School would be the right launching pad.

However, Urmila didn't think so. For her, an upbringing within and under the tutelage of his parents and close family would inculcate the culture and character suitable to succeed. She did not think it practical for Subendu to be distanced from his estate and its affairs, permanently or for long spans of time. It was a clash of opinions between a realist and a dreamer. In this case, the dreamer happened to be the male patriarch, and hence, his opinion prevailed.

Urmila played a happy mother and wife, and Subendu was excited at the prospects of something, the full gravity of which was yet unknown to him. In those times, the right to an education equivalent to one of the Chief's Colleges (Mayo College, Scindia School or Daly College), or on the pattern of Private Schools in Great Britain (of the likes of The Lawrence School. Sanawar or The Doon School) was only reserved for the elite Indians with a cultural, professional, and financial pedigree to boast of.

Narendra's family ticked all the right boxes, and hence, the Board of Governors of the Doon School didn't have any reason for doubt in unanimously registering young Subendu as one of their future probables at the Chand Bagh Estate Campus of the school in Dehradun. A proud and beaming Narendra put the registration papers safely into his cupboard, freshened up, and left for his HAM Radio session at Ishaq's mansion.

It was a reasonably long driveway from the huge ornate gates to the main edifice of Ishaq's mansion. The mansion was of neo-Muslim architecture, with arches and domes, and a fair bit of floral carvings and murals, both on the exterior as well as the interiors. Since the mansion was not very far from Narendra's bungalow, he had used his horse carriage as a transport, musing and looking around at the city's evening activities, while puffing at his pipe.

Narendra enjoyed his Thursday evenings with friends, which was not only the HAM session but also men's talk over a few rounds of whisky soda. The evenings were in rotation in each of the friend's houses, and it was Ishaq's turn.

Though drinks were not allowed at Ishaq's residence, by and large, this gathering was an exception. However, it was within the secrecy of the men's study, that too behind closed doors. Another attraction was the very ethnic and ornate hubble-bubble, which took rounds amongst the men present, making the room a bit smoky, albeit with fragrant tobacco smoke.

Apart from Ishaq and Narendra, the rest of the group present were Dr Ajay Singh, Dr Madan, Dr Caroli, Sultan Singh, an industrialist in whose business Narendra had heavily invested, Professor Dutta of the local university's botany department, and Virender Singh, an eminent lawyer of the district courts.

The HAM radio was tuned in. The session had already commenced sometime back and was pertaining to the preparations for the 'Quit India Movement'. The British Government had gone off the hook in imposing the unnecessary New War Tax to generate as much revenue as was possible from their Indian Colony to augment the huge deficit created on account of World War II.

As if this was not enough, they started exporting huge quantities of Indian rice without indulging in any kind of impact research on the grain stock available to the natives. Both availability and prices of the staple, as well as those of the other alternative grains, shot up, leaving the poor far more impoverished than what had been seen in ages. Theft and violence were on the rise, and the peasants revolted.

Hence, the Quit India Movement became a medium of protest to which the poor natives took to instantaneously, to give vent to their sufferings, angst, and frustrations.

Narendra and his group of friends did their best to avoid violent situations, at least in Meerut, as far as possible. Nevertheless, what gained momentum was the desire for complete freedom from British rule.

***

The desire for freedom simmered in other parts of British India as well...however with varied content and actors....

CHAPTER 6

Jai Hind! Jai Garhwal!

The pradhan's nationalistic ambitions had slowly started showing their true colours. He was more involved in managing the village affairs and the grassroots level politics. His main objective was to create a rural support base for the Congress and represent his constituency when India gained its persevered independence. He was a confirmed Congressman and had serious political ambitions, discretely hidden behind a veneer of simplicity and light-hearted indulgence in fun and frivol.

Kadam was controlling their farm and its produce and helping his father in the larger game, wherever required. He was attached to his village, and it was clear in his mind that it was here that he would be for the rest of his life. Trilok was working for a senior officer at the Government Accounts Service in Delhi, with a confirmed job now.

Hence, he had taken up the position of an anchor man in Delhi for his family and all others of his village. He was happily married with a son and a daughter, and both husband and wife knew that Satendra would be joining them for further studies and then a career in Delhi, preferring a government department once he completed his primary education at the village school.

Trilok had no love lost with politics and was confined to the happiness of his family and his village community. He had to work for them, succeed for them, and live for them.

Satendra had started going to the village school. He was good in mathematics and sciences and dreamt of continuing to study them till he possibly could. He was too young and naive to know exactly what to make out of himself as he advanced in life.

He knew, as he had been told, that he would have to migrate to Delhi, to his elder brother, once he had exhausted his studies in the village school, which was just another few years. There, he would study further and get a good and steady job to support his family, and do charity in his village, along with his elder brother.

Naresh Bhandari, the schoolmaster, was sure that Satendra would be the jewel in the village's crown, in climbing the success ladder. Till then, the highest achievement amongst the villagers was that of Trilok, who had a permanent job as a personal assistant to a senior officer with the British Government's Accounting Service in Delhi. The village also boasted of a few sepoys in the British-Indian Army, including one of the pradhan's nephews.

However, the pradhan, along with Negi and Bisht, were the trio who had decided to dedicate themselves to the cause of Garhwal's freedom from the King's nepotism and corruption, as also a larger picture of India's independence.

***

It was an early crisp Monday morning, and the pradhan had a visitor—a trader from Srinagar, who had some serious business with him and his team of friends.

Harideo Jayal was not only a businessman, but also a serious activist, closely linked to Srideo Suman, a leader, editor, writer, and freedom fighter, and through him to the great Govind Vallabh Pant, a leading national-level Congressman of great repute and respect from the Kumaon region of Himalayas, adjacent to Garhwal.

Srideo Suman was looking for leaders at the local level to collect and agitate against the feudalism and nepotism prevalent throughout Garhwal and Kumaon and integrate with the freedom fighters at the national level to actively support the cause of complete freedom from the British.

Harideo sat on a reclining cane chair, waiting for the pradhan while his porter sat on the floor with a large baggage of spices, fabrics, and woollens. These goods were bartered for vegetables, pulses and paddy from the pradhan's farms, and at times some surplus livestock as well. He had been dealing with the pradhan, his friends, as well as the whole village for years now, and had a close relationship with the pradhan. He was the person instrumental in keeping the pradhan in touch with political developments outside of the village and giving him and his friends a more regional and national perspective of the freedom struggle to overthrow British rule.

That day, he had come not only to barter, which was more of a cover but to extract action. The time had come for a collective show of strength alongside Srideo. He also brought along with him some editions of the Karam Bhumi Saptahik. a regional weekly of which Srideo was on the editorial board and wrote stirring articles regarding the socio-economic realities of Garhwal and Kumaon.

Pradhan came out of his room, neatly dressed for the day, and greeted Harideo with a warm embrace and a loving smile. They sat down to have some tea, sweetened with a generous helping of jaggery.

'We need to talk in private, while Kadam takes care of the barter,' spoke Harideo with urgency in his voice, which was low in tone, almost a whisper.

'As a matter of fact, I would prefer that we congregate at the village office along with the rest of your friends, Bisht and Negi. It needs to be highly confidential. Not to be disclosed even to your family,' whispered Harideo, talking rapidly, leaning close to the Pradhan.

'Kadam!' shouted the pradhan, 'come here immediately and take charge of the barter for goods brought by Harideo Uncle, while we take a walk to the village office and meet up with Bisht and Negi for further business. Once you are done with this, please come and inform us there.'

Saying this, he gulped the remainder of his tea and got up to go. Harideo followed him along the dirt track to the village office. They were silent, in their own thoughts and space, through the half-kilometre distance to the office, passing by Negi's and Bisht's houses.

The pradhan had a premonition that he would have to leave the village for a reasonably long time, though how long was too early to tell right then. The only matter of concern was how efficiently Kadam would run the family, farm, and the affairs of the village, in proxy and in his absence. Also, what would his wife Vimla's reaction be when she learned of her husband's departure for an unknown destination? She was the closest to him in every way and would surely be able to hazard a guess. He hoped that Satendra would be well looked after in his indeterminate absence.

With all these thoughts playing riot, the four of them reached the village office. The pradhan took a bunch of keys out of his pocket and opened the office for them to enter. There were charpoys placed around in the hall, where they sat down in hushed silence, waiting to hear from Harideo.

'As I told you earlier, pradhan, the time for action has now come. Srideo has organized a *praja mandal* (commoners' organization) at Tehri to protest for ending the feudal rule of the king and also to participate in the Civil Disobedience Movement called for by

Mahatma Gandhi to move towards complete independence from British rule. He is organizing a protest at Devprayag, the day after. So, all of you need to be there to add to the strength; and be willing to endure pain, arrest, and trials in the process,' spoke Harideo in a hushed yet audible tone.

There was a rush of excitement and emotions within the three friends from Gawana. They were the chosen few from not only their village but also the region. The pradhan's integrity was unquestioned and widely respected. This was the time to serve the country and grow larger than life in their self-esteem.

However, what troubled all of them was the reaction of their families when they came to know what the three were up to. Till then, they seemingly went to the towns below to settle deals on livestock and their surplus farm produce. It usually took them a couple of days, which was a usual routine followed every year, at regular intervals.

'We would need to identify at least one person from within our family who should know what we are up to, and against. He would be our contact point for all our families when the need arises,' whispered the pradhan, and it was agreed upon by all in the room.

Harideo had some reservations about confidentiality and the fact that these areas in Garhwal had a good number of people who were loyal to the British sahibs. They could not understand the efforts made by the freedom fighters and felt their lives would be no different with a change in government. They were certain that the British were better administrators than their fellow Indians, and they seemed reasonably snug with their sycophancy-driven feudal relationship with the king as well. What kept them busy was their daily existence and enjoying their present.

Taxes and levies did frustrate them, but some periodic relaxations in terms of doles and occasional festival celebrations gave them the necessary break from their daily fight against poverty. Then there was local hooch—a great equalizer. It was a popular saying in those areas: 'At sunset, Garhwal is at its best.'

What sealed the deal was Kadam. All agreed that he was a befitting successor to the pradhan and, in all probability, would take over the mantle once his father hung his boots. He knew how to keep to himself and had ample leadership qualities. He would be the person who would have a regular update from the three of them and deal with their families accordingly. As soon as they had decided upon this, they saw Kadam walking in to update his father on Harideo's barter.

Kadam had mixed reactions and feelings upon hearing his father's decision to play a larger role in the ongoing freedom struggle, along with two of his close and inseparable friends. The path of the freedom struggle had a very risky existence. One's life would be for the country and not for the family once one took the plunge. In a way, it was a proud, happy and yet solemn occasion.

However, Kadam knew his father's adamant nature very well. He also knew that pradhan had been toying with the idea of a larger role in the country's polity, suiting his values and passion, and had already decided along with his two friends quite some time back. Both father and son looked intently at each other followed by an intense embrace. Kadam broke down, and tears started rolling down his cheeks while his father kept patting him on his back, taking time to gain control over his own emotions.

'What will I tell my mother, and young Satendra, who is so attached to you,' spoke Kadam haltingly.

'Right now, they need to know that I am going on my regular business trip along with Negi and Bisht, and will be returning within a week,' declared the Pradhan in a controlled and certain tone. 'In case we are late to return, you will be updated by a messenger arranged by Harideo, and you should disclose accordingly,' carried on the Pradhan with the same steely certainty.

Harideo informed all that the team of three would be leaving the next morning to be in Devprayag by the evening. There would be a horse carriage waiting for them at the roadhead, which was about eleven kilometres of uneven walk through the forest from Gawana.

'Kadam, you have the mandate to be the acting pradhan in proxy, till I return to resume my duties, I will inform the village elders of this personally during an evening get-together, which you would need to plan,' instructed the Pradhan in one breath. He was in complete control of himself and the situation, which is why he had been the pradhan of the village, and one of the most respected leaders of all the villages in the surrounding area for a reasonably long span of time.

'Excuse me, gentlemen, I would have to leave now and, unfortunately, would not be able to participate in the dinner banquet tonight. Have a lot of work to do in too short a time,' spoke Harideo with the urgency of a man harassed by a packed schedule and walked off with his Man Friday and a mule carrying the goods of barter.

***

About ten village adults had assembled at the pradhan's courtyard along with Negi and Bisht and their immediate families. Kadam had announced this sudden invitation and the banquet to his mother, Vimla.

'Father is going for a week-long business trip along with Negi and Bisht Uncle, to the river valley towns below, which might augur well for our entire village. It is a crucial string of meetings; hence, he is calling the village elders along with both his friends' families for dinner and a small parting celebration,' Kadam explained to his mother, without directly looking into her eyes.

Vimla was a bit surprised by the suddenness of the journey and related activities. Her husband was a very fastidious gentleman who liked to plan everything well in advance. Unscheduled events upset him and were generally avoided unless it was an emergency. What emergency could it be in this case that had escaped her husband's vision? In case he knew of it, why hadn't he shared it with her in proper time, instead of taking her by surprise? Why did he not break the news himself, instead of using Kadam for it? Why was he calling a sudden dinner meeting of all the village elders? These were some of the many questions doing rounds in her otherwise simple mind, giving rise to certain uncalled-for apprehensions. However, putting all the complex thoughts aside, she yelled for Nirmala, Kadam's wife, to help her arrange for the dinner and the rest. Dhanua was asked to arrange for the vegetables and mutton from the village butcher.

***

The invited gentry arrived at about half past seven in the evening, almost walking in together, as a group. However, Negi's and Bisht's wives had come in earlier, along with their respective daughters-in-law, to help Vimla and Nirmala in the cooking and arrangements.

They were as surprised as the pradhan's family at this sudden decision of the group of friends to travel to the river valley towns for business and discussed this internally amongst themselves. Clarity eluded them, so they decided to move away from reasoning, concentrating on serving a good and enjoyable meal to the guests and family members assembled.

The males grouped together at the pradhan's front courtyard around a bonfire, dragging at the hukka and pouring gulps of country liquor down their throats, enjoying the burning and numbing sensation it caused. However, the pradhan and his two close friends were far more sedate and introspective than the rest of the gang, and so was Kadam. The four of them were privy to what lay ahead and were bearing the burden of concealing vital information from people nearest and dearest to them. While the congregation drank, munched on vegetable fries and nuts, and smoked the hukka, the pradhan got up to address the guests.

'Friends, Negi, Bisht, and I are making a trip to Rudraprayag, Srinagar, and Devprayag to strike certain long-term business deals with regard to our agricultural and livestock produce. I am sure that the whole village, and some of the surrounding villages, are going to benefit from it. At this point in time, it is only this much that we can safely reveal; the rest you will come to know very soon.

Also, I propose that in my absence, Kadam takes over as the acting pradhan since he is in close touch with all the activities and responsibilities, having supported and assisted me for a reasonably long span of time as an apprentice. In case you have any objections or a better idea, please do come up with it now. Otherwise, I would treat the proposal as having been accepted.'

The gathering was taken by surprise at the suddenness of everything. Some of them were a bit confused as well. They looked at each other, expressionless. Whispered consultations followed, after which Kunj Behari, one of the most experienced village elders after the pradhan, and a respected priest in the vicinity, responded on behalf of the others.

'Pradhan and friends, first we would like to express our surprise at this sudden journey, wherein we have not been given any time to discuss our village's requirements from a commercial standpoint. However, with experienced and able people like the pradhan, Negi and Bisht, we are left with no doubts that we are very well represented, and nothing contrary to the interests of the village will be committed.

'Secondly, as for Kadam as our acting pradhan, during the pradhan's absence and on his suggestion, I am sure that none of us have any problems. We are all there to assist and advise him in performing his duties. His capabilities as a pradhan are also not in doubt. He is young, energetic, and focused. Hence, we are happy to accept the pradhan's proposal.'

Everyone stood up, hugged and congratulated Kadam. Overnight, he had transformed from a happy-go-lucky youth, farmer, and a hunter, working under his father's guidance and tutelage, to a responsible adult, looking after the interests of not only his family but also of the village. He was excited at the new-found respect which accompanied his recent, albeit temporary position, but also nervous and sad at the prospect of his father's absence, hopefully for a short time.

The pradhan got up with folded hands and thanked everyone for accepting his proposition and reposing so much of trust in him. Another round of bottles of the country brew followed with some more drags of the hukka and animated discussion on various subjects, including Srideo Suman's call for a revolt against the nepotism of the Raja as well as Gandhi's call for total independence of India from the British.

The pradhan and his friends also participated in the discussion nonchalantly without anyone even guessing their involvement or role in the bigger picture. He was sure that his village would be proud of its sons, who were willing to sacrifice their lives for the respect and esteem of their land of birth and work. He was also sure that had his parents been alive, the blessings he would have received would have been a priceless talisman, motivating and protecting him in his trek to greatness.

A few drops of tears rolled down his cheeks, which he captured with the palm of his right hand into the privacy of his own sacred space. He then looked up with a smiling face towards all present, gulping down dredges of the liquor at one go before embracing Kadam in a congratulatory paternal hug.

***

The guests left well after the dinner. It was past midnight, and the pradhan had to leave at the crack of dawn, a few hours later. Vimla had already packed the pradhan's clothes and his shaving kit, soap as well as a bunch of neem sticks to clean his teeth. She had also packed a lot of potato-stuffed fried breads, pickles, sweetmeats, nuts and salty fries, for his friends and him to consume during the course of their journey.

The pradhan changed into his night attire, splashed his face with some fresh, cold water and sat down on the side of his charpoy. Vimla came and sat by his side, holding his hand in hers, pressing it ever so slightly, to quietly say it all, what words just couldn't express.

'Do well what you are going to do and succeed for yourself, your proud family and your beloved village. I know your capabilities and honesty in efforts,' said Vimla softly while enfolding the pradhan in a soft and loving embrace. Tears rolled down Vimla's eyes and made their way down while she managed to wipe them clean with the back of her hands so as to keep them discretely hidden from her husband, not knowing that he was doing the same.

The pradhan loved Vimla with his whole heart and respected her dedication and sacrifice for him and their family. He knew that it was not very easy to be the wife of Pran Singh Rawat. One of the requirements of being the pradhan's wife was to understand his larger-than-life size passion for his village, his state and his country. He was a people's man and his wife had to make compromises accordingly, and she came through in all respects.

He knew fully well that Vimla was not convinced with his alibi of the business trip, and suspected a hidden agenda. He lay down with Vimla closely snuggled by his side, enjoying the warm breath she released on his face.

Aaahhh! How much he was going to miss this....

The lovers did not realize that dawn was upon them, making both the pradhan and Vimla blink and get up with a jerk into reality from the dream world of soft and beautiful love.

The pradhan got up and stretched himself to activate his sleeping muscles, while Vimla went off to make tea and breakfast for him, exchanging a knowing glance. Fresh after a quick cold-water bath and a short meditation dedicated to the gods, the pradhan came out onto the veranda, twirling his majestic moustache. Dhanua had placed his piping hot sweet tea and stuffed fried bread on a small table placed in front of his favourite cane chair. After saying a small prayer, thanking God for the meal and the wellbeing of his family, he devoured the bread laced with his wife's love, gulping it down with the tea, comforting and warm to his throat that was dry and choked with emotions. No sooner had he finished this morning victual, there was a knock on the front gate of his house.

Negi and Bisht were there with a few porters who would be carrying their luggage down to the road-head, where they would be met by the horse carriage to take them to Devprayag, quite some distance away.

Dhanua handed over the pradhan's trunk and a pack containing perishable edibles to the porters, while the pradhan was bidding his final goodbyes to Kadam, Nirmala, and his wife.

Kadam's eyes were red out of the night's exhaustion, as well as overwhelming emotions, since he was the only person who carried the burden of knowledge of reality.

'For heaven's sake, be careful in whatever you do. Please do remember your family and your village. Both need you as much,' he whispered and turned away immediately to go inside the house. The stress had distinctly broken him down.

Negi's and Bisht's families had also assembled at the pradhan's house to bid goodbye to the departing group of friends. What no one noticed was that all three of them had discretely hidden their shotguns in their attire, fully loaded, and had also secretly kept quite a few rounds of ammunition in their respective luggage. The pradhan carried his smaller radio along with him, leaving the larger one at home for Kadam to operate.

They disappeared after being reduced to a speck from the village's line of sight, but not psyche....

***

It was reasonably windy, and there was a chill within the dense forest on the way down to the roadhead. The path downhill from Gawana was steep, cutting past streams on quite a few occasions. The pradhan and his two friends were soaking in the jungle lore echoing in the forest—birds, barking deer, monkeys and, at times, the crisp call of a leopard lurking around nearby, invisible to the eye. It was almost midday and they had walked at quite a steady pace for almost five hours with a few halts to drink water. They estimated they had another three to four kilometres to cover before they reached the roadhead, arriving before time, since the horse carriage would not arrive at the designated spot before three in the afternoon. So, they found a flat bit of terrain beside a stream, shaded by oaks, and decided to camp there for lunch and a short nap before they took on the last segment of the trek to their first destination.

One of the porters spread a cotton sheet on an even grassy patch, where the pradhan, along with Negi and Bisht sat down for lunch. Potato-stuffed fried bread, along with pickles and spicy cooked mixed vegetables, dal, and curd was the spread from the joint store prepared by the women of the three families. All of them were hungry and the food was tempting and tasty. A generous portion of the store was devoured in a short time. The three friends got up to have some fresh stream water and wash themselves up, while the porters had their lunch. They then squatted there to discuss further plans in secrecy from the accompanying porters.

'What would be our exact role in the agitation, Pran?" asked Negi, who like Bisht, depended on the superior intelligence and understanding of the pradhan.

'From what I could gather from Harideo, we would be regional representatives in the agitation covering the whole of Garhwal.

We would just follow him and Srideo in the protest, and fight shoulder-to-shoulder with our leader to achieve the objectives of freedom from the King and then the British.

'We need to realize that a free life without sycophancy towards the King or the oppressive Britishers is the dream that all of us deserve. It is our land where we labour to produce wealth, not to be consumed by the King or the British and given a few bits and pieces out of it in accordance with their desires, naming it social justice.

'The King or the British have not worked for the fruits of our labour, then why should they enjoy the primary produce?'

Pran was passionate in what he spoke, stirring the emotions of his friends to do or die for a free land which they could rightfully call theirs.

'We totally agree with what you are saying, Pran. We are the owners of what we produce. We are the owners of our labour. We are not slaves, or in any way subservient to the King or the British. We want to breathe easy in our own land of birth and work. This right has been given to us by God and can only be snatched away by him,' spoke Negi with passion and in agreement with Bisht.

They were prepared to clash with the mightiest and victory was the only objective. The three of them joined in a tight embrace and took an oath—freedom or nothing. They returned to snatch a bit of rest and energize themselves for the days ahead.

It was almost two in the afternoon when one of the porters woke them up. He could guess the time with the movement of the sun. The pradhan checked his pocketwatch and marvelled at his precision. They brushed their clothes clean, stretched their muscles, and started off towards the roadhead.

Within the hour, they were at Sharma Sweet Shop, the most prominent landmark on the mountain highway. The horse carriage was waiting to carry them to the next stage of their lives, shrouded in a mysterious veil. After having some steaming hot tea at the sweet shop, they started off on their journey to Devprayag.

The porters bid their pradhan and his two friends an emotional goodbye, before turning around and vanishing into the forests on their way back to Gawana.

***

The journey to Devprayag was long, arduous, and bumpy. However, being tired, the three friends were soon fast asleep, bumping along with the carriage, up, down and sideways. Negi was the first to bump out of the long slumber. A fiery red sun was setting over the horizon. It was beautiful.

The carriage man called to apprise them that their lodge for the night was about five minutes away. They were in the holy township of Devprayag, where the Bhagirathi and Alaknanda rivers met in a passionate embrace to lose themselves in one another, emerging with a new identity—the Ganga.

As the temple bells tolled, the carriage came to a standstill, accompanied by the tired grunting of the two large and healthy horses. Harideo was standing at the entry of the lodge, by the roadside, to greet the three with a smiling face.

They embraced each other with slogans, 'Jai Garhwal!', 'Jai Hindustan!', and walked inside the lodge.

The front door led to a corridor, which further led to a large, open, cemented courtyard bordered by double-storied rooms on three sides and toilets and baths on the fourth. The courtyard was already busy welcoming many visitors, who were coming in and settling down on the carpeted floor to listen to the speakers on the occasion.

The pradhan, along with Negi and Bisht, also settled down amongst the larger gathering after putting their luggage in one of the rooms on the first floor allotted to them by the praja mandal. The whole lodge was lighted up with kerosene lanterns, their sheer numbers making the whole area bright. Each of the rooms also had a lantern for use by its inmates.

In a while, Harideo came up in front of them and announced the schedule. It was already nine in the night.

'Srideo Suman and his team are mostly here, and he is going to address the gathering with the scheme of events and the objectives for tomorrow. He is also going to apprise all of us on the activities of the praja mandal from here onwards—and on our responsibilities and expected participation.

'This address by Srideo will be followed by dinner, after which we should have a much-needed rest to be energetic and fresh for tomorrow since it would be a long and tiring day.

Hope it is clear to all. In case there are any questions at this stage, please feel free to ask.'

Everyone was quiet. Harideo started to leave the dais when the pradhan got up to talk.

'I have no questions but something to say....

'We are all together in this freedom struggle, till death or liberty....

'Jai Garhwal! Jai Hindustan!'

The pradhan shouted, followed by the whole congregation including Harideo, as well as Srideo and his team, who had arrived by then.

Srideo embraced the pradhan, admiring his enthusiasm, motivation, and passion.

'You will be with me, my dear sir, tomorrow and thereafter... as my immediate support and compatriot. It would be great if you could introduce yourself to all of us,' said Srideo in a patronizing and amiable tone.

'He is the pradhan of Gawana, Pran Singh Rawat, Srideo,' spoke Harideo, 'and a close friend of mine for a very long time. A man with a lot of respect and credibility in the whole region.'

'And we are his childhood friends from the same village, Ajay Singh Negi and Bhim Singh Bisht,' shouted out Negi in a proud and elated tone.

Srideo acknowledged both with an embrace.

For the three of them, it was the proudest moment for Gawana, thanks to the leadership qualities of the pradhan. Srideo, moved on to the dais, in the front of the courtyard, to address all.

'Friends, I think everyone knows why we are assembled here. Anyone who doesn't need not be a part of this congregation since I do not want anyone joining us without the desire and passion for freedom. If a person doesn't feel the pain of captivity, he should not waste his time and life to fight against it.

'So, people who truly have the zest, to the extent of sacrificing their lives for a free Garhwal and Hindustan, would wake up at the crack of dawn and get dressed in neat and clean clothes, to walk with me to the Collectorate.

'There we are going to put forth our point of view on the atrocities of the Raja and the British regime. We would communicate the pains of abject poverty we have to deal with on account of high taxes and deficiency of staple grain.

'Even though we labour in the fields to grow the crop, it is enjoyed by people who do not even know from where and how it comes to their plate. We refuse to be providers for the King, the British and the world, while our women and children languish in abject poverty.

'We would communicate our resolve on peaceful non-cooperation, as has been dictated by Mahatma Gandhi. We will not pay taxes and share our produce with the King or the British Government. Who is with me on this resolve?' shouted Srideo.

'All of us are with you in this resolve, in life as well as in death,' shouted out the rest, led by the pradhan and Harideo. The congregation, which mostly comprised of Hindus, with a small group of Muslims, were unified in cause. The differences between the Congress and the Muslim League at the national level were not at all evident in this part of India.

The gathering dispersed for a traditional Garhwali dinner of rice, lentils, mixed vegetables, and mango pickles. It was a spicy and enjoyable fair for the tired and hungry revolutionaries.

***

The pradhan stood by the window of their dormitory, which housed seven beds and seven occupants, including his two friends. He had scarcely slept, with thoughts intermittently merging into dreams. He idly gazed at the newly born Ganga, with her parents meeting only a few yards back. She played childish pranks, full of energy, gushing down to her increasing age and maturity with a deafening sound. Playing a blissful orchestra with the sound of the Ganga were the multiple bells tolling at the numerous temples, welcoming and anointing the sun, fresh from sleep, announcing a new dawn.

The pradhan habitually twirled his moustache and thought of his new struggle, his new responsibility and passion—freedom. He sincerely felt that the idea of a whole unified India would become a reality for his children to see and breathe in. They all deserved to call it their motherland and mould it the way they wanted to—create wealth in it and generate prosperity for themselves and all fellow Indians.

What would be the expanse of India, what would be its boundaries, was something the pradhan could not quantify. However, he knew it would be huge, with people of all races, religions, and creeds residing within its embrace. He knew it would be a welcoming nation, governed by Hindu philosophy, open to and respecting all religions as its own.

In his village and all the surrounding villages where he had travelled, he had never seen people fighting over or disputing gods and goddesses. Ram and Rahim stayed amicably together. When the Muslims had invaded from the northwest and ruled Hindustan from Delhi, they had all assimilated into the singular idea and concept of India as one nation, which unified, was now craving for a free existence from the British.

He wanted an elected government governing this extensive motherland, instead of being ruled by multiple kings taking their kingdoms in varied directions, always at war with each other, ruling by exploiting their subjects, enjoying their efforts and prospering on their account. He was loath to pay undue obeisance to the King and his degenerate family, who lived on the wealth created by him and his likes.

The pradhan was fascinated and drawn towards the great stalwarts like Mahatma Gandhi, Jawahar Lal Nehru, Govind Vallabh Pant, Bal Gangadhar Tilak, Gokhale, and Maulana Azad, who had decided to sacrifice their lives and freedom for Independence. He had heard that Jinnah was musing on a separate nation for his Muslim brothers by forming a Muslim League. But he also knew that not many Muslims were with him in this. At least not the ones he knew, directly or indirectly.

He was jolted back to reality by Bisht, who stood beside him, informing him that everyone was ready for the march. There were about thirty men assembled in front of the lodge, all excited and ready for the charge. Some policemen could also be seen lurking around in close vicinity, sceptically observing from a distance. Being natives, they were praying to God to avoid any untoward incident so that they would not be compelled to use force or open fire.

Srideo was all geared up in his crisp white cotton kurta pyjama. Standing along with him were Harideo and the pradhan, in the same dress as Srideo. Most of them were attired similarly.

Srideo started the day's proceedings without delay.

'Friends, we all know our objectives. We would not indulge in any violence. These are clear instructions from Gandhi ji and Pant ji. We would be moving in a single file, chanting our desire for a free Garhwal and a free Hindustan.

'I am carrying our charter of demands, which include freedom from the King's rule in Garhwal and the British Rule in Hindustan. It also contains a request for an end to the War Tax, as well as proper availability of food grains at reasonable prices at the local markets.

'Harideo, Pran Singh, and I will lead the praja mandal, holding placards calling out to free Garhwal from the King's rule, corruption and nepotism; and to free Hindustan from the British. The rest of the procession will follow our chant. In case we are stopped by the police, we will continue to walk without creating violence or retorting back with aggression.

'Finally, as a mark of our protest, we will all court arrest. Anyone who wants to withdraw should please do so now since one step hereafter will be one step too many to withdraw later.'

The assembly had already made up its mind to go the way to complete freedom, with the necessary passion, zeal, and sense of sacrifice.

'We want freedom from the King and the British!'

'We want freedom from corruption and harassment!'

'We want freedom from arbitrary taxes!'

'We want grains at lower prices!'

The praja mandal shouted slogans in a chorus as they progressed, walking rapidly with long coordinated strides. The procession walked up to a crossing on the main highway about half a kilometre away and then turned left, along the hill face, straight to the court complex and the Collector's office. The police followed at a discrete distance but had increased in numbers.

Suddenly, they found barricades, with armed police standing in an attack position to welcome the procession. They already had the necessary information through local intelligence gathering.

The pradhan, along with Srideo and Harideo, had gone into a passionate trance, working up the same with the rest of the procession. The protest had reached a crescendo, and a barricade was the least of their worries. The pradhan was secretly carrying a holstered shotgun around his waist over his pyjamas, discretely hidden by his thick cotton kurta. He knew it would not be wise to expose it at this juncture since Srideo had time and again warned against any act or show of aggression whatsoever. He perceived it to be nothing but a passive security measure that might come in handy under extreme circumstances. He had no way of knowing that the tool of destruction could have a mind of its own.

By the time the procession had reached the barricade, every member of the procession was one with the issues and they pierced through the obstruction like a sharp knife making its way through a slice of soft butter. The police started a baton charge lashing out at the group at large.

Srideo was the first to get a blow on his shoulder but moved on grimacing a bit. Harideo got it on his shin, with a cracking of a sound and heaped on to the ground. However, he got up with the support of the pradhan and limped onwards. With the pain and swelling, a fracture was obvious. The pradhan turned around to rally the rest of the procession including his friends, Negi and Bisht. Negi was on the ground with a gash on his head.

The pradhan hoisted him up and tied his handkerchief tightly on Negi's head to stop the bleeding and requested Bisht to take him along to the Collector's office with the rest, while he supported the remaining people. What Pran did not realize was that his shotgun holster had come loose in all the activity and frenzy, and the revolver was hanging out. One more jerk and it fell loose on the ground, catching the pradhan's attention. He looked around and picked it up immediately. What he did not notice was that a policeman was staring at the pradhan throughout this activity of the falling revolver and his picking it up.

He charged at him with his gun and bayonet when the nervous pradhan opened fire with his shotgun. A bullet struck the policeman on his right thigh when he fired at random at the pradhan. Within a flash, the pradhan was riddled with bullets, his blood all over, including a neat hole in his temple.

Some of his colleagues caught hold of him and placed a stumbling pradhan on the ground. Harideo and Bisht looked back to witness all the action and rushed towards their beloved friend. The pradhan lay there with the world ebbing away from his eyesight. Morphing, distorting and then disappearing.

Negi and Bisht, along with Harideo and now Srideo sat beside him, comforting him with assurances of a free country and Garhwal. The two friends howled and yelled, catching hold of their dear friend from childhood, to jerk him to life.

'Jai Hind! Jai Garhwal!' murmured a fading Pran.

'Jai Hind! Jai Garhwal!' rallied all, including Srideo, Harideo, Negi, and Bisht.

'I.... I...gift my freedom to all of you.... To my wife...my children...my friendssssss....'

He breathed his last, unfortunately, before he could taste the fruits of freedom. Before he could felicitate freedom as Gawana's living pradhan. However, he would be honoured and cast in history as one who fought valiantly like a true Rajput, for the peace and prosperity of his beloved village, his Garhwal and his country.

They carried the valiant son of the soil in their arms, with his spirit now soaring in ether, giving them all the strength and rejuvenation to fight till their end or freedom, which ever came earlier. The gathering was arrested, while the pradhan was free—entirely free from all the dirt and humility of bondage.

The Collector promised arrangements for Pradhan's body to be transported to his village, and cremated with full honours. Srideo's protest had made them agree to allow Negi and Bisht to be present, under police guard, at their friend's cremation in Gawana. They all pledged to renew their struggle for freedom with much greater vigour and determination, with tears pouring down their cheeks.

***

Life flows its own course.... Joy and sorrow coexist...it is nothing but a universal law of existence....

CHAPTER 7

Beraham Angrez

It was about four on an August morning, and Urmila was not well at all. She had general body swelling and fever and was unable to digest any solid food. She had been restive the whole night, moaning with pain and discomfort and had vomited a few times. Narendra was awake throughout, looking after her, with Chameli, one of the female attendants close by.

He finally got out of bed to freshen up and prepare for another tough day ahead. The Civil Surgeon, Dr James Rutherford, was supposed to be visiting him to look up Urmila and discuss the prognosis and future course of action, at about seven. This was to be followed by breakfast for Urmila and himself, and the morning shift at the dispensary. Lunch again would be with the family giving him some time with his wife. The evening shift at the dispensary was to be followed by an important meeting scheduled with his close group of friends.

A lot depended on this meeting with respect to the future course of his life, as well as those close to him. Nevertheless, the day would start with a couple of rounds of steaming hot, brewed Darjeeling, his favourite beverage of the morning.

He normally sipped his tea slumped in his armchair on the veranda adjoining his bedroom, partnering it with pensive drags on his Briar filled with some exquisite tobacco with an intoxicating aroma. This half-an-hour company with himself was critical for him to gear up and gain direction and motivation to steer him through the day.

Narendra was very disturbed by his wife's state of health. As a doctor, he knew that the body swelling was due to dropsy—a condition in which there is fluid secretion and retention under the skin in the body. It was caused by some more serious underlying organ condition. Urmila was also having frequent palpitations when she exerted herself, even a bit, which meant that the condition of her heart was not sound at all.

Of late, she was almost on complete bed rest, with the only movements being to use the washroom, or being helped to change clothes by Chameli and Sharmila, her sister.

God bless Sharmila, mused Narendra. What would have been the circumstance had she not been there, he thought and shuddered. She was one of the very few people he could count on his fingertips who genuinely cared for her sister and the family. Otherwise, the whole household was populated by the 'what is in it for me' category of relatives and friends.

Narendra was aware of the profile of each one of them and was careful enough to extract the best out of all of them, controlling the bounties they received in lieu with shrewd alertness. He was large-hearted and magnanimous in approach. He loved his entire family and found his world and solace within them. Friends, though important, came after his family in matters of preference. Right now, he was a worried man, on account of Urmila and his son, Subendu.

Subendu was an innocent fun-loving child, bordering around an early boyhood. Everyone in his large family seemed to love and admire him; at least, that is what his innocence could perceive. But Narendra knew it all, with scare and apprehension. He had a strange fear lurking at the horizon—what would happen to Subendu in his parents' absence? Who could he really trust and rely on to guide him to a stage of maturity?

Sharmila, Surobee, and Professor VR Mukherjee, his cousin and the first Indian principal of a premier college in Meerut were closest to him, whom he could trust with his heart and soul.

He was not aware of tears dropping out of his eyes and rolling down his otherwise stoic countenance, as he puffed on his pipe and sipped the last bit of his tea, which tasted salty, mixed with his stress and anxiety. He quickly wiped his moist eyes and face, yelled out to Babu Lal to clear up the tea-set while he shuffled into his flip flops and went to the washroom.

***

At sharp seven, Dr Rutherford was at the front door; and Babu Lal announced his arrival to an already dressed-up Narendra, who walked up the corridor to meet the Civil Surgeon and bring him in. Narendra's expressions clearly showed anxiety, nervousness, and tension. His forced smile could be easily identified even by a novice, and the Civil Surgeon was an expert. He patted Narendra on his back in a brotherly gesture.

'Doctor, you are a brave and reasonable man and a respected scientist. The human body's complex anatomy and physiology is not hidden from you. Hence, let us be precise and frank with each other and take the best course to get the lady out of harm's way, giving her a comfortable life,' spoke the Civil Surgeon in a soft tone.

Narendra nodded in affirmative, squeezing Dr Rutherford's hand symbolizing agreement and understanding, while keeping the false grin pasted where it was. They walked into Urmila's bedroom, where she was waiting for them with a hidden angst, more potent than a seething volcano. Chameli was asked to wait outside the room, while the Civil Surgeon did his clinical examination. The ones who remained were Narendra and Sharmila, his sister-in-law.

The Civil Surgeon turned around after his detailed examination of Urmila and nodded to Narendra to follow him outside.

They went into the privacy of Narendra's study down the corridor, calling out to Babu Lal for some coffee. Once in the room, the door was closed behind them, for extended privacy.

'Doctor, Urmila's prognosis is not encouraging at all. It is a case of dropsy on account of an underlying cardiac malfunction, which, I am sure you would have already guessed, looking at the medicines which are being already administered to her. The pulmonary oedema is reasonably acute, and unfortunately, we have very little to do apart from 'posture therapy', minimal exertion, light diet with a very reduced salt regimen and the medicines which she is already taking.

'You are a man of means and can afford to take her to England to get her heart treated by one of the specialists at Harley Street, but unfortunately, she will not be able to sustain the long journey, looking at her current conditions. Hence, let us monitor her well and do what we can here. I will send over a trained and specialized nurse, who will, in turn, train the lady's attendant as well as her sister, since I presume, they are the ones who will be primarily taking care of her.

'I have seen, in some cases, with these medicines and therapy regimes, patients getting out of the agony of oedema and surviving well for a reasonably long time. So, let us not lose hope.'

The Civil Surgeon spoke with a good measure of professional confidence and assurance while holding Narendra's hand between his two, leaning towards him in a friendly and affectionate gesture.

While they discussed, they hardly noticed Babu Lal bringing in the coffee tray, which lay there in neglect. Finally, they turned their attention to their respective cups and sipped the now not-very-steaming brew with indifference, gazing abstractly in different directions.

'Realistically speaking, Dr Rutherford, how much time do you give to my beloved, under the current circumstances, as an average instance?' enquired Narendra, with the anxiety of a layman, knowing the statistics fully well.

'Six months to a year, unless we are looking at God's Grace,' responded the Civil Surgeon, not looking at Narendra, who broke down into his handkerchief.

Dr Rutherford caught Narendra in a tight embrace, reassuringly, as best as he could, and then walked out of the study, with Narendra following him to the front door leading to the entrance porch.

Narendra entered his bedroom, appearing jovial and happy, an art which he had perfected over a period of time, being in a position where he was supposed to conceal his feelings and emotions. Urmila and Sharmila were waiting for him to have their breakfast together.

Subendu was dressed up for school by Sharmila and Chunni Lal and forced to have his daily quarter-boiled egg with a couple of toasts followed by a glass of milk. This he consumed with a total lack of relish and visible disgust, but his love and loyalty for Sharmila, his favourite aunt and chhotee ma (younger mother), were immense enough for him to endure this as well.

He had just left for school before Narendra entered the room for breakfast. These would be Subendu's last few years in the local school before he joined the Doon School according to his father's wishes.

A breakfast of steaming hot porridge with milk, followed by an omelette and toast, topped up by a banana, was what Narendra consumed almost daily. The only change would be the egg preparation, changing to a sunny side up, a fully boiled, or a quarter-boil as the day's choice.

Sharmila preferred her *roti* (fresh Indian roasted bread) and some cooked vegetables and jam, topping it up with a banana like her brother-in-law. Urmila was given some diluted, sweetened milk and mashed banana as advised by the doctors, something which she could digest without throwing up. Sharmila sat beside Urmila, helping her to eat, while she consumed her own breakfast. Narendra sat by the coffee table having his fare in silence.

'What did the Civil Surgeon say about my condition?' asked Urmila feebly, gulping down some milk and banana.

Narendra smiled, 'What you already know, my dear wife. You need rest, medicines and healthy, digestible food to recover. I want you healthy, up and about for our autumn break to Dehradun and Mussoorie.'

Urmila smiled back at him, however, not very reassuringly, while Sharmila commenced her chatter on what both the sisters would do when they went to the hill station.

'Sharmila, will you attend Subendu's parent-teacher meeting today since I seem to have absolutely no time for it? From what I know, he has been fairing reasonably well in his class, albeit not topping.

'Also, Virendra will be joining us for dinner today and visiting you, Urmila. We are having a citizen's meeting in our outhouse in the evening, after which he will come along with me for a quiet family gathering. Ruma Devi would also come along and join both of you while we are in the meeting.'

Narendra spoke while having his breakfast, noting the look of pleasure on Urmila's face on hearing of having people whom she liked visiting her.

Virendra was the professor-cousin of Narendra and Ruma, his wife. Narendra held both in very high esteem and respect and so did Urmila.

'Sharmila, please see to it that there is some spicy fish curry, rice, and mashed potato for Virendra da. He is very fond of this combination. Also, have some kheer made. Ruma has a sweet tooth. Rest of the fare is your choice,' spoke Urmila, with a bit more life and enthusiasm in her.

'Didi, we all will have our dinner in this room, along with you. Is it fine with you Narendra da?'

'Absolutely,' exclaimed Narendra, smiling in return, as enthusiastic as the two sisters. He got up to leave for his dispensary. On his way out of the room, he discretely nodded at Sharmila to follow him, concealed from Urmila.

Sharmila took a different route to the corridor to avoid any suspicions in Urmila, to meet her brother-in-law, who was waiting for her by the telephone stand. Narendra came directly to the point without any element of drama.

'Sharmila, my dear, I require you to book a call to Purobee and Surobee and apprise both of them that their mother is suffering from dropsy on account of an acute heart ailment, which is irreversible. Medical science does not give more than six months to her. So, they should make necessary arrangements to be with their mother as much as their respective families can afford.

'Also, I would like to have an internal meeting with Surobee, her husband and you, once together. I do not want to put very many responsibilities on Purobee, on account of her children and family circumstances. And please keep this confidential, even from your husband, Amarendra, as of now.

'I know, it would be difficult for both you and Surobee. But at the same time, I am confident of the strength and resilience which you two have in dealing with hard times.'

Sharmila broke down. She caught hold of Narendra, sobbing uncontrollably, with her whole body shaking convulsively, however discrete enough not to howl and make Urmila aware, who was sleeping in one of the rooms adjoining the corridor.

Narendra maintained an expressionless yet hard countenance with dry eyes. He just tapped Sharmila lightly on her shoulders, in a loose embrace, helping her internal emotional storm to pass. Sharmila, composed herself, wiping her face dry with her handkerchief, looked at her brother-in-law and nodded in complete agreement. She respected and marvelled at Narendra. For her, he was a giant of a man with immense capacity to absorb grief, crisis, and responsibility, while keeping stoic and composed.

***

Narendra walked into his dispensary, which was already full of patients, waiting their turn. Nathua was Narendra's compounder—a young boy of about fifteen, hot-tempered, energetic, and brash. The patients thought him to be only next to God, and so did he. A few swigs of medical spirit made him even more omnipotent.

'Next to God' was at work, dispensing already prescribed medicine to repeat patients while singling out the ones who would require a clinical check-up by the doctor. One of the patients was bleeding profusely, having been brought in by his mother. She wanted to skip the queue on account of the emergency, while Nathua was adamant about not letting it happen. It was then that Narendra walked in.

Hearing the ruckus in the patients' area, he walked out of his chamber, witnessing the ongoing argument between the wounded man's mother and Nathua, and immediately instructed the man and his mother to be ushered in.

'Nathua, you should be sensible enough by now to judge an emergency, instead of foolishly trying to follow rules without empathy. Help them into my chamber right now. I am sure the other patients would understand the situation.' Saying this, Narendra disappeared into his chamber.

The frail lady came in supporting her grievously injured and profusely bleeding son. She was howling and cursing the perpetrators as well as her son.

'*Ye beraham angrez.*' (These unsympathetic Britishers.)

'*Aur mera bewkoof beta.*' (And my stupid son.)

'*Dono aafat hain mere liye.*' (Both are a pain for me.)

'What exactly happened? Would you please compose yourself and tell me?' enquired Narendra softly while examining her son's wounds.

Her son was one of the student agitators of the leading degree college of Meerut, of which his cousin, Virendra, was the first Indian principal. The agitation had been motivated by one VS Dublish, a prime activist of the region, spearheading the Quit India Movement there. The students at the college were led by this young gentleman whom Narendra was examining as he was the college student union president.

Section 144 of the Indian Criminal Procedures Code, prohibiting unlawful assembly, had been imposed by the District Magistrate on account of the growing unrest. The police had orders to immediately enter the college premises and take necessary legal action. The Inspector, an Englishman, thought it to be prudent enough to first approach the college principal since he would be nearest to the administration on account of his status and would also be able to control the crisis. However, Professor Mukherjee had differing thoughts.

'Respected Inspector Sir, with due regards, I find this student agitation not without its merits. Undue suppression, vexatious taxation, increasing prices of grains, as well as its paucity, are reasons enough for rising frustrations. And I for one cannot come in their way. Hence, you are most welcome to arrest me as well, in case your law and administrative ethics do allow.' Saying this, he had closed his chamber's door on the Inspector's face.

The Inspector was snubbed as well as frustrated since he did what he thought was in accordance with protocol. He had expected to avoid any violence by getting support from the principal and was not amused at all by the way he reacted to his honest overtures.

The Professor was a much-respected person of the district, famous far and wide for his scholastics, intellect, and professional integrity. Therefore, attempting to arrest him was not only far from wisdom but also bordering on impossibility. Hence, the only option left with the Inspector was to relieve his angst and frustration on to the agitators.

'Break the agitation and arrest those who oppose!' the Inspector had bellowed out to the force accompanying him. Fifteen were injured grievously, many getting minor injuries and about a score of them had been arrested. When the Principal had walked out and waved to the Inspector, he had complied forthwith and walked up to him.

'Kindly stop this senseless bloodbath immediately. I have had a talk with the District Magistrate. You are supposed to leave the arrested students with a warning. The Magistrate is on the phone, kindly walk into my office and take the necessary orders directly.'

The Inspector had waved out to his forces to hold fire till further orders and maintain the status quo, after which he walked into the principal's office to talk to the Magistrate.

The Inspector had complied reluctantly, seething with anger against the principal, and silently walked away. The student leader's family were old patients of Narendra, so his mother preferred to get him there.

'He has a gash on his head, which I have stitched up. Apart from this he also has two broken teeth and a fractured left hand, for which I would recommend getting it plastered at the government hospital. I am giving you a note for the same, and also administering some injections and giving you some pills to look after infections as well as inflammations.

'Also, I would like to advise that non-violence is what the Mahatma favours and he is the person to have called for the Quit India Movement. Hence, a rush of blood and useless confrontation is not going to take us anywhere.' With this, he called out to Nathua for the next patient and to help the mother and son out of the chamber.

Dinner preparations were in full swing; and both the sisters and his son were looking forward to having some light moments with Virendra, Ruma, and their sons. The youngest of them—Ajay Raj Mukherji—was almost Subendu's age and a close friend of his.

'Sharmila, any news from Surobee and Ajit?' enquired Narendra since she was given the task of contacting his two daughters and their families.

'Narendra da, Ajit has decided to leave the Army and get into private practice under Dr Bidhan Chandra Roy, in Calcutta. He has put in his papers sometime back and is expecting release soon after his annual leave, which starts at the end of September,' replied Sharmila, knowing fully well that this was going to please Narendra and his scheme of events.

Narendra had already started toying with the idea of influencing Ajit and his father to let him assist and finally take over his immense practice in Meerut and the surrounding region. He was aware that many doctors would line up the day they came to know that Narendra was planning a succession. Further, this move, in case possible, would solve the problem of looking after Subendu also. Nevertheless, many in his own large family would not be very pleased with this scenario. Narendra got up, satisfied with himself, and proceeded to his evening meeting in the outhouse after freshening up. In the meantime, he could hear the cacophony of Kalu, his black Labrador.

Ruma and her kids had arrived, which also meant that his evening meeting guests had already started to make their presence felt in the outhouse. By half-past seven in the evening most of the Indian elite—businessmen, professionals and leaders of the region—had assembled in the drawing room of Narendra's outhouse.

Cars and horse carriages were parked by the roadside, flanking the 'In Gate' of the Banerji mansion. If one watched keenly, there was a discrete presence of plainclothesmen loitering around the mansion aimlessly, trying to sniff the action and, if necessary, act as themselves. Vishnu Sharan Dublish and Raghukul Tilak were among the leaders present at the meeting. Professor Mukherjee and Professor Dutta were amongst the leading educationists of the region and present. Nawab Ishaq, Mirza sahib, and Salim were the prominent citizens representing the Muslim community. Narendra, Dr Madan, Dr Ajay Singh, Dr Caroli, and Advocate Virender Singh were representing the professionals' caucus, while Sultan Singh, Vijay Pal, Yudh Raj, and Jodha Mal were present from the business forum. It was an important meeting, which also had certain visitors from the Congress office in Delhi.

The drawing room was large enough to accommodate all, and liveried waiters were already circulating beverages—whisky soda, juices, buttermilk, tea, and coffee, accompanied by a range of vegetarian and non-vegetarian snacks. Cigars were also seen to be in circulation. Narendra, being the host, opened the meeting session.

'Gentlemen, today's meeting has no guests as well as enemies. All are hosts and friends,' commenced Narendra, with a soft smile.

'We are assembled here to take certain strategic decisions on the way forward, considering the growing unrest and impatience for freedom. I am sure, that here amongst us as well, we would have varied opinions on the issue of our beloved country's future.

'In my opinion, all are unified to the cause of freedom, and I am sure, with the approach and attitude of our British rulers, even they are looking at self-rule by the native Indians.

'Hence, the question which arises is whether it is necessary to use violence or confrontation as a tool under such circumstances. We might make the transition a bit more vexatious by antagonizing a force that already wants to transfer power.

'Another important issue which needs to be discussed in the course of this meeting is the Muslim League's demand for a separate nation-state, Pakistan. What should be our region's approach to this? Are our Muslim brothers amenable to this course of action?

'Friends, these are issues to be discussed today, as understood by me. None of them is my point of view or opinion. Also, whatever is decided in this session will be recorded and strictly adhered to. Any amendment or change of stance will be reviewed by the minimum quorum agreed upon by this elite group.

'I hope I have made myself clear. In case there are any differences, please do feel free to address them now. Amarendra will be recording the minutes of this meeting, which will be circulated to all the members of the group.'

Narendra, now, took his seat, to let the session begin.

Nawab Ishaq was the first to address the issues.

'Friends, quite a few members of my community and I are impassionate and devout followers of Maulana Abul Kalam Azad as well as Mahatma Gandhi. However, there are also many among us who will blindly follow Jinnah since he is charismatic, and they are insecure, more on account of their ignorance and misunderstanding of reality.

'We are trying to have meetings in every locality and street corner to spread the message of peace and sanity. Some are understanding and coming around. Our objective is to protect the community in this region in a way that they do not think of leaving their homes and migrating to a future Pakistan.

'The Lahore Resolution of 1940, adopted by Jinnah and the Muslim League, calling for a Two Nation status, has moved a huge number of Muslims in East Bengal, United Provinces, and western parts of Punjab. It has resulted in a giant increase in the Muslim League membership. I have personally requested Maulana Azad to visit Meerut once and address our people here. It might have a very positive effect.

'Our Muslim brothers here feel very vulnerable ever since the partition of Bengal on communal lines by the British, and the backlash it provoked.'

The Nawab sat down and took a few contemplative drags from the hukka. Sultan Singh was more abrupt in his philosophy. Being a businessman, his focus was on commerce.

'Gentlemen, I have a thriving business and the support of the government as well as infrastructure. What we need to grant to the British is that they have been very good with policies and processes and developing the necessary institutions. We would not have had the Railways without them, nor metaled roads and electricity. The ports are very much improved in their regime.

'I agree that we must claim our land, self-esteem, and freedom. However, we must focus on maintaining what has already been created and improve upon it. My call is that we must endeavour to scale up into a developed nation with its own pride of place. In case Jinnah does desire a Muslim nation, we should not obstruct it and divert our focus from development. Let India be what India can control. Let us maintain peace and avoid any kind of violence and confrontation unless it comes onto a critical path.'

With this Sultan Singh went back to his whisky tumbler, taking a cooling sip, satisfied that he had spoken his mind. Dublish and Tilak were in favour of no compromise in the path to Sampoorn Swaraj as well as a complete India. They were for a mass campaign to convince their Muslim brothers of the positive points of being together, and to convince them of the prime motive of Jinnah to gain power and control, rather than the benefit of the masses under his influence, to assure them of safety, security, and a home for all. They were sure that Mahatma Gandhi would be able to derive an administrative solution of cooperation between Nehru and Jinnah.

Professor Mukherjee had a wider view of the current situation and a futuristic vision on account of the extensive travelling he had indulged in within the country and outside, including the enigmatic China.

'I have personally met and talked to many of our Muslim brothers in Bengal, the United Provinces as well as Punjab. The majority seem to be blindly following Jinnah. They see and are convinced that mayhem and genocide of Muslims will occur once the iron hand of British rule is lifted. Distrust within the two communities is clearly visible from the sporadic riots bursting out.

'Hence, our role is limited to creating sanity and brotherhood in our region, to restrain any violent backlash or impact. In case we can achieve this, it would be a major success towards setting up an example for the rest of the nation to follow. Jinnah should do away with the two-nation objective he has resolved to undertake at the Lahore Session of the Muslim League. Maulana Azad should be given a larger role in addressing the followers of the Muslim League, supported by Jinnah.

'An agreement, even at the cost of placating Jinnah with a premier leadership role in the new nation, should be looked into. In case these steps are not taken at the respective levels, we are surely gazing into very violent, painful, and torturous birth pains.

'Let me be abrupt, for which I am reasonably unpopular in some segments of our society. Socio-religious unity and integration in our country is not a favoured notion with either the British or some of our neighbours. It is a common human tendency to profit out of the problems of others, and I am not talking Greek when I say that quite a sizable part of the world will profit from our miseries for a long time to come.

'We, as a nation, should comprehend this at the highest level of leadership, and deny the world their piece of cake at the cost of ours. As far as I am concerned, I would continue to express my displeasure on this politics of Divide and Rule, albeit passively, yet surely.'

Jodha Mal, a leading grains and edible oil trader of the United Provinces was feeling restive, wanting to speak his mind in this august company. He had pestered Sultan Singh for an inordinately long time to get an invite and, finally, succeeded. He had radical views, those of a devout Hindu.

'With due regards, friends, I really cannot understand what the fuss is all about. In case the Muslim League wants a separate Islamic nation-state, so be it. That way we live in peace here, in Hindustan, while they can happily build their own nation. The only issue of prime importance is the boundaries and the area demarcated for the new nation. We need to see that regions demarcated as India are in continuity, and no region which is primarily and historically Hindu-dominated should become a part of the Islamic nation-state. Finally, I am assuming a separate Hindu and an Islamic nation, post-partition.'

All those present in the gathering were well aware that Meerut was too close to Punjab, in the northwest, for comfort and that Punjab would be one of the major areas of partition-related activities, apart from Bengal in the east.

Finally, Dublish summed up certain action points and approaches in a very concise manner quite inimical to his profile.

'Friends, we in Meerut have a great responsibility of moderation on our shoulders. We must act firmly, yet with patience and forbearance. I would propose that we follow the directions of Mahatma Gandhi in their entirety. Further, I would propose the name of Tilak, Professor Mukherjee, Dr Narendra Nath Banerji, Nawab Ishaq, and Sultan Singh as our representatives to collectively bargain on our interests, with both the British as well as the domestic leadership.'

Finally, the host, Narendra, got up to speak.

'Friends and Dublish ji, it is an honour and pleasure to have all of you assembled here, at my residence, today. And it is a bigger honour for Mr Dublish to think of me as capable enough for the responsibility he wishes to bestow on me.

'However, my professional dedication to my patients, growing family requirements and my contract with the British establishment in Meerut Cantonment make my acceptance of his kind offer difficult. There are complications on account of which I would request a modification in my critical duties and responsibilities.

'Whilst family requirements are something which all of us have to bear with pleasure, my patients and my professional relationship with the British cantonment in Meerut is to be looked into more incisively and clinically. I have an ethical and professional contract with both these groups, and as a doctor, I would have to give it my first priority, before anything else.

'Hence, I would propose a more diplomatic stance in the scheme of events. Due to my closeness to most of the officers, bureaucrats, and soldiers of the establishment in this region, I hear their voices, and they hear mine. I am surely a storehouse of a lot of private information, good or bad. Also, they do have a sympathetic ear to my suggestions, which, till now, they have had reasons to believe to be mature and on the right path.

'My importance to our aims and objectives springs out of this vantage point which I exclusively enjoy on account of my position. Friends, let us use this to our region's and our country's advantage, to the extent we can, without my coming out actively into the open. I hope all of you understand the nuances and the best way to gain out of it. You would surely agree that a horse in the opponent's cavalry is better than a hero in prison.'

Narendra looked directly at all his friends present to judge their mood after having spoken his mind. Dublish and the rest were looking positive and satisfied by Narendra's analysis and suggestions.

'I am absolutely with you, honourable doctor. We would keep your critical role a secret, however, we shall lean heavily on you for your support.'

Dublish's point of view was endorsed by everyone present, unanimously. All voted for him to lead the representation, which was accepted graciously by him. It was further decided that Tilak and Professor Mukherjee would assist in the absence of Dublish.

The meeting ended, and the participants started to make their way out of the outhouse.

***

It was half past eight in the evening when the professor and Narendra strolled back to the main residence. Narendra gave Virendra a brief on Urmila's health condition, with all honest details, wiping his eyes while confessing the grievousness to his best friend and brother.

'Virendra, I am tired, stressed, and broken down carrying a perpetual load on my shoulders. I am anguished by the future. Although Purobee and Surobee are both married and well-settled, Subendu is still a naive kid. We have a reasonable amount of assets under our control and a large extended family, with some lurking around for the right moment, not with the noblest of intentions. There are very few I can trust, my dear brother, and you lead this negligible minority. I shall rely on you heavily in a situation of my absence from this puzzle of life.'

Saying this, Narendra caught hold of his younger cousin and broke down into sobs, with increasing intensity. Virendra kept silent to let the emotions flow. When Narendra had gained control, Virendra spoke.

'Narendra da, you are going nowhere, and I am always with you, by your side. Pondering on the way forward—Ajit is also in the medical profession and well qualified with immense experience, at such a young age. I have also heard from the grapevine that Ajit has put in his paper with the British Indian Army Medical Corps, and is contemplating setting up his private practice in Calcutta under Dr BC Roy. In which case, wouldn't it be judicious on your part to engage with his father, Bijoy, and him, to influence them to settle Ajit down in Meerut and gradually take over your practice? That way, you would have the required support and much more in your personal and professional life.'

Narendra, for a change, had a glint in his eyes when he spoke.

'My dear brother, I have been thinking along the same lines and have asked Sharmila to contact Bijoy da and Ajit to apprise them of the situation. Also, I have requested Surobee and Ajit to plan a trip to Meerut, so that we can work out the feasible details. Let us hope for the best. Ajit is returning home from Malaya next month, after which he will continue to stay on to settle his practice.

'Further, for your knowledge and consent, I would also be proposing your name as the legal guardian for young Subendu till he comes of age and can make his own decisions. We shall discuss the details later when we meet for this purpose.'

Saying this he patted Virendra on the back and gestured to enter the main house. Virendra gave a sanguine grin, looking at Narendra and entered the house along with him.

***

The telephone bell was protesting shrilly and continuously, till it caught Narendra's attention. He rushed towards the phone kept in the corridor outside his bedroom. Getting a call so early, at four-thirty in the morning, always made him anxious. More so, he did not want to disturb Urmila from her sleep.

He picked up the receiver as quickly as was possible for him.

'Hello…hello…'

'Hello, is that Dr Banerji, I am talking to?'

'Yes, it is. May I know who I am talking to and what is the emergency for which you have called at such an early hour of the morning?'

'Doctor sahib, Dublish ji and Tilak ji have been arrested and taken to the police station about half an hour back. The inspector accompanying the arresting team was talking about you as well. They were also referring to yesterday's meeting at your residence, of which they seem to have complete knowledge and awareness. I am Dublish ji's nephew and have been asked to call you up and warn you in advance since you are also very much on their radar.'

Narendra listened with complete attention, without interrupting. His mind was rapidly analysing the future course of action at the same time. After Dublish's nephew had completed what he wanted to say, Narendra spoke haltingly, not showing the anxiety which was invading his psyche at that time.

'Thank you, dear son, for the call and the warning. Kindly tell Mrs Dublish that I will be on my way to your residence in a short time. And that we are all together in this hour of crisis as well as in what is to follow.'

With this, he kept the receiver down and went straight to the dressing room to get ready for the day. Urmila had woken up on account of the activity.

'Where are you going at this early hour, Narendra?'

Narendra was truthful and non-evasive.

'Dublish and Tilak have been arrested, I need to stand by their family at this hour of crisis and render all help which is possible.'

Saying this, he rushed out to call for Babu Lal for a quick cup of tea and alert his driver to get the car to the front porch. Within a short time, he was making his way through the empty streets of Meerut, sucking on his Briar and musing on what lay ahead.

***

In about ten minutes, when he arrived at the Dublish mansion, there was already a reasonable collection of relatives, neighbours, friends, and colleagues sitting and standing on the front veranda. Rose *sherbet* and tea were doing rounds while Mrs Dublish sat on a chair with anxiety and nervousness writ large on her face. The people made way for Dr Banerji to walk through to her.

'*Bhabhi* (sister-in-law), everything will be alright. I will be visiting the senior officers of the local government and working out modalities, along with other eminent and respected citizens of the city. I am very confident that we will have a positive result before the end of the working day.'

Mrs Dublish, feeling very relieved on seeing Narendra walking in, had a lot of confidence in his capabilities and the influence he wielded with the government machinery of the region.

'I am sure that everything will be taken care of with you there, Doctor sahib. But please see to it that Vishnu is not inconvenienced with rough behaviour.'

Narendra nodded with a smile and looked towards the gate, seeing Professor Mukherjee and Sultan Singh walking in from the front gate. Virendra had a concerned look on his face and was directly looking at Narendra while walking towards him. He gestured to Narendra to meet him away from Mrs Dublish. Narendra took leave from her and stepped down from the veranda, walking towards the gate, to catch up with his cousin.

'Narendra da, I am just coming from your house, hoping to have accompanied you here, but you had left. Also, I met a messenger from the District Magistrate's office, who had come for you. Evidently, the DM wants to have a word with you in his office at ten sharp. Since the messenger's son is studying in my college, he was kind enough to tell me that it is concerning your role in the Civil Disobedience movement in the region. I shall accompany you. and I have assured Urmila and Sharmila of the same, since, frankly speaking, I am apprehending the possibility of some discomfort.'

Narendra had an expression of mild nervousness when he queried Virendra.

'What is the discomfort you are apprehending?'

'Putting it straight, the DM might be thinking of some way to dilute your patriotism to a controllable limit. He cannot do very much more, considering your significance and status in this town,' replied the professor very nonchalantly.

'I cannot gather what is in the DM's mind. Anyway, let us go there and check it out. It will be very kind of you to accompany me. I need your moral support and confidence.'

Narendra checked his pocket watch while talking to the professor. He still had time to go to his clinic, check on a few serious patients and leave necessary instructions for the rest while he was away at this curious destination.

'Doctor sahib, Professor Mukherjee has told me all, and I will most certainly be present with both of you, at the DM's office. After, Dublish's arrest, we are not going to take any chances.'

Narendra had no way of reasoning out in front of Sultan Singh's determined posture. Hence, he just nodded with a touching grin, patted him on his back and walked out to his car, having communicated to Mrs Dublish that he would be visiting her again later that day.

At about five minutes to ten, Narendra walked into the DM's office flanked by Virendra and Sultan Singh on either side. By this time, he was completely composed, even sharing a joke with both his companions, with a toothy grin.

The DM's *shreshtadar* (assistant) walked up to them as soon as they entered the office to escort Narendra to the DM. However, he requested the professor and Sultan Singh to wait outside. Narendra, too, gestured them to wait.

The Collector was perched on his majestic chair at the centre of the room, with a large, yet methodical and clean table in front of him. He got up to greet the doctor as he walked in, with a firm handshake followed by a respectable namaste, with his hands folded in the typical Indian manner. The Collector and his family were Narendra's patients as well, the doctor being on the government panel for treatments pertaining to general medicine.

Narendra bowed to the Collector, giving due respect to protocol, and perched himself on one of the chairs in the front row, next to the table. The Collector initiated the dialogue and pleasantries.

'It was very kind of you, doctor, to have come at such short notice. However, the matter at hand is of immense importance to the Government as well as you. Hence, I had no other alternative but to have you called.'

'Your Lordship is at complete liberty, official and otherwise, to have me summoned. And I am duty-bound to obey the missives. Also, I am very sure that the issue in hand must be of importance enough, to have me called during clinic hours,' replied Narendra with perfect graciousness and civility, as desired by the circumstances.

'Well then, coming to the point straight away, doctor, I have orders from Delhi to arrange for your detention. They are aware of the meeting of some eminent local activists at your residence yesterday. They are also aware that it was attended by some Indian National Congress workers from Delhi, and action points regarding a civil disobedience movement at the local level were a part of the discussion. We even have a declaration by an eyewitness to the proceedings, whose identity is not to be declared according to our agreed-upon procedures of conduct. Hence, your detention is legally enforceable.'

The collector, while speaking, offered Narendra a cigar before lighting one himself. Narendra refused with thanks and kept on listening with rapt attention, albeit without any expression whatsoever. He kept silent for some time after the Collector had finished what he wanted to say. Evidently looking for a response and reaction from Narendra, the Collector kept looking at him. Finally getting none, he went on to ask him for it.

'Doctor, could you understand what I wanted to communicate to you?'

After what the Collector thought to be a never-ending wait, Narendra moved to have a glass of water, kept for him on the office table in front. and drank to the last drop. He was taking time to compose his thoughts and absorb the impact of what he had just heard.

Narendra was not inclined towards declared and acknowledged activism, which would take him away from his family and patients, who had as equal a stake in his life, as patriotism and nationalistic leanings. Or maybe slightly more.

'Your Lordship, you are at complete liberty to detain me or, more plainly speaking, arrest me immediately. I am well prepared mentally. and I have two witnesses to the process, in the form of two leading luminaries of the city. They can go back from here and declare the news to my critically ailing wife, the rest of my family, my patients and the citizen's forum, of which, currently, I am an office bearer of sorts.

'However, I am sure you are not going to hold me responsible for the reactions and outcome of my arrest since they could not possibly be guided by me.

'Hence, to help your Lordship to fulfil his responsibilities, allow me to call my two witnesses to apprise them of the administration's decision and enable you to initiate the arrest proceedings.'

Narendra had gambled on what he just communicated to the Collector. Before the doctor could move to get his intentions into practice, the Collector sprang up to interject.

'Doctor, I think you have thought quite a few steps ahead. It was never my intention to arrest you. I just spoke of the views in Delhi, who are not aware of the local nuances in Meerut. I have apprised them that the issue will be put to rest by me, after my conversation with you, and all misunderstandings will be cleared.

'Doctor, you are too important a man in this region to be disregarded with as brash and childish an action as an arrest. We know your significance to the society as well as the establishment here. You are a busy man with very little time or inclination to be instrumental in obstructing law and order in the city.

'Hence, kindly, not even for once believe or think that the request to have you with me in my office was the initiation of arrest. It is just to apprise you of what has transpired internally, as well as the trust that the establishment has in your integrity and persona.

'However, it is my request and advice to desist from having such meetings at your residence, as well as be seen to be a part of the so-called Quit India Movement called by Gandhi. We are aware of the influence you wield on the Meerut elites, who would listen to every word you utter to them. And it is our expectation that your presence would bring sanity to the current situation. I hope you understand our expectations from you?'

'I surely understand the establishment's expectations of me. However, you should also realize that I am a native Indian, and my fellow Indians also have expectations of me. The administration should be sensitive to this. It is not possible for me to take an open stance against the patriotic activism of my friends like Dublish or Tilak. They believe in me, and I cannot breach their faith or the likes of them.

'What I can assure you of is the calming influence I would be on such activism, as well as my role in controlling violent reactions. What the administration needs to assure me of is not to create a hostile situation soliciting a reaction, wherein it would be outside my purview and control to bring about any peaceful reconciliation.'

Narendra now accepted the offer for a cigar. He needed it badly and the Collector was more than happy to oblige. He took a puff and carried on.

'Moreover, sir, you are also privy to the fact that the British Government is thinking along the lines of local self-government, in which case a more benevolent approach of the administration towards the natives can be afforded. Rest you would be the best judge.'

'So, you want a trade-off to gain credibility with your people?' questioned the Collector, looking Narendra directly in the eye.

'Primarily, I want justice, and what is rightfully due, as also, yes, what you call credibility.'

Narendra was looking right back in the Collector's eye, who could easily ascertain the genuine emotions of a truthful and plain-speaking man.

'Okay gentleman, you shall have your way, and I will set the process of releasing Dublish and Tilak in motion. However, with a strong and enforceable warning.'

Narendra now let his face crack into a good-natured smile. He was relieved...very relieved.

'I would also like to meet our other friends waiting outside over a quick cup of tea before we pursue our respective callings of the day.' Saying this, he rang his desk bell to have the other guests ushered in.

'What was going on inside, doctor sahib?' enquired Sultan Singh, with a confused expression on his face.

'The Collector seemed to be very effusive in his trust and praise for you. Very friendly as well. However, outside, we had some guests in khaki, to escort you to prison. At least, that's what the shreshtadar said. They were waiting for the Collector's nod. Strangely, they left at the same time we were called in, on the instructions of the shreshtadar. Both Professor sahib and I were reasonably nervous and were planning out the next course of action, with you also in prison.'

Sultan Singh continued to blabber, till he was silenced by Virendra, who evidently had something important to say and ask.

'Narendra, it is evident that they had prepared for your arrest, but your shrewd negotiations have evidently turned the tables. But what were Amarendra and his friend Ravi doing here at the Collectorate? I suppose both were present at yesterday's meeting, at your residence? They avoided me and moved themselves from my sight in a huff. I did not quite like what I saw.'

Narendra recalled the eyewitness the DM was talking about. and winced at the thought. However, he kept the discussion entirely to himself. He made a note of not involving Amarendra or Ravi in the sensitive decision-making of the core group, and deal with the situation discretely and personally, without involving anyone. After all, Amarendra was a close relative and had many positive qualities, and Narendra had an intrinsic nature of sizing out all, taking their positives, but guarding against their pitfalls.

'Virendra, both of them are mature individuals having their own occupations. So, they have the liberty to move around and meet people at will. Let us not bother too much on such trivialities.'

One look at Narendra and the Professor could immediately make out that his cousin had not only processed the information but also decided upon the wisest course of action. He suppressed a smile and kept walking silently towards Narendra's car.

'By the way, Dublish and Tilak are to be released soon. Let us go by Dublish's residence and give the good news to his family members. The information would ease them considerably. And Sultan, would you please convey the same to Tilak's family straight away?' Narendra enquired.

Sultan nodded in affirmative, looking admiringly at his beloved and respected doctor and business investor.

'Definitely, doctor sahib. You have a very intelligent brain working there. Far above our comprehension.'

Narendra got into his car, along with Virendra, reclined back and gazed out of the window. It had been a tough day so far with tougher times ahead....

***

British India was a strange mosaic of activities, emotions, philosophies, and thoughts...every part was different than the others....

CHAPTER 8

The Khannas

About 500 kilometres from Delhi, Sialkot nestled peacefully, not far from the Pir Panjals—the middle Himalayan Range that guarded the picturesque Kashmir valley—oblivious of its future, smug about its past and enjoying the present. Expanses of bright yellow Canola blooms added to the beauty of the region, and the oil from its seeds gave the commercial necessity of its presence.

The city was quaint, yet industrious, with business, industry, and trade in its blood. The robust and hardworking Punjabis of the region toiled and enjoyed their lives, yet religion was precious to most of its peaceful and accommodating residents.

The businesses were generally controlled by the Hindus, while the craftsmen and shop floor expertise was with the Muslims. So, it was a team effort, which had been prevalent in Sialkot, with both communities depending on one another.

However, there had been a desire for a separate homeland hidden in the hearts of the Muslim population of the city and the surrounding rural belt on account of political debates and

Allama Iqbal's inclinations—a great poet and an acclaimed writer. Nevertheless, it had not gained giant proportions to disturb the social fabric as it then prevailed. For them, two nations existed only in their political masters' minds, distanced from reality and virtually impossible to achieve. Hence, Delhi was still not far, and still the capital city of the sub-continent.

Sports was the industry flourishing in Sialkot, and so were those making leather accessories, surgical equipment, arms and poultry. On the genesis of the sports goods industry, there was a myth that an Englishman had happened to break his tennis racquet, and it was given to a local craftsman for repairs. He did such a perfect job that a skill was discovered in the process.

Mulk Raj Khanna, amongst others, having capitalized on it down the line, was a renowned sports goods manufacturer in Sialkot. When it came to quality cricket bats, balls, and gear, Mulk Raj was the person to turn to. His fame rang a bell as far as England, where quite a few used his prime produce.

Having done his primary schooling at the Scotch Mission College at Kanak Mandi in Sialkot, he had gone on to complete his 'A' Level from Aitchison College in Lahore. He was a passionate cricketer, having represented his House and School teams at all levels, and this passion later converted to manufacturing cricketing equipment. Mulk Raj had started his entrepreneurship with a few local craftsmen within Sialkot, manufacturing bats and balls for local schools and children, and then scaled it up to a reasonably large factory employing a few hundred craftsmen and employees, manufacturing the whole range of equipment, feeding numerous families. His father was a prosperous landlord, while he turned out to be a prosperous businessman. With three healthy sons and a beautiful daughter, who had taken after her worthy mother, his family was complete.

It was a happy household, with great emphasis on core family values and education. Ladies had a complete say in the affairs of the house as well as the general well-being of the family. The eldest son, Ashok Raj Khanna, was studying at his father's old school, and was preparing to go to Dehradun, further to the east, in the Garhwal Himalayas, to a well-known boarding school, Colonel Browns. He had already cleared his admission registration.

The second son, Vikas Raj, had commenced schooling at the same school as Ashok, whilst the youngest, Vijay was enjoying his childhood with his family and neighbours, pampered by one and all, including his sister, Kamla Rani Khanna, who was studying in a girls' missionary school, not far away from their house.

The Khanna mansion itself was an impressive double-storied structure, with a semi-circular driveway connecting the 'In' and 'Out' gates and the front porch enclosing a lawn in its sweep. There was a backyard housing a kitchen garden and an internal courtyard surrounded by living rooms in two stories. The courtyard had a square-shaped cemented enclosure, the core of which was filled with fertile clay. A holy basil plant sprouted out from within it, spreading umbrella-like over a Shiv Ling.

The basil plant and the Shiv Ling were the centre of religious activities early in the morning, with Jaya, Mulk Raj's wife, bathing it with milk and water every day. This ritual was performed by Kamla as well, the Khanna household being a religious and devout Hindu family.

From the terrace, one could clearly view the famous Sialkot landmark—the Clock Tower, from where the Khanna House was just a short walk away.

***

Mulk Raj had returned from Lahore by the Allama Iqbal Express, which was running late as usual. It was almost five in the evening. He was in Lahore for a couple of days, on work, also meeting some important people in government, politics, and business.

His factory's horse carriage had come to receive him at the railway station, which was about twenty minutes from his house. He was lost in his thoughts, while the carriage jerked its way through the crowded streets of the vegetable market, through which he had to go on his way to his house.

What he had heard on his grapevine was not positive at all. Jinnah and his fellow Muslims were baying for an Islamic nation for the Muslims of the subcontinent, which could mean that Hindus would have to move out and Muslims would move in to replace them. It is what he could gather in a nutshell.

How would all this be facilitated?

How would businesses be relocated and compensated?

How would the new governments affect the migration and housing for the displaced?

These were just a few of the many questions which were furiously inundating Mulk Raj's already cluttered mind. He was planning an expansion, another larger factory premise, to house increased orders of cricket gear. Would it be prudent to go ahead with it, or somehow manage with the space restrictions already asphyxiating production? He did not have the answers at the moment. Suddenly, the sight of the Clock Tower appeared in front of him, and his confusion vanished, giving way to pleasant thoughts of his family and his prosperity today, tomorrow and many more days to come.

He glanced at all the gifts he had purchased for each one of his jewels from the fascinating Anarkali Bazaar of Lahore. He also tenderly picked up a properly sealed packet of succulent kebabs, which he had purchased from one of the fine barbeque joints in the market, and smelled them to judge the freshness. They were mouth-watering. So excited was he that he jumped out of the carriage as soon as they reached the gate of his house, and almost ran in….

'Ashok! Kamla! Come here with the rest; see what I have got for all of you from Lahore...,' yelled Mulk Raj from the courtyard.

Jaya came out from the kitchen, with the children streaming out from their common study room, all excited for their pot of gold. The children knew how much their father was obsessed with them. They were aware that he lived for them, toiled for them, and spent most of his spare time planning their future.

'Why don't you first go and freshen up while I fetch a cup of tea and samosas? We can then enjoy the moment with more energy and freshness,' said Jaya, softly. However, she knew the response.

'No! First, papa will show us our gifts, plan for the remaining evening, have tea and samosas, and then go to freshen up,' said Kamla in her love-choked voice. This was unanimously endorsed by all, and grudgingly accepted by Jaya, who went back to the kitchen to get the refreshments with snacks.

The first box was for Ashok. He grabbed it, unwrapped it in the same motion and gasped. It was a Brownie Reflex Camera, fresh, shining, and new. He had tears in his eyes while embracing his father. Photography was a passion with him, and till now he had stroked his hobby with borrowed cameras from his father and uncles. The photographs he took were very mature for a boy of his age. Once, he had also expressed a desire to own a camera of his own, to which Mulk Raj had promised him one after he succeeded in gaining admission to one of the good boarding schools they were trying for. He admired his father's character of being truthful and remembering to keep his promises. He had been successful in his admission tests for Colonel Browns, Dehradun, and here was the best gift he could have asked for. With the camera were four photographic reels to enable him to get into action immediately, which he did.

Ajay's gift was a licensed radio, with both medium and shortwave bands. He was very fond of tuning in to various stations and could play around with it for hours. He kissed his father and vanished in search of a plug point.

Vijay got a carom board set, British-made. It was his initiation into something more serious than his present occupation of puerile fun and frivol. However, he was expecting some more car toys, which he already had in plenty.

'Papa, I do not know how to play this game,' Vijay blurted out.

'Don't worry, Vijay, we will all play it together, and you will pick up the skill much better than any of us,' assured Kamla, with more excitement about Vijay's gift than him.

For Kamla, Mulk Raj had got a new Hawaiian guitar. She was very good at it, and the older one was in bad shape.

'Why did you take so much trouble, papa? I have been doing very well with the old one, and my music teacher is also very happy with my progress on it,' said Kamla, albeit very unconvincingly.

'My cute little *bitiya*, I want to see you giving a public performance soon. That is what you have to aspire for with this new guitar,' said Mulk Raj, petting his favourite jewel.

In the meantime, Jaya had put out the spread of tea, *lassi* and samosas on the table kept at the centre and sat down on one of the cane chairs beside her husband. Mulk Raj, handed over two packages to her, one after the other.

The first one, Jaya soon discovered, was a beautiful magenta and pink *Banarasi* saree, richly brocaded and embroidered in the city of Benaras.

'Why did you have to spend so much? I already have so many of them,' Jaya responded, yet loving every bit of her husband's gesture, as well as what he had got for her. Mulk Raj held her hand and gave a satisfied smile, observing the happy atmosphere in the house. It was exactly what he had imagined on his way back from Lahore.

'And all of you, the last packet in your mother's hand are kebabs from the famous Khalid Chacha's joint at Anarkali Bazaar! Today is a full moon night, and as per our family practice, we are all going for a night picnic at Head Marala. We would have these kebabs, *paranthas* (fried Indian bread), pickles and daal as a packed dinner. Ashok would be our official photographer.' Mulk Raj spoke while picking up a samosa.

'Yippee!' was the common cry from the children, followed by a condescending nod from Jaya.

'So, Ashok, tell Magan Lal to clean up the car and keep it ready. I will drive. Also, tell him to get paranthas and daal from Khadim's at the Clock Tower. Jaya can give him an idea of the quantity.'

Mulk Raj got into the excitement mode, looking forward to a lively family evening ahead, and with this, he added a wish for Kamla, his dear daughter.

'Kamla, you will play some good music on your guitar for all of us at the picnic.'

Kamla smiled and agreed. The family got into motion, getting ready for the excursion.

***

Head Marala was an expanse of a water body on the Chenab River. The headworks were situated there, with two main canals branching out, about twenty kilometres from Sialkot City. The road connectivity was good, and it took the Khannas about forty-five minutes to reach.

Parking his Morris on an empty patch of grassy land, under a peepul tree, Mulk Raj got out of the car and stretched himself, breathing the fresh and pleasant autumn air. The children and Jaya also got out, looking around for a good spot to settle themselves down.

There were ten steps leading to a lower landing, about four feet above the water level. The landing was almost seven feet wide, running along the circumference of the Chenab reservoir, and was entirely covered by well-kept cushion grass. There was a rear flowerbed full of colourful seasonal flowers adding to the manicured beauty. The entire area was passionately maintained by the British-Indian Irrigation Department.

The Khanna family descended onto the lower landing, spread their durries, kept the two folding chairs, and placed the food and utensils and the other accompaniments to complete the picnic atmosphere. The full moon was generous with its luminescence and bathed the entire area with its shine. That, along with the sound of the breeze, moving and lapping water, comprised heaven's contribution to the Khannas' picnic. They just couldn't have asked for more.

Soon, the family settled down on the durries while Mulk Raj and Jaya took to the two chairs. Ashok was busy with his new Brownie Reflex, clicking away at almost everything. Kamla, along with Vikas and Vijay, helped serve some orange juice in glasses to the family.

Mulk Raj drew out his whisky flask and spiced his juice with some of it, sipping it with a satisfied relish.

'*Waaahh*! What an atmosphere! And Kamla is going to add on to this with her guitar recital.'

Kamla smiled coyly while bringing out her new instrument and starting to tune it. However, instead of the sonorous sound of the Hawaiian guitar, there was an interruption of the sound of another car coming and halting on the landing above. Mulk Raj had a frown on his face when he heard car doors opening and closing and then heard animated voices moving towards them.

Soon, the figures appeared climbing down the steps to where the Khannas had parked themselves. There was a burst of laughter and loud expletives from both the groups. The Uberois, another leading family in the sports goods industry of Sialkot had just joined the Khannas.

Having heard from Magan Lal at the Khanna residence that they had gone for a night picnic to Head Marala, the Uberois decided to do the same. So, packing up some kebab rolls and fruits, they reached where they were now.

'You bloody fool, Mulk Raj, can you just slyly run away without taking us along…ha ha ha! *Teree toe, behen ki* (a compromise on a Punjabi abuse)…,' guffawed Lalit Uberoi.

Lalit was accompanied by his wife, Mohini, and a son and daughter. All of them were very close to the Khanna family, and the whole group was happy in each other's presence.

While the families bunched together in their respective pursuits, Mulk Raj and Lalit went off for a walk with their respective whisky and juice, accompanied by a cigarette.

'*Yaar* Mulk, the environment is not very healthy, and I am not hearing the right noises,' spoke Lalit in a relatively hushed tone than he was generally used to and coming straight to the point.

'What context are you talking about, Lalit? Is it the Two Nation Proposal of Jinnah?' Mulk Raj enquired, though guessing it to be what Lalit was talking about.

'Absolutely, boss. I have had an extensive talk with my foreman, Abdur Rehman, who, though very much in favour of a separate Muslim homeland, talked sense in whatever he said,' responded Lalit.

'What did he say?' asked Mulk Raj.

Lalit took a swig of his whisky and a long drag from his cigarette and then spoke on.

'Well, Mulk, he has categorically advised me to start shifting business to either Amritsar, Jalandhar, Ludhiana or Delhi, if not anywhere else where we have relatives or known people. The hint comes from the fact that Punjab has been reasonably apathetic to Gandhi's call for the Quit India Movement.

'The only active response has come from Khan Abdul Ghaffar Khan from the Northwest Frontier Province. The majority of the Muslims are following the call of Jinnah to boycott the movement.'

Both friends had the need for another whisky, which Mulk poured from the flask he was carrying in his pocket. After a swig, Lalit carried on.

'Rehman has information that the British are going to transition power to two national governments instead of just one, which means that there would be a Muslim migration into the demarcated Islamic nation and Hindu migration out of it.

'And, dear friend, we are in that part of Punjab which would form a part of the proposed Islamic nation. So, we need to strategise when and how to move. Both of us have a reasonably large infrastructure, and it is going to take us quite some time to conclude our migration plans.'

'I totally agree with you Lalit *bhai*, and I am also thinking on similar lines, having almost similar patterns of information through various sources,' said Mulk Raj, flushing the remaining whisky down the hatch.

Mulk Raj had always been a very silent and introspective visionary. He liked to set objectives and achieve them with the most confidential and uncomplicated approach. Moreover, the Uberois were competitors, apart from being friends. Hence, there were a lot of areas of his business and life plans that he needed to work out within himself. In such cases, his wife, Jaya, was the only person he could always depend upon and confide in. She knew virtually everything that he was thinking of at any point in time.

Ashok being sent to Colonel Brown's in Dehradun was a part of the plan to kick-start the migration process. It would be slowly followed by the rest of the family. He was already researching Amritsar, Delhi, and Agra as areas to relocate and had been talking to his various close connections in all these places.

Mulk Raj was sure that the Two Nation plan as envisioned by Jinnah and the Muslim League, and also adopted as The Pakistan Resolution Day on 23 March 1940, would take a long time to materialize, if at all. He gave it at least a decade, which meant that there was no immediate stress. However, he was smart enough to keep a finger on the political pulse, both at Delhi and Lahore.

'Mulk, where are you lost *yaar*?' spoke Lalit in a bit of a loud tone, startling Mulk Raj out of his chain of thoughts.

'We are being called by the ladies for dinner, and we need to finish off the contents of your flask, whatever little is left,' spoke Lalit, with a twinkle in his eyes.

They finished the last dregs of whisky in silence, gazing at the outlines of the Shivalik Ranges in Kashmir. With a full moon and a clear sparkling sky, the visibility was enthralling. The rest of the gang was busy serving kebab rolls and daal to all.

***

The Idea of Independence is spreading throughout British India...with varying intensity...objectives...self-interests....

CHAPTER 9

Gawana

Pran was no more. His mortal remains were sent to his village, Gawana, with two representatives of the British Government, and with Negi, Bisht, and three armed guards accompanying them on the solemn journey.

Both friends of the pradhan were now prisoners and had been allowed to accompany Pran's body and attend his funeral as a special case by P Mason, the Deputy Commissioner of Pauri Garhwal. Mason was a popular officer amongst the natives of the entire region, sympathetic to their cause, righteous, and always readily available to anyone who required his support or presence.

He had decided to attend Pran's funeral and be with the grief-struck family for the entire day. He was genuinely fond of Pran and had many a discussion with him on earlier happy occasions. His death on account of the unintentional yet fatal bullet was a setback for Mason sahib (as he was popularly referred to).

What made Mason's visit to Gawana more painful was the absence of Pran and having to face his family and the village folk. Negi and Bisht were grossly overwhelmed and could not help breaking down in short bursts. After all, it was their childhood friend they had lost. Pran was their rudder, who gave them direction and motivation. He was the single factor behind their limited successes in life. It was Pran who forced Negi's elder son to migrate to Delhi, where he was under the guardianship of Trilok, Pran's second son. Negi's son had done well in his studies and secured admission to the University of Delhi, from where he got into a government job after having completed his graduation. Bisht's second son had also parked himself with Trilok and completed his Diploma in Mechanical Engineering, before getting a foreman's job in an English tool manufacturing company in Delhi.

The journey continued, till the police one-tonner reached the roadhead in front of the sweets shop from where the three friends had first begun their journey to partake in the fateful agitation.

***

'Hey Kadam, there seems to be a group of people coming towards the village entry,' said Pochi, Bisht's eldest son.

Kadam was sitting in the courtyard of his house, along with his friends and some village elders, discussing the status of the agitation in Devprayag. Each had their version and interpretation. However, all the versions ended with the heroics of the pradhan and his two close friends. They were proud of their sons of the soil and were sure that Gawana would be known for their bravery. On hearing the approaching crowd, they headed towards them. They could see Mason sahib leading the group, which made Kadam a bit anxious.

He was the acting pradhan now, and any official visit should have been intimated to him at least a day in advance, giving the village panchayat ample time to prepare an appropriate welcome. A sudden visit was unsolicited unless there was an emergency or else an approaching catastrophe. As they came closer, Kadam could see his uncles, Negi and Bisht following, wearing distraught expressions. Policemen and many others followed them. They seemed to be carrying something amongst them, which till now was hidden from Kadam and his group's view. And what was further confusing was the absence of Kadam's father.

Slowly, everything came into view. Pochi was the first to cry out, sighting his distraught father. Kadam's legs buckled and he collapsed to the ground.

***

Mason sahib, stood with his hat in his hand and head drooped. He had bloodshot eyes, with fresh tears rolling down. His friend's body was placed in the courtyard of the house, where Pran spent his childhood playing and growing up, where many a bottle of liquor was consumed…many a prank played, where many decisions were taken for the family and the village, where Mason sahib had sat with Pran discussing Garhwal, its village fabric, and soliciting support for his schemes over a few rounds of drinks. His friend had departed to a plane far above him and his comprehension. This simplistic, yet truthful son of Garhwal showed great courage and patriotism, for which his family, village and the whole nation would be proud of in times to come.

Vimla, Pran's wife, stood quiet and tearless, in one corner of the courtyard, consoling Nirmala, who had been Pran's favourite in the house. She had looked after all his needs, quietly, yet efficiently—from his morning tea, breakfast, meals, snacks, and drinks to cooking for his parties—the list could go on.

'Could someone, for heaven's sake, tell me what happened to my husband that he lies here, still, and silent? Why isn't he bellowing and shouting at all of you, to be behaving like such idiots?!' Vimla shouted out at all assembled, and then suddenly rushed to her husband and fell at his feet, howling inconsolably.

She then banged her fists on the courtyard floor, breaking her glass bangles, while she continued to talk incoherently. (The breaking of bangles was an age-old Hindu custom for a widow to perform just after her husband has departed since they are a sign of being a married lady.) All this happened so suddenly that it took some time for Nirmala to react and get to her mother-in-law.

By this time the whole village had assembled at the pradhan's house, shocked and bereaved, since Pran was genuinely and deeply loved by all. It was then that Mason sahib took control of the situation and described what had happened to his brave friend—how he saved Negi, and rallied around his friends and comrades.

'He died like a true and valiant Rajput (a Hindu warrior clan), being shot at from the front, and not caught running. He breathed his last, helping and rallying his brethren, in protest against what he felt was unjust to him and his nation. Gawana should be proud of a pradhan of the likes of Pran.'

Mason concluded with a salute to the great soul lying in permanent meditation on his beloved soil.

'The administration has decided to give him an official and honourable cremation befitting a man of his stature—one of the most popular and well-known pradhans in this region,' said Mason further, walking up to Kadam to console him and consulting on his father's cremation proceedings. He had called his office staff to be present and arrange all that was required, including a parting '3-Volley Salute' generally conducted for military or police funerals. However, Mason had ordered this honour as a special case for his beloved friend and pradhan.

'He deserves every bit of it and more, which is outside my reach of command. The grand man from Gawana,' spoke out Mason, before breaking down at the loss.

Pran was cremated with full honours in his village at about 5 pm the same day. People from all the surrounding villages, as well as from as far as Devprayag attended the funeral. The mood was somber and there were tears in every eye.

After the '3-Volley Salute' and the cremation, Kadam addressed those present, giving them the schedule of the ceremonies to follow, ending with a community lunch on the thirteenth day after his father's death. He had gained complete control of himself, befitting a person who would take over his father's responsibilities thereafter.

Trilok and young Satendra had bloodshot eyes and stood beside him. Trilok had been informed earlier in Delhi through the good offices of Mason sahib. He knew of the tragedy well before his family in the village and had made immediate arrangements to rush back, along with his son, infant daughter, and wife. He had been shocked by this unexpected news since he had no idea of his father's intense involvement in the freedom struggle. The extent of his knowledge was about his father's involvement in regional politics being a pradhan. It was his vision to see his father as a regional-level leader in independent India, as and when the time came, not to remember him in retrospect.

Satendra stood close to him, sobbing intermittently. He was flanked on both sides by his two elder brothers, who were now to take care of his career and future, in his father's absence. It was a patriarchal and male-dominated society, hence, although his mother's shelter would always be there with him, the substantive movements in his life would be decided by Kadam, supported by Trilok. At his tender age, he was more shocked on the sudden uncertainty and insecurity he could perceive in his life, more than the unceremonious removal of his father from the family equation.

Kadam, Trilok, Satendra, Vimla, Nirmala, and Vandana (Trilok's wife) were all assembled in the room. Realities had to be discussed, hence the atmosphere was heavy. Everyone waited for Kadam to start the conversation, since he was the head of the family now, being the eldest son. Kadam finally cleared his throat and started speaking.

'Losing *babu ji* is a great shock for all of us, and we are trying to find our own ways to fight the loss. So, I would not like to increase our pain. There are a few things that need to be decided now which I am going to put forth.

'First of all, despite my being the head of the family and thereby being responsible for babu ji's estate, the ultimate decision-making would remain with *ma ji*. We would follow her decisions and will.

'Secondly, it was babu ji's will that Satendra be imparted further education in Delhi and study to become an engineer. Hence, Trilok would take up his responsibility after he takes his final exams for third grade in the village school here, which is another three months from now. We will compensate Trilok, as much as possible, in cash and in kind, to augment the cost of Satendra's education and living expenses in Delhi.

'These are the immediate important decisions which need to be taken before we discuss certain other issues of importance.'

With this, Kadam concluded the first part of his thoughts, to be put to rest by others. Vimla had tears in her eyes at Kadam's decision as the successor to her husband. She knew that he was a stepson, but she was convinced that their family honour was in the right hands. Her expressions conveyed her satisfaction to whatever Kadam had just said. Trilok spoke, after looking around at his mother, brothers, and wife.

'I am totally with *bhayji* (referring to his elder brother Kadam) and trust his abilities to run our farm and village affairs. He is the most competent to do so.

'I also have implicit faith in his decisions on our family affairs, henceforth. He is, to me, what my dear babu ji was. I am also sure that *ija* (referring to his mother) would have all the empowerment from all her sons to be the real head of the family.

'As for Satendra, he is as good as my *chewl* (son in the region's colloquial usage) and will be taken care of accordingly.

'Vandana and I are already prepared and looking forward to greeting him in our household in Delhi. I am also sure that both Vandana and I would be able to take care of all Satendra's needs on our own. However, what I have always depended on from our farm is the fresh produce, which, I presume, will continue to come my way.'

While speaking, Trilok drew, Kadam, his *bhayji*, near him.

Both broke into sobs. Bitter sobs. The brothers loved and cared for each other and their families immensely. Satendra clung to his ija with remorse at not having his father's patronage any longer, but at the same time, getting more and more comfortable with both his brothers. He was also looking forward to his journey and living in Delhi with Trilok bhayji and his family. However, he was discrete enough to guard and confine his excitement within himself.

Finally, the complete family unanimously declared Kadam to be the next Karta (head) of their Hindu Undivided Family (HUF) to close the procedural formalities, as well as support him to be the next pradhan of Gawana. An era had ended, and another had begun.

***

Another loss...at another place and time....

CHAPTER 10

Bittersweet

Narendra sat in his armchair upright, in a white kurta and dhoti. He was gazing at a distant horizon, lost in his own thoughts. Intermittently, he would take off his spectacles and wipe his moist eyes. Around him, on the veranda, outside his bedroom, were all his close relatives and friends. In the courtyard, three steps below the veranda were seated a whole lot of others on durries spread on the ground. It was a huge gathering.

Inside Narendra's bedroom lay his wife, Urmila, peaceful and relieved of all her maladies, once and for all, with sindoor (vermillion) in the mid-parting of her hair.

It was about five in the morning on March 24, 1945, when Narendra's wife had breathed her last in her mortal existence. Ajit, Narendra's son-in-law and Surobee's husband was the doctor who had checked her pulse and other vital symbols before declaring her dead.

Purobee and Surobee were uncontrollable. Surobee started beating her fist on Ajit, who took it all stoically, with tears rolling down his eyes. Sharmila sat beside her sister with a blank expression and wet eyes, getting hold of herself. She had a lot of responsibilities and work on her frail shoulders, starting with consoling her two nieces and looking after Subendu, just nine years of age, who was in a daze, asking naive, yet obvious questions to gather the impact of what had just occurred but not succeeding in it at all.

She also had to be by her brother-in-law, Narendra's side, and provide him with the necessary support he required to navigate through his great loss, as well as tide through all the rituals attached to his wife's departure for the two weeks to follow.

Narendra was with Ajit when Urmila had left him alone in her spiritual quests. As a doctor, he knew this would have to be the way it would end, but he remained in a state of denial and escapism till it finally shook him up. He tapped Ajit on his shoulder, asking him to take charge along with Sharmila, and walked away towards his study.

Once inside, closing the door behind him, he sat down by his study table, cupped his face in his two hands and started shaking convulsively. He cried out loud and banged his fists on the table. Salty tears streaming down his tired and fatigued countenance. He let them flow without any checks. They needed to since he could not afford tears thereafter.

After quite some time, he got up, composed himself, took out his pipe, tucked it with tobacco, lighted it with his Zippo, and sucked hard. A few long and hard drags. Then he walked out straight into the gathering, a changed and composed man who would take life by its horns and allow his immense grief to be a very personal friend.

***

In a Bengali household, the thirteenth day after a soul departs is called *niyom bhongo* (the breaking of rules that prevailed for the previous twelve days after the death of a person). A community dinner is spread out and served by the very close family members of the departed soul. It was the niyom bhongo following Urmila's death, and Narendra took it upon himself to lead his team of relatives in serving food to the invitees, comprising Ajit, Amarendra, Bijoy, Virendra and his other nephews and cousins. All were in traditional white dhoti and kurta. Their smiles clearly concealed their grief and the solemnity of the occasion. The food was typically Bengali and served using large containers and large ladles.

The seating arrangement was split into two segments, with the larger group seated on the ground on durries and served using traditional plates made from dried leaves, while a smaller group of close friends of Narendra and some British Officers were seated on chairs along the large dining table. However, all were supposed to use their fingers to eat—no cutlery, as the custom directed.

There was a large portrait of an effervescent and laughing Urmila propped on a pedestal at one prominent end of the gathering as if she was overseeing the feast and welcoming the invitees.

'*Kripa koray Urmilaar atmaar shanteer jonnay prarthona koroon.* Please pray for the departed soul of Urmila,' spoke Narendra in a raised albeit solemn voice, both in Bengali and English, to initiate the dinner.

***

The next day was a day off for Narendra from his clinic, and he decided to devote the morning tea, with a fresh mind, to conclusive talks with Ajit and Surobee, as to what lay ahead in his vision and scheme of events. The three of them assembled at the front veranda, outside his bedroom, while Babu Lal got a tray of tea and placed it on the table, leaving them to talk. Narendra started the conversation and eased out apprehensions.

'Your ma has now left us in her physical form, but her wishes continue to be a part of our lives. Also, the fact remains that even

I have a limited time with you all. Being doctors, both Ajit and I are aware of my hypertension and cardiac ailments. Diabetes does not make matters simpler.'

'But baba, we should also be aware that all the critical parameters have been kept in check through regular medication and dietary lifestyle, the sole problem being your obstinacy in not giving up smoking,' interjected Ajit, while Surobee agreed with a nod, stroking her father's hand at the same time.

'I agree, Ajit, but I also know the limitations of options which medical science provides us here in this country. We are a vassal colony of the British, and the government's primary focus has its limitations. What is available in the developed West is available only there,' spoke Narendra.

Ajit cut him off again.

'Baba, you are a privileged member of the Indian society, being one of the empanelled doctors of the Meerut Cantonment. The establishment knows and respects you and would be more than pleased to arrange for your passage and treatment back in London. You even have a few friends at Harley Street, and so do I,' reasoned Ajit.

Narendra disclosed a knowing grin while embracing Surobee with evident fondness.

'Ajit, I am fully aware of the vistas of possibilities available to me by virtue of my position, but I am equally aware of the limitations in my accepting the same.

'The situation in our country is very unstable, wherein anything can happen without the semblance of a notice. I have a tremendous number of responsibilities within my family and to society at large.

'My absence for months, even stretching to a year is unthinkable and impractical.'

Saying this, Narendra sipped his tea and picked up his Briar, which was immediately snatched and taken away by Surobee. He responded with a loving and patronizing look, while Ajit looked on and spoke.

'So, what is in your mind, Baba? Let us know so that we do our bit accordingly and as much as possible.'

It was the moment, and Narendra's instincts and experience prompted him to close the decision now, or it would be never.

He already had had a detailed conversation with Ajit and his father, Bijoy, in terms of his son-in-law's taking over his practice in Meerut and, in the process, settling himself down there.

Composing himself, after taking another sip of the morning brew, Narendra spoke, 'Ajit, I have already spoken my mind to you and your father more than a couple of years back, when you decided to quit the British Indian Army and set up your own medical practice.

'The matter was put to rest then, with the thought that you were getting a great opportunity to be trained under one of the most illustrious members of our profession, Dr BC Roy, in Calcutta. Hence, we would take up this offer after you have gone through a reasonable period of this experience.

'Now the time has come to take a call once and for all, since I would need to initiate the process of your introduction to the city and my patients. I would also be settling quite a few issues of our family's future, accordingly. The prime in my mind is Subendu.

'I can trust Surobee and you to carry out my wishes, both in my presence as well as absence, not only in matters relating to young Subendu, but also overseeing my estate and its complicated affairs. Of course, under the able guidance of Virendra da, whom I plan to appoint as the legal guardian and caretaker of Subendu.'

With this, Narendra sat back, pouring himself another cup of tea from the pot, helped by Surobee. He now waited for Ajit and Surobee to declare their joint will for the future.

Both looked at each other and decided that Surobee should take the lead and talk on their behalf.

'Baba, we have had a very long discussion with Ajit's father, mother, and my eldest sister-in-law. They all had mixed opinions since this would be a major change in not only Ajit's but also the complete family's life.

'At some point in time, both my father-in-law and mother-in-law would have to shift where Ajit and I finally settle down, after Ajit's sisters are all married off and *bapi* (Ajit's father) retires from his college in Assam.

'Hence, we would also have to have a house of our own to accommodate the family since staying in the Banerji residence is out of the question and against bapi's and Ajit's principles. So, baba, this is not as simple as just saying yes and that's it.'

Narendra looked at his daughter adorably. She had grown up into such a mature girl—the same hot-headed and spoilt younger daughter of Dr Narendra Nath Bandhopadhyay.

Composing himself for a moment, he spoke slowly.

'Surobee, I decided to talk to Ajit and not anyone else on this for a few valid reasons.

'To start with, I respect Ajit and his family to the core. Their values and integrity are of the highest pedigree. Then, Ajit is from the medical profession like me; hence, the only person at this moment to take over professional responsibilities from me.

'Finally, your immense affection and caring for your younger brother is not hidden from me. I will be a happy man seeing Subendu in your and Ajit's care and tutelage.

'Both of you are also aware of our larger family, which remains dependent on me and our household, in some form or the other. They all have their hidden interests, which might not be aligned with our own. I need not go into further details on them.

'The only people whom I can trust explicitly without raising an eyebrow are Virendra, Sharmila, and both of you. I know that the four of you would think of nothing else but the best for my little son and protect his interests to the best of your ability.

'Also, in Virendra, I find a very intelligent and thinking man who would guide our affairs in the right direction in these changing times, with the British indicating handing over power to a native government.

'We have complicated times ahead, and I need my chosen kith and kin by my side, to face it together.'

With this, Narendra picked up his pipe and clenched it between his teeth without lighting it. He knew it would be immediately snatched by Surobee.

After some silence, Ajit finally spoke.

'Baba, I know what you want and expect out of us, and we are willing to take up that responsibility.

'The only favour that we are looking at is your guidance in buying a piece of land, which we can afford, so that we can gradually build our house there and shift. Naturally, it should be near to this place and the clinic.'

With this, Ajit, who was a man of very few words, gave Narendra more than what he could expect. Narendra had already planned out where Ajit and Surobee would shift from Calcutta, as well as the plot of land, ideal for them to spend the rest of their lives.

***

Virendra turned up on the dot at ten in the morning. Narendra had called him over on a breakfast discussion. He was in his crisp white dhoti-kurta, which suited the somber occasion in the Banerji household.

Apart from Narendra, seated at the table were Ajit, Surobee, Sharmila, Purobee and Sujoy (Purobee's husband). Narendra did not waste further time and made his declaration during breakfast.

'Virendra, I have a request to make and do hope that you would be in a position to accept my desire,' spoke Narendra to initiate conversation and create an opening for himself.

'Narendra da, you know very well that unless it is a grave impossibility, I will be always happy and eager to be of any possible help and support to you. So please do tell me what is in your mind,' responded Virendra.

All present at the table already knew of Narendra's mind, as also what were the changes happening after the passing away of his beloved wife. Subendu was purposely kept away and was happy playing with his young cousins in the guest wing of their house.

'Virendra, there is a spot of good news in this grave tragedy, which has afflicted us. Ajit has finally decided to support me and take up my practice and improve upon it. I am very sure that the city is going to get a great doctor and scientist who would revolutionise clinical practice in this region.

'I have also identified a dwelling for Ajit and Surobee to start with. Ajit has also decided to buy a piece of land somewhere nearby and build a house for his family. I would lend all possible support to make that happen.'

With this, Narendra looked at the rest with a satisfied smile on his face and, after having a few bites of his *luchi-tarkari*, continued with the remaining part of his scheme of events.

'Ajit's decision to shift to Meerut is a very significant happening in our household. However, that is not all. I need to fit in another important piece to make the picture complete.

'What is also very critically required is to have a legal guardian for Subendu. Ideally, I desire both a protector and guru to my tender and young son and also a guide to me in today's complex times.'

Virendra was wise enough to guess and remembered having had a conversation with Narendra on this quite some time back when Urmila was suffering. However, he didn't want to jump the gun and preferred to hear it before he spoke his mind.

After having a sip of some sweet tea, Narendra continued.

'Virendra, I remember having already spoken my mind to you on this, so that I could have your opinion when the time was ripe.

The legal guardian I am referring to is you, and as a matter of fact, I have not been able to conjure up a more suitable option.

'I am more than sure that your commitment to this extension of your family is second to none, not even to me. So, pray, do give me your final response now, so that I can plan out all processes accordingly.'

'Narendra da, it is always an honour to have your trust by my side, and I will try to do justice to it. I am a man of few words; hence, my response is 'yes', in agreement with your desire," replied Virendra; after which he got up, reciprocating Narendra's gesture, and they embraced each other.

Getting back to where he was sitting and acknowledging the acceptance and smiles of all assembled, Virendra carried on speaking, 'I have some information from my grapevine that Meerut, along with Delhi and some of the surrounding areas will also witness relocation from West Punjab, apart from what East Punjab would be experiencing. After all we are not very far away from the dividing line.

'Hence, we as a family need to be very careful of all the assets which we already have and are thinking of procuring, now onwards, till the dust settles down.

'I am sure we are going to have quite a few permanent guests and varied vocations amongst us, in this very city.'

This was agreed upon and acknowledged by all.

Change was inevitable, and freedom would be sweet but with a bitter core.

***

Elections...approach...voters...and the voted.... All would define India of the future....

CHAPTER 11

On the Brink

It was the third week of September—pleasantly cold and slightly windy, and the sun's warmth was welcome and soothing. Being a Sunday, it was an off day for Narendra, as well as most of his relatives and friends.

Virendra, Sultan Singh, and Ishaq were seated on garden chairs out in the front courtyard surrounded by beautiful and colourful blossoms. The table in front of them was laden with fresh salads and fruits of the season, interspersed with glasses of chilled beer and juices, according to the taste of the people around. The topic of discussion was the announcement of nationwide elections made a few days back by Lord Wavell, on September 19, 1945. The air was replete with excitement, debates, and discussions. The election would clearly decide the roadmap of India's future. Rather, the future of an independent India.

'The passage is clearly indicating a Hindu-Muslim divide, friends,' stated Sultan. 'Congress and the Muslim League in the fray is a clear indication of what I say. Jinnah is openly stating it to be a two-nation referendum, and the British Government is also looking at it that way.'

'Sultan is right in what he has noticed and saying, but the complete mass of Muslims in the nation are not with what Jinnah and his followers desire,' responded Ishaq.

'But Ishaq, we all know that you have also formally joined the Muslim League and are supporting their campaign in Meerut and the surrounding area,' retorted Sultan.

'You are right, Sultan, but my ideology falls short of the desire for a separate nation for our community. As a matter of fact, let me make it very clear, here among friends, that in case Pakistan does happen, I will stay where I am. In Meerut. My first loyalty lies to my city and India, as is the case with our respected Maulana Azad,' stated Ishaq quite vehemently.

The atmosphere was getting a bit charged with Sultan's taunt, and Narendra, like a good host, intervened.

'My friends, I have absolutely no doubts about Ishaq's integrity and love for our nation. His leaving Congress and joining the Muslim League is a matter of his community ideology, which is personal to him and his strategy.

'We favour and support the Congress, likewise, he supports the Muslim League. He is not asking us our reasons to do what we are doing, and we should not be questioning him on his decisions in so far as there is no dent in our personal relationship.'

'Thank you for your understanding of my situation and internal struggles, Narendra. I owe the reason for my happy existence in Meerut to all of you,' spoke Ishaq, shifting a bit and holding Narendra's hand in a gesture of brotherhood.

Virendra was watching everyone quietly with absolutely no expressions on his face. However, the position in which he was and his hobby of interacting and researching all sociological as well as political activities going on, had blessed him with an uncanny sense of vision.

Narendra looked in his direction and asked him for his opinion on what could be expected in the near future. Virendra started to speak, softly and slowly.

'The divide between the two communities runs very deep, as the situation now stands. Bengal in the east is simmering and so is Punjab in the west. Whether we like to acknowledge it or not, trust runs very thin between the Hindus and the Muslims, even in the United Provinces, of which we are also a part.

'I am more than convinced that the eastern part of Bengal and the western parts of Punjab are surely going to vote the Muslim League into power. We would also have certain other Muslim-majority constituencies peppered around British India, which would vote for the Muslim League.

'Likewise, all the Hindu majority constituencies are going to put their weight behind the Congress. However, the Congress would have a clear majority in the Central Legislative Assembly, but the divide would undoubtedly be favouring the two-nation aspiration of Jinnah.

'Apologies, but Jinnah and his close team of followers have done a sound job in convincing the majority of Muslims to a feeling of abject insecurity in being a part of a Hindu majority nation.'

All of them knew this to be the truth but did not want to accept the facts. Narendra, for one, knew that there were some Hindus from the western part of Punjab who had been making discrete enquiries around Delhi and Meerut for land and shop space. As a matter of fact, one of his patient's relatives from Punjab had also deposited some money in a bank in Modi Nagar. The patient confided that the family was planning to migrate there and relocate business.

There were quite a few such cases, signalling that some people with a vision of the future, as well as authentic information from their grapevine, were already planning far ahead of the forthcoming birth of the two nations. Narendra snapped out of his thoughts and jumped into the present. At that moment, he was a man with a lot of questions, and he had a lot at stake as well.

'Friends, what I am visualising is that there would be substantial migration into our region, which is Delhi and Meerut. I can also foresee a lot of associated problems, the exact nature of which I cannot fully comprehend right now.

'But surely, tough, and expensive times are ahead of us, and we need to be very careful about our assets, businesses and callings. So, let us all bind together and support each other and stay afloat, while our nations get freedom and start life afresh.'

After speaking, Narendra looked around for comments.

Everyone was thinking along similar lines, and a joint plan of action was on the cards.

'Doctor sahib, we are all together and will face the challenges similarly. Our political ideologies may be different, but our fate lines do merge,' spoke out Ishaq.

Everyone nodded and shook hands. Virendra, however, had the last word.

'Friends, the coming few years are going to be very challenging. Situations will be very complex and stressful. We would need to maintain our cool and have a helpful attitude towards the weak, the displaced, and the poor.

'I would continue to give you all information and visibility I would have of the political scenario and the risks approaching us, and I expect the same from all of you. As of now, it seems Congress from Meerut.'

With this the friends disbursed, lost in their own thoughts.

Narendra and Sultan gulped down the last dredges of their remaining beer. Ishaq stayed back to have a private conversation with Narendra, to whom he confided almost everything which went on in his mind.

'Doctor sahib, things are not very good between the two communities here in Meerut. Muslims feel threatened by the Hindu majority, and there is a complete lack of faith and trust between the two.

'You might be getting some information from the patients of the two communities that visit your clinic. Otherwise, the upper segment of our city's society may not be that much aware of what is going on in the lanes and by-lanes and in the ghettos.

'As a matter of fact, there is a substantial mass of my community who are planning to migrate to Pakistan, as and when they are sure as to what and where Pakistan will be. Some are already communicating with their friends and relatives in Lahore, Sialkot, Rawalpindi and surrounding areas to help them resettle there.

'We would need to assuage this feeling of insecurity, and I had the good fortune of explaining this to Nehru ji and the Maulana when they visited my residence a fortnight ago, as you would be knowing since you were also present then.'

While saying this, the stress and earnestness on Ishaq's face were clearly visible, and Narendra could understand his emotions rather too well.

'Ishaq, I can say with utmost confidence that our complete circle of friends and I are with you and the complete community you represent. We are all Indians and brothers. So be rest assured,' confirmed Narendra yet again as they parted for the day.

***

It was a cold morning at Gawana where the only comfort was the sun outside. Kadam Singh Rawat, the village pradhan, sat alongside his uncles, Ajay and Bhim, the village schoolmaster Pandit ji and a few other village folks outside the village panchayat hall. They were all enjoying the sun, the hukka, bidis and *khaini* (a kind of chewing tobacco), while *chaha* (tea) was doing the rounds.

The topic of discussion was the impending elections declared by the British Government and communicated to them by Mason sahib. The only exciting point of discussion amongst the village folk assembled was whether their portion of Garhwal (Tehri Garhwal) would be allowed to participate in the elections by their King, HH

Narendra Shah. What Kadam and his coterie had heard was that most of the kingdoms under British rule and protection had refused to participate in the elections declared by the British Viceroy.

'Bhaeeyon, Tehri vote *naheen dega. Maharaj kee yehee ichhaa hai,'* stated Ajay Singh Negi. (Brothers, Tehri will not vote. It is the wish of the King.)

'Mainay bhee yahee suna hai, chacha," responded Kadam. (I have also heard the same.)

The remaining part of Garhwal, the Pauri region, was a cakewalk for the Congress since it was almost completely a Hindu mega constituency. There were no communal tensions there. Gawana, or any other village, or the larger towns of Rudraprayag, Srinagar, or Pauri had no choice of voting for a party apart from the Congress.

Kadam was listening to the radio regularly, and so were the others who visited the village panchayat office quite often. They had heard that things were not at all going well with the Hindus and the Muslims, down south, in the plains after Haridwar, in the east, in Bengal, nor in the west, in Punjab.

'They are not only fighting for freedom from the British but also for separate countries for the Hindus and the Muslims,' spoke Kadam. 'Here, we simply want a free Hindustan. Free from both the British as well as the King. The British, from what I have heard, are already planning to leave our country, and (Govind Vallabh) Pant ji will see to it that Tehri becomes a part of Hindustan.'

Saying this, Kadam, his uncles, and the others assembled to go to their fields for their work of the day.

Kadam and his uncles, Negi and Bisht, were still passionate about freedom from British rule, but their enthusiasm to lead from the front, alongside the other freedom fighters, had greatly diminished with Kadam's father's death.

Pran had become more of a local folklore—a great freedom fighter who sacrificed his life for the freedom and prosperity of his village, his Garhwal, and his nation. His name came ahead of all the army jawans who fought and gave their lives for the British in the two World Wars. Kadam was proud of his father and actively supported the Congress, but it all ended there. As a pradhan, his priority was the prosperity and well-being of Gawana and the progress of his family. He did not seem to have any further ambitions. Negi and Bisht had also settled down in their comfort zones after their dear friend Pran's death, and after being prematurely released from prison for good conduct. They had not got over losing their best friend and mentor. It was a big gap in their lives. Both had stopped drinking since there was no fun in indulging in such frivolities without Pran.

Overall, Garhwal enjoyed a simple life of day-to-day existence, with few activists among them. They believed belonging to the Devabhumi, nothing untoward would happen to them or their clan.

***

Work was on in full swing at Khanna Sports, with cling! clang! bang! sounds coming into Mulk Raj's cabin, while he was busy scanning through his accounts and order book, along with his accountant and cousin, Sanjay Kapoor.

Business was brisk and orders kept on increasing by the day. His main problem was keeping pace with the growth.

'*Yeh sab hogaa kaisay*, Sanjay?' asked Mulk and carried on. (How will it all happen, Sanjay?)

'We have Muslim labour, and Allama Iqbal as well as Jinnah are not making lives easy for us. Elections have been declared by Wavell. The whole of Punjab is already talking of a divide on Hindu-Muslim lines. It seems clear that the western part of Punjab, including our Sialkot, Lahore, and Jhelum, which is Muslim dominated, will vote for the Muslim League. Our votes here are in minority, while Eastern Punjab, including Amritsar and the surrounding areas, on the other side of Jhelum, will vote Congress in.'

'Toe issay kyaa pharak padtaa hai, Mulk bhai? *Yahaan Congress ho ya Muslim League, aap ko thoe ballay hee bannanay hain na?* responded Sanjay, while flipping pages of the ledger. (So how does it matter Mulk Brother? Whether it is Congress or the Muslim League, you only have to make cricket bats, isn't it?)

'Sanjay, to me it is very clear that this is also going to be an endorsement for the two nations of which Jinnah and his team are hankering about. Which means that Sialkot and Lahore will become a part of the future Pakistan,' Mulk asserted vehemently.

Sanjay was a bit confused when he responded questioningly at what Mulk Raj just said.

'So, we would become citizens of Pakistan. What difference does it make to be governed by a non-congress government?'

'I don't know, Sanjay. At present, I do not have a certain answer to your very simple question, but from what I hear, the situation will become quite complex, with the two communities not being in the best of terms,' replied Mulk.

'What are you saying, Mulk bhai? I stay at a place which is predominantly Muslim. And believe me, they are the best of neighbours and friends which I can have. Asif, who stays in the house next to mine, was telling me just the other day that no partition of this nation is going to affect the people staying in the cities or the villages, whether they are Hindus or Muslims.'

Sanjay's reasoning was so very innocent, naive as well as gullible, thought Mulk, who knew more, much more.

A close family friend of his, Ajit Kohli from Jhelum, about 90 kilometres northwest of Sialkot was even making plans of resettling near Delhi. He had sent his eldest son to Delhi to explore business opportunities and the availability of shops and residential space there.

On the advice of his father, Vivek had also opened a bank account with a bank in Modi Nagar, near Delhi, depositing more than ten thousand rupees in it, through the introduction of a relative of the Kohlis there. Ajit had clear indications that quite a few of the local Muslims were just biding time, so as to grab the assets created by their Hindu neighbours at throwaway prices when the right time came.

Similar information was also given to Mulk by many of his business friends in Sialkot, including Lalit Uberoi of Uberoi Sports, who had also created separate business units in Delhi and Calcutta; and was slowly transferring his bulk of manufacturing there. Mulk had discretely secured admission of his eldest son, Ashok, at Colonel Browns in Dehradun and had plans to do the same for his remaining two sons. However, he kept on denying to himself that he would ever have to move his business and factory from Sialkot. He had even purchased a larger bungalow in the Civil Lines area, shifting from his old residence near the more congested clock tower. He looked up from his order sheet and spoke in a hushed tone to Sanjay.

'Sanjay, would you be interested in travelling to Amritsar and Delhi and exploring possibilities of opening another factory there? Get a feel of house rentals and availability in some good localities in those cities?'

Sanjay looked at Mulk closely to judge the seriousness of his request.

'Mulk bhai, in case you are seriously considering such an option, I am definitely with you, as a support and your right-hand man.'

Mulk had already had serious conversations with his younger brother, Jai Raj Khanna, on a possible shift of business into the Hindu-dominated Delhi or nearabout.

Jai had suggested Jalandhar, Agra, or Meerut since they had relatives, suppliers, dealers, and friends in all three cities. He was also of the view that serious thought and follow-up action needed to be taken since a complicated process of partition could be easily sniffed. Both the brothers were also discretely exploring the price their business, factory, and houses would fetch in the Sialkot market.

'Yes, Sanjay, you get your train tickets booked for next week, in case it is possible for you. Consult with your parents and family today. We should not be wasting much time,' instructed Mulk with a tone of discernible urgency.

It was a strange mixture of excitement as well as nervousness in Punjab. The excitement was that trading, business, and agriculture would all become easier and more profitable with the suppression of high taxes, and with duties being removed by the free government of Hindustan. Or that is what they believed. The nervousness was there because Hindus in Punjab had a lot at stake in terms of wealth, running business, and assets. Most of them were sceptic of what lay ahead but comforted themselves with the rosy picture they liked to believe in and what they were made to understand by their Muslim neighbours.

Some of them were gifted with practical vision and guts to act out of their comfort zones. They were making plans and executing them silently and, in some cases, very efficiently.

***

Clement Atlee was clearly of the view that India was too immense to handle. The World Wars had left Great Britain with no energy, inclination, or funds to run this huge colony for its benefit or that of the colony. Discontent between the Hindus and Muslims was a clean divide and was being exploited by multiple stakeholders for their own benefit.

The Muslim League was baying for a separate Muslim nation where the elite wanted power, and the local populace of both East Bengal and West Punjab wanted to get rid of their day-to-day problems, including the clutches of the local money lenders. The much-talked-about elections were conducted by the British starting in December 1945.

The Central Legislative Assembly had 102 seats, out of which the Indian National Congress, headed by Sarat Chandra Bose, won 59, the Muslim League, headed by Jinnah, won 30, the Europeans got 8, Akalis 2, and 3 went to the Independents. Since the Princely States had not joined the elections, the seats had dropped from 375 to 102. It was a clear majority for the Indian National Congress, but what also became clear was the reality of the formation of a separate Muslim nation.

What had just started as a divide-and-rule convenience of the British administrators was seemingly ending in a complex scenario of a partition.

In July 1945, Atlee, after the victory of the Labour Party and his becoming the Prime Minister of Great Britain, declared his nation's intention of withdrawing from India. An act of Parliament proposed June 1948 as the target for British withdrawal. Hectic parlays towards a two-nation split took momentum.

However, it was the northern part of India, south of the Himalayas, extending up to the Central Provinces and including Bengal and Punjab, that began facing the heat of communal turbulence on account of the call for partition.

The southern part of British India and the northern Himalayan parts of the Colony had complexities of a totally different nature, not directly related to the call for a separate Muslim nation. Further, the multitude of Princely States had different dreams to weave.

All of them together were heading towards a chaotic advance to an exciting freedom where, apart from the unified desire for freedom, very little else seemed to be common. The British also wanted just that but in a different way. They desired freedom from having to rule India.

***

While Partition continued to be the principal speculation in eastern and western British India.... Resettlements carried on for a better future in other parts....

CHAPTER 12

Head Sahib

Satendra sat by the side of the stream bordering the village and the forest beyond with his feet dipped in the ice-cold water. Though his teeth were clattering, he liked the moving water over his submerged feet. It was just him and the ever-faithful old Shera, their Bhutia dog, from the days of his father. Shera had been left alone after his partner and soulmate Bela had passed away a couple of years back. Since then, his attachment to Satendra had grown immensely, and he followed him wherever he went, especially on his grazing trips to the jungle. Satendra had slipped out of his house immediately after lunch and wandered off to the stream without any purpose with Shera at his heels. He sat there chucking pebbles into the stream and saw them bouncing off the surface of the gurgling water. Shera also followed the trajectory of the pebbles, as a purposeless activity, happy to enjoy the companionship of his young friend.

Satendra was excited at the prospects of a changed life awaiting him in Delhi but screened behind this enthusiasm was the loss of the simple joys and pleasures of his existence in his beautiful village—of playing with his friends, going off in a group to graze their cattle, the excitement of encountering and safeguarding from the bagh, of hunting expeditions and gorging on the freshly roasted *kachmoli* (chunks of meat carved out from the hunted game), of the warmth of his mother's love and her delicious home cooked food, the comfort of his village school, where he was supposed to be a role model, and of the importance of being the famous late pradhan's son and the current pradhan's younger brother. The thoughts of the losses kept on pouring out, till they condensed into tears, which slowly became uncontrollable. Before he could realise it, he was weeping, holding Shera in a tight embrace. He let the emotions flow unabated since showing off the same in front of his mother was unpardonable.

She was holding up very strongly with a superficial sense of joy hiding the pathos within.

***

It was a sunny winter afternoon in 1945 when, with a cloth bag slung on his shoulder, a medium-sized steel trunk in his hand, and after touching the feet of his mother, Kadam, Kadam's wife, Bhuvi (his maternal uncle), Negi and Bisht, young Satendra took leave to start off on his long journey to Delhi.

'Theek cha, ab main chaldu chaan,' he said to his elders, before departing. (Okay, I will take your leave now.)

He had kept his slippers in the cloth bag to wear them later when he reached Kotdwar to catch a train to his destination. Till then, he would have to walk barefoot and save his slippers from the snow and moraine on the way. They were all that he had in terms of footwear. Trilok would buy shoes for him in Delhi later.

The village trader brought stock only on demand, and the simple village folk purchased footwear or clothing strictly according to requirements, which were few and basic. Restraint was in their value system. So Satendra, with his few essential possessions, had the advantage of travelling light.

The load that he carried were edible items packed by his mother and sister-in-law, Kadam's wife. That food should never be in short supply was the basic theme of the simple village folk. They lived off the land, and the land provided them enough to stay healthy and for people like the pradhan's family, much more.

A few of his friends accompanied him on his walk out of the village to the end of the nearby jungles, which grew dense from the first stream bordering the village clearing. For his friends, Satendra was somewhat of a hero. They were envious of his going to study in Delhi. What fortune and luck, they thought, which evidently did not quite favour them. Satendra knew this, and already behaved like a superior.

'Arey, bidi ko bundal nikaal na,' coaxed Satendra to one of his village friends, with a wink and glitter in his eyes. (Take out a packet of cigarettes.) They sat down under an oak tree and one of the boys drew out a pack of the local cigarettes. Acting and feeling like adults, they took deep drags and blew out the smoke in rings, looking at the horizon with dreamy eyes. Satendra took drags without really inhaling, which he could never manage to do, unlike his other friends. However, he felt great about it.

While taking drags in turn, he told them about what little he knew of Delhi, his city of the future—the large schools and colleges there, cars, carriages, buses, and other modes of transport, the wide, metaled roads, neat and clean bungalows, beautiful gardens, and monuments. His friends swallowed it all in amazement, their eyes and mouths wide open. Satendra had pulled some fried bread stuffed with potatoes and pickles out of his cloth bag, and they ate together.

'Ab chaldu cha,' said Satendra, getting up and dusting his haunches off the forest debris. (Let us go now.)

Satisfied after finishing a cigarette and food amongst themselves, they all got up to venture further. Satendra was to reach Pauri by the same evening and stay the night in one of the hotels, which had been arranged by his uncle—a walk of over twelve kilometres. So, he needed to hurry. Satendra finally bid goodbye to his friends, who left him on the fringes of the dense green oak forests. They had tears in their eyes. Years of playing, cattle grazing, and studying together were coming to an end.

Satendra walked into the unknown future, feeling the strong pangs of separation yet again, leaving his friends behind and walking alone. His separation from his mother, elder brother, friends, family, and village came back to him as a griping pain, an overwhelming longing. He knew that this intermittent suffering would continue to haunt him periodically, way beyond into the future.

After the first patch of jungles, there was a neighbouring village from where one of his uncles joined him, taking him under his care and tutelage. He was popularly known as Head Sahib, being the head mechanic at the Delhi Textiles, a large cloth mill in the city. It was Head Sahib's duty to drop Satendra at the Trilok's doorstep, while Trilok waited for his younger brother's arrival with both anxiety and excitement. Head Sahib would go back to work after a vacation in his village and having cast his vote. Head Sahib was already waiting outside his house gate, which opened on to the bridle path which ran through the entire length of the village. He waved to Satendra as he saw him appearing in his line of vision. After a brief touching of feet and minimal dialogues of well-being, both walked on, carrying their respective loads. The goat track was what they had, to lead them through forests, shrubs, and rocky terrain of the Himalayan region, right up to the roadhead, ultimately leading to the Pauri town.

The snow in some patches on the track had solidified into a harder surface due to constant footfall, and Satendra's feet were numb by the time they reached Pauri. It was a blessing in disguise since he could walk without feeling the freezing chill and debris bites on the soles of his hardened feet. Head Sahib was taller than

Satendra and walked at quite a brisk pace, forcing Satendra to almost run to keep up. The goat track was a regular descent into the valley and an easy passage for both.

Satendra almost ran down with gay abandon at the excitement of his first journey out of his village and of seeing large towns like Srinagar, Pauri, Kotdwar and then Delhi for the first time, of then getting on to a bus and then a train, also for the first time. He had only heard of them and seen some pictures in his house on paper bags which carried edible and other items. He used to gaze at them for long spans of time, dreaming to be a part of them. He distinctly remembered flipping through a newspaper that his elder brother got from Delhi. He saw ornate and fancy horse carriages with huge, healthy horses, being ridden by white sahibs with colourful clothing.

'Wow! All this is going to be a reality around me, and I am going to be a part of it,' thought Satendra, with immense excitement, which made him walk even faster, without realizing that they were now climbing a steep uphill slope and he had left Head Sahib quite far behind. Breaking out of his wonderland, he looked back to see his uncle labouring up with his backpack. Satendra stopped and waited till Head Sahib caught on.

'*Ye bag mithe de dyo*, Head Sahib,' spoke Satendra, courteously. (Give this bag to me.)

He knew that Head Sahib was much older than him, and the climb would sap his energy. Head Sahib handed over the satchel to his young nephew with a thankful smile. Satendra strapped it on his back, and both started to climb along to the Pauri Township. By early evening, they had reached the bustling mountain township of Pauri, walking and on carriages. Satendra was staring at everything he saw, with his mouth wide open and expanded pupils.

He was seeing so many horses, horse carriages, wheelbarrows and carts for the first time. British Soldiers, officers and Indian sepoys kept going about their daily chores. The huge marketplace went on and on with so many goods to sell, right from eatables to footwear, clothing, utensils, hardware, and toys...one had to just name it. Many people were buying so many things.

Satendra, almost banged into a cart, walking straight while staring all around.

'*Arey beta, dekh kar chal, bazaar baad mien dekhna,*' Head Sahib chided Satendra, who snapped back to reality. (Son watch and walk. Look at the shops later.)

'*Kitnaa badaa bazaar hai na,*' said Satendra with loving innocence.

Head Sahib embraced him with affection and told him that that was just the beginning of the wonders of their great country. He would have to see Delhi to believe it. Satendra was excited, very excited.

Soon, he found himself walking into a queer kind of house, which had many small rooms with two or more beds in each. Some faced the road and valley, and some faced an inner courtyard. Every floor had common toilets and baths at each end.

Head Sahib approached a room, where some people were sitting on proper chairs facing tables and appeared to be busy working and talking to people surrounding them.

'What is this, Head Sahib? Is it some kind of a big house belonging to a friend of yours?' enquired Satendra.

'Ha! Ha! Ha!' guffawed Head Sahib, 'this is a hotel, Satendra. Travellers come and rest here, to move on once their work in Pauri is over. We will stay the night here and leave for Kotdwar tomorrow morning. Let us take the keys to our room, put our luggage there, and freshen up. We can then go out to a restaurant to have an early dinner and go to bed. We have a long way to go tomorrow.'

It was a small room with two beds and chairs, a table and a wall-mounted cupboard. The floor was cemented. A window opened to a valley view below from which came the last rays of the sun and the creeping chill to greet the uncle and his nephew.

Satendra sat down on one of the chairs and pulled out a packet from his bag containing pieces of *gur* (jaggery). He offered some to Head Sahib and then nibbled on a couple of pieces. Head Sahib had ordered some steaming hot tea.

When Head Sahib went to freshen up, he picked up a newspaper, which was lying on the table. It was a few days old. He flipped through the pages and skip-read news from here and there. It was all about the Congress and the outcome of the recently ended World War II. Satendra had larger interests in mind—Delhi, and his new school, admission to which had almost been secured by Trilok, made easy by the good marks he had in his third grade, especially his keen interest in mathematics. The struggle for independence, the World Wars, the British Government, and the Indian leadership were only of academic interest to him, as should have been for a boy of his age. At that moment, it was his exciting journey and a new life, and right there, the good food.

Head Sahib walked in. He clapped in front of Satendra's eyes to take him out of his stupor and asked him to move.

'Let us go for dinner, young boy. We need to sleep early. A tiring journey ahead tomorrow, starting at the first crack of dawn.'

'Yes, Head Sahib, I am ready,' said young Satendra, following him out of the room, closing the window as it was snowing now.

The road was laden with a thin carpet of fresh snow and had become mushy brown with mud and dirt. Satendra was wearing his sandals now, and looking amazed at the traffic and people, even after seven in the evening, despite the drizzle of snow. There was a reasonably plush restaurant near to the hotel where Satendra was staying for the night; and he looked towards Head Sahib to know whether that was where they were going.

'Not that one, young boy. That is meant for only the *goras* (the British) and their official invitees. We will be turned out, even if we try to enter. Also, it would be far too expensive for our pockets and budget,' responded Head Sahib, guessing Satendra's query.

'But why would we not be allowed? It is our country and place after all.' Satendra spoke with a reasonable amount of amazement at the whole idea. This was the first time that he was exposed to such racism. They walked leisurely down the market area, window shopping.

Head Sahib stopped at a dingy outlet with a reasonable local crowd at the entrance and gestured for Satendra to wait for him outside while he disappeared into the crowd inside.

Satendra gave vent to his childlike curiosity, quite natural for his age. He ventured forward and tugged at one of the locals of the crowd.

'Bhai oo kyachh?' enquired Satendra. (Brother, what is that?)

'*Oo Daru k'dukaan ch,'* replied the man and rushed forward in a hurry to grab his entry into the shop for his fill. (It is a liquor vend.)

Satendra had a sweet and naughty grin playing on his face, realizing that Head Sahib had gone for a few quick shots to come out warm and reinforced. He, too, had an urge to try a few slugs of the fiery liquid. He distinctly remembered smuggling a bit out of Kadam's bottle, kept on a shelf in his room, back in Gawana. He had almost choked on it after having a large gulp, but the after-effect was rather pleasant. He had felt groggy and happy. He checked his pocket to see how much money he had on him and realized it to be good enough for a quarter bottle of the local fare.

His feet moved towards a small counter outside the shop to quietly buy a quart and gulp it down before Head Sahib came out of his revelry from inside the vend. However, his fear overtook his desire for adventure, and he froze where he was, with his teeth clattering in the cold. He pulled the monkey cap over his mouth to keep cosy and watched amusedly the people coming out after their affair with their bottles. Some staggering, some very cautious and some almost falling over.

Head Sahib came out resembling a rope walker on his trick. Satendra giggled within himself, concealing his laughter, while Head Sahib felt guilty that his young nephew had caught him in a nefarious act. Looking straight ahead as seriously as possible, he gestured for Satendra to walk along.

They reached a seemingly popular joint in one of the by-lanes, exuding a mouth-watering aroma of all kinds of food. The restaurant was full of garrulous men, talking away merrily and loudly.

The umbrellas, including the ones they carried, occupied a lot of space in the seating area. A Garhwali could forget his trousers but not his umbrella, so went the saying. Very much like the British. But that's not how they carried them. Their umbrellas would hang at their back, with the handle tucked into their jacket or shirt collar.

They were lucky to get a table with two semi-broken chairs and they balanced themselves rather well, with Head Sahib wobbling a bit like a ship in a bit of a choppy sea.

'Arrrreee doe meat ko thhali dyoch,' ordered Head Sahib with the authority he exuded at his workplace on the factory floor. (Hello, give us two meat meals.)

It was Satendra's first meal in a restaurant, outside of his village. They were served the typical local fare—*Mandua kee roti* (bread made out of a local cereal), *bhat* (rice), mixed *bhaddu dal* (dal made out of a mixture of local pulses), *urad dal ke pakore* (urad pulse fries), *bhang ki chutney* (sweet chutney made out of cannabis) and meat curry (mutton) with *sani hui mooli* and *nimbu* (grated white radish with lemon and red chillies). This sumptuous meal was topped up with *jhangore ki kheer* (a milk-based sweet dish). The elaborate dinner cost them less than two rupees, a stuffed stomach and a few belches apiece.

They walked back to their room, feeling the biting cold a bit less, with a satisfied stomach. While Head Sahib enjoyed the walk puffing an after-dinner bidi, an Englishman, in his place, would have been smoking his pipe or, maybe, a healthy cigar. Sleep came easily to both.

It was still dark and cloudy, having snowed for quite a part of the night, but it was not snowing any longer. They were ready after having cold water baths, which was common with the villagers from the Himalayan countryside. It protected them from the bitter cold and kept them healthy. Satendra was carrying parathas, some of which they devoured with some jaggery to fill them up for the long and arduous walk ahead. With his *chappals* (flip-flop sandals) back into the bag, Satendra followed Head Sahib, who wore a pair of half-worn-out sneakers, which he would discard at the end of his journey. After all, he was a working man, and this was the least he could afford at such a senior position and age.

About a kilometre from the market, there was a narrow trail leading down through slope farms growing vegetables and potatoes, the staple in these areas. It was a sharp decline at places, and they walked and slid at quite a steady pace. The path was more slippery on account of the snow, and they had quite a bit of company.

There was constant migration from these parts of the hills to the plains down below, with people migrating to Haridwar, Roorkee, Muzaffarnagar, Meerut, and right up to Delhi. This mass migration had nothing to do with politics or the freedom struggle. It was purely economic, for jobs and other earning opportunities. From Delhi, people from Garhwal further fanned out into other areas of British India and the Princely states. One could see them aplenty in the British Indian Army, with a full-fledged Garhwal Regiment forming a part of the establishment. Their presence could also be felt in the various Princely State armies. They were a trusted choice as clerks, working staff of government establishments and at homes of the elite since they were loyal and hardworking. However, climbing up the employment ladder was still a dream with the people of the region. Few, indeed, had risen to the seniority of a head clerk or a supervisor.

The economy of Garhwal and adjoining Kumaon was also popularly referred to as a Money Order economy, with the working migrants sending regular money orders back home to their families. The pradhan's larger family had a few success stories who had risen slightly above the rest, though not to very senior positions—a lower division accounts clerk, at the maximum, like Trilok, Satendra's elder brother.

Nevertheless, within the group that was walking as a team on their journey to Dugadda and then on to various parts of the plains and some eventually to Delhi; Head Sahib and Satendra walked tall and proud. The group was about fifteen strong, and the primary topic of discussion was employment, with studies and the freedom struggle taking the second and third priority. The British had given them job opportunities and a semblance of discipline and orderliness. A working government and an army with immense job potential were a boon for them. They did not want to slide back to an era of multiple power centres and internal wars and strife. Getting a government job was their ticket to success, glory, and respect.

The group had decided to walk about thirty-five kilometres and camp in the forests surrounding Dharasu. It would be arduous ups and downs throughout the day, and their destination would be reached only late in the evening. Walking down in a group protected them from the abundant wild animals, the most dangerous being the big cats and the great Himalayan Bear. There was also a lurking fear of man-eating leopards and tigers prowling around. Quite a few villages on the way had reported cases of their kith and kin being mauled or killed by the man-eating cats, some of them even dragged away. Some British hunters and renowned Indian shikaris risked their lives in hunting these animals down. They were sponsored by the government, as a measure of social service and maintaining the forest-human equilibrium. Groups of men and campfires generally discouraged wild animals from lurking nearby.

By midday, the group had come to the last village before the thick jungles made their presence felt. They decided to stop there, rest a bit and reinforce themselves with a quick lunch, some tea and a smoke before they walked through the jungle trail and camped for the night at some appropriate clearing in the forests near Dharasu.

There was a small outlet open on the main village track, serving hot meals and beverages to travellers, doubling up as a meeting point for the village males. The sun had shown up, giving respite from the intense cold, and the village folk were trying to make the best of it. A group of them were playing carom on a table spread out on the village road, outside the small restaurant, while some youngsters watched a team of four play, shouting 'hurrah' when someone pocketed a carom disk.

Head Sahib led the group to this outlet and requested a hot vegetarian lunch. He served all some *kafuli* (spinach cooked in spicy gravy), *bhat* and *koda ki roti* (baked bread made from a locally available cereal), accompanied with some sweet and sour *til ki chutney* (chutney made from roasted sesame seeds and yoghurt). The food was freshly cooked, spicy and delicious. More so, they were all hungry and tired. The fare was followed by piping hot sweet tea, with the intoxicating smell of charcoal on which it had been prepared. The elders accompanied the tea with a bidi smoke, while they chatted with the locals.

'You must move through the dense part of the forests within the next few hours, say, in about three hours. There are a lot of baghs and bears in there. Very dangerous,' warned an old man, sitting by the carom-playing group of youngsters. 'After about fifteen-odd kilometres, there is a *bugyal* (green pasture), at about five thousand feet, near a village, Varali. It will come after a short but steep climb of about a kilometre or so. That would be the best place to camp for the night.'

Head Sahib heard him out patiently, even though he had been on that route so many times that he could move blindfolded. He was the only person in the group who was so well travelled. The others were first-timers.

'I presume that we are not going to encounter any habitation from here to Varali, baba?' Head Sahib asked the old man who had volunteered to advise.

'No. And I hope that all of you are carrying some food to eat for dinner and breakfast tomorrow morning since you will not be staying in the village (Varali). In case you are not, buy some from here. Or kill an antelope or wild boar in the forest before entering the bugyal and roast a meal out of it. You would enjoy it,' advised the old man, with a toothy grin.

Head Sahib was carrying his alcoholic reinforcement, which he had purchased from Pauri, being a seasoned traveller, while some of the others were making discrete enquiries as to where to get some in this last village before the jungles.

It was late in the afternoon when the group started walking towards Varali, reinforced with requirements for the way and satisfied in the stomach. Soon, they were surrounded by forests and pines to start with. The ground became slippery on account of the carpet of pine needles moist with melting snow.

'No bidis' was the strict dictate while walking through pine forests. The trees and the needles were highly inflammable, especially the pine oil, which was tapped from the tree trunks by adjoining locals. The oil had tremendous medicinal, cosmetic, and industrial value, and some locals were venturing around for the purpose. They warned the group to be careful of a leopard doing rounds in the vicinity of a small Shiva Temple, near a water body, which lay ahead.

Head Sahib chatted with this small group of villagers in rapid local dialect and found out that, fortunately for them, the leopard was not known to be a man-eater and had not caused any major casualties. Picking up a dog here, or a sheep there was all it had done. But they needed to be careful, and a small stop at the Shiva

Temple, a short prayer to the great lord, would carry them safely through.

The pine forests were on an incline, however, on account of sparse undergrowth and less snowfall in the area, the progress was fairly smooth.

'Bhedu pako baromasa, kaphal paakay chaith meree chhailaa' was the group song while they laboured their way up the forest slopes. (Himalayan fig ripens throughout the year, while kaphal berry ripens in springtime, my love.) It was a pleasing, popular, and romantic folk song that the locals sang on many occasions, and this walk to the land of jobs and fortune was one of them.

Singing and chatting, they reached the Shiva temple, standing lonely by a stream that was hopping and skipping down to join some river on its way down below. The water was clean and cold, having its source from the freshly melting snow. They first washed in the cold water, drinking it to their heart's content, then dried themselves up and proceeded to the temple to pay obeisance to the mighty lord.

Satendra prayed for all his dreams to be fulfilled with regard to his education and career and for happy days ahead. All of them prayed for a safe journey to their respective destinations.

The forest was serene and quiet, with an intermittent cacophony of monkeys, chirping of birds, and sounds of the barking deer common in the area. While they sat and puffed bidis, a herd of *chital* (spotted deer) came down from the forest to quench their thirst, while their leader stood guard, hearing and smelling around. A cat on the prowl could be distinctly made out by the movement of animals around, and a sudden urgency in the jungle lore. All seemed to be quiet, so the cat must be resting for a busy night. The group flexed themselves and, with a final bow to the Lord Shiva, started off on their way to the bugyal for the night's stopover.

The temple demarcated the top of the mountain slope hosting the forest. From there it was downhill and an easier passage.

However, the pine forests dramatically gave way to deodars, and then silver oak and the undergrowth became more luxurious and denser. The redeeming feature was the absence of snow.

Satendra and another boy, slightly taller and older, were given the responsibility of leading the group with long knives in their hands to chop off troublesome undergrowth and weeds as they walked to safeguard others from the danger of snakes, scorpions, and insects.

The last bit of walk before they reached the bugyal was uphill and rather steep. The forest was also quite dense there. Dusk was showing its presence, with dimming sunlight and murky surroundings.

The Head Sahib and another tough youth from a village adjoining the Pauri town, separated from the rest in a pre-decided move. Head Sahib had taken out his gun and quietly crouched into the thickets.

The rest of the group walked on, including Satendra. The bugyal was supposed to be just a few furlongs of climb away, and they reached the beautiful green and undulating expanse by about half past six in the evening. Head Sahib and the youth had yet to show up. About an hour later, the group could see two shadows and more, labouring towards their campfire. Satendra ran towards them to help and greet them. They had a chital amongst them, still warm and fresh after the kill. Head Sahib and the youth had to wait, crouching in the undergrowth for almost half an hour before they saw a herd walking up to the same stream that flowed by the Shiva temple. With a simple experienced shot, the kill took less than a minute. There was a roar and cheer in the group when they saw the victorious team walk up to the campfire.

Some men from the group volunteered to skin and prepare the chital to be roasted and cooked over the campfire, while a few others started to prepare a wooden stand out of stout oak branches collected from the forest, wetting them so that they did not catch fire. After skinning and cleaning up the game, they marinated it with various spices, salt, and red chilli powder before settling it on the stand over the raging fire. Almost everyone in the group carried spices, condiments, pickles, and various other products from their respective villages.

While the meat was being cooked, the men, boys, and Satendra freshened up and settled down by the warmth of the fire, enjoying the aroma of the meat. Most of them, apart from Satendra and the other young boy with him, sipped into a couple of bottles of country liquor doing rounds among the group.

After a few swigs, Head Sahib came into his own and broke into a Hindi film song, while others followed. One after the other songs kept on pouring out with the right or wrong lyrics. The enterprising folks of the group carved out pieces of meat for themselves as well as others.

Satendra picked up some slices of the roasted antelope and walked off alone, away from the merry-making crowd, into the dark yonder, and sat down peacefully to have his meal of meat and some homemade parathas with spicy pickle. He topped it up with some jaggery and washed it down with some cold stream water stored in a steel container. With a belch of satisfaction, he sat back quietly, gazing at the distant mountains and hearing the banter and songs floating through from the direction of the campfire.

He braced himself within the warmth of a blanket that he had wrapped around to safeguard against the chill and, very soon, was lost in the romanticism of the prevailing quietude of nature. This was the environment he was used to and felt comfortable in. He felt safe in its tender embrace. The other world in which he would be treading would be more exciting, albeit totally unknown. What gave him strength was that he was just another face in a large crowd of migrating multitudes. His weakness was the warmth and care of his mother's love and his village and its surroundings, which was a whole big home for him. Thinking, with slowly moistening eyes and a surge of forlorn longing pushing from inside like a tidal wave, he transitioned into a state of blissful slumber, cuddled into his coarse warm blanket.

The next thing he knew, he was being woken up by Head Sahib. It was time for morning ablutions, a quick prayer, tea and parathas, and the move towards Dugadda, with a short break en route at a village called Verkhal.

By seven in the morning, the group was ready with their baggage, fresh for another long day of walk. The redeeming part was that this leg of the journey was that it was mostly downhill. They would be able to cover a longer distance with less effort and negotiate more shortcuts, decreasing the overall distance. Forests and streams, the chill and the undergrowth, flora and fauna continued to accompany them as before.

After walking for about two and a half hours, they could hear an absolute ruckus created by the monkeys. They could see antelopes rushing away, and the barking deer calling at the top of their voice from a concealed destination in the adjoining forest slopes. Almost everyone in the group was an expert in deciphering the jungle lore. It was a matter of survival for them. The noise opera was a clear indication of the lurking presence of a large cat.

They froze where they were, and complete silence prevailed. Taking discrete positions, they hid themselves as much as possible in the surrounding shrubbery.

Satendra dashed behind the lantana bushes by his side, with his young friend following. They settled with a bated breath. All was still, till Robert Browning's poetic creation slipped out of the nearby bushes and majestically walked off towards the direction of a distant water body. It didn't seem to be in any hurry or under any threat. However, it could sniff smells, which it must have been curious about. Nevertheless, with a full stomach and daytime laziness, the tiger focused on quenching its thirst and taking a long nap to reinforce for the night.

The hidden men and boys could see the tiger and its acute smell slowly fading off into the distance. After some time, they moved out of their perches, dusted themselves and commenced their onward journey. Four hours of walking later, with some smoking breaks to punctuate, the group reached the Verkhal village, where Head Sahib had planned a lunch break.

As common in this part of the country, a successful person was well-known throughout the region and had well-wishers wherever he went. So was the case in Verkhal.

'Namaste Head Sahib, *kakh jaanrhee chha?*' was the common question. (Good Day, Head Sahib. Where are you heading?)

'*Ma Dilli jaanrhh*,' replied Head Sahib courteously. (I am going to Delhi.)

Satendra was surprised at the popularity of his uncle, and a bit amused too. He half thought that the tiger they had sighted sometime back must also have known the Head Sahib and walked away in reverence. He grinned to himself while concocting the scenario. The pradhan of Verkhal was well acquainted with not only the Head Sahib, but with Satendra's family as well.

He embraced Satendra affectionately and told him about the great reverence he always harboured for his late father as well as Kadam, his elder brother. He was more than happy to host the whole group at the only village restaurant.

They were served *kapul and bhat*, along with *bhang jeera* chutney and real hot green chillies (rice and curry along with cannabis and cumin chutney). The food was piping hot, fresh, and tasty and the tired travellers lapped it up, doing complete justice to the cooking. The local sweet dish, *kandku*, vanished before anyone could count seven. The pradhan of the village also had his lunch with Satendra and Head Sahib. Satendra felt proud and good to belong to the famous Rawat family of Gawana.

There was a courtyard in front of the restaurant, and after their post-lunch smoke, everyone sprawled there to take a quick power nap and start moving towards their final destination of Dugadda before nightfall. The forests after Verkhal were denser and lusher with wildlife, including the big cats.

On the way, Satendra and the rest sighted tigers and leopards on multiple occasions, but neither seemed to be ruffled in the other's presence. Both lived off the jungle, and for both, towns and cities were alien and uncomfortable.

Moving at a steady pace, with very short breaks, mostly by streams and rivulets, the group finally arrived at the second town after Pauri, Dugadda. It was not as large as Pauri, but very picturesque and less cold as well. It was not snowing here, though the night temperature was below five degrees Celsius.

The river Malin meandered through the city, slicing it into two halves. Surrounded by dense forests, which were frequented by many a famous shikari, including the likes of Jim Corbett, who had quite a few trophies of man-eating tigers and leopards to his credit. The locals knew him and his exploits more in the form of popular folklore. He was very much a part of them.

The group reached the marketplace on the northern side of the river Malin, a somewhat smaller one compared to that of Pauri, selling mostly vegetables, cereals, pulses and spices. Down along the river was a liquor vend and, further down, a basic travellers' inn. Since it was reasonably late in the evening, all of them headed to the inn to grab a bed, while Head Sahib and another man walked off to the other side of the river to enquire about the morning bus to Kotdwar. It had to be early in the morning since they had a train to catch from there by about twelve noon.

The man at the small makeshift ticket counter informed them of a bus which left at six in the morning and reached the Kotdwar Railway Station at about nine. This suited them since they would have some time for themselves in the town.

Most of the people in the group were going to Delhi, while some would get down midway to go to Meerut, an important town before Delhi, which had a big British Cantonment. However, they would all be taking the same train.

Head Sahib and Satendra expected to be in Delhi at about five in the morning the next day, which being a Sunday meant that Trilok would be at the Old Delhi Railway Station to pick up young Satendra.

Head Sahib reached back to the inn to find Satendra in deep sleep, while most of the gang were reinforcing their appetite and soothing their nerves after a hard day of walking with the country liquor brought from next door. After having a few drinks of his favourite rum, which Head Sahib was carrying all the way from Pauri, he woke up Satendra for a meat meal.

It had to be an early night and a long sleep, after an exhausting two-day journey on foot through difficult terrain and intensely cold weather. Satendra, however, knew that for him, it would be a long night of a single dream—his first bus journey leading to his first train journey and, topping it all, the excitement of a railway station....

***

It was half past five in the morning with the group assembled at the small bus stand across the river Malin. Yawns, tea and bidi smoke constituted the immediate ecosystem with animated discussions of various hues adding to the audio chorus. The avian population had also decided to commence activity. chirping, singing, and fleeting around.

Satendra sat on a boulder, cupping a steaming hot kulharh (earthenware cup) of tea and then sipping from it. The hot earthenware also helped to keep his palms warm in the biting chill of breaking dawn. He was aimlessly gazing at the river flowing by, while multiple thoughts were being processed in his little brain.

Suddenly, there was a shrill honking sound, followed by a strange kind of roar, which shook Satendra out of his stupor.

From around the bend of the road ahead, he could now see a vehicle labouring uphill from the Kotdwar direction, belching out black smoke. It was green in colour, large, on four wheels, with some designs of mountains and flowers painted on its body, and a projected front, like a snout. It approached in the direction where Satendra was now standing and gaping.

He had seen it in magazines and newspapers and had heard a lot of stories about it, but he was physically looking at it for the first time. He walked up to the bus mesmerized, touched the vibrating body, and peeped inside through a big door from where passengers were streaming out.

The carbon-infested smoke was burning Satendra's eyes a bit, so he blinked. In the meantime, he was pushed in by the crowd getting into the bus. He stumbled into it and almost fell onto the first vacant seat. It was by the window, next to the entry and exit. The passengers were mainly his group with some others. Head Sahib came and sat next to him.

'Here, take some freshly roasted monkey nuts,' Head Sahib offered to Satendra. He took some willingly while looking out of the window. Satendra was in a trance, a world of his own.

The bus driver had not stopped the coal-fired engine since it was quite an effort to crank it back into action. He gestured to the conductor, who used his shrill whistle to alert all passengers to get to their seats as the bus was about to set off back to Kotdwar from where it had come and where it would settle down after another round to Dugadda, for the rest of the day and night.

Apart from the ones sitting, there were quite a few people standing in the aisle. The vehicle was packed like sardines in a tin, and Satendra was fortunate to have the choicest seat, having been pushed onto it by accident.

Throughout the jerky, bumpy, smoky, and noisy ride, he kept on looking out at the mountains and nature he was leaving behind, all moving away from him. He would miss them all.

The journey to Kotdwar was along the Malin River. Narrow and winding roads cut through the rocky Lesser Himalayan range and surrounding forests. Adding to the frenzy of motion were many of the passengers vomiting out through the window, unable to endure the continuous turns, bumps, and smoke. For them, walking would have been far more comfortable an option had it been given to them.

Finally, they came to a bridge across the Malin, to their left, which also marked the exit from the mountains, into the plains of the bustling and noisy city of Kotdwar, on the foothills of the great Himalayas, which housed the many Gawanas and Pauris and Dugaddas in its labyrinths, protecting them from the tense and complicated world below and out. Within the Himalayan fort lay the mysterious, legendary, and simple lives of the mountain people; outside lay the equally mysterious, legendary, albeit complicated lives of the people of the plains.

The mountain people in the bus were now transiting from one lifestyle to the other within a short distance spanning just the length of the bridge.

So was Satendra….

***

After crossing over the Malin River, the hustle and bustle of Kotdwar town came into perspective. The presence of the British officials, sepoys and the police was quite distinct.

Satendra was a busy boy. He had too much to see and observe, which he could never have imagined a week ago. Tongas, bullock carts, cabriolets, and horse-mounted officials crowded the narrow road on which their bus also competed for space. The sides of the road were choc-a-block with street hawkers—permanent, semi-permanent and mobile—selling various kinds of commodities and wares. Multitudes of locals were on foot, preoccupied within and without. Satendra could also see a reasonable gathering approaching them shouting out something which he could not discern in the audio-visual frenzy surrounding him.

'*Inquilab Zindabad!*

'*Firangion, Bharat Chhorho!*

'*Swaraaj hamaara janamsidhh adhikaar hai.... Hum issay le kar rahengay!*'

The slogan shouting was now reasonably clear to Satendra. He knew about them through reading and hearing about the exploits of his father and his two friends from his village. This was the first time he had seen it in action. He had also heard that the elections which had just been completed were a clear victory for the Congress.

'Head Sahib, why don't we have this excitement in our villages?' enquired Satendra.

'*Beta,* we have many other problems to deal with than agitate against the British Government to leave India. We want peace, we have it. What else do we waste our time on?' explained Head Sahib and kept looking on.

'But Head Sahib, I have heard that our country is very big. Much more than from Gawana to Delhi. It is far beyond,' spoke Satendra, full of inquisitiveness.

'Yes, it is beta. It is far too large for you to comprehend. The British rulers have got a huge area from further north of our village to further south of Delhi. And further east of Calcutta to further west of Lahore. That is all I know, and all I can tell you at present,' replied Head Sahib with all the patience he could gather.

While both were absorbed in their conversation, the bus came to a sudden halt and the conductor blew his shrill whistle to tell the passengers that they had finally arrived at the Kotdwar railway station. Satendra and Head Sahib gathered their respective belongings and filed out of the bus along with the others.

It was a substantial parking flanked by shops on the right and left, with the station building in front. The building itself had a tin roof, with Kotdwar Station written in bold, at the entry.

There was a huge crowd in flux, getting in and out of the station, some hauling their own luggage, while others were being helped by porters called *coolies*. They were mostly helping the *firangis* (the British in colloquial language) as well as some very prominent-looking Indian people, possibly senior government servants. The parking area was replete with horse carriages of various kinds, bullock carts, and a few buses.

There also was a cordoned-off area where some cars were parked. They must have come to drop off some VIPs who would be travelling by First Class, thought Satendra.

The station had two distinct entry and exit points. One for the First-Class travellers and the other for the Second and Third Class. Satendra kept gaping at the First Class entry and exit points from where he could see a white lady with a small pet dog in her arms coming out and being followed by a few sepoys from the British Indian Army and a bunch of coolies carrying her luggage. He could make out that she must be some senior Army officer's wife coming to join her husband in one of the nearby cantonments. Maybe Lansdowne.

Head Sahib held Satendra by his hand and guided him towards the general entry to the station platforms where they would be expecting their train. He decided to put their luggage in one of the cloakrooms and then go out into the city to meet some of their relatives who were staying in Kotdwar. Both Satendra and Head Sahib had quite a few of them.

***

After visiting their relatives in the city and having had numerous rounds of snacks and an early lunch, Head Sahib and Satendra reached the station with just fifteen minutes to spare for their train's departure.

A smoke-belching, yet shining and well-kept black steam engine with a long cylindrical snout attached to numerous brown carriages, with yellow bands running through their length, stood next to the platform. There were many windows in each carriage on either side. Head Sahib told him that they were called bogies of which there were three classes.

The First Class was neat and clean, with independent coupes, reasonably segregated, with an aura of snobbery surrounding it. The Second Class was more crowded yet appeared to be more comfortable than the Third Class, where most of the crowd on the platform seemed to be heading towards. There were more bogies for the Third Class and only a couple of them for the First.

'Why didn't we take the First Class, Head Sahib? After all, we are from a village pradhan's family, and you are such a successful person working in Delhi,' enquired Satendra, while following Head Sahib to one of the Third Class compartments, which was allotted to them, according to their tickets.

'Beta, locals are not allowed in the First Class, and we are one of them. It is only for the *firangees*. Also, it is far too expensive for our pockets. Even the Second Class is more expensive, and it is mostly reserved by officers and government servants. So, Third Class it is,' replied Head Sahib, assuming he had satisfied Satendra.

However, Satendra made a resolve, one of many, that First Class would be where he would travel after he had graduated to be an officer with the government since he was sure that an officer he would become. He took in one last glimpse of the formidable steam engine and the impressive drivers and helpers inside it, before getting into his allotted compartment.

Sitting on his wooden bench next to the window, he looked out at the humanity on the platform. Families squatted on the concrete floor of the platform, using their luggage as props, some sleeping peacefully, oblivious to the crowd and cacophony. Hawkers yelled out to the public at large, selling their wares and eatables, and dogs, wagging their tails, sniffed around for just a bit more to eat.

'Wooooooooooooooooooooooo!' the train hooted.

The Guard blew his shrill whistle.

There was a jerk, and Satendra saw the people outside through his window frame moving backwards and slowly disappearing. A new frame, and then gone…and this continued, till the station vanished from sight.

The train had picked up speed, passing through the rest of the city, as a VIP, with people stopping what they were doing and taking time off to look admiringly at this majestic creature of human engineering passing by. Some waved at the passengers inside and Satendra waved back at them. He was feeling proud and excited being one of the passengers, journeying into the future, leaving the past behind.

***

The forests in the plains were so different from those in the hills. So was farming, as were the towns, cities, and the houses. So were the people. Satendra was drinking them all in. It was an education in motion.

The Sun was setting, and the clitter-clatter of the metal wheels of the train on the metal tracks and the slow rocking motion of the bogies added to the electrified romanticism of this great first journey for Satendra. He was in his own world when the train slowed down to move into a city after passing over a broad and mighty river—the Ganga.

Almost all around him bowed and said a silent prayer of respect to their mighty Mother Ganga. The great river, which apart from being what it was, was also the bedrock of Hindu philosophy, as old as Hinduism itself.

Satendra was seeing this great river for the first time. What followed was the quaint and religious city of Haridwar, crowded and congested with all the paraphernalia of religion, from *sadhus* (godmen) to every kind of religious offering and wares. Satendra gulped it all gaping out of the window of his bogie.

The train finally came to a halt at the Haridwar Station, with the inimical whistling sound of friction between the wheels and the track, on account of the master brake being applied by the engine driver.

It was evening, and soon the bogies were surrounded by all kinds of hawkers, selling tea, snacks and water from the Ganga.

'*Chayai chayai!* (tea, tea)…*garam samosay*! (hot fried vegetable dumplings)…*tazaa pakoday* (freshly fried vegetable crisps)… *tazaa barphi* (fresh sweetmeats)….'

The cacophony continued. Head Sahib picked up some samosas and hot tea for them. After taking Head Sahib's permission, Satendra also ventured out of his bogie on to the platform, looking around while stretching himself after long hours of sitting on the hard wooden surface of his berth.

The platform was as full and busy, or maybe more, than Kotdwar. However, he could find more native tourists here. Saffron seemed to be the colour of choice to wear, reminding Satendra of the air of religiosity suspended all over.

'Wooooooooooooooooooooooooooooooo!' The engine went ballistic again, and Satendra jumped onto his bogie near the entrance where he was standing. The train moved on into the night, while Satendra transitioned into the world of sleep and dreams.

***

Satendra woke up in Delhi. Or rather shaken up in Delhi.

Head Sahib had to push him hard into action.

It was somewhere around five in the morning and the train was temporarily parked in the outer area of the grand and huge Old Delhi Railway Station, awaiting passage to enter its hallowed portals.

Satendra jumped up from his berth and rushed to the toilet to freshen up before the train docked at its allotted platform. He was lucky to find an empty toilet as soon as he reached it.

He picked up his pillow and sheet, folded it up neatly and stuffed it in his cloth bag, after which he pulled out his trunk from under his berth, and was ready to get down. So was Head Sahib, who was travelling light as a seasoned traveller needed to.

The train entered the allotted platform to crowds, sounds, chaos, and confusion. However, adding sanity to the prevailing insanity was Trilok's presence, whom both Satendra and Head Sahib could identify in the crowd, even before getting down, while they were standing by the exit. They waved at each other, and Trilok started moving along with the now-stopping train to be next to the door, where his younger brother stood, to step into a new life.

***

A huge platform, with high ceilings and grand arches—this was many times the railway stations he had seen on his way to Delhi and with many more people of different races and nationalities. The station also housed pigeons, crows, and sparrows. To Satendra it seemed that he had come out of a small room to the huge world outside.

Trilok had him by his arms and was pulling him along to the giant staircase, leading to a bridge on top, which ran from one end of the huge station complex to the other. There were many staircases from all platforms leading to quite a few such parallel bridges, meant to go from one platform to the other, as well as the final exits from the station complex. Satendra was lost and aghast and left himself to Trilok as well as destiny. Both Trilok and Head Sahib kept on walking and talking without noticing all the conundrums around as if all this was as natural as forests, mountains, and wildlife. Outside the station lay the sprawling capital of the British India. Bharat.

The whole country was governed from there, which included Gawana. This was Gawana's capital, Satendra's country's capital.

It was from here that the thousand mutinies originated, ended, and re-originated. This was where pradhan ji's source of political power resided. Satendra's mind was bursting with all these thoughts rushing through.

Trilok and Satendra bid goodbye to Head Sahib. Satendra, as he had been taught right from childhood, touched Head Sahib's feet and thanked him for his guidance and company throughout this momentous phase of migration. Then, holding Trilok's hand, he alighted on a tonga to become a part of this great city, where he had made a personal resolve to prove himself to be a worthy son and brother of his successful family of pradhans and his beautiful village of Gawana. He would only return victorious to his village.

***

So many Indias within one...and each one so different than the other...each one leading different lives than other lives in the other India....

CHAPTER 13

Across the Seven Seas

Mulk Raj, his younger brother, Jai Raj, and family friend Ajit Kohli were in Mulk's drawing room at his Civil Lines house in Sialkot.

Almost the entire year of 1946 and the first quarter of 1947, commencing from the declaration of the Central Legislative Assembly Election results, were the dark days of pre-independence, in substantial stretches of the northern part of British India. Turbulence had spread in the entire band from the Northwest (Punjab) to the Northeast (Bengal). United Provinces and Bihar were also a part of the disturbance, and Bombay also felt the tremors. The clashes were arising out of insurmountable gaps between the Muslims and the inclusive corpus of Hindus and Sikhs.

Jai had all the reasons for being agitated and frustrated with the inactivity in the Khanna household, despite continued indications of Hindu insecurity prevailing in Punjab, right through 1940, when the Muslim League clearly declared their intention of having a separate Muslim Nation-state, and all the virulent deliberations between the two communities in carving out their own spaces as a continuing activity thereafter.

Jai desired an unambiguous plan of action of migrating to either the eastern part of Punjab or further down east into the Hindu majority heartland of British India.

He was sure in his thinking that they would be losing it all to the Muslim locals of Sialkot in case they did not start the process immediately. According to him, they were already a year late, and should rapidly get their act together.

Ajit, who was visiting them from Jhelum, having come to meet some suppliers in Sialkot and Lahore, also agreed with what Jai had to say. He had already initiated the process, having identified a shop, residence, and a plot of land in the vicinity of Delhi. Ajit had also started negotiating with buyers in Jhelum to sell his shops as well as a residence there so that they could use the capital to purchase assets near Delhi. His target was to leave Sialkot in another two months, latest by May or June.

August 1947 was supposed to be the month of independence for the two newly carved out countries, and the Kohli family was unanimously targeting to be well and safely settled in their new home and environment before that.

'Mulk bhai, *humnay toe ye tai kar liya hai...Dilhi ya Dilli kay naal basnay da,*' said Ajit with certainty and confidence arising out of sound planning. (Mulk, we have decided to settle down in or around Delhi.)

'*Magar humaaray pind kay musalmaan mushkil paidaa karaangay.... Vaddee mushkilien,*' warned Ajit. (However, the local Muslims will cause grave difficulties.)

He apprised the Khanna brothers of the tough negotiations and the humungous difficulties they were facing in selling their assets in Jhelum. While some of them were genuinely well-meaning, however, the ones who were not could not be identified.

Ajit's family also resided very close to where Ram Autar Gujral (Advocate) stayed and had some knowledge of the freedom movement, as well as political manoeuvres taking place in the leadership circles courtesy of his son, IK Gujral, being an active part of the freedom movement.

'*Humnay bhee Amritsar tay Dilli kay aas paas tehkeekaat karaaee hai aur jald hee kuchh phaislaa kar levaangay*,' responded Mulk. (We have also made some enquiries on properties in Amritsar and Delhi region and will come to a conclusion very soon.)

Mulk continued, as many others, to believe that Jinnah, Suhrawardy and others were in favour of a separate Muslim-majority nation, where the minority Hindus and Sikhs would peacefully coexist and prosper. He strongly believed that all of them would remain where they were, as bona fide citizens of Pakistan. However, Ajit and many more appeared certain that Muslim-dominated states would transform into sovereign Islamic entities, where the Hindu and Sikh minorities would have no rightful existence. They would have to migrate to the Hindu-dominated Hindustan to survive.

There were many people among the Hindus and Sikhs, in some surrounding villages of western Punjab, who were being forced to convert themselves to Islam for future safety, which included some workers of Mulk's factory as well. Parallelly, there were also large masses of Muslims who were concealing their Islamic identity in fear of being isolated and manhandled in many rural Hindu-dominated belts, specifically in Bengal, Bihar and east Punjab.

One of Mulk's Muslim suppliers in Western Uttar Pradesh, near Meerut, had been fatally injured in one of the many sporadic communal clashes taking place in various scattered belts of northern India stretching from northwest Punjab to northeast Bengal. It was a sense of denial and utter confusion that made many people believe this to be transient.

Mulk caught hold of his younger brother's hands within his own, looked straight into his eyes and assured him that he was trying to follow Ajit's line of thinking, and had already sent his accountant to Amritsar and Delhi to identify and settle matters pertaining to their migration.

'He should be back from Delhi within two weeks or so, Jai,' confirmed Mulk. 'I am sure that he will bring positive news, my dear brother,' he continued with a twinkle in his eyes.

Jai broke into a smile after a long period of stress and embraced his elder brother. Ajit also stood up, gulping his tea and patted both the brothers before bidding them goodbye to get back to where he was putting up for the night.

'Why don't you stay back for dinner, Ajit?' requested Mulk, which Ajit courteously turned down on account of many other preoccupations he had to attend to before leaving for Jhelum the next morning.

***

Sanjay had just returned from his long trip to Amritsar, Jalandhar, Agra, and Delhi. He had a lot of information to report. The trip had been a success, but also confusing.

He sat across Mulk and Jai and commenced narrating the details of his encounters during his official journey.

'There is a lot going on in all the places I have visited. Apprehensions and confusion are aplenty, and so is sporadic violence. I faced riot-like situations on multiple occasions and am fortunate to be alive.'

He had gone right up to the cantonment town of Meerut, about forty miles further north of Delhi, as directed by one of Khanna's close family friends and business associates. He had advised that it would be a good place to relocate a business, being close to Delhi yet distanced enough not to be disturbed by intense political activities happening in the British capital and soon-to-be free India's capital. On his way up to Meerut, Sanjay's bus had been stopped by an agitating group of Hindus, who were in search of Muslim passengers, to be pulled down and taken to task. It was said to be revenge for what they were facing in other parts of the country—in Bengal and Punjab. Someone in the bus had pointed out towards Sanjay shouting that he was from West Punjab. Members of the belligerent crowd had immediately rushed to him to verify his credentials, and after quite a bit of argument, they were finally convinced that he was not a Muslim but a Punjabi Hindu. To Sanjay's great relief, he was spared... maybe of being hacked or torched to death.

The most alarming thing to notice, according to Sanjay, was that the police were not playing an effective role at all in quelling these widespread communal disturbances. It seemed that the British administration had lost interest in governing the nation after having decided to transfer power to the Indians.

What was further evident to him was that the whole of United Provinces and Delhi was seething in communal tensions on account of rumours filtering in from Bengal and Punjab.

'I got stuck in Meerut for a whole week on account of a curfew-like situation there. Both the communities are baying for each other's blood, while the administration and some local elites are trying their best to bring sanity between the two. During my stay there, I met some businessmen and was also invited to a gathering of some leaders. The situation, according to them, is grim, and they have already contacted senior national leaders to intervene, lest it gets out of hand. I was even discretely asked by some Muslim shopkeepers about the situation in Lahore and Sialkot. As a matter of fact, one of the Muslim businessmen also offered to swap properties with us.

'I was very lucky to have met two distinct personalities of this city in one of their informal gatherings over lunch, where I managed to get an invite—Sultan Singh and Nawab Ishaq. I introduced myself, our family as well as our business in Sialkot to them. Sultan Singh was very positive about our relocating the business from Sialkot to Meerut, and even offered to help us with the process. Nawab Ishaq introduced me to a few more Muslim businessmen, who engaged with me on offers of swapping assets since they were intending to relocate to the Muslim-dominated western Punjab. They seemed to be sure that our part of Punjab would be forming a part of the new Pakistan.

'I also met an influential and elite doctor of the city. He is supposed to be very well connected politically, being a Bengali and having close relations with many Congress leaders hailing from Calcutta and other parts of Bengal. The Nawab, along with many others, are regular visitors to his huge mansion. Sultan Singh introduced him to me as a major philanthropist and a helpful person. However, he did not talk much, just kept on listening. While parting, he told me to meet him before leaving the town, which I did.

'He has a huge establishment, and good connections with the British Government. He is of the opinion that independence and partition would be a painful, complicated and confusing event. There would be a fair amount of violence, enough to leave a permanent scar on the divided countries. Many Muslims in Meerut and around were planning to move in large lots, both to East Bengal and West Punjab. However, his team was trying their best to convince them of their safety and security. But the communal violence seemed to be picking up by the day, which made settlers like him nervous about the fast-approaching date of independence and partition.

'He also gave me some insight that their small group of influential people of the region were having extensive talks with Congress as well as the British establishment to earmark certain areas in the vicinity for the purpose of relocating migrants, especially from the nearby west Punjab. They were also working out certain support plans to make it easier for the moving population.

'I was finally treated to one of the finest lunches I have had during my complete trip. It was attended by Sultan Singh, Nawab Ishaq, and some other dignitaries. Waiters in uniform were serving hot and delicious vegetarian and non-vegetarian ranges, ending with excellent sweet dishes and coffee or tea.

'Dr Bandhopadhyay...yes...that is his name. I have noted down his address and phone number for the future.'

'That is a good job you have done, Sanjay! Could you give me the address, so that I can express my gratitude to him by post, as also get in touch with him personally?' Mulk spoke enthusiastically. He had a gut feeling that something important might come out of this contact.

Sanjay handed him over two pages of addresses he had collected on his trip to Delhi, Meerut, Agra, Amritsar, and Jalandhar. He had straight gone to Mulk's uncle in Agra, who was of the strict opinion that the Khanna family should shift to Agra and relocate their business there. He had even sent a note of invitation through Sanjay for all of them to make his home their base and then settle down gradually. He was a renowned lawyer of the city, and had ample contacts there to make things happen, both with the administration and important businessmen. His name was Adhiraj Khanna, the direction to whose bungalow could be procured as soon as one got off at the Agra railway station or the bus stand.

'*Bahut vadda aadmi hai, Adhiraj...aur uska dill sonay da hai... bilkul chaubees karat da,'* said Mulk, while going through the letter sent by him. (Adhiraj is a very big man with a heart is of old. Absolute twenty-four karat.)

Mulk had already thought of visiting Adhiraj *chacha* (uncle) and taking his guidance on the new scenario that all of them were to face in just a few months. Sanjay had reached Amritsar and then Jalandhar on the first leg of his tour, and after having talked to quite a few of his and Khanna family's contacts, had got the information that the Jalandhar administration and the Business Association were taking proactive steps in inviting businesses from western Punjab to relocate there. Like in Meerut, they had identified certain residential as well as commercial areas for people migrating and setting up work in the city.

While Mulk, Jai, and Sanjay sat in Mulk's study listening to Sanjay's experiences, Magan Lal entered with tea and the day's post. Mulk started sorting out the mail while listening to the conversation, and Magan Lal left the room after putting the tea tray on the table. All of a sudden, Mulk leapt out of his chair with joy, catching hold of Jai's hand and pulling him up as well.

'Kee ho gaya Vadday Pra, bilkul bachhay ban gaye ho tussee?' responded Jai, while grinning and embracing Mulk. (What has happened, elder brother, you are behaving like a kid?)

'Array, Khanna Sports ko villait da direct order mill gayaa hai Jai! Bhagwaan da lukhh lukhh shukar hai!' Mulk cried out animatedly. (Khanna Sports has got a direct order from England. Praised be the lord).

'Oh Ballay Ballay, khush kar deetaa mainu, Vadday Pra!' shouted out Jai. (Wow! You have made me so happy, elder brother!)

Sanjay also got up and congratulated both his cousins. All of them finally settled down on their chairs and Mulk spoke after a few gulps of the now lukewarm tea.

'It is a big order of cricket bats, balls, and protective gear. The best part is that it is a recurring order, and the contract is for a three-year period. However, considering the political situation here, we would have to work out how we are going to make this happen.

'The business house in England is aware of the fluid political and social situation in India, including the declaration of independence. As a matter of fact, they have specifically asked us for a plan on how we are going to manage the delivery, given the situation on the ground here.

'So, we need to get out of our excitement and work out a plan, since we under no circumstances can afford to lose this order. We all have worked very hard for it.'

Jai responded while Sanjay remained passive.

'Elder brother, it is for the first time that we are getting a direct order from outside our country, and it surely is a matter of great pride. But we are in a great political problem, leading to a shortage in investible funds, as well. I think Sanjay would be well aware of it.

'We will need to borrow at a very heavy cost. Then, in case we have to relocate, which we would, how will we maintain the continuity in production?

'Also, I am assuming that my elder brother would arrange for his visit to England to negotiate and start the formalities of the contract, including document preparation and signing.'

Mulk was hearing intently and was happy to see Jai having a full grasp of the business situation. This would help in relieving quite a bit of his burden in the complex times ahead of them. He had built up a complete business scenario in his mind on what would be required to execute the order, at least for the immediate future. Mulk also knew that once he could deliver the test consignment and get the quality approval, everything else would follow. He now spoke up with a certain and well-thought-out game plan.

'Jai and Sanjay, you are my core team without whom I cannot dream of building up our business. I am completely seized by the situation in our country, as well as our financial conditions. We have a substantial amount of money receivable from the domestic market. I have decided that Sanjay and I will take charge of recovering it with immediate effect. Even if we can get back half of that money, our external dependence on finance from the money lender would be negligible. I have a target of redeeming at least seventy per cent of the receivables.

'As for completing the contract negotiations and documentation with the buyer in England, Jai, there is none better than you. Since you have been dealing with them directly, they know you very well by now. So, please start preparing to sail off as soon as possible, without wasting any time.

'Finally, to maintain the continuity of our production, I have decided to talk to Adhiraj *chacha ji* in Agra to hire a factory shed so that we can hire some workers and train them to start manufacturing our range of cricket gear there. I am targeting a parallel production in two to three months from now in Agra. While we get going in Agra, we will jointly decide where to permanently settle down. Back to Sialkot, Agra, Jalandhar, or Meerut.'

Jai intervened.

'But elder brother, relocating from Sialkot itself is a very major piece of work. With me away, you will be left all by yourself to manage the entire family, selling off assets here and deciding upon a permanent place to do business in the newly independent India. I am very nervous and feel that my presence is definitely required at this stage of our lives.'

Mulk had a loving expression on his face, as he looked at Jai while he spoke.

'Jai, we must divide the work between us and take up extra responsibilities. The purchase order from England is important for our survival, and so is my presence here. My signatures and presence are not necessary in England, while here I need to be present to fulfil all legal processes and to deal with the newly formed governments.

'I have the able Sanjay with me, as well as our other friends and relatives, who would be relocating along with us. There would be quite a few of us. So, Jai, please do not worry, and focus on getting things right the first time with this foreign order. Come back as fast as possible to take up your responsibilities here. Speed of work is of utmost importance.

'Chhetee kar mere veer chhotay pra, aur Vilayat jaanay kee tayyaree kar. Tere Vadday Pra ka asheerwaad tere naal hai.' (Make haste, younger brother, and prepare for your travel to England. Your elder brother's blessings are with you).

Within his heart, Jai was excited about the prospects of his travelling across the seven seas. He would be the first in his family to be travelling abroad, and the thought made him almost jump with joy. He hurried out to go and break the news to his wife. His kid was too young to comprehend.

CHAPTER 14

The Road to Kud

Vikas and Vijay were attending their last day at the Scotch Mission College before the summer vacation started. It was the June of 1947. There was a sense of suspense and uncertainty in the air, which could not only be sensed by the teachers and the management of the school, but also by the children.

The principal had asked all the pupils and teachers to assemble in the auditorium at 1 pm sharp after the school ended for the day. The principal's cough was followed by an immediate pin-drop silence—a silence of anticipation as to what was so important to hold back the whole school after the last bell. He finally spoke.

'My dear students, teachers and rest of the staff, it is and always will be a pleasure to be together as a team in the golden period of our association. We have enriched ourselves from each other's intelligence and intellect, and have, together, weathered many a storm.

'We all must be aware, to a lesser or greater degree, that the independence of our great nation is fast approaching within the next couple of months. It is a happy as well as a sad occasion.

Happy because very soon, we would be free of British rule and occupation. Sad because, as the scheme of events suggests, this beloved nation of ours will be partitioned into two—India and Pakistan.

'We are also more or less aware that where we have congregated today, will be a part of the new nation-state of Pakistan. What effect the partition is going to have on us, the common men and citizens of the presently united nation of British India is most confusing and blurred as I speak.

'We may continue as we are, chances of which are reasonably fair. Also, we might migrate to a country which suits us and our family better. The latter also might hold true. In short, our school, in whatever form, will again reassemble in a new country.

'I would be happy to have all of you back here to spend the joyous schooling together, as before. However, in case that does not happen, may God bless those whose families chose to move to greener pastures.

'To conclude, I announce that the reopening date of the school is not certain as of now. It will be declared once the future of the independent nations and their respective status becomes clearer than what it is today. With a heavy yet positively expectant heart, I wish all of you goodbye and God bless!

'I would also like to announce that all students and their respective parents can collect the final examination results and transfer certificates from the school office, two weeks from now. The exact date will be displayed on the notice board outside the school gate.'

With this talk and announcement, the principal dismissed the congregation. The humming, buzzing, and whispering commenced, leading to loud banter as soon as the students emerged from the school auditorium. It was a mixed feeling of excitement, apprehension, and some amount of sadness which had afflicted the students. Vijay was more excited and Vikas was more apprehensive. At the school exit gate, they were greeted by Magan Lal.

Kamla was already sitting in the back seat of the tonga, waiting for her two brothers. As soon as the three climbed onto the horse carriage, they immediately broke out into an animated discussion, all of them trying to narrate their part of the experience first. However, their experience of the last day in school was identical. In Kamla's school also, their principal had announced to the same effect as in Scotch Mission College. It was about twenty minutes later that the three children reached their bungalow in Civil Lines.

Jaya was waiting for them with their customary glasses of freshly extracted orange juice, and the three entered as usual banging the front door open and shouting at the top of their voices. Vijay, the youngest of the lot, rushed up to his mother and engulfed her in a loving embrace.

'*Ma, ma! Aaj hamaaray school da akheer din thhaa. Kal se hamay phir kabhee school naheen jaanaa.*' (Mother, today was our last day at school. From tomorrow we would never need to go to school again).

'Chup rahay, khottay! Hamaraa school ab desh kee azaadee kay baad khulaygaa, aur khulnay kee tureek hamay baad mien pataa chalyegee. Aur ma, hamaraa school hamay result kay saath transfer certificate bhee de deyegaa. Iss tarah hum kisee aur school mien bhee dakhilaa le saktay hain,' clarified Vikas, with Kamla endorsing with a nod. (Shut up, donkey! Our school will now open after independence, and we will come to know about the dates later on. Also, they would be giving us our transfer certificates along with our results so that we are able to seek admission in any other school as well.)

Jaya was tense with all that was happening. She was worried about the well-being of her family and their business, assets, and earnings. She had been through their growth bit by bit, sacrificing many of her pleasures and personal dreams, being the senior wife of the family. Just when everything was going well with them—the new bungalow, their eldest son doing his schooling at a well-known boarding school, the huge business order from England… the uncertainties of independence from British rule, as well as the impending partition of the country had to happen. Her premonition of what was to follow was not good at all.

Pushing the dark thoughts back into a recess, she embraced all her children together, kissing each one of them, with a smile of love on her face. She then guided them to the dining table to have their glasses of juice and some warm snacks.

'Finish this off, children, and then freshen up and change into your home clothes. Your father and uncle will be joining us for lunch in another half an hour and want all of us to be together. They have some interesting plans for your summer vacations.'

While speaking, Jaya looked at her children with as much reassurance and excitement as possible, putting some crisps on each of their plates. The children polished off what was given to them, more out of excitement about their vacation plans than anything else and ran off to take a bath and change into some fresh clothes.

***

The whole family was present. Mulk, his younger brother Jai and their families. All were looking expectantly at Mulk to disclose the action which lay ahead in the coming trying months, the children with excitement and the elders with scepticism. Mulk looked at Jai and continued.

'Well, all my dear ones, we have a lot of work ahead of us, and a lot of responsibilities to share. Jai is going to England as soon as he gets his documents cleared and a round ticket for his journey. He is going to firm up some good business orders we have managed to win there.

'The ladies, along with kids, are going for summer vacations to Kud, in Jammu. I have managed accommodation there, in the bungalow of one Mr Gupta, who is one of our customers in that region. They have an independent portion which they let out during the season.

'Sanjay and I would be looking into the future of our business in Sialkot, as well as moving a part of it to some other safer parts in India. I would like to share with all of you that we are going through critical and confusing times with independence and partition, both just a few months away.

'We might remain and do business where we are today once everything settles down. At the same time, there is a probability that we might have to shift to some other safe city and continue what we are doing in Sialkot.'

The ladies, Jaya and Kiran (Jai's wife) were disturbed for quite a few months by what they heard from various quarters and what they overheard from their husbands. However, neither of them could sum up the courage and ask a man's question, as to what would be their future, their family's future. Now that they had the opportunity to do so. Jaya, being older, immediately took the lead rather animatedly.

'Are we going to leave Sialkot and this bungalow for good?'

'Well, there are chances, Jaya, yes, for good. But in case what our neighbours say turns out true, we might come back after a short gap,' replied Mulk.

'And where would we be for that short gap, *bhai ji*?' enquired Kiran.

'Most probably in Agra with Adhiraj chacha ji. I have already made the necessary arrangements with him,' spoke Mulk with a confident smile, giving the ladies all the comfort of sound planning.

Vikas, Vijay, and Kamala were secretly excited at the thought of Kud and the other new places where they would be travelling to in the next couple of months. The best prospect for the kids, however, was the absence of school from their life's equation, at least in the near future. No studies. A lot of surprises and play.

After having finished their lunch, Jaya and Kiran went off into Jaya's room; the gents sauntered off to the factory while the kids decided to go to their neighbours to play for the afternoon.

***

Jaya being elder and with primary responsibilities of the entire family, had quite a few loose ends tormenting her—the journey to Kud with the kids and Kiran, the listing and packing of essential and household items as well as valuables, the decision of what to carry along to Kud, and what would be transported when they move to Agra. And then the multiple consequences…what ifs….

'I have planned to pack up all my belongings, including valuables, and all the utensils and artefacts, in separate identifiable boxes. Why leave anything to chance of coming back again since my gut feeling tells me that we would never be able to come back to collect our belongings after independence,' Jaya shared with Kiran, being her closest as well as a trusted confidante.

Kiran was busy packing for her husband who would be away to England for a couple of months, including the return voyage. He just might not be back with them when the clock strikes independence. She was confused about what all to include for Jai, for his voyage, and what all to carry with herself to Kud and, further on, to Agra. However, Jaya's decision made matters easier for her.

She had been in the habit of following her elder sister-in-law blindly, with implicit faith that she could do no wrong. Kiran finally spoke about her plans.

'I am packing all of Jai's clothes and fineries with him for his trip to England. He would need all of them for his multiple business meetings and social calls. As for the rest, I would do just the same as you, didi. Frankly, I am excited, and so is Jai, on his foreign trip. He would be the first in our family to venture out across the *kala pani* (black waters—what the Indians used to call the seas leading to voyages to the West).'

Her eyes were glittering, and her voice quivered while she confided her excitement to Jaya. Jaya clasped Kiran's hands within hers and pressed them, expressing her happiness in her joy. What she artfully concealed, as an elder, was her feeling that Jai should have been with his elder brother, during these difficult times, come what may.

Whether she was right in her way of thinking or not, was something which only the future had answers to.

'Kiran, in the times and destiny which are fast approaching us, both of us would need to be together always, taking care of our children, our husbands and our belongings like hawks.'

While telling this to Kiran, Jaya, for the first time betrayed her emotions. Her eyes moistened and a few drops of pearls rolled down her cheeks. Kiran embraced her elder sister-in-law, assuring her support at all times to come, while Jaya broke down, with stress, insecurity, and apprehension.

'Didi, whatever we are and wherever we are, we will be one family and support each other at every step, like we are today, and like we have always been. Can I ever forget that this opportunity of going across seven seas has been given to my husband by none other than Mulk bhai ji? Both of you are more than our parents. You are our gurus, our god on earth, didi,' replied Kiran, with tears in her eyes.

***

It was way past factory hours, and the dusk had set in. Khanna Sports was silent and empty. Well, almost.

Inside, the shop floor was dark, with the only light coming from Mulk's office, and the pathway leading to it. The office had a few visitors, apart from Sanjay and Mulk. They were from outside Sialkot—from Karachi, wearing a loose *salwar kameez* (a local dress of the region), tall and well-built. All were talking in hushed tones, with a confidential veneer around.

Mulk asked Sanjay to get the Stock Valuation Register.

'*Kinna hore kee kee stock hai zara bataaee, Sanjay?*' enquired Mulk. (How much and what stock is there with us, Sanjay?)

'*Bhai ji, ai lo. Iss register wichh sub kuchh clearly calculated hai, hore up to date bhee hai.*' replied Sanjay while handing over the Stock Valuation Register to Mulk. (Here Brother, this register has all the updated values in it.)

Mulk went through all the figures while jotting down the totals and sub-totals on a separate sheet of paper. The visitors sat quietly, looking around Mulk's office, aimlessly, biding time. Finally, he looked up from the registers and the sheet and spoke.

'Sirji, sorry for the little delay in matching numbers, since *mai ik sahee figure dasnaa chahtaa hoon* (since I want to state one correct figure). Hope it is fine with all of you?'

'Yes, of course, that will suit all of us present,' spoke Aftab, who seemed to be the senior most of the three others present.

Aftab Alam was the founder of one of the largest sports goods distribution companies in British India, especially Punjab and further west, those portions of British India, which, in all probability, would come under the newly formed Pakistan.

Mulk was in talks with quite a few sports goods outlet owners, including Aftab, on liquidating his finished goods stocks. At the same time, he had slowed down on the production of cricketing equipment, keeping it strictly as per orders in hand and putting a freeze on any further orders. Aftab had quoted the best price per piece, and hence they had reached the second stage of their negotiations. Mulk spoke softly so that his voice would not carry beyond his cabin.

'Calculating according to the price list which we have agreed upon, the total for the complete free stock is coming to approximately three lakh and seventy-five thousand rupees.'

'I am supposing that the stock is entirely of cricketing equipment and gear?' clarified Aftab.

'Yes, of course. We do not make any other product in our factory, as of now,' responded Mulk. 'Also, you would already know that we are putting a special price on each of the goods, which is handsomely discounted, even on the wholesale price. We would like to bring our stock position to *sifar* (zero) before independence day.'

'Mulk bhai, we do not doubt your integrity, and we have already decided upon the pricing. Now, the next steps we need to take are the goods inspection as well as agreeing upon the mode of payment. Since this is a large sum of money, we would be able to make the payment in stages. I would be making an agreement advance of fifty thousand rupees right away, which I have with me.

'The final amount would be arrived at post-inspection, which I would pay in three stages. The next payment of one lakh and twenty-five thousand would be immediately after the inspection and finalization of the purchase.

'Another one lakh on delivery acceptance; and the last one lakh, one month later. Considering that you will make the delivery by the first week of July at Karachi, you will receive the last part by the first week of August.'

While spelling out his terms of payment, Aftab took out wadded currency notes from his cloth bag and put them in front of Mulk to count and keep. Mulk, on his part, was reasonably expressionless and did not show any excitement whatsoever.

He spoke in the same measured tone as he always did.

'Aftab bhai, the first week of August will be cutting it a bit too fine since the date of declaration of independence will be very near, if not earlier. We should finish all our transactions by the last week of July, at the latest.'

'Inshallah! I will try my best to arrange for the money according to your wish. You know our reputation, as well as that it has the guarantee and assurance of Sardar sahib (the president of the Punjab Chamber of Commerce).'

Saying this, Aftab got up and shook hands with Mulk, who had also risen up. Both embraced each other. The deal, negotiations for which had been going on for over a month, had been finally agreed upon.

'Aray Sanjay, kuchh mithhai shithhai ho jaaye. Aur chai kay liye bhee bole deyeen,' bellowed Mulk enthusiastically, while pocketing the currency bills in his cloth bag. (Sanjay, let us have some sweets and also call for some tea.)

Mulk was a happy man on his way back home. He had a smile playing on his lips after a long period of morbidity on account of the rapid and negative developments in his part of the country.

He requested the tonga driver to take him to the famous sweet shop near the clock tower, from where he got some hot *jalebis* and *kachoris* (an Indian combination of fried sweets and spicy fried breads) for everyone at home.

He wanted to relax the atmosphere in his family and also wanted to celebrate Jai's leaving for England, via Bombay, his first ship journey. Jai had to catch the train to Bombay the next morning. The two prices of good news made Mulk think positively. Finally, all is shaping well…he thought to himself while twirling his moustache as a matter of habit whenever he was happy or felt proud and arrogant.

***

The family had assembled at the central courtyard of the house where they used to generally have their tea and snacks, cut and shell vegetables, and make family gossip and take important decisions. That day it was more of an update and a sendoff congregation for Jai.

The low table at the centre was already full of teacups and plates with fresh and hot jalebi and kachori. As everyone picked up their teacups and started devouring the victuals, Mulk informed them of positive happenings in the factory and business, although superficially.

He then turned to Jai and enquired about his preparations for the journey, and whether he required anything of Mulk.

'I have all the files and documents in order, packed in a separate suitcase. I have also procured some foreign exchange, according to the budget which we had discussed. Our buyers in London and Birmingham know the precise date of my arrival. They have also arranged for my boarding,' replied Jai.

Mulk wore a satisfied expression on his face. Jai had surely grown up to be much more than what he had expected.

'*Shabaash* Jai!' exclaimed Mulk, patting him on his back. There is nothing much left for me to add, except that I have communicated to Mr Brown of Moore Sports to extend to you any advance sums of money that you might require in case of an emergency or extended stay, which can well happen. Also, let us decide to write to each other every day about the activities of the day. In case of emergency send a telegram.'

Jai caught hold of his elder brother's hand and assured him that everything would be as per plan and that he should not at all be worried or tense and instead concentrate on the family, the factory in Sialkot, and tackling the partition of the country, which was a handful.

Mulk smiled and invited Jai to his room on the first floor.

'Jai, come up to my room in an hour. I think Lalit (Mr Uberoi of Uberoi Sports) will also be dropping in. We will have some men's enjoyment as a token of your sendoff. However, we need to be very tight-lipped on the business contract that we have already won. I have told him that you are going on a business exploration trip without anything firm in your hands,' said Mulk with a grin.

Jai smiled back and gestured his happiness to attend.

Whisky was always welcome, especially on such an occasion. It would soothe Jai's nerve, which was pacing far over its prescribed limits.

***

The days leading to August 1947 were turbulent and confusing. There were signals of camaraderie as well as animosity. Sometimes, one felt safe, and sometimes equally vulnerable. People with vision and gut feelings were moving to safer regions according to their religions. On the other hand, there were those afflicted by a sense of denial and continued to stay in their perceived comfort zones, delaying destiny bit by bit. Mulk was a balance of the two.

After Jai left for England, times were moving at breakneck speed. Incidents of communal violence continued in Mulk's neighbourhood, specifically in congested and poorer localities, which were not endowed with the sane effects of education. He also encountered similar incidents in Lahore as well as Amritsar, both towns that he visited quite often.

In the meantime, he had managed to successfully send his family, including Jai's, off to Kud, as planned. It was a summer vacation as well as an opportunity for the women and children to stay away from the not-so-pleasant realities of the day.

He was also, very confidentially, in progressive stages of negotiations to get a good deal on his factory land, building, and machinery as well as his current residence, in case they would need to leave all permanently and migrate further east into a Hindu-dominated locale. These negotiations were not that easy, and many times, he felt that he was being taken for a discrete ride by the majority community in Sialkot and its vicinity.

Like Ajit Kohli, his friend from Jhelum, he had received a meagre advance, with continuous delays and further promises to pay the remaining sums due, for their shops and house.

Mulk was left alone to tackle the sale of the factory and house with all the uncertainties of the present, and the days to follow.

***

The entire British India and the Principalities were a confused lot…happiness continued to be shrouded by dark grey clouds of the fear of the known…as well as the unknown….

CHAPTER 15

Fanning the Embers

It was a grey evening on June 15, 1947. There were reasons to rejoice for British India since she had started moving towards independence. The countdown to August had begun. Yet there was a pall of gloom, a morose depression, a spell of morbidity and strain in the eyes of every Indian.

The All-India Congress Committee (AICC) had concluded its session a few hours before, in which it had accepted the plan of 3 June to partition India and create Pakistan. The session also rejected any notions of independence or autonomy of the Princely States, which were basking in the glory and protection of the British Raj.

Narendra, Professor VR Chatterjee, Ishaq and their complete group of Meerut elders were present in a small room adjoining Narendra's Clinic. Dr Ajit Chatterjee, Narendra's son-in-law, was in the clinic, busy attending to the steadily growing number of injured patients. The trend, to the experienced eyes of a doctor, was clear. There was trouble in the city, violence was fomenting, and the cause could be anyone's guess.

In the adjoining room, the only sound that could be heard was coming out of a radio kept on a centre table, encircled by all those present. Ishaq was a troubled man, with his problems increasing every second as Nehru charted out the action plan as approved by the preceding AICC session.

The Muslims were in the minority in the region and were petrified at the scheme of events that had led to the approval of partition. The environment, which had been simmering till then, had exploded into violence, loot, and arson.

Many families with foresight and insider knowledge of the unfolding geopolitical scenario had already moved towards Lahore, West Punjab, and some had even journeyed towards East Bengal. Trains leaving towards the two destinations from Delhi were overflowing with people climbing onto the roofs. The exodus resulted in casualties and accidents every day.

Ishaq was in tears, trembling out of fear, frustration, and rage.

'Ya Allah! Yahaan kay muquami baashindon ko kyaa ho gayaa hai? (Oh God! What has happened to the residents of this place?)

'Jo hamdard thhey is mulk kay mustaqbil ko lekar, who ek doosray kay khoon kay pyaasay kyun ho gaye hain?' (Those who were well-wishers of the nation, how come they have become thirsty for each other's blood?)

He was sobbing convulsively. Professor Chatterjee patted Ishaq on his back, consoling him, while Narendra got him a glass of water. Suddenly, Ajit rushed into the room from the clinic. He appeared to be both nervous and scared.

'Gents, there is a mob at our clinic's doorsteps that is demanding custody of all our Muslim patients. They are not amenable to any peaceful conversation. I need your support immediately.'

Loud slogan-shouting and banging of doors could be heard outside. Narendra got into his act, barking out orders to his friends assembled in the room.

'Ishaq, please get inside my house from the back door, immediately! We will join you once the crisis has been doused. Also, try contacting the police through the internal telephone line provided to me once you are inside my study, for precaution.

'Virendra, Sultan Singh and I are going out to reason with the agitators, while Ajit, you continue your good work inside the clinic.'

Narendra did not wait for any response or debate and rushed out with Ajit, Professor Chatterjee and Sultan Singh following. There were over seven members of the agitating crowd in the outer waiting veranda of Narendra's clinic. The rest of the crowd was standing outside the gate near the road.

'Musalmaan *haaye haaye*, Musalmaan *haaye haaye*!'

The crowd was shouting in unison, making a rather formidable noise. Narendra decided to take a strong approach instead of a reconciliatory one.

'*Aap logon ne ye kyaa tamaashaa machaa rakkhaa hai?*' he shouted out. (What ruckus are you people creating here?) 'Don't you understand that this is a clinic; and we are doing serious work here, saving lives?'

The leader of the group, who had come into the clinic veranda, spoke up in a high and excitable pitch.

'Doctor sahib, we have come here for the Muslims. They have wronged us and our families in Punjab and Bengal. Taking revenge is our duty towards the Hindus. They plundered our shops and homes in the walled city area here in Meerut, Ghaziabad, and Gurgaon. So, please hand over all the Muslim patients to us, as a devout Hindu Brahmin yourself. We respect you and that is the minimum we expect out of you.'

Sultan Singh was about to speak, but Narendra gestured for him to leave the response to him and spoke slowly without any sign of agitation, excitement, or nervousness.

'Dear friends, as you know, I am a doctor, and for me all are patients. That is the only religion I know in the clinic, or else care for. Right now, my duty is to cure my patients of their suffering and not to make them suffer. So please leave my clinic in peace and carry on your duties outside of my premises.

'Also, as an elder, I would advise you that with a violent attitude towards your fellow countrymen you all are doing a disservice to your nation and delaying independence. The rest is up to you since you yourselves are grownup people. However, please clear out from here and let me perform my duties in peace.'

The doctor and his friends stood there looking directly into their eyes. After a while, the assembled group relented before the respect and personality of the doctor and his group of influential elites, all of whom were Hindus.

Their leader spoke again.

'We truly hope that there are no Muslims hiding here, who are not patients?'

Narendra again responded without the slightest hint of excitement.

'All of you are most welcome to be my guests and look in for yourselves.'

There was a sudden, loud public announcement from a passing Jeep outside that declared any public gathering, carrying or using arms & ammunition, and any inciteful activities as illegal and leading to immediate arrest. An hour was given for compliance and curfew was to be enforced from midnight onwards.

The crowd dispersed immediately, and the clinic was left in peace for the doctors to do their duty. An army flag march was also announced. The group retired into the safety of their anteroom, behind the clinic where they had originally assembled. By this time, Ishaq had also come back from Narendra's study and spoke shakily.

'I did not call up the police immediately. Thought to wait for some time. Has the crowd left?'

'Yes, Ishaq. You needn't worry anymore. We assure your safety for now and always. In case the need arises, you are most welcome to stay with any of us here during critical times. We are a family.'

Sultan Singh spoke with all the warmth of a close friend and clasped Ishaq's hand within his to comfort him.

'There is violence brewing in the walled city. However, Khoonee Pul onwards up to the Cantonment is untouched, apart from minor incidents of groups coming and enquiring like the one we just faced here at Narendra's clinic,' said Professor VR Mukherjee. 'I know a few Muslim families of my students and staff from the college who have decided to migrate to West Punjab beyond Wagah. They have arranged a bus and are going in a group for the sake of safety. Anybody that any of you know can go along with them. They are leaving late tonight so that all of them can catch the early morning train from Old Delhi Railway Station to Wagah and beyond as per arrangements with their relatives there.'

Narendra scratched his chin, in a pondering mode, gazing at the wall ahead, and then called for Ram Lal, the compounder.

'*Arey* Ram Lal, Khan sahib *ko zara bulaayeeyay,*' requested Narendra and then spoke to his group of friends. (Ram Lal, call Khan sahib for a bit.)

'Khan is one of my horse carriage drivers and has been with me for more than a decade and a half. He and his family have been very nervous about the threats they have been receiving from some radicals in the local Hindu community. Frankly, I have been regularly donating to some politically active groups in Bengal, as well as the Congress, but never have I favoured any partisan or secessionist activities. We are but one people of the same stock, and can achieve no sensible purpose by separating into two nations.'

While the conversation was in progress, Khan sahib had arrived at the clinic, with Ram Lal announcing his presence to Narendra.

'*Ander bhejo Khan sahib ko,* Ram Lal,' called out Narendra. (Send Khan sahib inside, Ram Lal.)

'*Jee,* sahib,' replied Ram Lal, gesturing Khan to walk in. (Yes, sahib.)

'Jee, doctor sahib,' Khan bowed in respect. '*Aap nay humay bulayaa,* sahib?' (You called for me, sahib?)

'*Haan,* Khan sahib. Professor sahib *ko toe aap jaantay hee hongay*?' enquired Narendra and carried on. (You must be knowing Professor sahib?)

'Some people known to him are leaving for Wagah and beyond by train from Old Delhi Railway Station on the day after tomorrow, early in the morning. To catch the train, the group will be leaving for Delhi by a privately hired bus late tonight. Since you and your family have made all arrangements to shift near Lahore, it would be a good opportunity to leave safely with a group. Although I would hate to lose you, your services, and comradery so soon.'

Khan had tears in his eyes. He had never wanted to leave the services of such a kind employer. But he was facing unfortunate days, and this seemed to be the only viable option for a person of his meagre standing. He could not fight the system.

'*Theek* sahib, *hum in logon kay saath hee chalay jaatay hain. Kharchaa bhee kum hogaa aur safar mien mehphoos bhee rahengay,*' replied Khan, with his head bowed in respect and gratitude. (Agreed sahib, will go with them. It will be less expensive as well as safe.)

'Done then. Virendra, please convey to me the cost of Khan's complete journey to Lahore. I have decided to bear the whole of it. And Khan sahib, here take this also, you will need it during the journey and to set yourself up in your new home.'

Narendra had kept aside five thousand rupees for Khan sahib, which he extended to him. Khan broke down while accepting the gratification from his employer. His God. His Allah....

Narendra wiped his moist eyes and turned back to his friends for further discussion on the prevailing situation.

'We, along with some others, have been called for tea on the day after tomorrow in the morning by the Collector. I presume it will be to discuss the future course of events and our roles and responsibilities as known citizens.'

At that moment, Ajit walked in to tell them that the Inspector of their police station had visited and requested them to shut down the clinic. They could look into emergency cases only.

The assembled gents got up to leave. It was quite dark outside now, and in these troubled times, their homes would be the safest place to be in.

'Let us keep in touch in case of any emergencies. No news will remain to be good news,' was Narendra's bidding to all.

***

Babulal knocked on the door of Narendra's study before entering.

'Sahib, we would have to pick up Naseem, the barber, from his place since he is scared and too nervous to come to our house by himself. He told me that he would surely be done in by Hindu miscreants on his way here. There have been threats in his locality.'

'Ask the coachman to take the single horse carriage and get him over. I need a haircut, and the only time I have is the next hour. So please hurry,' Narendra ordered Babulal.

He turned to his radio to tune in for the morning news. The radio crackled….

'There is an important announcement to be made. A private bus carrying Muslim passengers to the Old Delhi Railway Station was blown up near Modinagar in the early hours of this morning. A couple of country-made bombs were hurled onto the bus by an unidentified group of men emerging out of the jungles and disappearing immediately thereafter, as reported by the conductor, the only surviving person during this dastardly act of violence. All traffic has been stopped on this route till further notice.'

Narendra was stunned, as was Naseem, the Barber, who had stepped into the door of Narendra's study.

'Khan sahib!' cried Narendra in anguish and in pain.

'Abbu...Ammi...!' cried out Naseem, his face contorting, and tears and sweat mixing on his pained face. (Father...Mother...!)

***

The capital and its share of migrants...their lives....

CHAPTER 16

Radcliff's Doodle

It was the last day before the summer break at DAV School on Chitragupta Road at Paharganj in Delhi. Satendra Singh Rawat had finished with the last paper of his final exams amongst all the chaos and pandemonium in the city as well as the whole of British India. After the last exam, he, along with all the other students at the school, congregated at the playground to listen to their principal speak. They were told that he had some important announcements to make, hence all should be present to hear.

The principal started without delay once he saw most of the school already there.

'Students, your summer breaks are to begin from tomorrow. However, right now we are not able to declare the date for the reopening of the school. As all of you know, our beloved nation is moving towards full independence from British Rule on a date to be specified in August. There would be a change in government, and we are also expecting a division of the entire British India into two nations. India and Pakistan.

'We are already getting numerous new students from western Punjab almost every day. The numbers are going to increase even further after independence and partition. I would expect all of you to be cooperative and kind to them. Help them out in what they have missed in class.

'For students who would be leaving the school and migrating to Pakistan, they can collect their Transfer Certificates after two weeks from today. We are declaring early results this time considering the abnormal circumstances. They would be displayed on the notice boards exactly after two weeks.

'The date for reopening of the school will, of course, be declared later, and all of you need to be in touch with the school office for the same. I wish all of you the very best for the vacations as well as life. Keep safe and out of trouble. Be good and worthy students of DAV in this hour of need and change.'

Satendra gulped it all down as he listened to every word of his principal and got pushed out of the ground with the rest of his fellow students amidst loud noises of various degrees of excitement. He and his friends from neighbouring villages started walking back to where they lived...as neighbours in the amazing megapolis that was Delhi. Walking was the only option they had, living on shoestring budgets with a long way to go in life.

However, they never minded walking. Even in the muggy and sweaty summers of Delhi, walking came easily to them. It brought them nearer to their beautiful village days, where they walked for miles through tough yet enchanting terrain, and at times in very rough weather indeed.

Satendra was in love with his village, its mountains and dense forests. Yet he found Delhi amazing in different ways—its heady mix of people, the pace of life, and the many kinds of transport on its streets. So many kinds of lives people lived there. The confusion, fear, competition, struggle...and so many things happening at the same time....

***

It was about an hour's walk to his living quarters at Panchkuian Road, which bordered Connaught Place, Delhi's premier business and commercial centre. Since Trilok, Satendra's elder brother, had a shortage of space in his quarters not far away, he had arranged for a room shared with another boy from their neighbouring village in these barracks. Satendra had taken to it at first sight. It was a nice, clean locality surrounded by a lot of shady green trees—*neem* (Azadirachta Indica-Margosa) and *jamun* (Syzgium Cumini). There was a lot of space to play and run around since the barracks were set off from the main road by quite a distance and well concealed. A bonus for young Satendra was lots of company for his age, and that too from Garhwal and Kumaon, sharing the same language and culture. They played games together, shared similar memories and village delicacies, and four of them even went to school together.

On the road adjoining the barrack compound, two electricity poles with affixed loudspeakers stood on either corner from which periodic news broadcasts could be heard. The pavements were areas of social gathering where the inmates of the barracks and people from the neighbourhood sat together listening to the news, debating and analysing consequences, and sharing a smoke together. Satendra and his playmates remained busy in their world, enacting their plays while the elders keenly listened to all the announcements and news making its way through the speakers. What interrupted the children and turned their excitement to fear were the army and police rushing past the street and gunshots and the periodical 'boom!' of the bombs exploding in the vicinity.

On one such occasion, Trilok whisked away Satendra to his living quarters and made him stay there for some days. On 23 June 1947, by midday, the date of independence for India had been announced. It was to be 15 August, while Pakistan would come into existence on 14 August, a day before.

Delhi and all the adjoining regions were put under virtual curfew. Day after day, they were holed up in their quarters, not seeing the roads at all, which got frustrating and boring, especially for Satendra, who daydreamed about being an important government officer and kept on talking to himself.

The enthusiasm of mono-acting could not survive long and gave way to depression, despair, and longing for the carefree and independent life of the mountains and the jungle, where the only fear was that of predators, giant bears, and stray elephants, none of whom took lives without reasons or a genuine threat. There, in Delhi, being a Muslim was a crime to the Hindus and vice versa.

'Why, bhayji?' Satendra had questioned Trilok once when he had warned him to stay away from Yusuf, his very close school friend. 'Why is Yusuf dangerous? He just calls Bhagwan Allah because that's his language, that's all. Is it reason enough for him and his family to be asked to leave the city? Is it reason enough for Hindu mobs to come and torch their house and inflict pain and injury on them? Do you remember Ajmal and his father, Asif, the tailor in our village? We used to have such good food cooked in their house. Delicious and spicy mutton. They were invited to all our weddings and functions, and we lived so peacefully in each other's company. Have they been asked to leave the village?'

These were times when Trilok found it very difficult to handle Satendra's innocent, yet truthful inquisitiveness. However, in his younger brother, he could clearly visualize what educated citizens of a proud and free India would be like....

***

Delhi was also seeing loads of Hindu refugees coming from Punjab, especially from the western parts. Special camps were being set up in various parts of Delhi to accommodate refugees who had no arrangements there.

Satendra and his school friends had befriended some young refugee boys and girls who had arrived by trains and buses and had traumatic tales to tell. One boy was older than Satendra and far more mature on account of what he had gone through during his journey from Jhelum to Delhi with his ageing parents, and he narrated that most of the people of their community continued to stay there, hoping that all this violence and confusion was just a temporary phenomenon.

'They are making a huge mistake and will lose every possession they have. Maybe even their lives,' he said with a very remorseful expression. 'Our community is being targeted everywhere in Punjab. We are suffering more towards the west of Amritsar, while Muslims are suffering more towards the east of Amritsar. There is open killing going on. I have seen them in hundreds, on our way to Delhi.'

The feelings of hurt, denial, and confusion had led to violence of a grave kind. The Hindu refugees were moving towards the east, while Muslims towards the west. Riots were being reported from Amritsar, Lahore, Gurdaspur, Sialkot and other surrounding regions.

In Delhi, two provisional governments had been formed on 19 July 1947—one for India and the other for Pakistan. Lord Mountbatten, having been declared as the Governor General of India to guide the two nations to independence, was a busy man, overseeing the complete range of hectic parleys.

Cyril Radcliffe, a lawyer by profession, was given charge of drawing out the boundaries on the western and eastern parts of undivided India to carve out a sustainable West and East Pakistan and was appointed the chairman of the Boundary Commission.

On 22 July 1947, the Indian National Flag was finally approved by the Constituent Assembly, after being proposed by Pandit Nehru. Satendra was excited about getting a sample and was flaunting it around to his friends and some other elders. He also got a pamphlet bearing the flag from one of his schoolteachers who stayed close by and told him that the flag was designed by Pingali Venkayya, a relatively unknown congress member from Machilipatnam in coastal Andhra Pradesh.

Delhi, the capital city, was where all activities were converging. The loudspeakers attached to poles on the streets were hubs of excitement. Locals of Delhi listened with rapt attention to every bit of news and announcements coming out of them. There were vociferous discussions and debates among the listening crowd, which included Trilok and his community working and staying in Delhi, having adopted it as their city of destiny. However, what the destiny would be like in independent India was something which the coming month would unfold....

***

Independence and Partition were two sides of the same coin...to be traded together in Independent India...in times to come....

CHAPTER 17

Goodbye Dear Land

Mulk was sitting alone in his small cabin, in one corner of the factory shed. It was in the afternoon, but activities in the factory were at their lowest. There was confusion, protests, and violence on the streets of Sialkot, which had kept most of his workers and other employees away from the factory.

'*Fakru kay allawah ik bhee karigar naheen aaya! Humnay toe kissee ka kuchhh naheen bigada!*' (No other worker apart from Fakru has come to work today! We have not harmed anyone!)

Mulk muttered loudly in frustration, anxiously playing around with an oval paperweight lying on his table. Sanjay walked into the cabin, his expression showing that the news was not good. Mulk's anxiety went up. He had sent Sanjay to Aslam Sharif, the local labour leader at Sialkot. Aslam commanded respect from the workmen, not only in the city but right up to Lahore. He had his finger on the pulse of the political confusion and violence.

'*Buree khabar hai, veer ji,*' started Sanjay with a very grim expression on his face. (There is bad news, elder brother.)

'Chhetee bol oye, Sanjay, kee khabar laya hai Aslam nal,' retorted Mulk, with unusual impatience and irritation. (Tell me quickly, what news have you got from Aslam.)

'Mainu ik ik din mehenga pad rahaa hai…inna order kaun pura karegaa!' cried out Mulk in anguish. (Every day is adding on to my expense…who is going to complete all the pending orders!) Mulk could sense foul times and felt frustrated that solutions to his problems were outside his control.

'Veer ji, Aslam has clearly said that the majority of the Muslim workers are feeling very unsafe working in the Hindu factories and establishments hence they have decided to abstain from work. Moreover, he says, that our factory is in a totally Hindu majority area of the city, so their attending to work is out of the question,' updated Sanjay avoiding Mulk's eyes. He was apprehensive of his elder cousin's mood swings of late.

'Hore ye silsila kab tak chalega, mainu das, oye Sanjay!' exclaimed Mulk. (And tell me Sanjay, how long will this situation continue!)

'Aslam has also advised that we should transfer the factory and assets to local Muslims here as promptly as possible before it is too late, and before we are stressed to sell at a throwaway price. He also told me that there are rumours in the market about Mulk Raj Khanna being in the final stages of negotiations to sell his factory, his shop in Lahore, and his house. And that the people he is dealing with are not to be trusted,' said Sanjay.

'These are blank guesses, Sanjay, which are doing the rounds in the marketplace for every Hindu establishment and known family. It is an open fact that all of us are not sitting with vacant minds, waiting for the future to guide our lives. We are all discretely viewing options, and surely, I am not an exception.'

Mulk was honest yet guarded in his conversation with Sanjay. There were certain matters of family and business which he liked to keep essentially to himself. Sanjay had an idea of the stocks being sold, but as for the factory land and building, the shop in Lahore and the residential properties, Mulk was negotiating alone, since Jai was in England.

However, the progress he was making in these negotiations was measured. Mulk felt played by the people of the other community who were making use of the uneasy circumstances. People agreed to certain sums of money and then disappeared. New people would materialize, there would again be multiple rounds of negotiations, and yet again, they would set off never to return, and each time, Mulk would be forced to lower the sale price. Each passing day made Mulk more nervous. The middle of August was only about a month away.

He turned back to Sanjay, who was staring at his thinking and introspecting cousin.

'Sanjay, look at the accounts and tell me the exact amount we have received from Aftab, what remains, and when it is due so that I can pursue the payments as a matter of priority.'

Sanjay nodded and got up to fetch the *bahee* (account book) to answer Mulk's queries. He soon returned with a red cloth-covered, stitched and folded traditional account book, which was used by the Hindu business houses and establishments.

Mulk had two such sets of books of accounts. One was personal which he kept confidential between him and Jai. The other was the one maintained at the factory office and regularly updated by Sanjay. When combined, both had the complete record of every single bit of his business.

Sanjay opened the bahee, flipped through the long pages by licking moisture from his tongue and arrived at the relevant accounting entries.

'Mulk bhai, we have received two lakh seventy-five thousand rupees from Aftab so far and have delivered stocks worth four lakh twenty-five thousand rupees, full and final. Aftab now owes us one and a half lakh rupees and has given us an IOU slip of that amount also.'

Mulk assimilated the accounts and asked Sanjay for the date of the IOU slip. It was 3 August 1947. He was satisfied with the progress and did not have any suspicions of default since the promise to pay was backed by the Chamber of Commerce. However, Mulk had quite a few loose ends to cover, and they were increasing by the day.

After the Noakhali and Bihar Hindu Muslim riots in the second half of 1946, and the news of massacres of Hindus in Bengal (Noakhali) and Muslims in Bihar, nothing was the same between the two communities.

Although there were good Muslims and Hindus all around, helping each other in times of crisis, the bigger picture was an ever-lurking suspicion. A definite lack of faith. So, when property dealers, direct purchasers, or their agents came to Mulk, he always had an apprehension of foul play at the back of his mind.

They were the new locals of tomorrow. The inheritors of a new nation in making. Mulk had suddenly become an alien in his home and place of birth. He was convinced of a rough ride to partition and the oncoming independence. There was a lot of negativities all around.

He had to finish certain orders for delivery before the cut-off date of 7 August as fixed in agreement with his buyers and the workmen in his factory. It would be the day to begin winding up the business in Sialkot and the subsequent move to Agra as had been decided and planned within his family.

That evening, someone referred by Aftab was to visit his factory and house to inspect and negotiate the purchase. According to Aftab, he was genuinely interested in both the properties as well as the business set-up.

***

Younus Siddiqui was a major scrap dealer living not far from Mulk's factory in a Muslim-dominated locality. Both Mulk and Younus knew each other in business. However, their acquaintance had been limited to that extent. Mulk knew Younus had a shrewd disposition and was a well-known personality in his community in Sialkot. Sanjay had left the factory premises reluctantly leaving Mulk alone. It was almost half past seven in the evening and dusk had set in.

Mulk was not very comfortable having to face Younus alone, especially in such troubled times. The vicious atmosphere had resulted in mutual distrust. The gap between the two communities seemed to be becoming more and more unbridgeable with each passing day. Mulk had started keeping a shotgun but had never used one, even for sport. He was a businessman focused on manufacturing and trade. Arms and ammunition were only to be read about and seen from a distance with the army and the police brass. He had never realized that a peace- and fun-loving person like him would have to acquire a gun.

When he had first taken the weapon in his hands and felt its contours, a shiver had gone down his spine, as if the gun would pump a bullet into him. He immediately put it away in his office almirah, locking it up securely, so that it didn't slip out and get violent by itself.

Toying with it gingerly, he remembered how he had kept the purchase a secret from his family and felt guilty about it as if he had already committed his first homicide. Slowly and steadily, he got used to the idea of loading and holding the gun straight and stable with the correct finger on the trigger. He acted to shoot in various poses and angles as if he were in a battle, ridding himself of his fear of the weapon. Now he felt confident in its presence.

Loading and cleaning it gingerly with his handkerchief, he kept it in one of the large drawers supporting the right side of his office table. No sooner had he completed this than he heard footsteps resonating from the workers' hall, at one end of which was his cabin. Peeping from the window, he saw his chowkidar leading a group of about five gentlemen towards his office.

Mulk was slightly confused, apprehensive, and tentative on seeing so many of them. He had expected maybe two, including Younus. Maybe he had been hasty in allowing Sanjay to leave. Also, he was missing Jai. Missing him very much indeed...he was unguarded and alone, an ideal time to be done in, with the factory snatched away. What he suddenly realized left him cold and his mind frozen.

***

Hamid Gul, the chowkidar, entered Mulk's office followed by Younus and the others. The average height of the group was above six feet, while Mulk was not more than five feet seven inches. They were all well-built and intimidating.

'Sahib, Younus Miyan *apnay saathiyon kay saath, aapsay milnay aayien hain. Kah rahien hain kee aapko iskee jaankaaree pehlay se hee hai,*' said Hamid Gul with utmost respect. (Sir, Younus and his friends have come to meet you, and are saying that you are expecting them.)

'*Bilkul* Hamid Miyan, *sahee kah rahay ho,*' responded Mulk. (You are right, Hamid.) With that, he shook Younus's hand and requested him and his friends to take a seat. He also asked Hamid to get two more chairs from the outside hall to cover the shortfall. He wasn't expecting a crowd.

'*Maaphee chahtaa hoon*, Mulk bhai, *ye mere partner aur rishtedaar hain. Vadaa mamlaa hai naa, toe saath aa gaye,*' said Younus in a soft tone, putting Mulk at some ease. (I apologize, brother Mulk, they are my partners and relatives. Since the business and transaction are big, so, they have accompanied me.)

'*Koee gal naheen, Younus bhai, is may maaphee kee kyaa baat hai? Aap log araam se baithien, aur main chaa shaa mangaataa hoon,*' replied Mulk, while turning to Hamid and asking him to get some tea and biscuits. (What is there to apologize, brother Younus? All of you, please sit comfortably while I order some tea.)

Hamid left immediately to fetch the tea and snacks while Mulk settled behind his desk with a hand on the drawer hosting the shotgun. Younus looked at a rather rough-looking man sitting next to him and gestured something, after which the man put his hand inside a cloth bag.

Mulk, by this time, had slowly opened the drawer and quietly gripped the weapon. He did not realize the sweat beads rolling down his forehead. To his utter relief, the rough-looking man drew out a few wads of currency notes and handed it over to Younus.

'Mulk bhai, *ye mere aur mere partner kee taraph se ek chhotaa sa nazrana hai, isko kabool karien, aapkee vaddee meherbaanee hogee,'* spoke Younus, while keeping the money on the table. (Brother Mulk, this is a small token from my partner and me. It will be kind of you to accept it.)

Mulk removed his hand from the drawer, with a smile of relief breaking on his lips. However, instead of picking up the token and keeping it in his drawer, he just covered it with a small towel kept on his table and made a silent note that the rough-looking man was Younus's partner. Hamid walked in with tea and biscuits as ordered.

'Lo jee, zara chaa pee lo, phir hum baat aagay badatay hai,' requested Mulk. (Here, please have tea, and then let us proceed with our conversation.) He ordered Hamid to stay just outside his cabin and wait for further orders. Turning back, he spoke to Younus.

'Younus bhai, this token is not really required, since we have not yet talked of the business deal, and I am not sure as to whether you know exactly what is up for sale.'

'Mulk bhai, I have done my homework well, through enquiries from Aftab and some other people of this town. We are aware that you are planning to sell your factory, residential, and commercial properties here and in Lahore in a single deal. That is why we have all come together, since we would be pooling in our resources and make one bid for the complete block,' replied Younus, with an air of superiority and confidence of a secure local.

Mulk had a strange feeling of insecurity welling up within him. He felt naked and small in front of this mostly alien group of people who already knew his mind…knew all of it. He thought deeply while discretely observing the five gents sitting in front of him, and then spoke purposefully, directing his speech towards Younus since he was the only person he knew at all.

'Younus bhai, I am surprised at your thorough homework. I am thinking of shifting from Sialkot to Agra since the rest of my relatives are already settled there and have been pressing me to join them for quite some time now. So, my family has made up its mind to take the plunge, keeping in mind the approaching independence and the proposed partition.

'It was indeed very hard for us to arrive at this conclusion, with a thriving business and a happy existence in this city of my birth and work. But I think life must go on, and we must adjust accordingly.

'However, I would finally make up my mind provided the deal is a good bargain, living up to our expectations. So, please keep the token with you till we reach a final satisfactory agreement, before which, I will not be able to accept anything. Please don't mind.'

Younus cast a glance at his friends with a perceptible smirk on his face and spoke on their behalf as well as for himself.

'Mulk bhai, you would have to take a call soon or else you and your family will be the losers. We, in the market, know of all that you have asked for and what you have been offered. Do believe me that with every passing day, the value of your transactions will keep dipping faster than what you can imagine, till you reach a stage when you will have no buyers….

'When your estate will be left to the whims and fancies of the new government of Pakistan….'

Mulk's fear and nervousness were now turning to frustration and agitation. He was feeling powerless and cornered and indirectly threatened to accept whatever Younus and his cronies were about to offer. In such situations, Mulk always liked to withdraw for another day, to do his homework and approach the negotiation afresh. He immediately distanced himself away from the ongoing transaction and spoke gently and slowly.

'Younus bhai, I am sure that whatever you are telling me is the correct situation. I also understand that the independence we all are earning comes at a cost. At a very grave cost.

'However, this move is very critical to me, my family and our future. Today, I am happy to leave it at a point where I know that you are willing to have a single deal on my estate with me. Now, we have to arrive at an acceptable figure by looking at the current market situation.

'Since it is reasonably late in the day, let us meet here the day after tomorrow, early in the morning at about six. Will it be fine for all of you?'

Younus was a bit flustered and taken aback by this sudden withdrawal by Mulk. He was smelling success when suddenly Mulk had called it a day. He made a last-ditch effort to regain lost ground.

'Mulk bhai, at least let us know what is your asking value for the assets you are thinking of selling? We must get an idea to think of and consult with our family and near and dear ones.'

Mulk had already got up while Younus was literally pleading to know his thoughts on the price. He started putting his documents and registers in the almirah while Younus continued his efforts to extract information.

After winding up, Mulk turned around and looked at Younus with a peaceful and brotherly smile.

'Younus bhai, it is just a matter of a day, and we will be ready with all the facts and figures to make a decision. I am sure that what we decide will make both of us and our families happy. And we would have reasons to celebrate. Come, let us leave for now, since I have some personal business to look into on my way back home.'

As they left, Younus and his friends had a somewhat anxious and disappointed expression on their faces. Evidently, they had come ready for the kill and were going away even without firing a shot!

Mulk walked down the lane leading out from his factory gate to the main road after having seen off his guests, locking his office and the factory shed, and handing over the keys to the chowkidar, his daily routine. He truly had urgent work before he reached the comfort of his house as he had mentioned to Younus. Mulk had to meet someone in private. Quite confidential and critical....

Deep in thought, he waited for a tonga after reaching the main road. It was not a long wait.

'Sadar *chalega*?' asked Mulk, in an authoritative voice. (Would you go to Sadar?)

'Jee sarkar, *bilkul challangay*,' was he courteous reply. (Will definitely go, Sir.)

Mulk hopped on, still musing on what had passed and what lay ahead....

***

The tonga stopped just outside the gate of a medium-sized bungalow near his old house, not far away from the Clock Tower. Mulk paid the tonga driver and walked up to the gate, gingerly opening and shutting it once inside, and then walked down the short driveway to the house within.

Aftab was already waiting for him on the porch rather impatiently. Mulk was about fifteen minutes late on account of heavy traffic leading through the Clock Tower marketplace. What Mulk had never realized, and what started off as a professional as well as suspicious relationship, had led to a strong bond of comradery and trust between Aftab and him.

Aftab was an influential man and a political heavyweight in the region, which in the very near future would become Pakistan. His key interest was to help Mulk smoothly sell his factory and other assets, realize their value, and safely move out into what would be India of the future.

On account of Mulk's simplicity and being a man true to his words, Aftab had developed a brotherly liking towards him. He had become a family member, having made frequent social visits to Mulk's Civil Lines house with his entire family.

Aftab had arranged Mulk's family's safe journey to Kud and hosted Jai in his house in Karachi before he embarked on his first sea voyage to England. Now, Aftab grabbed Mulk's hand and guided him towards his Sialkot residence guest room, bordering the veranda, which opened onto the porch. On his way inside, he advised Mulk to just be guided by his talks with the waiting guest.

They entered the guest room to find Aslam, the local labour leader already there, sipping tea from a small glass. This was a very confidential meeting, arranged with great difficulty by Aftab.

Aftab broke the silence, introducing them both.

'Aslam bhai, *aap Mulk bhai ko toe jaantay hee hongay? Yahaan kay achhay khaasay vadday karobaaree hain.*' (Brother Aslam, you must already know brother Mulk? He is a reasonably big businessman in Sialkot.)

'Jee, *bilkul zanaab, inko Sialkot mien kaun naheen jaantaa. Inkee factory mien banay cricket kay samman toe duniyaa bhar mien mashoor hain,'* replied Aslam. (Absolutely, sir, who doesn't know him? Cricket goods manufactured in his factory are well known all over the world.)

Mulk was rather surprised at meeting Aslam here and in this way. Although he knew Aslam very well, he had never met him. Sanjay, his nephew and accountant, was always the go-between.

Aftab explained the reason for the meeting, which was critical for Mulk. There were developments which could not be spelt out to people like Sanjay. Aftab also had to put immense pressure on Aslam to make him come out with information that would be crucial for Mulk to negotiate well and offload his assets here in Sialkot.

'Mulk bhai, I was the person who introduced you to Younus bhai, since I had good business dealings with him. But he turned out to be a true scrap dealer, shrewd and unscrupulous. He convinced Aslam bhai of the benefits of Younus's taking over your factory at a low price for the community at large. Younus promised all Aslam bhai's unemployed union members a job at a decent salary.'

Mulk was a bit confused now and queried on this.

'And Aftab bhai, what was Aslam to do in return?'

'Let me continue, Mulk bhai. Aslam had to instigate your factory's labour strike, and he did! I apologize for having introduced you to such a person, Mulk bhai.'

Aftab spoke with his head bowed, tears in his eyes, and clasping Mulk's hand within his two sweating hands.

'And I will correct this situation, which has been my creation in the first place,' spoke Aftab. 'I have had a lengthy talk with Aslam bhai and have offered him what Younus has already agreed with him, as well as a stake in the running of your factory, once it is purchased.'

Mulk was reasonably nervous, shocked, and irritated by this time, and his expressions showed multiple questions and emotions dwelling up all at the same time.

'But Aftab bhai, how are you supposing so confidently that the deal for my factory, leaving aside my other assets, will be transacted so smoothly? I have no reasons for any optimism about the way things are moving.'

Looking directly at Aslam, Mulk continued sternly.

'I am suddenly finding enemies and opportunists all around, making me a stranger in my own home! All for which I have worked so hard throughout my life seems to have become an easy target for people who just want to walk in and take over!'

While talking excitably, Mulk's voice quivered and then he broke down, unable to control himself. He suddenly started feeling the pain of being alone. Absolutely alone.

Jai in England. Wife and children in Kud.

He felt very vulnerable indeed….

Aftab got up and embraced the sobbing Mulk. Aslam, who had been sitting quietly with his head bowed down with guilt and remorse, also got up and crossed over to where Mulk was sitting. He stood there silently with a hand on Mulk's shoulders, embarrassed with the situation he was responsible for creating in connivance with the ruthless Younus.

Mulk recovered slowly from his bout of lachrymose inebriation, wiped his eyes and face with his handkerchief and took control of himself.

Aftab offered him a glass of water, which he took graciously, and gulped it down in one go. He turned towards Aftab enquiringly on what he had thought of in coming out of this useless trap Mulk found himself in.

Aftab could easily decipher what Mulk wanted to know. He took a chair beside Mulk and began rolling out his plan.

'Mulk bhai, I have decided to form a partnership with some businessmen to buy the running business from you since I cannot arrange all the money by myself. The price would include the factory land and building. I have also identified different buyers for your two residences, here in Sialkot as well as the shop in Lahore. This way you will get better prices for all your assets.'

While explaining his plans to Mulk, Aftab got up and crossed the room to go to the room inside, leaving Mulk and Aslam in the guest room.

Both sat in pregnant silence without looking at each other. Aslam wore a guilty expression, gazing at the carpeted floor of

Aftab's guest room, while Mulk looked out of the window, with storms of frustration sweeping through his insides.

Aftab returned soon enough rescuing both his guests from an embarrassing togetherness. He had a packet clasped in his hands.

Crossing the room with a sense of purpose, he took his seat beside Mulk and placed the packet in his hands.

'Mulk bhai, this is a small advance for the factory. We will have a meeting tomorrow evening here to negotiate the best price for the assets, any remaining stock, and the business goodwill. The other partners will also be present. So please come prepared with your account books and documents.

'It would be better to get Sanjay along since he has complete first-hand knowledge of the business accounts and orders in hand. I would also have an inventory of finished goods stock which I have already purchased from you.

'And tomorrow morning, you will have some guests at your house in Civil Lines accompanying me. They would be coming to see the property, having already made a reconnaissance of your other property near Clock Tower and the shop in Lahore. They are keen to strike a deal tomorrow itself, so it will be good to have your lawyer with you.'

Mulk was amazed at Aftab's speed of arranging all this, as well as his thoughtfulness considering the situation in which Mulk found himself. Restlessness was growing between the two communities. Mutual suspicion, rioting, and violence had become the order of the day. Every day being alive was a blessing of God.

With less than a month left for the independence days of the twin nations, Mulk did not have very much of a choice or time. He looked at Aftab with appreciation and gratitude. With folded hands and tears welling up within him, revealing a couple of drops through his eyes, he spoke, 'Aftab bhai, *jo tussi theek samjho....*' (As you feel right....) Saying this, he took Aftab's hand within his two, touched it to his forehead and started sobbing.

***

After having bid farewell to both Aftab and a silent and guilty Aslam, he walked off to the gate, and then the road, where he got on to a tonga to transport him back to the safety of his home.... God alone knew for how much more time. He felt alone, vulnerable, and depressed, and could not see a bright future ahead, with a lot of loose ends to tie.

Jai had to be informed of all that was happening and was going to happen. With the passage of time, getting a call through to him in England was getting more and more difficult, so Mulk used to write to him every day in the evening. He used to send another letter to his wife, also daily in the night. He looked forward to this only form of communication he had with his family and indulged in it as the last chore of the day. He accompanied this activity with a couple of whiskeys and water.

Mulk was slowly getting into the habit of drinking daily, a casualty of living alone. Magan Lal continued to be as faithful a retainer to Mulk as he was when he was introduced to their family as a kid, fresh from a village near Amritsar. He was the one who dutifully, yet very reluctantly, fixed Mulk's drinks for him, constantly reminding him that this was something he would never have done in Jaya bhabhi's presence.

Lost in the thoughts attacking him from all directions, harassing and choking him at times, he reached the front gate of his home of the present. Magan Lal was there to greet him at the front door. He took Mulk's umbrella, lunch box, and his favourite cloth bag, in which he kept required papers, reading glasses, and other articles of daily use—pencils, a sharpener, and an eraser among them.

'Sahib, Sanjay *bhaiyya baithey hain ander, drawing room vich,*' informed Magan, taking Mulk's belongings away. (Sir, Sanjay is sitting in the drawing room.)

*'Arrey Magan, meri whisky, paani aur do glass le aayeen...*Sanjay *bhi ik peg lagaa legaa mere naal,'* called out Mulk after Magan while he entered the drawing room. (Magan, get my whisky, water and two glasses. Sanjay would also share a drink with me.)

Sanjay had been waiting for Mulk for the past hour rather anxiously and was relieved to see him well and in high spirits.

'Mulk bhai, it is so good seeing you safe and sound. I was very worried about not finding you in the factory or in the house. Even Magan did not know your whereabouts. Please inform him at least when you are late. The conditions in the city are not good at all, with so much senseless violence all around,' blurted Sanjay in a single breath.

'Sanjay, calm down, my dear younger brother.... I am safe and did not encounter any such violence on the way. It is good to have you here since I need to share some information with you and need your support as well. Let us talk over some whisky. I am sure you also need it as much as me.' Mulk spoke with put-on good humour.

Sanjay nodded at the offer of whisky quite gratefully. He surely required the fiery liquid to soothe his nerves. Magan had come in with a tray carrying all the requirements, including some fries and peanuts as accompaniments. Whisky pegs having been fixed, glasses having been clinked, and first deep sips having been taken, Mulk proceeded to inform Sanjay of his encounter with Aftab and his settling out his deals. However, he shortened the narrative to the extent he desired to disclose to Sanjay.

The news was good for Sanjay since their objectives were shaping up. Nevertheless, he could not gather the risks that Mulk could foresee on account of being the man in the front.

'Sanjay, you need to be here tomorrow morning at about seven with our lawyer since we will be finalizing the sale of our houses with a single buyer. And then I also need you at Aftab's Sialkot guest house at five in the evening for the commercial settlement of the factory and the accompanying assets. So do get all the necessary account books and papers along,' instructed Mulk.

Sanjay gulped down his whisky in excitement and happiness that his elder brother had finally taken him into confidence after a long period of neglect. He gripped Mulk's right hand and shook it hard, emotively, with the whisky also playing its role. Sanjay had tears in his eyes, which played around visibly within.

Mulk gave him a tight hug and instructed him to leave since it was late in the evening, and the situation of the city, especially where Sanjay lived, was not at its best. There was sporadic violence erupting on and off.

Sanjay took leave, touching Mulk's feet, and walked away.

***

It was a balmy yet humid night without any breeze. It was too early to be so quiet in the city areas of Sialkot, which otherwise were fairly vibrant where people liked to both work and party hard. Sanjay, who had by now walked out of the gates of Mulk's residence, was also finding the quietness and peace unnatural, too.

He waited for a tonga or a rickshaw to pass by to hitch a ride back to his home further into the city, not far from the Clock Tower, also Mulk's old *kothi* (bungalow). But none passed by.

After waiting for about five minutes in solitude, he started to walk his way home. A walk, which under normal circumstances he would have enjoyed, but was now risky.

Many were using this politically created opportunity to settle scores with each other. New enmities were taking shape and finishing someone off had suddenly gained currency as the easiest form of revenge.

Sanjay could hear his footsteps, with the heels of his shoes clickity-clacking on the pebbled footpath bordering the street. What he did not notice was the sound of more footsteps.

The alien footsteps kept a discrete distance till Sanjay crossed a cigarette shop from where he purchased a packet of his favourite Panamas. He took out one and lit it with a match provided by the shopkeeper. Making polite conversation, the shopkeeper warned Sanjay to be careful while walking alone and suggested taking public transport as soon as he could get one.

'The conditions of the city are growing from bad to worse, sahib…so you better watch out for unruly mobs. They are baying for our blood. You must be a Hindu sir…at least you look so… take a tonga home, sir…my advice….'

Sanjay, taking a puff or two and relaxing in the process, wished the shopkeeper a good night and walked off, more comfortable and less apprehensive. God was with him, and no one could harm him.

He turned left onto a narrower lane, off the main road, on a shortcut to his house. A hundred yards on…there was a shuffling sound…and before he could react, a loud crack on his head made him stare into absolute darkness. His legs buckled as he collapsed on the road. He could hear muffled voices…till he could hear no more….

'Bloody fool, he has unnecessarily given his life for that selfish hi…nd…oooo….'

***

It was a depressing and horrific day in the life of Mulk.

He had already been through the cremation of one of his favourite cousins, confidante, accountant, friend, and brother-in-arm. At times, he felt closer to Sanjay than his younger sibling.

He had also faced the hostile and accusing postures of Sanjay's father, who was the only parent Sanjay had. He sat in his drawing room, surrounded by Aftab, Aslam, Lalit Uberoi and his area's police inspector—a good-natured, distinguished, and well-loved Englishman. The police were reasonably confident of who the men behind this macabre killing were.

Younus was not at all happy with Mulk's refusal and Aslam had also moved away. Aftab was a much stronger adversary who was openly supporting Mulk. Did he have any other way to spoil Mulk's plans, other than using the safest way of communal violence and the impending menace of partition?

The inspector, who was a well-wisher of Mulk and interacted with him frequently, especially with the level of his business engagements and the troubled times, spoke in a rather patronizing manner.

'Mr Khanna, you are alone right now, as well as targeted. The local people, and the ones in close vicinity know that you are a prominent Hindu and are most likely to leave for the newly forming India. You are already interacting with some group of people towards liquidating your assets; and already have liquidated some. You also might have refused some of their offers. Sir, you need to move as fast as possible, and certainly not stay alone in these circumstances.'

The Inspector was genuinely disturbed and concerned.

Aftab sprang into action.

'Inspector sahib, I am equally worried and concerned about Mulk bhai's wellbeing, and I am more nervous after this heinous killing of poor Sanjay. I am sure that Mulk bhai is a broken man. We will not leave him alone under any circumstances, till we have made sure that he is safe and sound with his family. I would request a couple of sepoys to be posted outside his bungalow for a few days, and I will be with him, till we have planned for his travel to where he has plans to go.'

The inspector looked satisfied and barked orders to a constable posted outside the room.

'Hari Singh, you, along with another of your team, are to guard Mr Khanna's residence till you get further orders from me. Do you understand?'

The constable nodded in affirmative, after which the inspector continued.

'Aftab, I am proud to have people like you around, and on you, I put a lot of responsibility and faith in seeing Mr Khanna safely through. You will have all the support of the police station, on demand. I promise that.'

With that, he requested leave and walked off briskly. The inspector had a very long day ahead. Both Lalit and Aftab supported a sobbing Mulk into his bedroom and made him lie down. Lalit asked Magan to get a glass of milk for his master.

Leaving Mulk to relax, Aftab and Lalit got back to the drawing room. Aftab apprised Lalit of some insider knowledge he had by virtue of his belonging to the other side of the divide.

'Lalit bhai, Younus and his group are after Mulk bhai and his assets. They now want to grab everything for nothing. Mulk bhai's life is in great danger, and we must shift him off as soon as possible. Maybe within a day.'

Lalit was in agreement but asked the most evident and burning question.

'What about Mulk's assets and money? His life's savings? What will he live by if he loses everything here? Unlike me, he has not planned much, and has been living by the hope that everything will get sorted out by itself. Please do let me know as to what possible help I can be of. You are much closer to him, yet I am of the same trade.' That was also one of the factors Aftab was apprehensive of.

Aftab was the closest friend and relative whom Mulk had at that point, and he would certainly not jeopardise Mulk's position in front of his competitors, albeit friends. He weighed every bit and answered.

'Lalit bhai, I am very close to him, and I have been a part of all that he has planned for his imminent departure. Believe me, he has a viable plan in place, however late. Bhabhi ji and the rest of the family have left for Kud. His elder son is already studying in a school in Dehradun, and Jai is in England on business. It is all in accordance with a well calculated plan of Mulk bhai.

'The only problem is that, unlike you, he started moving on his thoughts a bit too late in the day, and now this tragedy has really caught all of us off guard.

'Anyhow, since you know the manufacturing part of the trade very well, I would need your help to straighten things out for Mulk bhai, and I will continue to take your support as and when required, since you would be here slightly longer, having managed your affairs well in advance.'

Lalit left after assuring him to be at Mulk's residence whenever he called. Aftab, having asked Aslam to get as much information about the known and unknown enemies of Mulk, went inside to where Mulk was.

***

Aftab and Mulk sat in Mulk's drawing room, pouring over a survey map, while sipping some steaming hot cup of tea, which was in continuous supply, thanks to Magan. Mulk was tense and anxious with a lot going on in his life much before it had to.

However, he was sure of the safety of his dear wife Jaya, his sister-in-law, nephew, and his kids—his prize possessions—in Kud, the eldest son being safe in Dehradun. The family also had Hans Raj with them, another of his man Fridays, like Magan. He was a person on whom Mulk could leave the factory with all it stocks and cash, unguarded. Such was the trust, second only to Sanjay. Jai was busy and safe in England.

None of them knew what Mulk was stuck in all alone with life playing hide and seek with his mortal body. Tears rolled down his eyes, and, travelling down his cheeks, dropped onto the map below. Aftab embraced a sobbing Mulk.

'Mulk bhai, *apne aap ko sambhaliye, aanay waalay dina vich aap ke upper bahut zimmedaariaan hain...aisay kaisay kaam chalega... bataaiye*?' (Mulk bhai, take control of yourself, you have a lot of responsibility on yourself in the coming days...how will it go on like this...please tell me?)

Mulk took a few deep breaths, had a few gulps of water brought by Magan, and got back to what they were doing. He surely had a lot to be done in the hours ahead, with absolutely no time to think of options, which were conspicuous by their absence.

'To Jammu and then on to Kud would not be more than about thirty to forty kilometres, and hence the ideal route to join the family, and be in safer territory post partition.' Mulk spoke up looking towards Aftab for his endorsement.

'This is the best option, Mulk bhai. Let us wait for Aslam to come back with news of your mode of transport—truck, bus, or train. We would draw your exit plans accordingly,' added Aftab in a tension-filled low tone.

'Aftab, I have a few main worries which would need to be settled, and I really don't know how. Magan needs to go with me, and what happens to the sale of my factory, the shop in Lahore and the residences, is critical.

'Then my luggage, which I need to carry, and its safekeeping is something which also needs to be worked out. For the sale, I am totally dependent on you, Aftab bhai. I do not know how it is going to happen, with me in Agra.

'As for the rest, I would have to handle it singlehandedly, with whatever support I can get from Magan. Oh! How much I am missing Jaya, only I know.' Mulk spoke chokingly and started sobbing again.

In the meantime, Aslam rushed in without knocking, while Mulk gulped down some more water and steadied himself, to hear from Aslam, hoping for some good news for a change.

'Aftab bhai…Mulk bhai…!

'Mulk bhai has just time till midnight today to move out of here. I have heard with my own ears that they are going to attack. They want to kill Mulk bhai and take over all his properties.

'Aftab bhai, you need to do something fast to safeguard Mulk bhai. It is all my doing; I am completely responsible for all that is happening!

'Ya Allah, mainu toe dozhak mien bhi jagah nahin milegi, meri galat kartooton kee wajah se!' (Oh God, I will not even get space in Hell, for what all I have done.)

Aslam had gone hysterical, and Mulk had to move up to him, embrace and pacify him while he himself was a shattered man, not knowing what was going to happen the next moment.

Mulk called for Magan and gave him clear orders to pack up both their essential belongings. For the rest of his critical belongings, Mulk would have to pack himself, and having been a good manager of his business, he gave himself a target time of one hour for all this. Provided he survived….

He was lost in his world and had completely forgotten the presence of Aftab and Aslam in the room, till Aftab came to him and jolted him out of the stupor.

'Mulk bhai, please get back to the present and let us plan a time-bound programme. Just be sure that I am always with you till my life parts with me. Now, both of you, please listen carefully….

'I will be going back to my house in Sialkot and getting one and a half lakh rupees in cash that I owe to Mulk bhai. Aslam, you need to arrange as much as you can for now, with a minimum of what I am getting. We will adjust this in the sale proceeds of Mulk bhai's properties and business.

'Mulk bhai, once you reach Agra safely, we will communicate with each other in whichever way possible, agree upon and settle the remaining amount to be paid.

'Either I will come to Agra, or you will come to Sialkot for the final deal. I am also calling up one of my influential friends here, to see in case we have a safe house or arrangement for Mulk bhai and Magan to stay till we settle their transport to Kud."

***

It was 7 August 1947, and uncertainty and rioting in the district were on the rise. Aftab came back dejected since the district administration had still not created any safe dwelling infrastructure for any Hindu or Sikh refugees who planned to migrate into safer portions of India. While walking out of the Collector's office, Aftab had already made up his mind. Mulk would shift to his dwelling in Sialkot, and till he didn't safely see him off to India, he would continue to give Mulk company and delay his trip back home to Karachi. He had strong reasons to be sure that Younus and his henchmen would not dare to touch his house.

***

And the insanity...the bloodbath...the dance of the devil continued....

CHAPTER 18

Embers to Flames

A major part of Meerut was immersed in a senseless communal bloodbath. Dr Narendra Nath Bandhopadhyay, dressed in a finely tailored summer suit, settled down in his graceful horse carriage.

He was on his way to attend an invite by the Collector to all the distinguished persona of the city. The agenda was not made known yet was obvious.

Some sanity had to be brought about in the city from the frenzy. It had to be made more welcoming for the tortured and harassed refugees, mostly from west Punjab, who were pouring into Delhi and surrounding areas. The poor migrants had already had a harrowing time in the course of their morbid and dangerous journey, and the camps in which they were made to put up.

On his way up to the Collectorate, he could see some broken rickshaws and a smouldering tonga and…he asked his coachman to stop immediately. A young boy stood there, bleeding profusely through a nasty gash on his head and a serious wound on his knees.

Narendra got down, did a quick check-up, and found him with intense fever, which meant sepsis was already setting in.

'What is your name, boy?' he yelled out in local parlance.

'Zakir, sahib, mumbled the poor suffering boy, and painfully continued, 'Sahib, *woh bahut log thhe.... Mujhe lathiyon se aur hockey stick se maara...maine bahut haath jode...kah rahe thhe ki tera mur jaana hee achha hai.'* (Sir, they were a crowd...they beat me up with sticks and hockeys...I begged and pleaded...but they said that it is good for you to die....)

With this the poor lad started moaning and writhing with pain and broke down. Being a doctor, it was a split-second decision for Narendra. He passed immediate orders to his coachman to help put the boy on to the carriage and turned around to his clinic. He would put the boy in the safe hands of Ajit and then quickly get back to the tea meeting with the Collector. He was sure they would understand the critical and sensitive calling of a doctor. This boy had to be saved.

While they were loading him onto the carriage, one of the local Hindu leaders happened to be walking by. He stopped and asked Narendra about the boy.

'Doctor sahib, hope he is not a Muslim? Please don't land yourself into any problems, Doctor sahib. These are very bad days, and these *haramis* cannot be trusted....'

Narendra responded with a greeting, while packing the boy safely, sat next to the boy and moved on. He saw the man from the corner of his eyes...after looking at the disappearing carriage, the local leader moved on. After all, Doctor sahib was a trusted man in the city.

***

The District Magistrate was seated along with another gentleman who would be taking over from him on the date of independence of India. A sharp and congenial gentleman, the successor seemed to be aware of the challenges he was going to face at the dawn of independence.

All the invitees were present. Nawab sahib, Sultan Singh, Professor Chatterji, Dr Madan, Dublish and others were already there waiting for Narendra. They were rather worried about his being late since they knew him to be a person whom even the clock looked up to.

The incumbent Collector looked up to those present, enquiring as to when to start the proceedings of the meeting. Nawab sahib made a request to wait for another fifteen minutes for doctor sahib on account of the importance of his presence there. As there was general consent on this, including from the Collector, they waited, discussing the current situation; and sharing experiences.

***

'Hello, gentlemen.' Narendra's largish frame entered after a knock.

'Doctor, where the devil were you…we have been waiting for you since the meeting wouldn't have had much of purpose in your absence,' exclaimed the Collector, getting up from his chair and guiding the doctor to his seat as a mark of respect and protocol.

Narendra bowed and took his seat while apologising for the delay.

'I had to tend to a grievously injured young boy, a product of communal violence in the city.'

'Who was the boy? Where was this? Who was he…Hindoo or a Muslim?' The Magistrate rattled off all these questions in one breath, to order for action if required.

Narendra was by now composed and at ease in his cushioned chair and was in no way inclined to disturb the focus of the current meeting. Time was of the essence for all present, and he was fully aware of that. So, he thought it judicious to put the matter to rest then and there.

'Sir, I have taken care of the life and wounds in the capacity of a doctor, and my clinic will follow the medicolegal process as required and necessary. So, we have no reasons to worry and can go ahead with the agenda in hand.'

The Magistrate appreciated Narendra's wisdom and took the day's proceedings forward.

'Gentlemen, as you all must be aware, we are on the doorsteps of independence. Both India and Pakistan.

'The Boundary Commission, headed by His Excellency Sir Cyril Radcliffe, is in the process of giving the finishing touches to the award, which will be declared any time now. However, what we are sure of is that Meerut would be an integral part of India; hence, we should be going ahead with the transition, accordingly.

'We already have Jai Kirat with us, who would be taking over the reins of Meerut District from Friday, 15 August 1947. He is a bright bloke but would need support and cooperation from each one of you, to sustain the transition.

'Meerut is the proud district to have had Sir WC Bonerjee to have guided and shaped her psyche and bring about the necessary discipline, and I expect Jai Kirat to sustain the development, harmony, assimilation, and discipline very much required at this juncture.

'There is a lot of work in hand, but the primary task is to bring about peace in the district. We also need to make quite some guests comfortable, who have been left with nothing in their torturous, alarming, and pathetic journey from western Punjab all the way to the bleeding refugee camps in Delhi and nearby. We have decided to request help from some of the prominent citizens of the city, and hence, we are all here together.

'To start with, the administration proposes to form a citizens' committee to investigate all incidents of communal disharmony and problems related to citizens planning to migrate to Pakistan, helping the administration identify the ideal land to resettle the incoming refugees. And the list goes on.'

While talking, the Magistrate looked towards Nawab sahib and continued.

'Nawab sahib, I count upon your good offices to bail us out with your support. We all know of your splendid reputation and credibility, not only with your community but with the gentry of the city as well.'

The Nawab was touched with the kind words of the Magistrate. However, at the same time, he was reasonably tense and worried about the situation on the ground, with his scared and insecure community.

They were on the receiving end in the city and, hence, were resorting to collective counter-violence wherever they had the numbers to support. Most of the members of Nawab's extended family had left for western Punjab, in the vicinity of Lahore, and he had been unable to convince them otherwise. His wife was not inclined to stay back, too, but for the staunch obstinacy of her husband, totally under the tutelage of the great Maulana.

A nudge from Professor Virendra jerked the Nawab out of his thought jungles. He fumbled with a glass of water which he was unconsciously holding for quite some time, almost spilling it in the process. He drank a few gulps and responded to the Magistrate, who had been intently looking towards him.

'I am honoured, Sir, to have been trusted the way I have been. And I would like to bring to your knowledge that I am already doing my bit to achieve what the administration also desires to.

'However, what extra needs to be done, you can always trust me to be with you all, and I would be delighted to be a part of the team of citizens to support the transition.'

The District Magistrate knew and was sure of the Nawab's cooperation, as also of most of the others who were present there. Their presence itself was a sign of their cooperation.

So, finally, he put in his concluding bit.

'All of you present here have been invited on account of the trust the administration has in you, and we also are sure of your support. Hence, I would propose to name a committee and apportion each member with a specific responsibility. The role would be commiserated to your area of expertise, and you would have the right of refusal as well.'

***

Narendra, accompanied by the Professor and the Nawab, headed towards his clinic, in his horse carriage. They were silent and brooding, absorbed in their thoughts…and their responsibilities. Narendra, apart from being a member of the committee constituted by the District Administration, also had the responsibility of carrying out medical check-ups of the refugees coming into Meerut, primarily from the west.

He was a part of the sub-committee to oversee the allotment of plots to the refugees for their homes and small establishments as well. Nawab Sahib and Professor Virendra, along with Sultan and a couple more, were also members of the sub-committee to support the Administration in the allotment of plots.

The focus of Narendra's thought was to recollect where he had kept a small diary in which he had scribbled some names and addresses of businessmen from Lahore and Sialkot—the ones who had shown singular interest in settling down in Meerut.

The District Magistrate, during their meeting, had also expressed a desire to pitch for the sports goods manufacturers of Sialkot and around to settle down in Meerut, so that it could become a part of the sports goods cluster along with Jalandhar and certain other cities. He was happy to see his adopted city taking a strategic turn.

The Nawab's work was far more tedious, and his focus was to settle down the Muslims and make them more secure in the city.

The only positive point was that most of them who had decided to stay back were concentrated in the old walled part of the city. So, their protection would become that much simpler. However, the violence that was showing up as spasms was very disturbing and depressing for the Nawab.

The Professor was of the coolest temperament of them all and was humming a tune while looking around the city. He was gifted with a happy temperament by the divine and made the most of it. His main concern was to promote education and sustain the existing standards—a job that he enjoyed in its entirety.

The trinity landed up at Narendra's clinic for deliberations and a cup of coffee. Narendra jumped down from the carriage and rushed inside his now crowded clinic with a harassed Ajit, while the other two walked through to the anteroom and yelled for Babu Lal to fetch a pot of coffee with some sandwiches.

***

After helping Ajit with some complicated patients, Narendra went into his private chamber and pulled the small diary from his bottom right drawer.

There were small scribbles of various things ranging from insignificant to significant, which he kept as a record to be referred to in future. He was looking for the name and address of an industrialist from somewhere in Sialkot or Lahore, which had been given to him by his accountant and cousin—a man whom he had taken a fancy to, on account of his simplicity and loyalty, as well as his intention to settle his elder cousin's business in Meerut or its vicinities.

Sanjay Kapoor, Khanna Sports, Sialkot....

That's it....

Narendra pocketed the diary and proceeded to where his friends were, to have a quick bite, gulp it down with some hot coffee, and get back to the clinic. Life had suddenly become much more hectic than it already had been, especially with independence and the dark clouds of partition looming large on the horizon.

Meerut was a city not at peace with itself, as was true for most of the other regions of the middle northern region, east to west, of undivided British India.

CHAPTER 19

A Friend in Need

Satendra, squatting on a vacant piece of muddy area in front of the barracks where he stayed, was absent-mindedly playing with marbles, which had become an inseparable part of his psyche.

He was alone since most of his friends had ventured off to the safety of the mountains, to return only after the independence day once stability returned to the young country. Satendra and another family from his neighbouring village were the only people left in the otherwise jam-packed dwellings.

They had gone, along with Trilok, his elder brother, and his sister-in-law to the government's salary disbursement office to get their final accounts sorted before British India closed its gates to enable independent India (*swatantra* Bharat) to welcome its citizens. It was to be a whole day affair, so all of them had gone with packed lunch and fruits to sustain the ordeal of waiting in the huge queue.

Satendra had opted to stay back since he was expecting some friends who would drop by from the neighbourhood to play marbles with him. His sister-in-law had kept some spiced rice and dal, with some pickles, for them to consume. What Satendra had discretely hidden was that Yusuf, his Muslim friend from school, would also be one of the visitors.

Two of his neighbours had already arrived, and after waiting for a short while for Yusuf, they started their first game of marbles.

While they were busy aiming their marble shots, they did not notice a figure advancing towards them, crouching, limping, lurching, and hiding behind trees…until suddenly, a young body, sodden with old and fresh blood, fell in between them. It was a grievously wounded and bleeding Yusuf, who could not control himself any further and was now whining and crying.

'Mere Abba ko aisa naheen karna chahiye thha….dekho kya ho gaya!' (My father shouldn't have done this, see what it resulted in.)

Yusuf kept on repeating this and howling.

Satendra and his friends did not know how to react and what to do. They were terrified and sweating and kept on staring in disbelief for quite some time. However, the rest of Satendra's friends thought it prudent to slip out of the situation, leaving Satendra alone to face the heat.

'Bhai hum toe jaa rahien hain. Hamare Pitaji ko pata lagaa toe… bus.' (Brother, we are going. In case our father comes to know about this…that will be it.)

Saying this, they virtually ran away. Satendra was scared and apprehensive too. However, he needed to act, otherwise he was sure to be in dire trouble, even as Yusuf continued to whimper and grimace in intense pain.

Satendra propped him up and made him walk to the rear courtyard of their barracks, facing the government officer's bungalow in whose campus the barracks were located. It would be far safer than facing the road, which was guarded by just a few rows of trees.

He then went inside his room and fetched a brown sheet, one of the only two he had, and covered Yusuf with it. Yusuf was already shivering with the onset of fever…and moreover, Satendra did not want anyone to see a wounded boy on the campus.

He then rushed off to Hemu Kaka, a compounder with an Indian doctor, who lived a couple of bungalows away, with his elder brother, who was working as a cook for another officer. The clinic was closed because of all the confusion arising out of the fast-approaching independence day.

Satendra was panting and trembling by the time he reached Hemu Kaka, who also knew his family very well, as he belonged to a neighbouring village in Garhwal.

Breathing hard, he spoke.

'Kaka, please keep a secret of what I am just going to tell you…. I have my friend at my house who has been badly injured by a rioting mob…he needs immediate medical help…please come with me, along with your first-aid box immediately.'

Satendra blurted out all this in one go, and rapidly. However, what he concealed was that Yusuf was a Muslim. Hemu put his hand around Satendra's shoulders and picking up his box, guided him out of the house.

'Do not worry, Satendra, everything will be all right. I have been handling many such cases every day these days. These Muslims are surely creating a lot of problems for us by not migrating across to their new country to be…Pakistan.

'I am of a strong opinion that Sardar Patel and Nehru ji should force all of them to follow Jinnah's footsteps and leave us Hindus alone here in India.'

Satendra quietly digested what he heard and was scared even to think what lay ahead….

***

Yusuf had a very high fever when Hemu touched him on his forehead and was bleeding as well, though not profusely. The main worry after dressing up his wounds was to secure him from the impact of high fever reaching his brain.

Satendra had reached Yusuf ahead of Hemu and taken off the sacred amulet in black thread, which Yusuf wore as a symbol of his being a Muslim so that Hemu would be unable to identify his religion. Since Yusuf was semi-conscious, he was unable to utter anything more than a whimper.

Hemu was dressing Yousuf's wounds and talking to Satendra about what would be the future course of action, among other issues.

'Satendra, see what these Muslims can do, they are so barbaric. It is better that they leave our country alone and migrate to Pakistan, lock, stock, and barrel.

'Since he is your friend and must be a Hindu, I am not insisting on reporting this to the police. That would not only put this poor boy but also you into an immense number of unnecessary problems.... But which family is he from?'

Satendra was immediately under pressure since he was a simpleton from the villages of Garhwal, where telling lies and cooking up tales was not in their value system.

'*Mere school ka dost hai...main iske parivar ko naheen jaanta....*' (He is a school friend, that's all...I don't know his family....)

Satendra managed to mumble, and it was true since he had never ventured to enquire anything about Yusuf's family. He had implicit faith in his friends, and the suspicions—political, fanatical or otherwise—were miles away from his simple brain.

Hemu continued, 'The days are bad, and you must know the whereabouts of your friends, Satendra. Anyway, I am giving him a mixture for fever, as well as one for controlling the infection. Keep him here for a few hours, after which he would be strong enough to walk back to his house.'

In the meantime, Satendra's attention was distracted by some noise coming from a reasonable distance but approaching fast. He requested Hemu to look after the patient, while he would be back in a bit after checking out the commotion on the street outside. He scooted off to the front of the barracks.

When he reached the street bordering the campus of the bungalow, he found a mob, wielding sticks and daggers, fast approaching where he was standing. Soon, they were almost on him, with several voices exclaiming and asking him about the whereabouts of a fugitive.

'Did any Muslim boy come in this direction, or into this bungalow.... He and his father have burned down a hutment in our locality, and one woman has got badly burned.'

Satendra was very nervous and did his best to control his inner trembling. With a laboured yet normal tone, he replied in the negative.

'I.... I have not seen anyone since I was sleeping inside my room there....' He told the assembled mob, pointing towards where his room was.

They looked him in the eye, with a few of the men entering the campus and hunting around the front yard, amongst the trees. Finding nothing, they came out and aggressively moved on.

As soon as Satendra turned back towards his room, he found Hemu walking towards him with his medical box, and a concerned and confused expression.

'Who were these people, Satendra? Why were they talking to you? And who is this friend of yours, who calls his father Abba?

Hemu rattled out in concern and excitement, being a close friend of his elder brother. Satendra was tired by now under pressure and wanted an end to this as soon as possible.

'Hemu kaka, they were a mob looking out for Muslims, and as I told you, the boy whom you just treated is a friend from school, from the lower class. Maybe because of that he is addressing his father as Abba....'

Satendra's tired looks and a frank answer convinced Hemu, who patted him on his back and walked off, asking him to take care and be careful, since it was not safe out on the roads.

'Satendra, give the boy some water and another doze of the mixtures I have left behind when he regains full consciousness. And you can also give him some light food in case he feels hungry. After which, please let him go back to his parents since it is not safe to have a wounded person here. It may land you and Trilok into trouble in case the police find out. And yes...I will keep it a secret between you and me. Not even Trilok will know about it.... Isn't that what you want?'

Satendra bid Hemu Kaka a grateful adieu and walked back with much more confidence than just a moment before. He was confused at the growing hatred between the two communities. In his beautiful yet simple village in the Himalayas, this hostility was unknown; and to his simple mind, it was unknown still. How two human beings could kill or harm each other without any reason...and how someone could develop that amount of hatred as to butcher another unknown person, he was too young to comprehend.

What he was certain about was that this was not his life... his way. He was focused on becoming a government officer and helping his village and his people to rise above their lack of education and daily calls of poverty. Satendra had built a wall around himself and his world. It had to be his world first and then anything else.

He had warmed up the rice and dal left behind by his sister-in-law, and pouring it out into two plates, he carried it to the now conscious Yusuf.

'Le...issey kha le, aur phir ghar ja...mere bhaiyya aur bhabhi bhi aatey honge....' (Take this plate and eat...and then go back home...my brother and sister-in-law would also be back anytime.)

Both had their food quietly, spiced with their own thoughts. Yusuf knew that this would be his last visit to his friend's place for quite some time to come.

Satendra was sure that for him, these differences would never have any impact, yet he would have to secure himself to fulfil his ambitions, which is all that mattered to him. So, when his elder brother and sister-in-law came back, life was as usual, and the brief flirtation with danger had never happened.

Later in the night, while Satendra was having dinner with his family in Delhi, he came to know that preparations were on for the grand function of the independence of India, which was to unfold on 15 August.

His brother continued his update of whatever he had learned from his office and friends while taking morsels of rice and curry at the same time.

'Our leaders have gone crazy, it seems. I believe some of them consulted an astrologer, who has said that 15 August is an inauspicious day to have the celebration of independence.

'And in Pakistan, Jinnah wants to have the new country's independence day celebration on 14 instead of 15 August since it coincides with the auspicious day of Ramadan.

'Mountbatten is rigid on declaring the independence of both nations on 15 August. There seems to be a difference of opinion on every issue, big or small, between these leaders.

*'Inko logon kee koi chinta naheen hai, sub jagah maar kaat ho rahee hai, dar aur dahshat phailee hui ha*i. (These people have absolutely no concern of the masses. Everywhere, people are killing each other. There is a sense of fear and alarm spread all over.)

'And what the leaders of both India and Pakistan are bothered about are their chairs and the independence day celebration.'

Satendra was swallowing down all that his elder brother was saying, along with his food. He was aware that the independence of his country was coming at a great cost. The division of British

India was costing a lot of unnecessary lives, and the geographical divide was creating animosity and enmity of a kind which would be second to none in the world.

His young mind was sure that the way independence was coming to his nation would leave a permanent scar on both independent Indians and Pakistanis.

However, what he could not understand was how British India was being divided. Were the people deciding or was it the British who were drawing a line on paper? To his surprise, as Trilok confirmed, it was indeed a British gentleman, Lord Radcliffe, who was drawing lines on the existing map of British India. It further surprised Satendra to know that Lord Radcliffe had never really visited India before he was asked to take up the ownership of dividing British India.

Now Satendra looked towards his elder brother enquiringly and asked a rather naïve question but got a rather long answer.

'Dada, are you sure that independence day will be celebrated on 15 August? With so much violence and confusion and so much unfinished work, how is it possible?'

'It is Mountbatten and the British Prime Minister, Clement Atlee, who have forced this date upon us, which is what I learned from my office. Otherwise, this day was supposed to come next year. With Nehru and Jinnah not able to compromise on a single nation, both wanting power, we are going to face a very bad time. At least, that is what we ordinary people can think and understand.' Trilok replied to his younger brother's inquisitiveness and carried on to something more personal.

'However, today I got a big job done. I squared up my salary account with the British Indian government, and my savings have been successfully transferred to a new departmental account. Now I would have to wait till the new government gets hold of the situation and commences salary payment regularly. Till then, and I don't know for how long, we will have to continue living with what we have. I hope we do not have to sell our belongings.'

Satendra was apprehensive as well about his school and educational expenses. He, or for that matter, even his elder brother and friends, had no idea when their schools would reopen, and what would be the school fees to start with afresh.

'Why don't we get some money from our village, for the time being, or else go back to the village till your office and my school reopens? Most of my friends and their families have done the same,' suggested Satendra in his innocent way.

For Trilok, his next sahib was also an issue of grave concern. Would he be as good and understanding if he was different from his present boss, who was also a native Indian? Would he allow him to continue to stay in his present dwellings? Which was not of that much of a concern since it was settled according to his work charter.

Finally, Trilok spoke up.

'Satendra's suggestion may be right. I have been thinking along the same lines. Tomorrow, I will talk to my sahib and make a decision. In case we must leave for our village, it has to be in the next couple of days. So, all of you start packing up your important belongings. We would retain our dwellings, so you can keep the rest of your belongings wherever they are under lock and key. Sahib's guard will keep watch.'

With this, Satendra's family meeting was over, and after washing up, he spread his sheet and mat on the floor to bundle up into his world of dreams. That night he was not going back to his barracks, and he was happy about it as well....

***

The wounds and cost of independence were always borne by the man on the streets....

CHAPTER 20

Caravan to Amritsar

The road to Narowal was not one of the best. The good stretches had potholes staring up at periodical intervals. Some were positioned such that the vehicle had no other choice but to befriend them, with jolts, thuds, and all kinds of creaking noises characteristic of a senior automobile.

Mulk was looking out to see whatever he could through the dim headlights of the bus on a full moon night. His lap was over-occupied with a cloth bag stuffed to the fullest. The same was the case with Magan.

The contents were variegated…ranging from documents to artefacts. What both were worried about was the gold and cash at the bottom of the pile in each bag.

There were four trunks in the bus's hold that contained all the clothes and household items, again with precious items at the bottom of each trunk. Over and above this, both Mulk and Magan had small cloth bags strapped around their waists, containing cash. This would help them during their long passage to Agra, via Amritsar.

***

They had not taken the Jammu and Kud route on account of heavy rioting and violence throughout that way. When Mulk and Aftab had gone to enquire about the busses and their departure timings, they were shocked at the macabre sight they saw there. It was total chaos with dead bodies, grievously injured, and shocked refugees all around, and police, doctors and paramedics wading through them. A huge crowd was looking on as if it was a free show till they were pushed out by the police charging at them in intervals.

There were busses coming from Jammu and near about, including Kud, with massacred passengers. Similar was the situation of the passengers moving out from Sialkot and the vicinity. It was an insane, illiterate, and barbaric act of revenge, one following the other, not knowing the starting point.

A clerk at the bus stand, known to Mulk, had told them that this carnage had been going on for the last couple of days. It was not only hatred that was the cause. More than that, it was the opportunistic looting of valuables from the passengers that followed. Human greed and avarice were the cause of what was being attributed to the senseless political decision to split the country.

A shiver had gone down Mulk's spine, and Aftab had sensed it. He had put a hand on Mulk's shoulder and guided him out of the gory site. Mulk had been in convulsions as he walked along with Aftab.

'What is going to happen to us, and our belongings.... I can clearly see a scattered family...there is no way that we all can get back together...I will be killed here, along with Magan...Jai would not know any of our whereabouts, being far off in England...Jaya and his entire household would be all by themselves, with at least Hans Raj to protect them....'

Mulk had gone on rattling off while sobbing profusely, and Aftab did nothing more than try to console and steady him. He had understood that Mulk's vision and feelings were not far from the reality of the bad times that had befallen him and his family, and like him, on the multitudes in both the communities, for no fault of theirs.

Aftab was a good Muslim and a gem of a human being. He had resolved not to let any of this happen to at least his friend... his brother-in-arm.

Having dropped Mulk at his Sialkot residence, Aftab had ventured off to make arrangements for Mulk's departure to Indian territory after Radcliffe's partition was made known officially. On returning, Aftab seemed to be a more satisfied man, than when he had gone off. He was accompanied by Aslam.

'Mulk bhai, here are your and Magan's bus tickets to Narowal. From there, you will be crossing the Ravi River by ferry to Dera Baba Nanak and taking a bus or ride to Amritsar via Ajnala. From whatever information I could gather, you should be safe once you reach Dera Baba Nanak. Once in Amritsar, you can make enquiries about the whereabouts of the rest of the family and Insha Allah, you would be able to travel together as a family to Agra. I am sure.

'Mulk bhai, the bus journey from here onwards will not be easy. So please take proper care of yourself and your belongings, despite the support you would be getting from my acquaintances. Anyway, it would be far safer than going to Kud, as the situation is now.'

He had put his hand into his long shirt pocket and drawn out another piece of paper that had all the references of officials and influential people who would help Mulk, with or without costs, during the journey. Aslam handed Mulk a cloth bag stuffed with currency. It was what Aftab owed Mulk, plus an advance on his business, factory, residences in Sialkot, and the shop in Lahore.

'Mulk bhai, here are one and a half lac rupees I owe you towards the stock I had purchased from you, and here is a token advance on your estate and business, which I would adjust in the final sale amount.'

It was two lac rupees as advance, and Mulk had taken it with gratitude since he would need every bit of it, or even more, in the uncharted and unnatural journey he was about to make….

***

It was over four hours since they had been on their way to Narowal. Apart from the treacherous and sometimes narrow road, the journey so far had been uneventful. The only interruptions in the rocking motion were the multiple times the bust stopped for police checks. The policemen would board the bus with lanterns in their hands and pass through its length, looking at every passenger, most of whom were making their journey to what they were sure was the new India.

During one such check, the leader of the police group stopped at Mulk and Magan's seats and stared at them more closely. Mulk had almost stopped breathing, and beads of sweat appeared at the edges of his temple. After a brief look, the policeman moved ahead, to Mulk's relief, only to return. He then softly asked him as to whether he was Lala Mulk Raj Khanna, to which Mulk nodded in affirmative. The policeman then indicated to Mulk to follow him out of the bus.

'Arrey zara gaddi roke ke rakhna, mujhey in zanaab se thodi gallan karni hai.' (Stop the bus for a while, I need to talk to this gentleman.)

Saying this, the policeman guided Mulk out. Mulk was shaking with fear, with a dry mouth and palpitating heart. He kept on looking at Magan while he followed the policeman. Magan got up to come after Mulk but was firmly asked to remain seated. The other passengers on the bus remained silent and prayed to God that this would not be repeated with them.

Once out of the bus, the policeman took Mulk some distance away and enquired about his relations with Aftab. Mulk suddenly came back to life. Maybe the policeman meant no harm. The relief was Godsent.

'*Zanab*, he is more than a brother to me, and he only has arranged my journey to Narowal,' replied Mulk with warmth and confidence.

'Lala ji, the situation where you approach Narowal and cross the river after that is not good. You would require a lot of help there, which I have been asked to arrange for you.... But it will cost, as you can very well understand....'

The policeman spoke as if it was nothing abnormal, being a natural course of events in these complicated times.

Mulk was aware and had been adequately briefed by Aftab as well, that he needed to pay at certain points and buy his and Magan's safety. As a matter of fact, he had separately tucked some money around his and Magan's waist in cloth bags to cater for such situations. He had also been advised not to pay what he was asked at the first instance. He needed to bargain and to make evident that he did not have enough to go through his journey, hence mercy needed to be meted out to him.

'Jee Zanab, *dasso*...how much would be required, as a reasonable amount to pay for our safety and support,' enquired Mulk.

He was going through all this as a machine bereft of emotions. The last few days had sapped him in every way, and he had absolutely no notion how all this would end...would he remain alive or not was also neither known to him nor was he really thinking about it.

'*Pachaas hazaar* rupees should be enough to take you across the Ravi to Dera Baba Nanak. This would include the boat journey as well. I will give you a slip, which you would have to give to the policeman at the point from where the boats will be taking off. His name is Haneef. Just give him the slip and tell him that Arif has asked him to do the needful.'

Arif opened the negotiation without looking at him and knew fully well that there would be some hard bargaining by the Lala ji.

'Zanab, sahib, I do not have that amount of money, and I have a long way to go from Dera Baba Nanak...please have mercy on me and leave me with some amount to make the rest of my journey, have something to eat and find my family...without whom I will not be able to survive...Zanab, I am like your elder brother, and you can ask Aftab how close we are as a family....'

Mulk was virtually begging for mercy since fifty thousand rupees was a huge sum, which he would not be able to afford, considering the long way he needed to go...for he knew not how long.

Before the policeman could respond, Mulk moved away from him into the darkness, pulled out a wad of currency from the cloth bag around his waist, and started counting it in the little brightness of the taillight of the bus and some of the moon above. It was about nine thousand that he had drawn out.

He turned back to the policeman, and with tears of exertion and circumstances in his eyes, he took out five thousand from what he had in his hands and extended it to him.

'How much is it?' enquired the policeman gruffly, seeing that it was a fraction of what he had asked for. He snatched the amount extended to him by Mulk, who by this time was sobbing, and counted it under the lantern light.

'What the hell is this? I asked for dinner, and you are treating me to just water! Do you think I am a stupid fool to risk my duty for your safety!'

Arif shouted at Mulk, snatching the remaining amount from his hands. and inspecting him closely. While doing so, he could see two thick gold chains concealed around Mulk's neck, under his long shirt and vest.

'Give me those gold chains as well, which you have hidden under your clothes!' shouted Arif while physically snatching them off Mulk, who continued to sob like a baby, terrified by the trauma and humiliation of the treatment that was being meted out to him. Arif pushed him back into the bus with a signed slip to be handed over to Haneef at the river point.

'*Saala...chutia...humey bhikari samjhda hai kya! Jaa tu bhi kyaa yaad rakhegaa, dosti nibhanaa kissay kehte hain*!' (Bloody fool, have you taken us as beggars! Now go...and remember my show of friendship and comradery!)

Mulk stumbled into the bus, limped back next to Magan, and sat down wiping his tears and trying to control himself, while the bus chugged on....

***

As the journey to Narowal continued, Mulk was becoming more apprehensive. He had heard enough of the clashes around Narowal and Dera Baba Nanak to be sure that crossing the Ravi would be a game of dice, with his life and belongings at stake. He was also apprehensive for the safety of Magan, who was his responsibility and his only mate then.

Something about the way he had parted with the policeman was troubling him. It had not gone the way it should have. A fear lurked in his mind that the policeman did not have much control over what he was going to face in Narowal.

He took the slip given by Arif out of his pocket and read the contents for the first time. What was scribbled increased his fear and apprehension. Arif had communicated in Urdu that he had received his part of the money and had also mentioned the amount.

'I have received my money. Lala Mulk Raj Khanna is known to me personally. So, deal accordingly.'

The chit was ambiguous, and Mulk was sure of another payout at the river crossover point.

When Mulk and Aftab had strategised the best possible plan of travel, seeing violence raising its ugly head almost everywhere, and having ruled out the route to Kud due to the imminent dangers there, which, to Mulk's utter dismay, took him further apart from his family, they were left with two other viable options. One was to take the train to Amritsar, via Lahore and Wagah. The other was to take the Narowal route.

The second option, according to Aftab's study at that time, was less used than the Lahore route by the multitude migrating into and out of Pakistan. The trains to Amritsar were stuffed to more than double their capacity, with people willing to risk travelling on rooftops, open to all kinds of vagaries. While Mulk, because of his and Aftab's connections, would have got a berth in a first-class compartment, he could not have avoided being slaughtered, harmed, or looted by many groups with vested interests and passions running high.

So, they had decided on the Narowal route and that too by bus and not the train. Though it would be more tiring and cumbersome but, to their thinking, it would be less exposed to the ongoing turmoil.

The circumstances specific to Mulk were forcing him to withdraw from Sialkot much earlier, without waiting for the partition award to be officially released but, as both Aftab and he perceived, would be beneficial in beating the mass movement that would later take place when the alarm finally did go off.

Mulk had trusted Aftab more than his own kin and kith, more than people of his community who had warned him of the dire consequences he would have to face in the future. He had left behind with him a cache of gold, silver, and precious stones that he had collected as his savings from his successful business deals. He had also entrusted him with a power of attorney to transact the sale of his remaining business and personal assets in Sialkot and Lahore.

It was only a part of his gold, silver, and cash that he was carrying with him, to enable him to sustain, create a foothold, and keep his and his family's head above water with self-respect and dignity. After all, it was Aftab who had stood by Mulk in all his trying and testing times. He had gone to the extent of risking his life and making enemies within his own community, and Mulk knew that their relationship would always remain an estranging point between Aftab and his business community in the times to come.

So, why not trust such a godsend man…why not…thought Mulk…almost aloud…and jerked out of his stupor to gaze out of the window of his bus…in absolute horror of what he saw….

Bordering the highway to Narowal, which would be just about fifteen miles away, were a mix of paddy, sugarcane, and cotton fields. The bus in which Mulk was travelling was passing through a large patch of paddy cultivation, which was flooded with water and bound by ridges of clay.

Through Mulk's side of the window, he could see a long queue of people going in the opposite direction, towards Sialkot. There were men, women, and children, as well as old people constituting the sea of humanity. Some were slipping into the waterlogged fields, falling into the slush, with people behind helping them up again, while others managed to balance themselves. It was a moonlit night, and Mulk could see the distinct silhouettes. What he could also see were some people falling and not getting up at all—the ones who were being left behind.

Mulk got up from his seat, got to the aisle of the bus, passed by a sleeping Magan, and peeped through the other window, over the people sitting there. He could see a similar row of people walking towards Narowal in the direction of the bus. There, also, he could see bodies strewn about in the fields, apart from the ones that were moving. It was strange and confusing for Mulk.

By this time the bus conductor had also come by his side. Mulk turned around and enquired about this movement.

'These are all people migrating to and from what they can guess to be Pakistan. And the people falling into the fields, not able to get up are injured or dying. Massacres are going on in the villages and towns on either side of the assumed borders. The Ravi River would be the likely dividing line of the two newly independent nations, and Narowal would be the last township on the Pakistan side,' explained the conductor to Mulk. The bus driver yelled at the conductor to come near his seat. There seemed to be an emergency of sorts.

Mulk went back to his seat, virtually cold, and shaking. The driver could see silhouettes of a crowd with burning torches against the moonlit night. He, by virtue of his daily experience on this route, could smell grave trouble in case he carried on. He called the conductor to discuss options.

About a hundred yards ahead was a dirt track leading through a village, and would loop out onto the main road, hopefully bypassing the mob. That seemed to be the only chance the driver could take since going ahead into the mob would certainly mean a massacre of most of the passengers in the bus.

They decided to take the risk of the dirt track and swerved the bus to the left. The vehicle rocked and creaked, and the passengers rolled along with it. Those who were not properly anchored were hurled onto the aisle.

Mulk and Magan held on having guessed the move. They were in the front half of the bus and could judge from the driver's actions, though they could not see what was going on ahead in the distance. The lurching and rocking gained in proportion, spiced with shrieks of anxiety of the passengers. At times, the bus seemed so critically tilted to a side as if it would topple into the waterlogged rice fields.

After quite a distance, they reached the narrow lanes bound by hutments on both sides. The vehicle managed to graze through, with the driver intermittently jamming the brakes when he saw village folk, even if just outside their house doors which opened into the lane. Everyone had prayers on their lips when suddenly a group of villagers asked the bus to stop to enquire about its presence in their midst. Fortunately, the village seemed peaceful and not affected by the madness around. The migrants to India were more often taking the train route and going through Lahore.

When the driver told them that the passengers were mostly traders, some with their families, they bought his argument after some dilly-dallying. The journey commenced peacefully through the narrow winding lanes, slowly, haltingly, with lots of honking.

The bus was back again into the open fields after a while, leaving the lanes and dwellings behind, and almost immediately the driver had to jam his breaks, with the passengers all lurching forward.

Mulk was very anxious at each such stoppage and discretely peeped out of the window to identify a group of people with sticks, scythes, and sharp instruments in their grips. They looked quite belligerent in the way they talked to the driver.

After a vociferous discussion between the driver, conductor and the crowd, the conductor moved away from the quorum and went towards the front entrance of the bus, opening the creaking door, ajar.

'Lo, khud hee dekh lo kaun kaun jaa rahe hain Narowal haat naal!' (Come, see for yourself who all are going to the Narowal market fair!)

The conductor was loud and clear to the passengers within the bus, and also to the armed men entering it. It was a good move, which gave the passengers a headstart to have a common alibi for travel. There were about five men who entered the already overcrowded bus, two of them with lanterns in their hands, taking a look while making their way to the rear.

One of them, with the lantern, stopped a row in front of where Mulk and Magan were seated with their cloth bags on their laps to enquire where those people were going. The people in front were a man with his wife and daughter. He had two other sons sitting on the other side of the aisle. Fear was writ large on their faces. What and how they would answer would decide the fate of all within.

'Kahan jaa raha hai biradar, inna saamaan laike?' asked one of the men quite softly.

'Sahib, hum toe Muridke ke pass ek sabji aur anaaz ka haat lagdaa hai, audhron jaa rahe hain. Ussay pehle ik aadh din Narowal mien Ravi kinare bitaayenege. Humare rishtedaar rahte hain wahan.' (Sir, we are going to a local village market near Muridke. We will spend some time near the Ravi riverbank, where some of our relatives stay.)

The man continued to look at the passenger for what seemed like a long time. Looking at him in the eye, he talked rather intimidatingly.

'Kahaan se aa rahaa hai? Wahaan kyaa sabji naheen mildi, jo aisey samay mien Narowal ghumne chalaa aayaa?' (From where are you coming? Don't you get vegetables and grains there, that you are going to Narowal in such dangerous times?)

'Sahib kareeb ke gaon se hain....' (Sir, we are from a nearby village.)

While the passenger continued to mutter, the men with the lanterns and the others following them moved on. The bus continued its journey to the relief of Mulk and all the others.

After they hit the main road, which was clear of crowds or incidents, the conductor told Mulk and the others who had enquired why they had taken the detour, that a truckload of people who were leaving their homes to cross over across the Ravi, had been looted and slaughtered by local groups lurking around the area, avenging what was happening to people of their community migrating to west Punjab. The uncomfortable and longer detour through the village lanes had saved most of the passengers, who were nothing but sitting ducks for another bout of senseless massacre.

Mulk looked up to God with tears in his eyes, thanking him to be still alive, hoping to see another day or days and get closer to his family....

The sun was strong, accompanied by intense heat and humidity. Mulk was lying on his side, with his forearm protecting his face from the extreme elements. His hair, neck as well as the long shirt was drenched with his salty sweat. The shirt was muddy, blotched with spots of blood all over. There were cakes of dried blood on the exposed parts of his body. On the face and portions of his head, hair stuck to the clotted blood. Flies were hovering around him.

Mulk lay still for quite some time…dead to the world and himself. Maybe his soul did not want to have very much to do with his supine body….

The boat was rocking on the ripples of Ravi, which was agitated on account of the monsoons and heavy traffic that she had to support.

Mulk was shaken up by the rocking boat and could see two policemen guarding the fifteen-odd people packed in it like sardines. Mulk was in one of the corners, having some space to move. He moved…he was alive…but did he want to be was another question for which he had no answer nor inclination. He managed to get up, with a shooting pain in his head, shoulders, and legs.

It took some time for him to focus. Injuries on all his boat-mates…some minor scratches on exposed body parts, while some with gaping wounds. Clothes, mostly torn to various degrees, as if designed with blood-red blotches. Suddenly, he turned frantic as he looked around for Magan and his luggage. He remembered carrying a cloth bag, and one more with Magan. They both also had a small cloth bag with cash tied around their waists. Apart from this, they had four trunks, which he could distinctly recollect. What he could not find was Magan with his luggage and the three more trunks.

He looked around, and his gaze stopped at the two policemen accompanying the boat. Slowly, the whole scheme of events came back clearly…as a tragic and dark movie…the only difference was that when Mulk came out of the theatre, he found the events of the movie still haunting him as real…causing real pain…and making him burst into tears with a choking sensation which, too, was real….

He could distinctly recollect people following them down the lane, while they made slow progress with all the luggage. He could clearly see the policemen goading the mob to chase them…and then, in no time, the mob was on them.

Before they could gather themselves, Mulk had received a massive blow on his head with a blunt weapon, with a piercing pain in his right arm, then his left leg, before he crumpled into his pool of blood. Losing focus, he had seen Magan being stabbed again and again and again, till he fell unconscious, or maybe dead. By this time, the police had arrived, gaping over them and shouting indistinct words and orders, while the mob receded with Mulk's luggage.

Mulk had kept on crying hoarse, pointing at his belongings, which kept on going further and further away, till they had disappeared. What was left with him was the trunk next to him, his cloth bag, and the waist bag, which still loyally clung to his flat, hungry, and gurgling stomach.

The recollections made him weep and wail again. The person lying next to him on the boat jerked up at the melancholic sound coming from his left to see Mulk weeping incessantly. He, too, was wounded by the pains of life and the journey, yet he managed to get up to a sitting position and tried pacifying Mulk, rubbing his sore hands with his wounded ones.

Mulk wept even more, sucking in air intermittently, since he was getting breathless in the process. Seeing the pandemonium, one of the policemen came to Mulk's side of the boat, stepping over people, sitting or lying down.

'Kee gull hai, Lala ji, bachhon ki tarah ro kyon rahe ho…?' (What is the matter, Sir, why are you weeping like a kid...?)

The policeman enquired, with a hand on Mulk's shoulders.

Mulk's reaction was rather unwarranted and aggressive. He jerked the policeman's hand aside and caught hold of his belongings in a very tight embrace as if they were going to be snatched away.

'Please leave me alone now, as it is you people have ripped from me whatever I possessed...do let me live with what little I am left with!' cried Mulk. His voice was so shrill that the policeman backed off with surprise and apprehension, with an expression of confusion writ large on his face, as if saying, what the hell did I do for this shrill rebuke.

By this time the boatmen had docked the boat on the other end of the mighty Ravi...the Indian end....

'Get off the boat, one by one, please...we are now in India... Dera Baba Nanak....

As if Pakistan was already born....

***

It was already 12 August, a couple of days to go for the independence of the two nations, India and Pakistan. Most of the Indian bureaucrats were oblivious to the exact boundaries drawn by Sir Radcliffe and his core team, and there was confusion about when the 'Award of Partition' would be declared.

On the ground, this confusion resulted in senseless knee-jerk reactions from people of both major communities. Gaps were widening, and leaders were playing to the tunes of their ideologies, ambitions, and power-mongering.

In this atmosphere of confusion and aggressive posturing, yet another victim of the partition set foot on the shores of the Ravi at Dera Baba Nanak with a steel trunk, a cloth bag, torn, tattered, blood-stained clothes and a cloth waistband with a cloth pouch tied around. He limped and lurched forward, continuing to walk to the main road leading to the city.

Mulk knew the city well, having been there quite a few times before to deliver goods to a solitary sports shop in the main city. However, that day it had a different look.

He felt like a foreigner in a land that he never felt was any different to his Sialkot or else Narowal. Local people were gaping at him, and many of his kind were stepping onto this side of the Ravi along with him. At the same time, he felt strangely safe, as if he had just escaped from an enemy territory, which so far had been his home, all in a span of a few days.

Mulk's life had changed. He had no business…no family…his younger brother in England, out of contact for a long time, not knowing where the rest of his family was…his wife, kids and sister-in-law, who were supposed to be at Kud, from what he had last heard, but no longer knew…Magan, snatched away from him, by his own people and the police…more than half his belongings also gone….

Walking, limping, thinking, and lost to the world, Mulk landed into a crowd of people and bullock carts, full of people to the brim. There was a lot of noise and hundreds of voices talking of thousands of things at the same time.

For Mulk, it did not add up to anything. He was lost in his world, which now had only him and his memories…at this time, he was supposed to be at his factory, supervising production… then again, a jolt…which factory?…which production?…he was a man on the streets, with nowhere to go…. He sat down on the street, within the crowd, with his remaining luggage, tears welling out…and then, he saw a bright light approaching him…and then darkness….

***

Mulk had passed out, and when he regained consciousness, he found himself in a moving cart with a dignified-looking old man checking his pulse. Evidently, he was a doctor.

'Where am I? Where are you taking me to? And who are you all?' exclaimed Mulk, both with suspicion and apprehension. The doctor tending to him smiled with a reassuring expression and responded.

'Dear brother, you are now a part of a caravan which is moving on foot to Amritsar. Please do not worry, we are all from the same community and are being well guarded by so many of us, as well as a few policemen belonging to the Indian government-to-be. Going by bus on the main roads, or by train would be very dangerous now.

'We are all refugees from the soon-to-be Pakistan like you and have our own sufferings to suffer. But see, we are now all together and safe. Praise the Lord...Jai Sri Ram!'

Mulk, after a long time, felt safe. Looking around, he gave a hint of a smile. It was indeed reassuring to be in a friendly group of people, all tending to each other. He got up, but the pain in his wounds made his motions slow and jittery.

The doctor told him that it was fatigue and fever on account of infections in his wounds. He had been stabbed in his legs and right arm, but thank God, his stomach and chest were spared, because of which he was still alive.

Antiseptic had already been applied to his wounds, and Mulk found crude, yet effective bandages on his legs and arms. The doctor gave him a few tablets to control the spreading infection and advised Mulk to rest in the cart for a few more hours, after which he would find himself much more reinforced.

After having a few glasses of sugar cane juice, which some of the people had been serving on the way, Mulk dozed off....

***

Activities continue...and so does the process of Independence....

CHAPTER 21

Destiny

Narendra finally entered his study-cum-ante room where his friends were lounging and already sipping their coffees. He joined them, pouring some still-hot coffee for himself in dainty chinaware and picking up a cold cucumber sandwich simultaneously.

He then picked up the phone handset from its cradle on the table next to his chair to call up the District Magistrate, who would be taking charge on 15 August 1947. When he finally got through, he gestured at his companions to hush up, but be seated where they were.

'Can I talk to the Honourable District Magistrate, please? I am Dr Bandhopadhyay speaking,' requested Narendra to the Secretary, and then waited.

And then….

'Hello Mr Jai Kirat Singh, this is Narendra here…I wanted to share some information and need some support in connection with a sports goods manufacturer from Sialkot…I have information that he is a prominent businessman there and can resettle in

Meerut…I also help in convincing his colleagues to follow him in this decision….

'Can I give you his address and phone number to have your department find out his present whereabouts and get back to me if required, so that we can jointly convince him on this?

'I have already had some conversation with his accountant and cousin some time back, in course of a luncheon, where he was also invited as a visitor from west Punjab…at that time he was scouting for some suitable land and living accommodation, in case his elder cousin decided to relocate.

'OK…fine…thank you and so kind of you Sir…good day and goodbye….'

Narendra hung up and turned to explain to his companions.

'Do you remember this person from Sialkot, one Mr Sanjay Kapoor? He is a cousin to Mr Mulk Raj Khanna, one of the leading manufacturers of cricket goods in British India.

'According to Sanjay, his cousin has been looking quite keenly towards Meerut and its near-about to relocate his manufacturing base. In case they do so, others might follow, something that might be good for the city and its commerce. This is why I have asked our District Magistrate to connect with him through the Civil Service channels. And he seems to be quite excited about it.'

While the three friends were chatting about the future, Narendra's son, Subendu, walked in with a sheet of paper in his hands. He looked serious as well as apprehensive. As they soon found out, it was his final examination results, which had not gone the right way, and Subendu was scared of his strict father.

Narendra went through the contents. The frown on his forehead deepened as he progressed till his eyes looked from the top of his half-moons towards Subendu with an un-asked question quivering on his lips.

Surobee had followed Subendu into Narendra's study and was equally apprehensive of her father's reactions as her brother.

'How would you be able to seek admission into Doon School with such excellent performance, my dear loving son?' asked Narendra in a sarcastic tone. 'You do not expect me to call up the Board of Governors of the School and beg for your sake, do you?'

Professor Chatterjee took the report card from Narendra, and after looking into it for some time, he looked up with a slight smile on his face.

'Narendra, I think you are being unduly harsh on young Subendu. The only subject where he has not done very well is mathematics. His English surely seems to be above par. If you throw some light on your prowess with numbers, you will realise that you became a doctor because you could not afford to become an engineer.' With a chuckle, the Professor handed the result card back to Surobee.

The professor's gentle and good-natured rebuke had softened Narendra, and he dragged Subendu to himself and hugged him. He then instructed Surobee to look up a good tutor for Subendu for mathematics, since just about a year was left for his review for admission to the Doon School.

***

The professor and nawab sahib were about to depart when the telephone rang, and Narendra jumped to it. After a brief conversation and putting the receiver down onto the cradle, Narendra turned to his two friends. His expressions were tending towards a confused frown, while he narrated the gist to his friends.

'The call was from the District Magistrate's office. They had contacted the Sialkot administration to find out about the whereabouts of Mulk Raj Khanna and had shared his telephone number as well.

'After about an hour they got a revert from Sialkot that Mr Khanna's house was locked. However, the people who had gone to check met two private guards lounging on chairs, near the gate, smoking cigarettes. They reported that Mr Khanna had left for some city in eastern Punjab which would be a part of new India. His family had left long back, and his cousin, the one we met here in Meerut some time back was, unfortunately, killed in a rioting incident in Sialkot.

'Now, the District Magistrate has suggested that I give an identification certificate based on my meeting with Mr Khanna's younger cousin and accountant so that they can allot land to the Khanna family for their factory and residence once the areas are earmarked. He has also kindly verified Mr Khanna's residency in Sialkot and his immigrant status.'

Narendra took a few drags from his smouldering briar and carried on.

'Dada (Professor Chatterjee) and nawab sahib, it is my desire that this family settles down here. I have developed a strange attachment to them without really meeting them. My heart cries out for that young cousin of his whose life was destined to be a victim of the senseless violence going on throughout our region, from Punjab in the west to Bengal in the east.

'May God bless them and keep them alive to experience the benefits of our independence; and begin a good new life.'

The professor and nawab sahib were in total agreement with Narendra and promised to follow up, being members of the committee set up by the District Magistrate.

All of them had to meet again at the District Magistrate's office in the evening to finalise the preparations, roles and responsibilities for 15 August 1947.

Nawab sahib seemed confused by the uncharacteristic attachment shown by Narendra towards the cricket goods manufacturer from Sialkot, someone whom he had never met. For the professor, it was a clear case of the dynamics of destiny.

CHAPTER 22

Independence Day

It was a late Wednesday evening of 13 August 1947, dark and cloudy with a continuous drizzle, and the roads were full of locals, police and some scattered *firangees* (the British). Security was tight around the Collectorate as well as the Mall Road.

Within the Cantonment and the Collectorate, there was a surfeit of activities. Charges were being handed over to the Indian officers, and the British were packing up to go back to their native land. Mixed emotions could be seen—some happy and some grave expressions peppered amongst the motley crowd…some tears and some cheers….

The British in India were soon going to lose all the perks and importance they had in their vassal colony. Back in England, they would be by themselves, doing their chores with no one to order around, no one to serve them their morning and evening rounds of exquisite tea and cold sandwiches in dainty china. The *'koee hai'* would produce no response.

In all this confusion, the District Magistrate's large office room was filled with influential Indian citizens of Meerut. A lot of critical topics were being discussed and issues sorted out. Jai Kirat, the first Indian District Magistrate of Meerut in soon-to-be free India had a lot of stress to endure, but he also had dedicated citizens of the district to see it through with him. Narendra was a part of it, too.

***

At 10 pm on Thursday, 14 August 1947, Jawahar Lal Nehru declared India independent from British rule in his capacity as the first Prime Minister, in the presence of Lord Mountbatten, who agreed to remain the Governor General of independent India to oversee a smooth transition.

Narendra, along with some other city elites, had been invited to the 'State Council Building' in Delhi, which would later be known as the Parliament House. The District Magistrate was to go separately with the officers' entourage. All of them had to return to Meerut to hoist the tricolour on the subsequent morning. It would be hectic, yet exciting.

There was a continuous stream of refugees heading towards Amritsar, Jalandhar, Delhi, Agra, and many other surrounding cities, including Meerut. Large-scale violence in Lahore and Amritsar had been reported, with aftereffects throughout the northern belt of India. Meerut was simmering and erupting in waves, and there was heavy security and vigil in the city area.

Independence Day was nothing but a beginning of confusion and conflicts for the officials, politicians, leaders, and the multitude of kings and princes.

***

It was a strange mixture of melancholy, anger, excitement, and patriotic pride for all those present in the visitor's gallery of the Parliament to witness the first session of the Constituent Assembly of independent India. Narendra overheard various comments and views while being a part of the privileged gathering, waiting for the first prime minister of a 'nation to be' to address her citizens at large on the dreams and aspirations that all of them collectively harboured.

'We are attending the second independence of various dominions kept together by the British. The first happened yesterday in Karachi. God knows how many more independence days this region will see,' whispered a rotund and over-decorated member of the attending gentry, twirling his moustache as he spoke.

'India, as Nehru and Sardar sahib (referring to Sardar Patel) look at is every piece of land which is not Pakistan…they are not aware that the third dominion is that of the numerous Princely States, who would like to have their own confederation of states, independent of Nehru's India,' whispered a tall and lanky person sitting next to the rotund one, somewhat loudly. I guess you people are not aware that there are strong principalities like Hyderabad, Travancore, Jamnagar, and Patiala that are seriously mulling over standing apart, on their own, much like India and Pakistan. I have a highly confidential piece of information that they have the ears of none other than Lord Mountbatten, who has been unanimously accepted as the first Governor General of independent India to look over the complete transition of power till it happens,' responded a senior gentleman, wearing a black Jodhpuri with matching slacks, sweating profusely, yet refusing to open his collar.

'Friends, as we sit here, Jinnah is already negotiating with the Dewan of Junagadh to have his dominion under Pakistan, with the Nawab retaining his grandeur which he enjoyed under the British.,' continued the man in Jodhpuri, this time with more excitement and sweat, and a raised pitch in his voice.

Narendra had been patiently listening to his immediate and confused neighbourhood giving expert opinions on the beleaguered independence of a bleeding nation. He was amused at the erudite assembly of political scientists who, he felt, should have been Nehru's Kitchen Cabinet, rather than sweating and slugging it out in the Visitors' Gallery. Gandhi ji would have done well to hear them out before guiding the nation to '*sampoorna swaraj*'.

Or was it '*sampoorna swarajs*' for multiple nations....

Narendra could not control himself any longer, and leaning to his left, he expressed his opinion to the tall and lanky gentleman, who was talking of the third dominion of the Princely States.

'Sir, it seems that you have not been kind enough in making Gandhi ji, Nehru, Sardar sahib as well as Mountbatten aware of this well-guarded secret which weighs so heavily on your heart.'

The gentleman was rather surprised at this uncalled-for intrusion to which he did not know how to react, apart from stupidly interrogating, 'Which secret are you talking of, sahib, which is weighing so heavily on my heart?'

By this time Narendra was enjoying himself. With a naughty grin, he answered the gentleman.

'The secret of the three nations, which you seem to have been exposed to, by some divine providence. You must rush off to the entrance as fast as you can and make Pandit ji aware of it so that he can change his speech accordingly. Lest the world may laugh....'

The gentleman was blushing now and would have changed his seat if he could. However, the best he could do was wipe his sweat and turn the other way.

The august group of leaders of a great country-to-be...or not-to-be, arrived at the podium, creating a sudden hush in the huge hall. The historic moment had finally arrived. Irrespective of the British or world cynicism, the 'equator was in the process of converting into a nation'.

Like Narendra, multitudes of others who were assembled on this great occasion had full faith in Gandhi's aspirations, Nehru's romanticism, and Sardar Patel's iron hand.

After Sucheta Kriplani's chanting of *Vande Mataram*, and the opening speech by Rajendra Prasad, who was the president of the Constituent Assembly, Nehru evoked the birth of India with his famous 'Tryst with Destiny' speech…while frenzy, avarice, greed and xenophobia invoked the death of countrymen of a senselessly split-up country….

15 August 1947. Meerut awoke to incessant rain…the country shedding tears in grief or happiness…first steps in a confused freedom that it had been handed. A lot needed to be done. It was indeed freedom at midnight, but the dawn was nowhere to be seen.

The assembled gentry in Meerut saluted the national flag, sang the national Song with zest, and took the national oath with abject sincerity…yet none of them knew the colour of their future, and the future of their beleaguered, newly-born foetal motherland.

While the celebrations and speech took their course, the city remained seized in the grip of violence and tension. Narendra had to rush back to his clinic, along with his son-in-law, because of a rush of wounded patients at the clinic.

***

Celebrations of the likes of this were never seen before… or after….

CHAPTER 23

A Dervish's Word

Jaya was standing near the telephone operator at the post office in Kud, very near to where she was staying. She was nervous, constantly playing with her wrap-around, rolling the ends around her index fingers while waiting for the operator to get through. He was known to her family, which is why he continued to try all the alternative numbers which Jaya had given to him, scribbled on a crumpled piece of paper.

The crowd behind Jaya was getting more and more restive on this special treatment being meted out to her. All of them were equally on the edge…all had lost someone… quite a few did not know where to go…and who would be kind enough to give them refuge.

Jaya, her sister-in-law, daughter, and two sons were totally cut off from their husbands and all that they had. Hans Raj, their old family retainer, who had come with Jaya from her parent's house after her marriage as a child himself, stood as a shield between Jaya and the rest of the impatient crowd.

Finally, the operator got through to Aftab, who was about to leave his residence in Karachi for his office. Jaya screamed at the top of her voice over the loud din created by the collective murmur of the crowd outside.

'Hello…hello…Aftab bhai, *kaise hain aap?!* (Hello…hello… Aftab brother, how are you?!)

'*Main Jaya bol raheen hoon…aapki Jaya bhabhi*! (I am Jaya, your sister-in-law.)

'*Haan…haan sunayi de raha hai.* (Yes…yes I can hear you.)

'*Bhai ji, woh kithhien hain…. Unse kisi bhi surat-e-haal baat naheen ho pa rahi…Magan bhi phone naheen uthha raha hai…. Kar naal!* (Brother, where is he? I cannot get across to him under any circumstances…even Magan is not picking up the phone at home.)

'*Kya! Ye kya kah rahien hain aap?!* (What! What is this you are saying?!)

'*Chhorh kar chalay gaye…kahaan gaye? Kuchh to bataaeeye….*' (He has left and gone…gone where? Please say something at least….)

The phone got disconnected, and that was that….

Jaya, after paying for the call, followed Hans Raj, who cleared a way through the crowd and their stares. She managed to control herself for some time, but not for long, staring to wail, sinking next to a tree on the roadside.

'He has gone along with Magan…and I do not know where… what news to hear on our auspicious independence day…what the hell are we celebrating…and what for? I want to go back to my Sialkot…I belong there…my kids, my husband and my family belong there….'

Jaya screamed and cried while Hans Raj stood quietly, with tears in his eyes, since he could do nothing more.

***

Hans Raj convinced Jaya to get back to the house in Kud and discuss the next course of action with the rest of the family. Jaya sat down on one of the cane chairs in the veranda with her sister-in-law, Kiran, and Kamla, her daughter. They all bore an anxious look that arose from a sense of uncertainty...scared at being surrounded by senseless violence...and being separated from the males in their family without any news of their whereabouts.

What they knew was that Mulk was in India and Jai was in England. But both were huge geographies, and they were single men within those huge, crowded spaces. When would Jai come back to India? Where would he come back to? Sialkot in Pakistan? Or somewhere in India? Would he know where to find his family and how? None of the ladies or their children knew where to find Mulk. Where was he now? The only awareness that Jaya had was from the plans which Mulk had disclosed to the family—that he would reach Agra to his uncle Adhiraj. But how would he reach Agra in all this confusion and violence? Why hadn't Mulk called up the owner of the house in Kud where he had arranged for his family to stay? Mulk knew him very well and should have called him up, but he hadn't. Was he alright? Was he safe, sound, and alive?

Jaya broke down and started wailing, snuggling her head in her daughter's shoulder, with Kiran trying to console her, patting her on her back while crying herself. Their only consolation was that Jai must be safe in England and that Ashok, Jaya's eldest son, was safe in his boarding school in Dehradun—Colonel Browns.

***

While Jaya and her family were immersed in their destroyed world, a harrowed Hansraj suddenly appeared on the veranda, panicked and nervous. The landlord's servant had informed him that the landlord and family had driven off to Amritsar, all of a sudden, in the middle of the night, to his brother staying there. He had also instructed his man Friday to inform Jaya to make immediate arrangements to move to Amritsar with the rest of the family. Kud was burning, and soon their part of the city would be engulfed, which so far had been the safest area to be in.

Before Hansraj could react, there were people armed with sticks, knives and machetes who had come to the gate and called for him, sitting him from the driveway. He was warned to move the residents of the bungalow out of the city immediately. People from the other community were baying for Hindu blood and were moving towards this posh Hindu locality.

After what Jaya and the rest heard from Hansraj, their total focus got diverted to moving quickly, abandoning their self-pity. Jaya, Kiran, and Kamla had already packed up their entire belongings a day earlier, prepared as they were to leave at a short notice. Hansraj was asked to call for a horse-drawn carriage to transport the family and him to the bus stand to journey to Amritsar.

Jaya decided to go to their sister's place in Amritsar, where they might be able to get information about Mulk's whereabouts, or, in case they were lucky, he just might be there waiting for them. How uncertain the certainties of the country's independence had turned out to be. A paradox of euphoria and celebrations to cold-blooded butchering on the streets….

***

Jaya and her family stood on the road, while Hansraj ran around looking for a horse-carriage taxi. There was none in sight. But what was in sight was slowly turning fearful. A crowd could be seen, growing slowly in size…enveloped in dust and noise.

As it came nearer, Jaya and the rest could discern people on foot and some bullock carts. The people were a mix of men, women, and children. Some of the men were carrying knives, sticks and machetes.

Hansraj had gone a bit further to get information from the approaching group which, as was evident, were all Hindus. They were shouting *bhago! bhago!* (run! run!). They told Hansraj that all Hindus in the locality were welcome to join them to save their lives from the rioting people from the other community.

Jaya and her family had no time to weigh or analyse further action. So, led by Hansraj, they jumped in with the crowd, their hands occupied with pieces of heavy luggage. As they progressed, Hansraj managed to transfer their luggage, piece by piece, onto one of the carts, which still had some space. While walking alongside another woman of practically her age, Jaya found out the group was moving towards Amritsar on foot. The road in front of the bungalow where they were staying led straight through fields and forests towards Jammu. It was a lonely route that was only frequented by people of the nearby villages, mostly Hindu populated.

'Why are we running away like this, suddenly? It is a day to celebrate, rather than running for life.' enquired Jaya, innocently, unaware of the depth of the problem.

The lady walking alongside responded, panting for breath because of walking at quite a heady pace.

'The partition and the uncertainties have caused a cycle of violence, where people have forgotten the excitement of independence from the British rule. Hindus are butchering Muslims in Hindu-dominated areas, and the Muslims are doing the same in theirs. Kud has a sizeable Muslim population, which is now hounding every Hindu they can lay their hands upon.'

'But Kud is a part of India, isn't it?' asked Jaya.

'I don't really know...the Muslims are claiming it to be a part of Pakistan, which gained its independence yesterday...so it is better to get out of here...Amritsar is definitely a part of India, so it is safe to go there and wait...the Indian administration has set up camps in and around Amritsar, that is what we have heard... we will find out once we reach there,' replied the lady.

Hansraj, along with Jaya, Kiran, Kamla, and Jaya's two sons became a part of the group that would be their family till they completed their journey, or maybe even thereafter...the future was uncertain. Was it independence from British rule and slavery to anarchy, violence, and confusion? Would it have been better to be a stable British India, rather than an independent nation which did not know its bounds, where there were so many opinions of what India would become?

Jaya wondered and thought hard, till the fatigue of thinking and the monotony of walking took over, and her mind drew a blank...whatever would be...would be....

***

The sun was setting, and the caravan was crossing from fields into wild shrubs, and then into an area with large, wooded trees. There was a gravel trail crisscrossing the forest, and the caravan was also following the same curves. As Jaya walked along, with Kiran beside her, and the children in tow, she was focussing ahead on a male, ahead of Hansraj, walking along with a family. She had been trying hard to place them...had she seen them before? They looked so familiar. If she could get closer, she would be able to make out. She nudged Kiran and asked her to be close to her children while she moved ahead to have a closer look at the family in the fast-fading natural light.

Jaya reached where Hansraj was walking. Fortunately, he had managed a lantern, which he was carrying with him in the darkening forests. She took the lantern from Hansraj and came nearer to the family she had been trying to focus on for quite some time. Raising the lantern to see their faces more clearly.

'Savitri bhabhi! Varun bhaiyya? Am I correct in recognizing both of you? Were you not our neighbours when we were staying near the clock tower at Sialkot?' exclaimed Jaya, excited after a long period of time.

'And you are Jaya didi, aren't you? Mulk bhai's wife, from Khanna Sports?" replied an equally excited Savitri.

With this, the two families got together and exchanged as many notes as they could. Varun Malhotra had a workshop manufacturing surgical equipment. He had lost it all…gutted… but he had managed to escape. His elder brother, however, had not been so fortunate…he had burned to death in the workshop. His elder brother's wife had committed suicide, along with her daughter, but the son, Gagan, had gone to get some ration for home…and got saved. He was with them, along with their own son, Viresh. Savitri called for her son and Gagan and introduced them to Jaya, who in turn called for her children and Kiran. It was a comforting reunion under the circumstances. They trudged along, the children forming a group, the women their own, and Hansraj helping Varun look after the larger family.

A whole day of walking had taken its toll. The elders and the women were tired, and their grunts and panting were making a strange chorus. The night was dark, with below-par visibility. The caravan had reached a large clearing in the woods—a grazing area for the nearby inhabitants—an irregular circle large enough to accommodate the caravan comfortably. Varun went up to the leader of their group to request that the Malhotra and Khanna families be put together in a cluster.

The only members of the caravan who seemed to be having a rollicking time were the kids, for whom there was no school, no homework or discipline to follow. They were left alone by their parents who had so many other worries. However, there were a few children who were unfortunate to have lost their parents in the frenzy. One of them had lost both his parents and a grandmother and had seen them being butchered in front of his eyes, and he sat all alone with his back to a tree, traumatised and stunned, as if his brain was numb and dead.

***

Mulk woke up after what he thought was many days. The sun was shining—burning and sizzling all it surveyed, including Mulk. He was drenched with his salty sweat, and his wounds, under the bandage, were itching greatly. That had jolted him to reach out to areas of his body, wanting to tear apart the bandages and scratch himself crazy. But he couldn't stretch his arms around his body. His forelimbs seemed to have frozen. Any movement resulted in shooting pains, making him scream, to the discomfort of his co-passengers in the cart.

Suddenly, he saw a mongrel on the roadside throw his four limbs around in the air...cycling with them and rubbing his back on the muddy ground below. Mulk looked on with fascination and some amusement. This dog seemed to be celebrating his country's independence in his way and style, the only difference being that he would never know which country's independence he was celebrating. Mulk realised that he could learn a few tricks from this canine coach...and he started rubbing his back on the back lid of the cart to satisfy his itching body. He then took out his linen cloth from the semi-open duffel bag next to him and wiped off the profuse sweat on his face, hair, and neck. He decided to get off the cart to let some others rest in their long and gruelling walk. As he gingerly stepped down from the moving cart, he fell, making a soft landing without hurting himself more. He had forgotten his wounds, which caused a shooting pain all over as soon as he landed. The doctor was not very far off and rushed to where Mulk had fallen.

By then, Mulk was up, dusting the mud and dirt from his already dirty attire, smelling of sweat, dry blood and disinfectants.

'Khanna sahib, what are you doing? Getting down like that is going to damage your wounds further. You are supposed to relax till I tell you to...and I have yet not asked you to walk. So please get back to the cart!' reprimanded the doctor.

However, Mulk was quite reinforced with the rest and the cane juice he had before he had dozed off.

'Doctor sahib, I feel fine enough to walk and stretch myself a bit. Sitting in the cart is cramping me and increasing my body ache. So, please. sahib, let me walk a bit, after which I promise to get back to the cart and rest.' Mulk looked indignant, and the doctor relented.

Mulk discovered that they would reach Amritsar in the next few hours, and a camp had been made ready there for the contingent. They were also to be a part of the Independence Day celebrations, and the district administration had organised a special dinner for the occasion.

Mulk worked out a plan in his mind. He would celebrate with the people who had given him a new lease of life, after the harrowing losses, right from Sialkot to where he found himself now…nearing Amritsar. From a new Pakistan…to a new India. The next day he would leave for where his sister-in-law stayed to have more chances of finding out the whereabouts of his wife, kids, and his younger brother's wife.

The horrors he had gone through had affected his mind very negatively. He could only think of tragedies ahead, nothing good could happen to him. He was on a slide downhill. What if his whole family had been wiped out in Kud, where he had heard of gory violence between the two communities? No one had picked up his friend's phone at home, where his family was staying, in Kud.

There was no way of contacting his younger brother, and he did not know if he was still in England or had come back to Sialkot…in case he had come back to Sialkot…God! Hope the goons had not caught up with him and done what they wanted to do!

There were so many like him with their baggage. The person who had been trying to pacify Mulk had seen his family hacked to death. His shop, about twenty miles from Narowal, had been gutted, with all his stock of fabric consigned to fire. He had a princely sum of a few hundred rupees with him.

Mulk had more…much more. He had no information of his family having perished…his estate in Sialkot was in the safe hands of Aftab…and he had quite a few relatives scattered around in northern India. He slowly settled down with this new realization and embraced his accompanying friend warmly, and they walked on together into a new India…with new expectations and hopes. After all, it was simple…there was no other alternative….

***

It was a cloudy night, with the moon providing some visibility. Viresh was sitting all alone with his back resting against a robust tree trunk. The absence of the sun helped in suppressing the ill effects of the prevailing heat and humidity. He could not sleep. Too many things had happened in just a few days, taking him from a happy and relaxed childhood into a pseudo-adulthood. Death, violence, all shades of tragedy…he had seen it all. But then, he was not alone in this 'circus of violence', and that is what kept him mentally alive. Being physically alive was not in his hands, so it did not bother him at all,

There was the monotonous yet sonorous singing of crickets, the occasional hooting of owls, and certain other unidentified sounds of nature when suddenly he heard footsteps, trying to be as silent as possible, with only the jungle undergrowth giving way to the weight on it.

Viresh transitioned to alertness from his stupor and blinked his eyes to adjust to the eerie jungle night. He could see a shadow moving past about a couple of hundred meters ahead, towards the thickets.

***

Kamla had been feeling ill for a while. She had a full bladder and an intense urge to throw up, which was growing by the hour. She sat up to see all the ladies fast asleep after a very trying day, both mentally and physically. Without disturbing them, she got up and tiptoed past, and lifting the Bedsheet that hung like a partition between two trees, she walked across the opening towards the thicket.

Thank God, she thought to herself, that no one was awake to witness her embarrassment. She did not know anyone, and neither was she in any state of mind to do so. On reaching a few feet inside the thickets, she found a small space, enough to squat and ease her bladder. She stood up, walked a few paces further down and began to puke, trying to be as silent as possible, so as not to attract any attention.

Suddenly, she got sucked inside the surrounding thickets and pulled with extraordinary force, causing a shooting pain in her left arm, which was in a hard grip. Before she could shriek with pain and fear, she was gagged with cloth stuffed into her mouth. There was a strange smell, which made her feel more and more faint by the second. She heard strange noises as if coming out of a long tunnel, distorted and weird, and could feel multiple hands drawing her in different directions. There came another strong force that sucked her out of the same thicket in which she was sucked in. Then there was darkness....

***

When Kamla woke up, she was surrounded by her family, worried, anxious, and scared. Viresh was standing by the side of her makeshift bed—her clothes all soiled and torn, and at places marked with spots of dried blood. Varun, Savitri, Gagan, Viresh's parents and cousin were all there, apart from Kamla's own family.

Kamla herself was all soiled up, with scratches and bruises all over. However, she was covered with a clean sheet. God had been with her in the form of Viresh, who had followed her into the thickets. Confused as to why she was tiptoeing towards the thickets, alone, in the darkness of an uncertain night, he felt worried and strangely patronizing without understanding the reason. He felt a call of duty to his family-friends from his city.

Realising the reason for Kamla tiptoeing past him, he gave her the needed privacy and distance required to fulfil her calls, but soon he was terrified to find Kamla being pulled into the thickets, and before he could react, she had been consumed by the forest.

Viresh was well-built, athletic, bold in disposition, and an avid footballer in school. He took no time in jumping into the thickets. Behind a ring fence of bushes was a clearing, again followed by dense forests of tall trees and dense undergrowth, all darkened by the black paint of the night. A few oil-dipped lamps had been dug into the ground in the clearing using their wooden handles. Three locals from the other community had Kamala in their grip. In their lascivious moments, the miscreants had let go of their daggers, which lay on the ground not very far.

Viresh seized the opportunity and lunged at the man who had pinned down Kamla and was trying to lift her gown. The other two had grasped her hands, to enable the heinous act. Taken by surprise, the three left Kamla alone and focused on Viresh. As they grappled and fought with fists, one of the attackers managed to get hold of a dagger lying on the ground and lunged at Viresh. Viresh saw him from the corner of his eyes and shifted in time, getting brushed by the dagger. It tore a part of his long shirt and made a shallow gash on his skin. The momentum of the attacker carried him forward and he ended up plunging the dagger deep into one of his companions. Confused and afraid, they ran away into the darkness of the jungle.

Kamla was weeping and shaking in fits, while an injured and exhausted Viresh limped towards her to take her back to comfort. They made it back to where the rest of the family had camped carrying the remaining two daggers. These would come in handy for the rest of their journey.

***

Jaya stared at Viresh, her expressions revealing nothing at that point. Kamla was there because of Viresh. It was her second life, with her respect intact. Had the dagger landed where it was intended to, Viresh would have had a different story to tell. Unable to quantify her indebtedness in words, Jaya did not want the injustice of even attempting it. Viresh stood embarrassingly still, as did Varun and Savitri, choked in emotions.

'Varun bhai, I will never be able to forget what has happened today.... Why only I, none of us would. And would like Viresh and you all to be always a part of us. But we are in such uncertain times right now that we cannot formalise our desires.

'My husband is also not with us...so the only thing I can do now is to know your mind on a possible union of Viresh and Kamla, after we settle down in India, under these new circumstances....'

Jaya was holding Viresh's hand...sniffing and sobbing in the process. It was an emotive response by Jaya, not giving it a second thought...but it came straight from her heart...a genuine feeling, to fulfil which she was prepared to walk the distance.

Viresh was blushing, unable to grasp the intensity of the situation. He had done what was right, with no other thoughts crossing his mind. Kamla had to be saved...and that was it.

Varun and Savitri were surprised at the turn of events...and so were Kiran and Hansraj...but all felt happy after days of depressed uncertainties. Varun stepped forward and picked up the two daggers lying on the floor and gave one to Jaya and one to Savitri.

'This will continue to remind us of this day and the commitment that the two families have towards each other. I am fully with Jaya bhabhi, and if we are all alive and well, it will be my endeavour to fulfil bhabhi's desire and make this family into one big unit. And I am sure that Mulk bhai will be with us to make it happen.'

Viresh was embarrassed, and so was Kamla. He left the enclosure where Kamla had now propped herself up to a sitting position and tried looking in the other direction. But, at their tender age, both had committed themselves to each other.

***

It was still a long way to reach Amritsar. The caravan had to first reach Udhampur from where they would have to take a bus ride to Amritsar via Pathankot, Gurdaspur, and Batala. People would be leaving the caravan at various points starting from Udhampur.

The Malhotras left at Pathankot to take a train to Delhi from where they would meet Varun's cousin, who was a trader in the small town of Bareilly. The Khannas carried on to Amritsar in a rattling bus on the unevenly surfaced roads. Every turn and bend had a story to tell. Violence was writ large on the landscape, and the bus had to take bumpy and dusty detours through fields and villages to keep out of harm's way.

The Khanna family, with the remaining people of the caravan, spent a night at the Gurdaspur bus stand. They could get the flavour of new India, with its pains and pleasures of the partition and independence. Hansraj remained tense and watchful till they finally reached Jaya's sister's house in Amritsar, alive and safe, apart from the skirmish that had changed Kamla's way of looking at life...maybe forever.

***

Mulk sat on a large wooden log, along with two others, looking vacantly into the distance. Music was blaring from two loudspeakers diagonally opposite to each other on a large, flat, dusty ground with sparse, unkempt grass sprouting here and there. The ground, which people in Amritsar referred to as '*maidan*', was not far from the infamous Jalianwallah Bagh, and it was fringed with two concentric circles of small tent hutments to accommodate the refugees who were arriving in a constant stream from all over. The city had virtually become a major centre for those arriving from all parts of Pakistan, most of them with varied degrees of physical and mental injury.

The loudspeakers were blaring the recognised national anthem of newly-born India and other patriotic songs peppered with announcements from happenings all over the country. The focus of all those present was on the news from Delhi, the current seat of power.

The maidan was a mixture of pain, misery, separation, the elation of being free from the clutches of the dictatorial British, as well as the uncertainty of the future. All those present had been displaced from the comfort of their homes and cities. The sense of loss was immense.

The stink, lack of sanitation and drainage, and the constantly piling debris defined the atmosphere of the refugee camp. Flies, crows, swooping eagles, and scurrying rats also formed a part of the camp like their human companions. It was all collectively, albeit strangely, a part of the heady independence. Within this kaleidoscope, Mulk felt a change occurring.

At the entry point of the camp, there was a small crowd moving in, like a homogenous mass, a swarm of bees moving along with the queen. When the crowd came nearer, Mulk could see that the queen was really a king bee, dressed as a gipsy with earrings, necklaces, and rings. He was amused to see the king bee moving in his direction across the Maidan when he suddenly realised that the log on which he was perched with a few others was the only decent sitting spot in the camp.

'*Om namma shivai...alak niranjan,*' bellowed the king bee, shaking his head from side to side. The shaking was accompanied by the musical sound of all the trinkets on his sweaty and smelly body, with drops of sweat running off his unkempt, entangled hair and forehead. He took up space beside Mulk and made him his first focus in the camp.

'You have had a very trying time, son; and have lost a lot,' he started. Mulk was amused since that's what the camp was all about—everyone had had a trying time, and all had lost a lot. He began to move off the log when the clairvoyant caught hold of him, forced him to sit, and came straight to the point on what he could gaze into Mulk's future.

'You have borne enough in a short time…but you are a good and god-fearing man who has thought well for everyone…and God has not ignored this…right from today you would only move in the direction ordained by Him…a direction of immense happiness, peace, fulfilment, and success. You will be a leader in business, settled near Delhi….'

Mulk laughed aloud, yet there was a glint in his eyes…he suddenly felt light and full of hope as he walked out of the camp, not looking back at the gipsy, who by now was surrounded by almost everyone in the camp. What confounded him was how 'near Delhi' had cropped into the equation of his life. He had already advanced to quite an extent his deliberations to settle his business in Agra with the support of his uncle Adhiraj.

***

India was already a couple of days old, and yet directionless. People in the northern part of the country were all in a state of flux, either helping or being helped. The Indian police and other government officials were indeed helpful, doing their bit within their mounting limitations. Everyone was at their wit's end, with varying degrees of complications and violence all around. Amritsar was crowded, littered, confused, and seized with senseless violence.

Jaya, Kiran, and Kamla were sitting with Jaya's sister, Lata, in her bedroom in Amritsar and animatedly discussing the future.

Lata was of the view that once Mulk had been traced, they should go to Jaya and Lata's eldest sister and brother-in-law in Mathura, near Delhi, and look at avenues there, instead of Agra.

'Delhi and its vicinity would be far more progressive than Agra,' suggested Lata. 'Radha and her husband are also there. You must know that Radha's husband is a doctor, ex-army. He has a lot of influence there.'

Kiran was far more excited at the prospect of Delhi than Agra, but Jaya was circumspect and wanted to wait for Mulk to take the decision. Hansraj walked in to remind Jaya that she was to visit some of the refugee camps set up in Amritsar to enquire about Mulk and Magan Lal. Jaya got up to leave to go, while Kiran agreed to stay back in the house with the kids and Lata.

***

Mulk kept on walking in the direction of the Golden Temple, from his camp. It was a straight road leading to a crossing after almost three to four miles of a crowded walk. From the crossing, one turned right through a busy marketplace to arrive at the famous, or rather infamous, Jallianwala Bagh, from where Harmandir sahib, or the Golden Temple as it was also called, was just a mile away. Mulk had decided to go to the temple and pray. He was sure that a solution to unite with his family would show up there.

After almost half an hour of walking, Mulk arrived at the busy marketplace flanking the narrow lane leading to the Temple. His throat was parched, and shops selling *lassi* (churned and sweetened or salted curds) appeared tempting to Mulk, but the belief within prompted him to carry on—to pay respects, pray, take a dip in the holy waters of the tank, and then get back to the market to have a spot of lunch. So, he carried on till he reached the temple.

There was a huge crowd walking around the tank, as was the custom, taking a dip in the holy waters and then paying their respects at the Temple. Mulk followed and repeated all that the person in front of him was performing. His mind was focused on his family. Where would they be? How and in what situation?

He decided to visit Jaya's sister's house after his prayers and lunch. He was sure to get some information from them. Maybe he might also find them there.

From Kud, he had got information that the house where they were staying had been ransacked and burned down. The servant's body was found in the thickets behind the ruined bungalow. It had left Mulk desolate and scared.

He had also tried to call up Jaya's sister on quite a few occasions, but without luck...he could not connect...the phone lines and communications were in a mess. So, he decided to go there and find out for himself if they had any news. He had some idea where their house was even though he had visited their place quite some time back. He did not perceive it to be a major problem. What was scaring him was a niggling apprehension of the safety of Jaya's relatives themselves. They stayed somewhere between the Durgiana Mandir (temple of the goddess Durga) and the Sher Shah Suri Road, the main arterial road cutting across Amritsar town. going right up to Lahore, then in Pakistan.

The area was congested and had reported heavy communal violence leading up to Independence Day. The fear of sporadic incitements still lurked in the lanes and by lanes.

He walked around the tank, with all these thoughts clouding his mind. All his prayers were directed to the well-being of his family. He only knew of Jai, who was on his way to India on a ship sailing to the Bombay port. Jai would call up their uncle, Adhiraj, in Agra, to get further bearings once in Bombay. Lost in his thoughts, he did not know when he swooned and collapsed.

When he opened his eyes, Mulk saw an unfocussed image of a lady tending to him. Next to her was a familiar man...and then a crowd of onlookers, all around.

Slowly, he regained his focus and discovered that God was indeed with him, protecting him from all that was inclined to go wrong with his world. His head was resting on Jaya's lap, who had cupped his head in the warmth of her hands, with her tears of joy washing the heat and grime off his forehead. The man next to Jaya was Hansraj, who was fanning Mulk, with the cotton cloth he always carried with him.

An inner voice had dragged Jaya to Harmandir sahib before she could venture to the Refugee Office to gather information about the camps and the refugee list, which was being compiled by the local administration of Amritsar. It was the God within who had got Jaya and Mulk together, who got the falling and struggling confidence back in them, who changed their flailing lives within moments.... Mulk was certain that the Bohemian gipsy whom he had met at the camp was right after all. A good turn had just taken shape, and he was sure of greener pastures ahead, no matter how hard the climb.

***

There were tears in everyone's eyes, while Mulk narrated his days and journey right up to his sister-in-law's house in Amritsar. Magan Lal being killed was a tragedy for the entire family, including Hansraj. The family also said a prayer for Aftab. Had it not been for him, Mulk would not have been alive, and his financial interests taken care of. Jaya narrated her journey from Kud to Amritsar, and the role Varun and his family played in saving Kamla. Mulk endorsed Jaya's on Kamla's future with Viresh, Varun's son. They decided to call up Varun and convey their gratitude and agreement to Jaya's decision. They also decided to call up and remain in constant touch with Aftab.

Over dinner, that night, Jaya managed to convince Mulk to first go to Mathura, near Delhi, and meet their eldest brother-in-law, Dr (Major) Pratap Arora. He was influential and might be able to help settle them down near, or in, Delhi, which would be a better place to do business than Agra. In case things did not work out there, Agra and Mulk's uncle were always there.

***

New India and her new Indians struggle to come to terms with their new independence....

CHAPTER 24

A Generation Moves On

Dr Ajit Chatterjee finally got a break from his hectic existence with his father-in-law tending to the ever-increasing number of victims of arson and rioting that seemed to have escalated after independence.

Lord Louis Mountbatten had made the Radcliffe Boundary Award public. Punjab in the west and Bengal in the east had been virtually dissected into two, to be shared between the two countries. The British had made a hasty exit from their Indian colony, leaving the administration in the hands of the local people, both in India and Pakistan, all of whom were trying to grapple with the complex situation at hand. It was a steep learning curve, which had made the administration, as well as the police, quite ineffective.

Meerut was no exception, and doctors like Narendra were working overtime. Ajit was excited to make a journey to the nearby town of Mathura, where he was to meet his colleague and friend from his army days, Dr (Major) Pratap Arora who, like Ajit, had opted out and gone into private practice with one of his friends in Mathura. Ajit chose to drive down in his Austin—a long, vexatious, and risky journey.

Over rounds of steaming tea and coffee, the two friends discussed all that had happened and was happening, about the prevalent senseless violence where they were, and in Punjab, Bengal and Bihar. Their discussion and memory walk were suddenly disturbed by a shrill ring on Pratap's telephone kept close by on a side table. After a few minutes of conversation, disturbed by poor connectivity, Pratap got back to where he was sitting.

'A trunk call from my sister-in-law in Amritsar. We would be having guests from Sialkot, in a week or so. Jaya and Mulk Raj Khanna—my youngest sister-in-law and her husband. Poor chap had a flourishing business of cricket goods in Sialkot. Had to sell it off along with all his other assets to escape alive.'

As Pratap spoke, Ajit was visibly excited, his tea spilling over the napkin on his lap. He saw destiny right in the eyes. It was Pratap's turn to be amazed to know that Ajit's father-in-law had managed to get Mulk registered for land allotment without even knowing him for farthings. While they discussed this coincidence, the telephone rattled off again. This time it was for Ajit. No sooner had he put the phone down than he rushed out of Pratap's house, dashing for his car….

***

Ajit was always a rule-abiding and cautious driver, but that was a different day…he had to reach Meerut as soon as possible. Baba, Dr Narendranath, had suffered a severe heart attack. It had come suddenly, early in the morning, when he was in the bathroom for his morning ablutions. He had somehow managed to stagger out to his bedroom and raise an alarm. Surobee had rushed to her father's room in no time, and Babu Lal, Ram Lal, and the rest of the retinue were at his bedside. Nathua, Ajit's compounder, immediately administered first aid medicine and called Ajit, as well as Dr Caroli and Dr Madan from the neighbourhood.

Narendra had his head on Surobee's lap and was constantly calling out for Ajit and Virendra, his cousin, professor, and friend.

Being a doctor, he could feel and realise the paucity of time. He was frothing from his mouth and breathing hard...very hard....

Subendu, tapping on the doors of teenage, was confused and nervous. He knew that whatever was happening was not good. He started to sob, holding his attendant, Chunni Lal's hands, quite tightly. Narendra could just manage to speak a bit, in between gasps and sucking in whatever air he could manage to take in.

'Subendu...Doon School...must. Virendra will look...after all...of you.

'Will...in my study...drawer. Ajit...will lead...my practice... doctor....'

One immense gulp of air...a ghastly sound...and all was over.

Dr Caroli had arrived, but in vain, only to declare his close friend dead. Virendra, Nawab Sahib and Sultan Singh followed in quick succession.

Surobee sat still, stunned, with her father's body on her lap, and his soul in her heart. By this time Subendu was crying aloud, clinging to his very still father. He could faintly remember his mother lying as still...both his father and mother were still now.... It would take him quite a time to understand the enormity of the situation.

Ajit entered. By that time there was a crowd. His father-in-law was in a permanent state of peace on the green mosaic floor. His wife sat beside him, expressionless, warm saline tears dripping from both her cheeks. She held Subendu with her right arm around him. He seemed to be fatigued and sleepy with continuous sobbing. All the close relatives and friends sat around Narendra, shocked and broken. Narendra had beckoned all of them to his Quit India...Quit World....

'He has escaped the tragedy of our country's independence, leaving us to tackle the pain and misery, perched peacefully and snuggly in a heavenly corner,' spoke Virendra, before breaking down and banging his fist on his temple.

He had got up to embrace Ajit and guide him to where he should be. A whole generation of Bandhopadhyas had moved on.

Subendu was the heir to the family's pains and pleasures, surrounded and closely watched by a hoard of relatives…eager to guide, love, and be there…nearest to him…an unenviable place to be in….

***

Ajit and Virendra sat in Narendra's study, filling up forms and attaching necessary documents for Subendu's passage to The Doon School. Virendra was Subendu's legal guardian and Ajit was now his caretaker, along with Surobee. They were the people whom Narendra had left to guide and guard Subendu till he learned to fly. Outside the study, there was a huge extended family, whom Narendra had kept together with his love and magnanimity. All of them were being looked after by Sharmila, Surobee, and Purobee, who had come to be with her younger sister and aunt for some time till life returned to normal.

CHAPTER 25

Masters No More

While India underwent intense pangs of birth, there was a small and beautiful corner within its boundaries which continued its peaceful, pristine, and happy existence.

Trilok had the luxury of getting a long leave from his government job in Delhi. He had left for home while in British India and would join back a new and independent India under Pingali Venkayya's Tricolour. Right then, he was sitting on a crude bench, innovated out of locally available old pinewood under the pleasant Garhwal sun, which had peeped out of the dark monsoon clouds. Kadam and their other friends were doing the same, savouring the local brew with some hot and fresh potato fries and hot chutney.

There was a lot to discuss. The euphoria of an independent India was quite palpable. What was missing was the pain of the plains of the west and east—the riots and hate crimes prevailing in Uttar Pradesh and Bihar, the confusion and tension in Delhi.... The local brew made the peace seem even more real.

'Arrey bhayyon, ab to aap log kabhi bhi Dilli, mere ghar aa sakte ho. Apnaa desh hai, apni sarkaar hai.... Rokne wallah kaun hai.... Wahaan per bhi aisey hee baith kar angreji piyenge...,' babbled Trilok, the fiery country liquor making him far more confident and garrulous than he usually was. (Brothers, now you can come to my house in Delhi, anytime.... No one to stop you...our country...our government.... There too we will sit like this and consume English liquor....)

'Dilli mien hamaare bhai ki bahut pooch hai...sarkari naukari jo thehri...,' spoke out Kadam, patting Trilok on his back while the others nodded in confirmation, looking up to Trilok with immense pride. (My brother has a lot of say in Delhi. After all, he is a government servant.)

***

Nehru was a hero in Garhwal. He had led India to freedom and was now their first Prime Minister. Gandhi was like God. And Sardar Patel and Govind Vallabh Pant were the strong men, around whom fables were being woven. Partition was a necessity, and good for the new Bharat. This was a simplistic view of the people of the hills.

But these simple people of the hills had only heard of the pains of nation formation...romanticised on the tales they were hearing. They were happy to know that they wouldn't be harassed by the British sahibs for *lagaan* (taxes), which they were forced and loath to give. Their bigger angst was not to be under the Parmar Kings. They were happy to be directly governed by the Indian government, instead.

Kadam had been called by some other headmen of neighbouring villages in Pauri the following day. They were teaming up to raise a demand to be a direct constituent of the Indian Union, rather than to be a part of the Garhwal Kingdom. He was told that some important leaders from Delhi would also be coming to address their demands and show them the way.

Trilok had received a letter from his post office. He had been asked to join back in Delhi within a fortnight. It was good news, but he was sceptical because of the uncertainties. Trilok and his family, along with Satendra, planned to leave by the end of August.

***

On arrival, Satendra saw the same old Delhi Railway Station, the same crowded, dirty, and smelly platforms, coolies in the same red uniform, with a brass plate around their upper arm and over the uniform sleeve declaring their identity. The only difference that Satendra could happily notice was to see native Indians getting off from first-class compartments along with some English gentry. There was a new-found confidence in the local population...suddenly, the police were not harassing them to fall in line and exit from a different gate. Existence had levelled out. However, there was more indiscipline and a lack of proper governance.

With all this, the Rawat family led by Trilok and trailed by Satendra at the rear...made their reappearance in the capital of independent India....

***

The Rawats arrived at Trilok's dwelling quarters. They had vacated the quarter where Satendra used to live with his friends since they could always find a new one when they again got back. Post-independence.

While Vandana, Trilok's wife, settled down along with her children, Praful and Ankita, Trilok, and Satendra went out to the streets to look for some warm meal available from the numerous street-side vendors. The lane that housed them was dirtier, more crowded, and erratic. There seemed to be no policing, at least not at that hour in the hot and humid August afternoon.

Trilok and Satendra were greeted with a warm smile of recognition by their old vendor from whom they used to get some delectable Indian breads and a nice spicy daal. What surprised and excited both Satendra and Trilok was the presence of some English gentry partaking in the spread of spicy Indian food along with the locals. They were given warm welcomes, not only by vendors but even by the local customers. Satendra found guests who, till some time back, were their rulers. They were still sceptical about mingling with the dirty and smelling natives. The whole scenario seemed to have changed.

They were, like tourists, enjoying what was on offer in a country which was no longer their own. An Englishman recognised Trilok and walked up to him. They embraced each other in bonhomie, with the Englishman trying to converse in broken Hindi, and Trilok trying to converse in broken English.

Satendra found it amusing to see the effort both were trying to put in to make the meeting and conversation successful.

The chance meeting ended in the Englishman getting invited for lunch at Trilok's quarters, and the three of them walked towards their destination with some warm food in their hands.

The firangi was working as a supervisor in Trilok's office, and before this chance meeting, the only conversation they had was wishing each other a formal good morning when they first met, and a nod when leaving for the day.

'Sir, I joining office Monday,' stammered Trilok, trying to be as fluent as possible. 'You going office everyday?' he stammered again.

'No Trilok, I have been released from office here in India, and I will be leaving for England soon. My last day in office would be by the end of next week.

'Mai tum sab ko miss karega.... Bahut miss...jab hum England ko jayega...,' replied the British supervisor, with a lot of effort to make Trilok understand. (I will be missing you people...quite a lot when I leave for England.)

Trilok got up to serve his supervisor a plate of hot lunch, which he had got from the street hawker, along with some sweet tea in a steel glass brewed by Vandana.

The supervisor enjoyed each bit of the food, the steaming tea giving extra kicks, sizzling its way down his gullet. Beads of perspiration dripped down his forehead as a tribute to the chillies and spices. Satendra could hardly eat because of the excitement... being in such proximity to a white man...for the first time, meeting him informally as an equal. He had an innate desire to touch his skin and feel the similarities or differences. So, he got up, and sat down beside him on the cot, not looking at Trilok, who was staring at him, indicating his displeasure at this odd behaviour.

With a staunch determination, Satendra held his hand, and the supervisor, taking it to be a young Indian boy's inquisitive handshake, returned the gesture with an effusive, strong clasp and a pat on Satendra's back. His day was made in a way he had never thought of; Satendra felt close to the rulers.

'Are you going...to England...your home?' stammered Satendra, managing to communicate with a white man in whatever English he had managed to learn courtesy of Macaulay's efforts.

'Yes, of course, dear boy. I sure am, in a fortnight. However, I would be very happy to have you and your family over for dinner at my quarters, before I leave this great nation and its loving people,' responded the supervisor with a genuine desire that his invitation be accepted.

Both Satendra and Trilok got the gist of the conversation—they were being invited for dinner. Their acceptance couldn't have been any better than a nod since a conversation might have been disastrous in consequence.

'So, then I take it to be final. Dinner, the day after tomorrow, at my place,' stated the supervisor, with a sense of finality.

'Yes…me and him…,' replied Trilok with a lot of effort and courage.

The session ended, much to everyone's relief, and left Satendra excited and impatient to boast amongst his friends and relatives and convert it into a family saga for years to come.

CHAPTER 26

The Benefactor

It was late evening. The bus, rickety and old, was to rest for what was left of the evening and the night to take another journey from Mathura to Delhi the next day.

Amongst others, the Khanna family, minus their eldest son, Ashok, and including Kiran and her son, emerged from the creaky interiors of the rickety old bus. Mulk and his two sons got the main pieces of luggage down from the top of the bus while Jaya and Kamla helped with the pieces that the family had retained with them inside—a few bags, a bedding roll, and a cloth sling bag tightly hugged by Jaya. The sling bag had all that the Khannas had left to sustain themselves till Aftab could find a way to transfer them what remained. None of them knew when that would happen. Mulk stretched himself after a long journey and looked around for some mode of transport to take them to Dr Pratap Arora's residence.

There were a few tongas waiting for passengers, and Mulk walked towards them, only to be interrupted by a slightly familiar well-dressed gentleman. Mulk narrowed his eyes, focusing on him, and trying to make out who he was.

'Are you Mr Mulk Raj Khanna from Sialkot?' enquired the gentleman. It was the doctor himself, who had guessed the time of their arrival from his last conversation with Mulk. They hugged each other and moved towards where the rest of Mulk's family were waiting. It was a happy feeling after the family's tragic run from death and humiliation. However, Mulk mused…when… Oh God when…would he be able to settle down into a home and life of his own….

***

Like his friend Ajit, Dr Pratap also had an Austin…grey and shiny, and he was mighty proud of it. The car was his office and comfort zone while on his house calls to patients…he was quite well-known, popular and revered in Mathura. He and his wife always felt good to help relatives and friends.

Raveena was waiting in the house to greet and host her sister… so many stories to tell and hear…she was at the gate of their bungalow when Pratap's car came in sight.

The Khannas broke loose from the car, where they were all stuffed with their handbags and luggage. Noisy embraces followed between the sisters Raveena and Jaya as everyone looked on.

'Come on…we can have the second part of the emotional meeting inside, in the privacy of our house…the Khannas are a tired lot, need to wash up and then refresh themselves…,' Pratap said with a broad smile, and then chaperoned them inside, through the driveway, after which he got the car inside and parked it in the garage.

***

The centre table of Pratap's drawing room was full of tasty vegetarian and nonvegetarian victuals…mutton kebabs, tandoori chicken and spicy chaats. To wash it down, Raveena had kept different kinds of sherbets in jugs…and some stronger stuff for

Pratap and Mulk…a good, imported Scotch, presented to Pratap by one of his affluent patients.

After a couple of gulps of the smooth and inviting whiskey, Pratap asked about their escape from Sialkot—a conversation that would last late into the night after dinner, only to be resumed the next day…leaving the listeners with a heavy heart, moist eyes… and yet a positivity for what was to follow.

Pratap suggested that Mulk try and settle the second chapter of his sports business in Meerut, which was not far, and where the local bureaucracy had carved out a niche for the sports industry shifting out of Pakistan.

Mulk developed an inquisitive frown on his face at the name of Meerut…trying to recollect the old reference…was it Sanjay who had mentioned something…some person…from this city?

The clarity came suddenly…a Bandhopadhyay…an eminent doctor from Meerut…and he blurted out in excitement….

'Pratap, *aap kisi* Doctor Bandhopadhyay *ko jaante ho*…Meerut *ke mashahoor doctor hain?'* (Pratap, do you happen to know a Dr Bandhopadhyay…a famous doctor of Meerut?)

Pratap broke into a smile.

'Mulk bhai, I know the whole family. As a matter of fact, his son-in-law has been my course-mate and close friend from my Army Medical Corps days. We put in our papers together… his father-in-law expired some time back…he is the one…Dr Bandhopadhyay.'

Mulk tapped his knuckles on Pratap's desk showing growing excitement….

'Pratap bhai, Dr Bandhopadhyay had assured Sanjay, my cousin and accountant, help and support for us to settle down there. Unfortunately, Sanjay was killed in the communal riots in Sialkot…but I am sure that doctor sahib's family and friends would definitely have an idea of this…can you enquire?'

Pratap vaguely recollected Ajit mentioning something similar before he had rushed back on a family emergency.

'Sure, I would immediately call up Ajit, my friend.' Pratap began to dial Ajit's number. Fortunately, he got through without much struggle, and Ajit was there on the other side, despite shoddy connectivity.

Putting the phone down, Pratap spoke after a mischievous suspense.

'Mulk bhai, you will not believe this, but Dr Bandhopadhyay had got you registered for a piece of land to be allotted to you, to relocate your sports business in Meerut...and it is still available in your name!!"

'Kya baat kar rahe ho, Pratap bhai...*farishta hain ye* Bandhopadhyay sahib...nothing less than God, for me!' cried out Mulk.

Pratap asked Mulk to leave for Meerut the same day and take possession of his allotted land as soon as possible, to which Mulk agreed and took the first available bus. Pratap had already asked Ajit to wait for Mulk and lend him the necessary support.

***

Ram Lal, from Ajit's Dispensary, as what it was now known as, after Narendra's death; was detailed to receive Mulk and his wife from the Meerut Bus Stand. and escort them to the Bandhopadhyay residence, where Ajit, Surobee, Virendra, Nawab Ishaq and Sultan Singh were waiting for them.

Although it was a tad bit late for lunch, an elaborate tea, sherbet, and snacks had been prepared, as a welcome...so typical of the household.

A bus rolled into the Meerut Bus Stop with the insignia 'Mathura-Meerut-Mathura', and Ram Lal, who had been vigilantly looking out for the bus from Mathura, sped up to it as it was parking. He looked enquiringly at all the disembarking couples till he hit the bull's eye...Mulk and Jaya were only carrying a bag between them, with essentials and a box of sweets popular in Mathura that they had picked up on their way.

After initial enquiry and pleasantries, Ram Lal took the bag from Mulk's hands and guided them to the horse carriage. The uniformed driver saluted them and helped them up into the carriage, while Ram Lal settled down beside the driver...and they sped along.

Mulk was impressed. 'Personal Carriage,' he whispered to Jaya...who felt safe and satisfied, after such a long and torturous time. She had come into her element once with her sisters in Amritsar...and then...yesterday evening.

***

The road was sparsely populated, with a few more carriages, some people walking by, and a car entering a large gate to the right of the road, leaving dust behind. The carriage that was transporting Mulk and his wife followed into the same gate as the car. A huge bungalow, spread into distinct wings, with multiple inner passages leading up to different destination points, came into view. Mulk and Jaya were overwhelmed by the grandeur of the place they were entering...a few of the likes of Mulk's Civil Lines residence would have fitted within the compound in which they entered.

Once inside the gate, which was guarded, there was a wing facing them with a passage skirting a beautiful garden, taking them to an arched entrance coated with a healthy growth of ivy creepers, where the carriage stopped. Ram Lal jumped off and helped Mulk and his wife down the coach ladder. They were requested to wait there while Ram Lal went inside to let the people know of the Khannas' arrival.

Surobee, along with Sharmila, rushed out to greet the guests, supported by Babu Lal and Chameli...and after warm greetings, they were ushered into the front veranda of the main wing of the house, which overlooked another lawn, bedecked with colourful flowers and trees—jacarandas, magnolias, peach blossoms...and then, a courtyard beyond, where one could sit and enjoy the fragrance, riot of colours and varieties of birds, darting and flying around. There was also a bird cage with some exotic birds creating a symphony and some ducks walking around.

Mulk and Jaya were speechless and mesmerized.... After what they had gone through, they seemed to have landed in heaven, amongst such elite, albeit simple people.

'My husband, Dr Ajit Chatterjee, will be here in a bit, along with two other elders of this city, to help you with the proceedings you are here for...and in the meantime, Babu Lal is getting some refreshments, and we can chat over some tea.'

Surobee apprised them in an excited tone and, in the same breath, called out for Babu Lal to get the snacks, drinks and tea. Soon they had a lavish spread of cucumber sandwiches, samosas mixed fritters with spicy chutney, mango sherbet...followed by piping hot tea served in fine and dainty china to be stirred with silver spoons. The Khannas were overawed with the welcome and the niceties, restoring their faith in human values after a long and ugly gap.

They told Surobee and Sharmila their tale of woes through which they had waded till the gratifying present with such loving and hospitable people.

Surobee, Sharmila, and even Chameli, standing behind them, were in tears...Sharmila got up and embraced the weeping Jaya, while destiny connected the two distant dots together....

Tears were flowing down Mulk's cheek when suddenly he jerked back to the present with a hand on his shoulders...it was Ajit, flanked by Nawab Sahib, and Sultan Singh.

***

Mulk accompanied Ajit, Sultan, and Ishaq to Narendra's Study, now used by Ajit. Ajit called for Ram Lal and asked him to usher the Collector's clerk into the room.

Sultan Singh opened a conversation with Mulk, asking him about his existing business and about his plans of continuance in Meerut after migrating to the newly formed country.

Mulk had clearly thought-out plans of continuance and was even connected with many of his customers in the Indian part of the partitioned region under the British Raj. He also had orders in hand from England, which Jai had finalized while he was executing the torturous migration from Sialkot virtually singlehandedly. He gave broad details to the godsend benefactors sitting with him in the room.

In the meantime, the Collector's clerk entered the room and greeted everyone inside with folded hands, knowing all of them well, apart from Mulk. Ajit cleared his throat and explained why they all had assembled; and what lay ahead.

'Mulk sahib, it is an honour for all of us to have you here. We can't get you back your glory, happiness, and peace, which was once yours in Sialkot, but we can surely try to make amends as a recently independent nation to support you in building up your life again.

'Our Collector, on behalf of our fledgling government, has earmarked certain plots of land for migrating businessmen from west Punjab and the rest of Pakistan, as it now is, so that they can rebuild their lost glory.

'Sultan Singh ji and the rest of us here will help you and your family to establish yourselves here in Meerut and make it your home. I would also like to let you know that the government has established a decent fund to support people like you to start up your business from where you left off and help you prosper.'

Mulk had tears of happiness and trust in his eyes.

Ajit got up while requesting Mulk to stay on in their guest wing till he got all his papers and possession of the land in order.

Surobee had already taken his wife to where they would put up so that she could relax and rejoin the Bandhopadhyay family for a special dinner organized for them.

Mulk had nothing to add to this fairy tale, but to follow the gents out and move to where his destiny in this city was supposed to be. Even Ajit and the rest of the elders were going to see it for the first time….

***

They all moved out in two cars, Ajit's and Sultan's, with Sultan leading, since the Clerk was with him; and he knew the way to where the provision for the sports industry had been made. One of them was Victoria Park…a bit out of the main city, with fields all around, so as to provide for future expansion. Plots had been marked with single brick boundaries, and there were about 180 square yards to a plot.

An estimation had been made as to what was held by each of the sports goods industry refugees coming from west Punjab, and a proportionate compensation was being granted, in terms of land, as well as a starting-up grant. There were about fifty-seven such plots allocated at Victoria Park and about forty-three of them at Suraj Kund since this marked locality bordered a pond named Suraj Kund.

The Clerk showed the group both the allocated areas. Mulk's immediate preference was Victoria Park…he was excited as soon as he laid his eyes upon it. In quite a few ways it was better than the locality in Sialkot, and he would have the liberty to build afresh. Mulk was gifted with an active mind, wherein he could see the larger picture of what lay ahead, by delinking it with the past.

He had already taken a shed on hire through Adhiraj, his uncle settled there and had begun contracting skilled workers to train them and get production up and running to seamlessly complete orders in hand and remain in sync with his still active customers and dealers. That way, he would have time in hand to build up his Meerut establishment according to a well-thought-out plan and strategy, and not in a hurry.

Mulk suddenly remembered the gipsy whom he encountered at the refugee camp at Amritsar...how right he was when he prophesied that things would go only right with him thereon... he was reunited with his family...and had hired a workable shed through his uncle in Agra...and now destiny had brought him to Meerut, where he was looking at a property that he could call his own. God had taken a very tough test indeed, on him, his family, and associates...but he had never been the complaining or the cursing type...Mulk always believed that there was an element of sanity in the world's insane ways, and the Almighty's invisible hand always saved and directed the deserving.

After so many anxieties, losses of such great magnitude, falling to the bottom of the pyramid...and travelling the path of life with his family, he started smelling success and happiness yet again... leaving the dark cave behind.

Sultan shook him out of his spiritual thanksgiving....

'Mulk sahib, we need to work out details for your land allotment with the Collector...we have fixed a meeting with him after you get a fair idea of what suits you the best...the choice is between Victoria Park and Suraj Kund...both of which you have seen now.' They drove to the Collectorate, which was not very far away, and Ajit Chatterjee led the group up to the Collector's chambers to fulfil one of his father-in-law's last wishes.

***

Mulk had a habit of nervously shaking his legs while sitting on a chair at a speed in proportion to his state of nervousness or excitement...right now, although hidden by the table in between the Collector and the rest, Mulk's legs were shaking rapidly. He was staring at Mulk 2.0, in the story of his life....

Sultan put his hand on Mulk's thighs to calm him down, and Mulk took the hint. The Collector was going through pages of a file evidently connected with Mulk...he then looked up and smiled at Mulk with a welcoming gesture....

'Mr Mulk Raj Khanna, you are welcome to Meerut as a bonafide citizen of independent India...as a matter of fact, we have quite a few guests from the sports industry of west Punjab who have decided to make this city their business base and continue their journey of success.

'We are in the process of allocating all of them sufficient space and also deciding upon what other facilities are required by them to resume their lives in the right earnest.

I am sure that you have visited some identified sites, which we have earmarked for the sports industry, and might have found some suitable to your liking and requirement?'

Mulk had made up his mind for Meerut...it was a nice, neat and reasonably 'simple format' town, where he was already feeling very much at home. He preferred it to Agra since the authorities were trying to convert a part of this city into a sports manufacturing cluster, and he would have many neighbours and colleagues from the same fraternity doing business alongside him...the bond would be strong, which was more valuable than competition, having to start all over again at a new place.

The Collector was staring at Mulk for a response, while Mulk continued to be lost in his thoughts till Sultan gently nudged him into reality, yet again. Mulk got out of his thoughts with a jerk.

'Collector sahib, I found the first locality more suitable to my liking.'

'He means the Victoria Park area, Collector sahib,' interrupted Sultan.

'Oh! Okay,' responded the Collector, while going through the file of allotments. 'It appears that Victoria Park seems to be more popular amongst the identified sites, and as I can see from the file, we have more requests for Victoria Park than we can accommodate. So, we would be accommodating requests on a first-come-first-serve basis...wherein...you are in luck, Mulk sahib.

'We have considered your request date to be when the honoured and late Dr Bandhopadhyay had put in an official word about you to us...and we have such immense respect for him and his illustrious family, that we would consider that a request for Victoria Park.

'He must know you rather well to have called up specifically to make this happen...and had he been alive, I am sure, he would have been overjoyed to see it successfully through...however, he would be happy wherever he is to see you succeed and progress... good to have such a great human being as a friend, and I am happy to see Dr Chatterjee taking a personal interest to fulfil his father-in-law's last desires.

'I would request you to fill in your formal request form, which would include your business details of Sialkot, including your landholdings and business turnover with as much proof and substantiation as possible...since that would become the primary base for equivalent compensation. My clerk, sitting outside, the one who had taken you on the guided tour of sites available, would assist you with the format.

'I would also request Sultan sahib to help you in compiling a good case so as to help us to help you the best way we can...after all, he is a very successful businessman, local to this place.'

With this, the meeting was over quite successfully...Mulk was lost in his thoughts...so much was happening, and so rapidly, that he was not able to sit still and compose the direction his life was taking...he had so much to do and achieve...in such a short span of time...so much to tell his younger brother...his wife... his complete family.

Then...he had so much to thank God for...at the moment, the God he could perceive had a name, as well as a known shape...Dr Narendra Nath Bandhopadhyay.

CHAPTER 27

The Scholarship

Trilok was walking at quite a brisk pace, with Satendra trying to keep up. It was somewhere around half past nine in the morning...the beginning of the week, busy, with new hopes, new aspirations, in a newly independent nation.

Trilok was in semi-formal attire—a crisp white shirt and dark blue baggy trousers, with black shoes—the only one he had for office and wherever he needed to be formal. Satendra was in his khaki shorts and white shirt with freshly painted white canvas sneakers, which he generally wore to school, albeit not as clean as it was on that day.

It was a special day. They were going to his school to check the list of students who had applied and had been selected for admission to the Delhi Polytechnic, which had been created not long back at the historic Kashmere Gate area of Delhi.

Satendra was one of the sharpest students in his school, and his principal was very hopeful of his selection to this prestigious Polytechnic, created by the 'Wood & Abbott Committee of 1938'.

However, what Trilok was tense about was the cost of Satendra's education in this institution…would he be able to afford it… would he have to ask for help in the village…would Kadam or the rest of his family be able to fill in the gaps?

He did not want to put undue pressure on his family in the village. They were well off and happy, but as per their village standards. They sustained themselves from the soil they tilled and had enough to live happily there, but a sprawling city like Delhi was a different kettle of fish altogether. Everything was expensive here, including the day-to-day living. Moreover, the new government was coming to terms with the reality and the mess that the Raj had left the coffers in.

Trilok had requested his boss and chief, in whose outhouse he was staying, to refer some private scholarship that some affluent families had floated to help in educating the children and youth of newly independent India. The principal of DAV School, where Satendra was a student, had also guided Trilok to apply to such a private scholarship in case his nephew was selected at the Delhi Polytechnic.

Thinking of all these issues, Trilok and Satendra arrived at the front office corridor of the school…it was crowded with parents, guardians and students, trying to take a peep at various admission lists to various institutions where the students had applied.

'Cannot find any list from Delhi Polytechnic, bhayji,' exclaimed Satendra, looking both disappointed as well as anxious.

'Come, Satendra, let us go and talk to the principal…he would be having the answers, and I am sure…happy answers.' While talking, Trilok put a hand on Satendra's shoulder and guided him to the principal's office.

A few parents and wards were already there, and Satendra could identify that all of them were there to inquire about the Delhi Polytechnic results…making him relieved for not being the only one in the crowd.

As they entered, the principal was addressing the problem—the list had just arrived from the Polytechnic. There were just three students who had qualified from the school. He picked up the cyclostyled sheet and commenced reading out the names. It was in alphabetical order, and Satendra...was very much included! When he heard his name being announced by the principal, both he and Trilok choked with happy tears. This was the first step for Satendra to realise his dreams of being a government officer... travelling first class on a train...and having respect and power in his village and in society. He would lift his family and village up on the scale of recognition.

Most of the parents left disappointed, except for Satendra and another one of his classmates, who was accompanied by his father. Both were asked to report to the Delhi Polytechnic for the admission procedure as well as the fee payments.

Trilok got out of the stupor of happiness and pride for Satendra and inquired about any news the principal had regarding the scholarships that the students had applied for, including Satendra. The principal communicated that no one from the school had been awarded any government scholarships. However, there were certain private scholarships that had been awarded to some lucky students seeking admission to the Polytechnic, and that information would only be available there.

***

Satendra was lost in dreams of a classroom at the Delhi Polytechnic...being lectured to by learned professors...learning the practical and technical aspects of physics...doing complicated calculations...and....

Trilok was thinking and musing hard on how to collect the admission and tuition fees required to get Satendra into the fabled portals of the Polytechnic. Although the fee was quite subsidised, yet taking hard cash out of their life's systems was still very difficult.

Payment in kind was how their family carried on in these early days of a young country. Loans from local money lenders were the other alternative...although a tough one...accompanied by a high-interest rate, pushing borrowers to penury and bankruptcy. Trilok would finally have to depend on Kadam and his friends (Bisht and the Negis) to lend the amount required.

Both, lost in their own worlds, reached the gate of the institution, with the carriage jolting to a halt. They hopped down and walked in without any one of them conversing...still lost... sleepwalking...till they reached the corridor, where there was a crowd around a few frames...notice boards...with lists of names within.

Satendra was distinctly there in the list of admissions, and then...one of the frames had two lists...government scholarships...and private scholarships. There, in the private scholarship list, the first among seven entries was Satendra's...! However, the name of the person, trust or organization giving the scholarship was not mentioned.

***

India, immediately after independence, was a country struggling to walk, and then run. It was the nation's call to its affluent citizens to help educate the not-so-fortunate yet intelligent students to study further and increase the intellect of the country to establish itself in the world. The collectors of districts were given the onerous task of identifying such sources of funds within their respective jurisdictions.

Narendra was always inclined towards aiding young students in becoming educated gentry of the nation, having a keen interest towards Garhwal. He had already funded quite a few Garhwali students to pursue higher education in Delhi as well as Calcutta. He had created a trust with specific selection instructions for scholarships to pursue degrees in science, mathematics, engineering, and medicine as a priority over other pursuits. Virendra and Ajit were nominated as principal trustees, along with Sultan and Ishaq...this was finalized during Narendra's lifetime as per his desire.

Since its inception, the trust had grown considerably through family and friends' charity...and had become an accelerated pursuit immediately after India gained independence. The young Nation required many more families and individuals to fulfil the dream of a majorly skilled and educated India, which was also Pandit Nehru's focus.

One of the scholarships for that year from Narendra's trust was awarded to Satendra Rawat, to pursue his engineering diploma at the famed Delhi Polytechnic...being one of the brightest students from Garhwal, having topped his school in Higher Secondary.

So, it was Narendra again as the person behind the young Rawat's future...although Satendra or his entire family did not have a clue as to who the angel really was, at least for quite some time. It was in 1950 that India became a Republic, and Satendra entered his class at Delhi Polytechnic for the first time...still confused and thinking as to who his benefactor was.

Trilok, who now was championing the cause of his fellow Garhwalis in Delhi, was continuing to look around for the person who was and would be responsible for turning his youngest sibling into an engineer from such a coveted institution...must be a fellow Garhwali was his thought.

CHAPTER 28

A New Generation

The car carrying Subendu, Virendra, and Ajit stopped at the gate of Chand-Bagh Estate in Dehradun, which harboured the Doon School. Virendra handed over the entry ticket for the new student at the gate and was immediately ushered inside to the freshmen induction room, not far away. Subendu was in awe, and apprehensive of what came next.

The campus had a beautiful spread—verdant lawns, playing fields, pebbled pathways, ivy-covered main building block, hostel Blocks, teachers' quarters, some abstract sculptures, science laboratories...and it went on. The campus was dotted with students going about their routines of the day, and teachers and staff rushing around. It was rather tough to get a place at this elite institution, and Subendu had been lucky to have both the pedigree and the pluck to succeed.

There was another student from his native town, Meerut, who was also there with his father, a prince of a small fiefdom nearby. They got talking, since the families knew each other, being patients of Narendra and then Ajit. In times to come, the two of them would be the best of friends and be connected throughout.

Soon, Subendu met other students in his batch and got connected. Virendra and Ajit looked at each other, with a satisfied smile on their faces. Slowly yet steadily, Subendu started to enjoy the ecosystem of the school, his friends in his boarding house and his class, the activities that kept him busy throughout the day, and his sleep when he hit the bed at the end of the day.

On his way back home for his first term break, he jostled into another boy at the railway station, from another school…Colonel Browns.

'Hey, I am Ashok Khanna from Colonel Browns,' is how the conversation started, with Ashok taking the lead.

'Hello, I am Subendu from the Doon School and heading to Meerut,' responded Subendu.

'Wow, even I am heading to Meerut. My parents are there, my father has a sports goods factory,' commenced Ashok. 'We can catch up once we are in Meerut.'

'Well, I have a reasonably large family in Meerut, and I was born there,' said Subendu.

'Oh! I was born in Sialkot, now in Pakistan…my parents and our entire family shifted from there during the Partition and settled in Meerut in the same line of business as before,' responded Ashok.

Ashok was the first to depart from the overbridge, his platform was downstairs to the right. They greeted each other and went their own ways. Subendu soon joined his crowd of schoolmates, animated and excited to get back home with a lot of stories to share, ready to be pampered by his sister and the rest of the family.

***

Ajit and young Subendu's estate lawyer were waiting at the Meerut Railway Station for his school special to arrive while sipping some hot and sweet tea, so typical of a railway platform in this part of the country. They had also hired a coolie.

The school train chugged into the designated station platform, and soon there was noise all around...school students storming out...some to just buy something from vendors...and a few to get absorbed in the city where they lived.

Subendu was one of those who got out of his coach, looking out for Ajit and waving out to his friends who were traveling further to Delhi...or further ahead.

Ajit could track Subendu in the crowd and waved at him. Subendu waved back and moved towards him. Soon they jostled their way out into the car park and were on their way to Subendu's house, where his sister, aunt and the rest waited.

***

At the main front door of the Bandhopadhyay residence stood Subendu's two elder sisters, Purobee and Surobee, along with their maternal aunt, Sharmila, eagerly waiting for their VIP of the day, who walked pompously in, followed by Ajit and the estate lawyer. Surobee took the lead and embraced Subendu tightly. Both had tears in their eyes. They just couldn't do without each other, they were inseparable. They all walked inside to the main veranda facing the garden and the courtyard beyond.

Other relatives and the staff were waiting anxiously for their loved 'Khoka Babu' to come back from his residential school on his first break. All of them came and hugged him one by one. There was a spread of the most delectable snacks and sherbets laid on the coffee table...Subendu cut loose and charged...it was a war involving his stomach, mouth, food and a 'post-boarding disorder'.

'Khokon (Subendu's pet name), our estate lawyer and I will be waiting for you in the study once you are done with the snack pampering by your sisters,' said a grinning Ajit before he left the happy family for their love time together.

***

Ajit and the estate lawyer, Dinesh, were waiting for Subendu in the study, sipping a chilled glass of sweet lime water, when Subendu entered the room, after a discrete knock on the semi-open door.

'Dada, please make Subendu aware of the responsibilities we are going to take up on his behalf, and till when...and do make it simple so that his young mind can understand the gist,' said Ajit, looking at both Dinesh and Subendu.

Dinesh turned towards Subendhu and started to explain, 'Khokon, your father and your uncle have left you substantial assets to manage, which at your tender age, will not be possible. Hence, he chose Professor Virendra as your legal guardian and Dr Ajit to support him and you in making decisions that are favourable to you. I would give my approval to those decisions from a legal angle, and also see to it that all the compliances are completed in time. All documents on which you would need to sign would be signed by Professor Virendra on your behalf.

'Further, there are certain charitable trusts that were set up by your father, which are supposed to progress according to his will. Virendra, Ajit, and I are taking care of it as of now. We will continue to give you a summary of all that is going on from here onwards. Also, you would continue to receive pocket money, over and above your school and boarding fees. This is it for now.'

'Can I ask some questions, Dinesh da and Ajit da, to have a better understanding?' responded Subendu. 'The questions are regarding the charitable trusts...who are the beneficiaries...and how will the charity go ahead in future?'

He knew that he could only trust his sister Surobee, Ajit da, and Virendra uncle...and that his school was his only solace on which his persona would depend going into the future.

He also knew that Dinesh was the only person with some knowledge of the law, appointed by his father, and that he would have to depend on him, whether he did really trust him or not.

The wisdom that Subendu was acquiring in the process made him more interested in the charitable trusts…he wanted to know whether they had been handled well so far and what the trustees wanted to do going into the future.

He used to listen to conversations between his father, Uncle Virendra and Ajit da on these issues and between a larger circle of his father's friends, Sultan and Ishaq included…and gained a big interest in the concept of helping build up a robust society in the new India. It was developing into a passion and obsession in the young mind. He knew within himself that he would play a very strong role in building people around him into a strong, successful and happy lot.

Ajit took the lead in answering Subendu's query on the charitable trusts managed by the Bandhopadhyay family.

The family had its fingers in three charities. One was taking care of the refugee families that were settling down in the city and its vicinities. The second was providing higher education scholarships to students intending to pursue law, medicine, and engineering, in and around the northern part of free India. The third was to provide medical attention to the needy, in and around Meerut. The trusts were fairly cash-rich, with a major portion of the money being donated by Subendu's family and regular contributions coming from other friends and relatives of the family. The beneficiaries were selected in accordance with certain rules that were framed and agreed upon by the trustees and were well-kept secrets, known only to the managing trustees—Virendra, Ajit, and Dinesh. Quite a few beneficiaries were residing within Delhi and Meerut.

The knowledge of his family's activities satisfied Subendu's inquisitive mind. However, he wanted to know of the beneficiaries at a personal level…at some point.

The four of them wrapped up the session, and Subendu ran out of the room to his sister, excited to learn that there would be a party very soon before his school break ended, the occasion being his first homecoming from the boarding school. It was likely to be quite a big gathering with all the who's who of the city and nearby having been invited….

CHAPTER 29

Sialkot Redux

Mulk was sitting in the study of the Bandhopadhyay residence's guest wing, pouring into the form given to him at the Collectorate, and the official documents that were in his possession substantiating his ownership of business, land, and residence in Sialkot. Thanks to tips given to him by Aftab while preparing him for his fateful journey into the newly independent India, Mulk was carrying all his critical ownership documents and identifications that would clearly substantiate his existence and net worth back in Sialkot.

However, he got stuck at one of the sections in the form, which referred to a guaranty bond or an equivalent amount of bank deposit that would be released on the completion of his project. It meant that he would have to block a substantial amount of his scarce capital for more than a year or two to get the project rolling...and in case he did that, where would he arrange the capital to build up and kickstart his factory?

Could he contact Aftab...he had a substantial amount of his money in custody? Or could he take a loan from Adhiraj chachaji...or Dr Pratap...?

He filled up the rest of the form and attached all the necessary documents to substantiate whatever he had claimed. He then revised every bit of what he had declared, packing up in the early hours of dawn, satisfied with what he had achieved.

He went into the bedroom to catch his sleep for a few hours of what remained of the night. The next day would be another day…another long and trying day….

***

In the morning, while sipping a hot cup of tea along with Jaya, Mulk was musing aloud on the progress and roadblocks on their resettlement project in Meerut.

'I have completed the project form for land allocation and support, to be submitted to the Meerut district authorities. I intend to do it today after consulting Sultan sahib and Dr Ajit. However, the major hurdle seems to be the bank guaranty or deposit to be furnished, which would be released once the project is complete. I do not have that much capital to spare.'

'Oh! You can always ask Dr Arora or Adhiraj chacha ji for the time being and then replace it with your money when you get it from Aftab. Also, Jai should be able to help, he must have some tucked away for the rainy day. I can ask Kiran if you so desire?" responded Jaya.

'I was also musing on the same lines, but let us see what help we really get,' replied Mulk. Mulk got up to get dressed and to call up Pratap and Adhiraj from Dr Ajit's clinic.

***

Mulk walked out of Dr Ajit's clinic clutching hold of the project form in a file. Ajit was on a patient visit, and his compounder took Mulk to the inner study to make his calls in private.

Both Pratap and Adhiraj were sympathetic, yet very noncommittal…money supply was not all that great, and the future quite uncertain…was the standard response from both. However, both had promised to explore the extent and the nature of support they could possibly extend. In short, it was a 'no'.

What Mulk realised was that help was a very shy commodity. It had its limitations, and when one passes through a tempest, one encounters only broken shacks.

He told Jaya about it. She had also drawn a courteous blank from her sister, Dr Pratap Arora's wife. She confided their predicament to Surobee, with whom she was in continuous touch. Surobee heard Jaya out and took her to Ajit, who was in his clinic.

Ajit reassured Jaya.

'Jaya di, be rest assured, we have already spoken to the Collector, as well as the Commissioner, and I am sure they will find out a way. The authorities know that the Bandhopadhyay family is interested in this case, and we have not made a personal reference for any other person coming in from Pakistan, east or west. So please remain stress-free and let the process take its own course.'

With this Ajit rang the bell for the next patient to walk in. After all, he was a busy doctor in the city, with virtually a crowd jostling outside his clinic.

Jaya walked back to the guest wing with a queer feeling of being left alone in that very new city. She felt that they had already overstayed the Bandhopadhyay hospitality, and this big and busy family had a lot more to look upon.

What she had not been able to observe was that Dr Ajit Chatterjee was a man of few words, reserved, and at times quite reticent. He was not a person to openly express elation or excitement, and that too during clinic hours.

Both Jaya and Mulk decided to follow the process and see where it took them. They had fallen to the ground and seen a lot…it couldn't get worse. They also decided to rent a room and stay there for whatever time necessary. They had already stayed with this gracious family for quite a few days.

Mulk left the house for Sultan Singh's place from where he had to go to the Collectorate to submit his file with whatever he could manage to complete. If he could not submit a bank guarantee or arrange for the deposit at this time, so be it. He could not do more than that…so it was better to be truthful and upfront rather than elusive.

Sultan was waiting for Mulk in his drawing room with dry fruits and snacks laid out on a largish coffee table. He was reading the local vernacular when Mulk walked in, guided by a bearer. It was the first time Mulk had visited Sultan's house since they had always been meeting at the Bandhopadhyay mansion.

Mulk was embraced by Sultan as a gesture of welcome, and both of them parked themselves on leather sofas around the coffee table.

'What is the urgency that has brought you here, Mulk bhai? I was thinking of inviting Jaya bhabhi and you to our house for a home-cooked vegetarian meal along with our other friends. Anyhow that will still happen, soon, maybe over the coming weekend,' said Mulk, offering him some dry fruits.

'Sultan bhai, I am in a bit of a problem regarding my allotment application and the project,' replied Mulk.

'What is it, Mulk bhai? I will do what best I can, I assure you,' responded Sultan.

'The allotment application requires a bank guaranty or else an equivalent deposit for the tenure of the project completion. Now where do I or anyone in my position arrange for that? The partition and its immediate impact on all of us has left us hand to mouth. We had to literally run away overnight, leaving substantial portions of our belongings where they were.

'Those of us who had the vision were able to dispose of our properties but at heavily discounted prices, leaving us with a meagre sustenance. I have to start from scratch and do not have enough cash to do so, forget about arranging for a bank guarantee or else a bank deposit,' explained Mulk, almost in one frustrated breath.

Sultan was quiet and observant while Mulk rushed through his angst…and remained silent for some time.

He had answers to Mulk's problems, which would give him peace or even euphoria, but it would be better if he accompanied him to the collectorate and settled the issue once and for all. So Sultan decided to do just that. After tea had been served in exclusive silverware, Sultan offered to accompany Mulk to the collectorate and see what he could possibly do to solve the problem.

***

Sultan and Mulk reached the Collector's office in Sultan's car.

The Collector was in and so was his staff. They went straight to the clerk who had been entrusted to help Mulk out with his request application. Mulk submitted the file to him.

'Have you completed the entire application, along with all the required documents, Mr Khanna?' enquired the clerk.

'Yes sir. However, I have not been able to furnish any bank guaranty or any deposit in lieu since I do not have the necessary capital to do so, and it will not be possible to arrange the same at such short notice,' responded Mulk.

The clerk looked at Sultan, bearing an uncertain expression, and replied that he would have to consult the Collector and get back to them. He requested Sultan to follow him inside into the Collector's room.

Mulk spent what seemed to him an interminable period of time waiting for the clerk and Sultan to emerge from the room. In the meantime, he browsed through the local vernacular lying on the clerk's table for news of the city and its surroundings.

A lot of traders and businessmen were still trickling in from Pakistan, with a scarred past, leading to their transborder migration. A lot of them were still living out of refugee camps, in dirt, filth and grime…not yet breaking through to the starting point of a new life—doing manual labour in local factories and construction sites.

The clerk was standing beside Mulk and gazing at him and the newspaper that he was holding, yet not really reading.

'Mulk sahib, the Collector has called you inside…Sultan sahib is there with him,' the clerk addressed him.

'Everything all right?' Mulk asked him.

The clerk smiled and guided him in for Mulk to gather the rest himself. It was a make-or-break moment for Mulk. In case nothing could progress without the bank guaranty or deposit, he would have to press Adhiraj for momentary relief and somehow get in touch with Aftab for his own capital, which was in his safekeeping. Or else he would have to wait for his younger brother to arrive at Meerut to request him to try and get back to Sialkot and have his remaining money and certain other moveable assets hand-delivered by Aftab through him. However, the journey back and forth would have its inherent risks.

Mulk entered the Collector's office with the clerk behind him. He was gestured by the Collector to take a seat beside Sultan.

The Collector began without any preamble.

'Mulk sahib, we have an unconditional guarantee from Dr Narendra Nath Bandyopadhyay's trust which supports businesses and migrants here in this city and around, supported by their bankers. Hence, you no longer require furnishing any further guaranties. Also, you have been sanctioned a support loan to help you set up your business, on easy payment terms. This loan has also been guaranteed by the Bandhopadhyay Trust. So now just concentrate on setting up your project as soon as possible… commence business and see to it that your repayments are as declared in your loan document…and avoid defaults.'

In one stroke of human providence, all Mulk's woes were washed off. He was dumbfounded and stupefied…Dr Ajit, Sultan and their group of friends must have known all about it and yet were acting as if all this was new to them, not making him feel a wee bit embarrassed or humiliated.

Mulk yet again remembered the dervish's clairvoyant declaration on his future…from here on, everything will go right in your life…he had suffered enough…God had tested enough… and he had a firm feeling of having passed life's hard examination with flying colours.

Sultan came by Mulk's side and caught him in a tight embrace. 'Now, Mulk bhai, you will soon become an integral part of Meerut's growing business community, and we will be seeing more of you and your family.'

Mulk nodded, with tears rolling down…he really did not have much to say…he was overwhelmed.

***

Mulk finally reached the Bandhopadhyay residence guest wing where Jaya was anxiously waiting to hear from him. He had a bagful of delectable sweets and hot jalebis.

Jaya also had a surprise for him…their kids, along with Kiran and her kid, had all travelled to Meerut from Mathura to spend some time together.

It was feasting time with Mulk breaking the news that his project had been accepted, the bank guaranty had been arranged, and a further loan had also been arranged…and that he would get his land allotment within the week.

The entire family went into a huddle, and prayed to the Lord Almighty for all the good turns their lives were taking…all the good people who were connecting with them and helping them to restart their lives.

There was further news as well. Jai, Mulk's younger brother had contacted Kiran at Dr Pratap's residence and informed him that he would be reaching Delhi, from where he would take a bus to either Mathura or Meerut, wherever they all would be. The Khanna's just couldn't believe how incredibly bad times too had passed.

Jaya and Kiran brought in some steaming Punjabi tea, along with the sweets Mulk had got, and they settled down to share happy times together after such a long span of torture...leaving all that behind...and looking ahead to the positive hard-working days ahead.

While sipping their tea, Mulk shared his further plans. First, Jaya and he would go to the main house of the Bandhopadhyays and express their gratitude to them for the support they had extended and how effective it was in pulling them out of the virtual poverty that Mulk and his family had found themselves slipping into. Also, they would soon shift to a rented apartment from where they would monitor the rebuilding of their lives and careers...yet always remain in touch with this great family.

Once Jai got back, they would plan, amongst many other issues, to contact Aftab and get their money and other moveable assets back. This was of utmost importance since Mulk never liked to have loans in his name—their family had never lived like that.

Finally, he got up to freshen himself up and asked Jaya to dress up as well, to go and visit their hosts in the main house.

The children started to play carrom on the board that they had carried with them all the way from Sialkot. It was a gift from Mulk, who looked at them with moist eyes full of glee.

***

Jaya dressed in a dignified saree and Mulk in a Pathan Suit and made their way into the Bandhopadhyay main house.

Since Dr Ajit was already informed about their coming, his wife Surobee and he were waiting on the front veranda in their evening formals. Surobee sported a fresh jasmine flower band around her hair every evening and looked very charming indeed. It was the hallmark of every lady in the family.

The couple got up when Jaya and Mulk arrived. Mulk greeted Ajit with an emotional hug, while Jaya exchanged a *namaskar* with Surobee and her husband. Mulk broke the silence.

'Doctor sahib, your family has transformed our distraught lives by the immense support you people have provided us with. It seems to be a divine chapter, only seen and read in fantasy. It must be a divine intervention, to have had the support of the Bandhopadhyays and their helpful group of friends.

'Doctor sahib, you all have made us feel so much at home that I have not even thought of taking a break and visiting Jaya's sister and brother-in-law at Mathura even once.'

Surobee interrupted and spoke since Ajit would hardly have spoken a few words, if at all...and at the most, given a pat on Mulk's back. That would have been the maximum emotion he was capable of. Purobee caught hold of Jaya's hand and responded emotionally.

'Believe me Jaya, you are more than a sister to me. And whatever you see of us and our family, are the ethics we have in legacy from Baba, my beloved father. Had he been alive, he would have been forced to join politics by none other than Nehru ji and the Congress. They held him in high regard and depended on him heavily. He took it to be his duty to support any good human out of troubled waters, and had he been alive, he would have cared for you more than a younger brother. We are just following his wishes.

'He has been instrumental in creating some trusts to help businesses to develop in and around this city, and also educate the young India to brace up to the world. Mulk bhai sahib and his business is nothing but one of the results of that support. We are thankful to have such good people like you as friends forever, and look forward to a great time together.'

'Didi, since we would now have to stay on permanently in Meerut and build up our business and home, we are also looking out for rented accommodation somewhere around to have some kind of permanency. Doctor sahib can be of some more help to us to identify an appropriate abode.' Jaya looked up to Ajit expectantly.

Ajit finally spoke in a soft tone.

'Mulk bhai and Jaya bhabhi, Surobee has already told you of how much we feel for you, and I need not add very much to it... neither am I quite capable of it. However, I am sure that you should not be in any hurry to move to your accommodation. We are in no dire need of the guest wing as of now, and as you can see, we have quite a bit of spare space in our residential establishment.

'Anyway, I will tell my staff and friends to arrange for an adequate rented abode, which I am sure you would be able to have reasonably soon. Till then the guest wing is for you and your complete family. Please treat it to be your own, till as long.'

With this Ajit asked Babulal to pour them some hot tea and get some sandwiches and muffins to go along.

***

After a good early evening with the Bandhopadhyays, Mulk, and Jaya walked back to the guest wing, satisfied and free of stress.

They were also told that there would be a large party thrown by the Bandhopadhyays in a few weeks to introduce the next young Bandhopadhyay as the next master of the ship, under training. Subendu would be taking over the affairs of the family once he came of age.

The entire Khanna family, along with Dr Pratap Arora and his family would be invited to grace the occasion. They would meet the who's who of the region, and it would be a good occasion for the Khanna's to get acquainted with those they would like to be acquainted with. It would be an ideal occasion to launch themselves at their new home. However, as of now the Khannas had their hands full.

Jai would be arriving in two days; and would come straight to the guest wing of the Bandhopadhyay residence…fresh from England…having left British India a few months back…and arriving in a newly independent and divided India…months later.

The land allotment had to happen within a week, and the project was to commence immediately. Sultan had already acquainted Mulk with a contractor known to him, and Mulk appointed him by giving a token advance—his first investment in his new venture, at a new place, starting all over again.

He also wanted to visit Bareilly, along with Jaya, to meet the Malhotras, who had taken the journey from Kud to Pathankot, with Jaya, Kiran and their children. The two families had come quite close to each other, and Jaya had decided to make Viresh her prospective son-in-law. Kamla, Mulk's daughter, was quite aware of it and silently happy, too.

But right then, Mulk was in a mood to celebrate…and Hansraj, his old retainer already knew what to do.

'Hansraj, *hamara shaam ka saaman le aa yaar*,' called out Mulk. (Hansraj, please get my evening stuff.)

He had already told him to prepare for the evening some tandoori chicken, tikkas and paneer for the whole family, whiskey for him and some juices for the rest. Dinner was being cooked at home. They would all sit together and enjoy themselves as a family, thanking God to be alive and together, plan and dream for the future, sing songs and be merry….

It reminded Mulk of Sialkot when he came back from office or a tour with some success under his belt. They used to have family get-togethers, picnics by the Chenab, or parties with friends. After a long and dark gap of losses and tragedies, he could sense normality and happy days…now that the whole family would be together again…with Jai also back…and with new friends and relatives…a new social circle…a new life, more secure and safe.

He took a vow, holding hands with Jaya, Kiran, and the kids of never thinking of separating, to grow together, and get big together. He also took a silent pledge to add Dr Bandhopadhyay into his Hall of Gods…what a blessing to be under his secure shadow…what a family!

CHAPTER 30

The Invitation

The schedule in the Delhi Polytechnic was tough, and time was always very short. For Satendra, his day began with travelling to his engineering college near Kashmere gate, attending lectures, devouring his lunch tiffin, playing, discussing, and chatting around with his classmates, and pushing off to the library thereafter. He travelled back home after five in the evening.

Saturday evening onwards was party time. Satendra, his brother, and the family went out to the nearby market for weekly shopping, loafing around on the India Gate lawns, enjoying street food, and finishing with some freshly churned ice cream, then getting back home shrieking, laughing out loud…nudging around…continuing to gossip till late at night, before giving in to deep slumber.

Sunday. of course, was drinks day for Trilok. A few of his near friends used to drop in, all of whom were from neighbouring villages in Garhwal. Satendra enjoyed these evenings because of the snacks and nonvegetarian food…and also the importance he got from all on account of being the brightest boy around. It was fun seeing Trilok and his friends getting more and more jolly, with each sip of the Bacchus…finally breaking into Garhwali folk songs…and dancing.

One such evening, a close friend of Trilok and a regular at the Sunday parties, came home a bit earlier than the others. He had something important to discuss and had thought it better to do so before the rest of the gang arrived.

The friend was working in the Controller of Defence Accounts (CDA) office in Meerut, which had quite a few settler Bengalis, having migrated from the unified Bengal of British India. A couple of days prior, during the lunch break, one of his Bengali colleagues asked him offhand, whether he knew of some Satendra Rawat, under the guardianship of one Trilok Rawat from Delhi, since he was also a Garhwali.

'What luck!' Trilok's friend had retorted. Trilok is from near my village in Pauri Garhwal, and my neighbour in Delhi as well. I meet him every Sunday. Satendra is his younger brother, who is studying engineering at the prestigious Delhi Polytechnic. A very bright boy with a promising career ahead.'

The Bengali colleague extended an invitation card after taking it out from his satchel.

'Yes, yes! They are the ones I am talking about. I need to extend them an invitation from the House of Bandhopadhyays, one of the leading families of the city, and also a settler from Bengal…like me. I am also one of their relations to have settled down here, with the family's help. The family is throwing a lavish party to introduce the next scion of the family—Subendu Bandhopadhyay—still a minor, studying in school.'

He asked Trilok's friend that the invitation be handed over to Satendra after neatly writing Satendra and Trilok's names on the envelope.

Trilok took the envelope with curiosity as well as surprise while he went through the content.

'Why have we been invited?' Trilok asked his friend.

It was surely strange since Trilok knew no Bengalis from Meerut; he hardly knew any Bengalis at all.

The party was scheduled to be held in the next month. Satendra was excited, not only because of the invitation but also on account of a journey to another city, which he would be visiting for the first time. Soon Trilok's three other friends also trouped into the outer room of his house. Two of them got their sons along with them. Satendra and the two boys rushed out into the open, to enjoy a boys' evening, followed by their Sunday special eateries. The men sat down with 'Yo ho ho and a bottle of rum'.

***

Trilok, Satendra, his sister-in-law and the kids sat together for an early morning tea the following day before almost everyone disappeared to their respective callings after a hurried breakfast.

Trilok was musing aloud on various reasons as to why were Satendra and he invited to this grand feast by the Bandhopadhyay family in Meerut.

Even Trilok's wife, Vandana could not figure it out. Her guess was that the connection must be due to her father-in-law, who was a larger-than-life size pradhan and a freedom fighter hailing from their village. He must have been known in the political leadership of the northern part of India. But then, why was Satendra the principal invitee, and not Trilok...or Kadam...or else their mother, Vimla...it could not be explained.

What made it more confusing was when the principal of the Delhi Polytechnic happily patted Satendra on his rounds and informed him that he would be getting a day off to prepare to go to Meerut for the Bandhopadhyay feast. He further told him that it was prestigious for the institution and that he would also be there. It was beyond the Rawats, only time would explain everything.

Then came another surprise. Trilok was called by his boss in the main house to express his happiness and pride on Satendra being invited by the Bandhopadhyay family. It seemed that Trilok's boss knew more than what he was ready to disclose. He only said that Satendra was shaping up well, and if he continued to be as focused as currently was, he had a bright future ahead.

After returning from the main house, Trilok embraced Satendra, with joy in his eyes.

'You are surely doing us proud, dear brother…continue to do well…you are not only our family's hope but the whole villages' as well…. The invitation seems to be because of your outstanding performance as a student at your college.'

That day, the Rawat family in Delhi went out to have ice cream at India Gate and let their hopes run riot….

CHAPTER 31

A New Scion

The Bandhopadhyay household was in a state of frenzy and at the peak of excitement—the family members, relations, resident guests and the entire staff.

How the times had changed. Narendra and Debendra used to love hosting parties and organising them. Narendra had always been a man of details and managed each aspect of the party, right from the menu to the guest list, and the welcoming of every guest. The larger the gathering, the more exciting it used to be for him.

The current majordomo was Surobee, who was more than ably assisted by her husband, Ajit…in whatever time he could snatch out of his busy medical practice. All were working as a team, along with chirpy and happy Sharmila.

Dinesh was drawing out the guest list, supported and approved by Ajit and Surobee. It was the most tedious part of the party since the family had deep roots in many gardens…ranging from Narendra's close group of friends, political associates, business circles, and bureaucrats of the young country, including its capital,

Bihar, and their very own Bengal. The family were investors in many businesses and corporate houses, especially the Boxwallah-led companies from England and parts of Europe. Hence their senior executives would also be invited, well in time, to organize their travel plans.

Then there was that ever-growing family associated with the Bandhopadhyay trusts, which were so important to the family's objectives. It was the first occasion when Subendu would be introduced to their world at large and give all known a sense of comfort that the family's affairs were in safe hands, and they would continue to go on as before...even better.

Surobee was sitting along with Purobee and Sharmila, sipping a deserved cup of steaming hot tea, when Dinesh came in, walking up to the front veranda from the back entrance. He had a file in hand—the guest list. It had exceeded 500, which Surobee and Virendra were taking to be a budgetary benchmark. The Bandhopadhyay family's huge following made limiting numbers a sticky business and a maddening exercise. Surobee vaguely remembered Subendu's birth party, where certain families were lobbying for their inclusion in the invitee list...going crazy as if their existence depended on that simple invitation.

More than a hundred invitees were coming from far distances and would have to stay for a couple of nights in the city. It was a big order to arrange accommodation for them. The family's own residential space available was stretched, especially with the full strength of relatives who had already arrived. The Khanna family had vacated the guest wing and moved on, though, left to Ajit, he would have convinced them to stay on and on.

Sharmila's husband and Ajit were knocking on all doors, helped by Virendra's connects, Nawab Sahib and Sultan, to get hold of good accommodation, guest houses, messes, and inspection bungalows.... They also had to arrange for the Army Band, which meant talking to the new officers replacing the Royal British Indian Army and also inviting all the senior officers posted in the cantonment at that moment in time.

Amarendra, Sharmila's husband, was given the charge of creating the menu list and getting it approved by Virendra and Surobee. He and Purobee were to finalize the cooks who would be contracted to prepare the various cuisines on the menu, to be overseen by Bahadur and Nanu, the two main chefs of the Bandhopadhyay household. The complexities of organizing this gala dinner went on....

CHAPTER 32

Opportunity Beckons

The day of the 'mother of all parties' was nearing. Trilok had ordered his tailor to stitch a shirt, trousers and blazer for himself, while Satendra would be getting freshly stitched shirt and trousers and would top it with a sweater, being knitted by his sister-in-law.

There was excitement in the household. Kadam had also travelled all the way from the village to oversee the preparations. When in Delhi, Kadam met a few of his political contacts to find out about this party and his family members being invited there. His political contacts felt that they were too low in the political pecking order to know of the party and its whereabouts. They didn't even know of this family that Kadam was talking about. The closest information was with Trilok's boss and Satendra's college principal, both of whom were also going for this soiree. Trilok and Satendra had been offered a to-and-fro ride by Trilok's boss, which the Rawats had gladly accepted.

Satendra was living and reliving the party again and again, with his books open in front of him…imagining his interactions with important people...shaking hands...having a cold drink...being offered special snacks by liveried waiters...senior and successful people talking to him and interested to know of his educational achievements...maybe getting photographed for some newspaper or magazine...and the recognition he was and would be getting further in his college. He felt that this invitation was a gateway, an opportunity to climb stairs in his career path and life, to be known in this vast world outside his village, to have his own office room, assistants, peons...so that when he went to visit his village, he would be looked upon as a piece of history in making, whose lore would do rounds in generations to come.

His ego was growing...from a scale of non-existent simplicity to a sense of arrival—a process of successful growing up. Satendra was counting the days till it was virtually upon him.

***

The Khannas were so immersed in setting themselves up—the land allotment formalities, shifting to a new rented house, commencing the factory construction, and supervising order completion at the rented shed in Agra.

The Khannas had been allotted land at Victoria Park, their first preference, which was very fortunate on account of the administration's sympathy due to the influential friends they had connected with...destiny was the name.

Dr Ajit had managed to get him a fairly good, rented accommodation that belonged to one of his patients. No questions were asked...and no advance demanded. Even the rent was what Mulk could afford at that time.

Construction at Victoria Park had started almost immediately, thanks to some money which Mulk and his family could manage to safely wiggle out in the process of the grave and dangerous migration, topped with the resettlement grant and loan extended by the administration.

Jai, Mulk's younger brother, had the responsibility to connect with Aftab in Sialkot. One morning, there was a familiar voice on the other end of the trunk call, at the post office near to where the Khannas had made their first abode. Jai and Mulk were both there, and Jai immediately extended the receiver to Mulk.

'Hello…hello…Aftab…hello…Aftab!' Mulk was virtually shouting at the top of his broken and choking voice. It was quiet at the other end…some sniffs…muffled sobbing…and then distinct crying. Aftab was sobbing like a baby…and so was Mulk, while Jai watched.

'Mulk *birader…naheen rah pa raha twade bina…naheen rah pa raha,'* mumbled Aftab and kept on sobbing. (Can't stay without you…just can't.)

It carried on for some time before they realized that they had urgent work at hand and that the call had a time limitation and would get disconnected at any moment. Mulk managed to communicate and inquire about the status of the money and sale proceeds that he had left behind in a hurry. He was both apprehensive and grateful to Aftab for what he had already done for him. He also did not know in what state Aftab, his family and his business were at that point in time.

There was a pregnant silence for quite some time before Aftab managed to speak in between his emotional outbursts.

'Twadi amaanat mere naal hai, Mulk bhai…bahut samhaal ke rakhi hai….' (Your property is safe with me).

They decided to meet at Gurdaspur, where Aftab would transfer Mulk's assets to him, and meet him in the process. Mulk did not have the courage to ask Aftab about the amount and value that he would be getting from Aftab. It would have been a major insult to their relationship and faith.

The majority of his business friends and acquaintances had lost everything they had left behind, snatched by the waiting vultures there…and here, Aftab had kept Mulk's belongings safe, willing to risk coming up to Gurdaspur, to hand it over to him...whatever be the value...God was with him.

The dervish at the Amritsar refugee camp continued to be so right...he wished he could see him again...to embrace him and take his blessings.

Mulk and Jai walked back home, emotionally sapped, and grateful for God's mercy. They then narrated the whole conversation to their family. All were dumbfounded...and stayed quiet for some time...in silent prayer.

While sitting and sipping some well-deserved tea, Mulk was gazing at the Hindi calendar gifted by the Sultan when he suddenly jumped up. The Bandhopadhyays' party was nearing rapidly. The whole family had to organize themselves...clothes, gifts....

He looked at Jai—they needed to decide on so many issues ever since they had understood the importance of the event to which they had been invited in the city. The attendees would all be from the important circle of the region...with guests coming from far and beyond. Ashok would also be there in his term break from his school in Dehradun, which would make them a full family together.

CHAPTER 33

The Party

There were no holds barred for the Bandhopadhyay Party. The cooks had been contracted from Lucknow, Delhi, Calcutta, and locally—each was a specialist in their own niche. The menu was divided into vegetarian and non-vegetarian sections and then further subdivided into Awadhi, English, Italian, North Indian, and, of course, Bengali…how could a Bengali host not include the best of their cuisine from their land?

A few days before the party, the raw materials and other ingredients had started arriving and had been methodically stored according to their categories. The various meats and fish arrived a day prior in large ice containers. Bahadur and Nanu had their hands full.

Everyone else was rushing around for the least important to the most important errands, and the atmosphere was electric with excitement. Amid all this, Subendu was busy building structures out of the exhaustive Meccano set gifted to him by Ajit and Surobee. His concern for the party was limited to the excitement of being the prime object of this exciting confusion and making new friends of his age.

On the day of the party, Amarendra was to dress Subendu up in a starched dhoti panjabi (a thoroughly Bengali bhadralok dress) with a black jodhpuri coat, protecting him up from the wintery chill of the city.

Between dressing up and the soiree, a family photo session was scheduled with the famous Mathur Photo Studio. Mr Mathur was already there on the front veranda with his complete paraphernalia and two assistants. The photographer would remain till the end of the party and also assist the gentry from the press who were expected to be there, keeping in mind the nature of the get-together and the spectrum of gentry that were attending.

Quite a few of the Bandhopadhyay household who had arrived from Bengal could be seen dressing up—some trying to fit into English clothing, a suit with a tie or a bow, which seemed to get along with them as good as an ascetic in a tuxedo.

Ajit was as stereotypically dressed as he always was, though very dapper—tweed and woollen trousers, with a silk tie over a pin-striped shirt.

Purobee, Surobee, and Sharmila decided on elegant Indian silk sarees, bought especially with this occasion in mind. They were to finally wear the Bandhopadhyay women's signature—fragrant jasmine around their hair. The best jewellery was spread out for the three important women of the family to choose from.

The party was the first after a long period of turmoil and tribulations within the family and around the country. It was a statement from the Bandhopadhyays and their clan—a statement of relevance, trust, and power they still held in the society, a statement of what a migrant from British Bengal could achieve and consolidate in a new geography.

***

It was already half past seven in the evening, and the party was all set to roll at eight. The main gate was elegantly decorated with panels of assorted flowers…marigold, roses, and rajanigandha with lights focusing on them. The gate was manned by two ethnically dressed men who were to sprinkle rose water on all the guests coming in. The air resonated with lilting Indian classical melodies of the Shehnai recital by a maestro and his team, specifically called from Varanasi. They were setting up their instruments and warming up for the long and important evening ahead. The complete evening would be accompanied by an assortment of Indian and Western music with complementing acoustics.

The Army Band had arrived from the Cantonment well in time, courtesy of the Punjab Regimental Centre, and they were setting themselves up at the corner of the front garden, which had been allotted to them. They would begin at eight with independent India's national anthem. A dance floor had also been created adjacent to the band.

The caterers contracted from Delhi's Connaught Place were more British than Indian…a relic of the Raj, in their elegant white and gold livery and braided caps. They were setting up tables, cutlery and the works, both for sit-down as well as buffet meals.

From behind the main bungalow, in a canopied open field, different kinds of aromatic smoke were drifting with the wind, giving an exotic hue to the party venue, with live barbeque, snack counters, and the bar in the main soiree area.

The parking had been organized in two blocks. The chauffeur-driven vehicles of the elite gentry had a special invite to drop the living luggage at the entry of the soiree and then drive straight into an inner parking area, right behind the residential quarters, near the cooking canopy. The others needed to park their vehicles by the roadside, for which special permission had been procured from the local administration, the senior officials of which were all invitees.

***

A group of bureaucrats from Delhi were one of the first guests to arrive in different cars. The Rawats, Trilok, and Satendra were in one of the cars, travelling with Trilok's boss and his wife.

All of them got off at the entrance, while the driver, having the inside parking ticket, left to park, guided by the parking assistant. Ajit and Virendra, along with Amarendra, comprised the reception team, who greeted the guests while rose water was sprinkled on them as a sign of welcome.

Virendra spotted Satendra, while Ajit engaged with the accompanying bureaucrats. Trilok was the proud escort to his young brother.

Satendra was overawed as he was embraced by Virendra, who happened to not only know his name, but also his achievements and scholastic records. The photographer was at hand and clicked a group photograph with Trilok and Ajit, along with Satendra and Virendra. Virendra then patted Satendra's back again, guided him to Surobee and made the introductions.

'Surobee, this is young Satendra, one of the beneficiaries of our education trust…he is a real success who was so correctly chosen by our team and has been topping his class in electrical engineering at the famous Delhi Polytechnic. I would like Subendu to meet him as well…let me go and call him while you talk to this young lad here.'

Saying that, Virendra went off to call Subendu, while Surobee held Satendra tenderly, conversing with him in Hindi, then switching to English. Trilok stood close to his brother, answering some of the questions asked by Surobee, regarding their origin and their ancestral village.

Through Surobee, they came to know that Satendra's scholarship was awarded by their family education trust, started by her father, Dr Narendra Nath Bandhopadhyay and that his selection was based not only on the recommendation made by his school and that of a senior bureaucrat—Trilok's boss—but also on his belonging to a proud and well-known freedom fighter's family. It made both Trilok and Satendra feel proud indeed.

While they were conversing, Virendra came back with the young dhoti-clad bhadralok, Subendu, holding him lightly by his shoulders.

'Here, Subendu, you must meet young Satendra, a brilliant scholar from Delhi Polytechnic and one of our higher education scholarship awardees. We are so proud to have him and his elder Brother with us.'

Both Subendu and Satendra shook hands and got photographed again, this time by a press photographer. Subendu took Satendra along with him, while Trilok remained with his boss, sipping a bowl of soup and taking rounds.

It was a singular experience for Satendra. He had not experienced a matching glamour, decoration and such an elite circle of guests ever in his life...never had he experienced the luxury of freely flowing exquisite snacks, drinks, and what not in abundance, being served by smartly dressed waiters.

The Khannas also arrived along with Dr Pratap Arora and were guided in by Ajit. Mulk was introduced, amongst others, to Trilok as well, while Ashok, Mulk's elder son, could spot Subendu looking around and walked up to him.

'Hey Subendu, what are you doing here in that fancy dress... dhoti and all!'

'Hey Ashok...hope I am right with your name...the guy from Colonel Browns?!' waved Subendu. 'And this is no fancy dress...it is a Bengali attire, and I am a Bengali...remember, my full name is Subendu Bandhopadhyay.'

Ashok scratched his chin.

'Oh yes..., you are the bong guy I met from The Doon School at the railway station...great catching up with you again! But...

is this by any chance...I mean, the hosts of this party, are they related to you in any way?'

'Of course, mate...this party is hosted in my honour...at least that is what has been communicated to me by my elder sister and brother-in-law,' responded Subendu, a tad animatedly.

'And yes...come and meet another of my friends, Satendra Rawat, from the famous Delhi Polytechnic...he is pursuing electrical engineering there...an intelligent guy, having already achieved so much.'

Ashok introduced himself to Satendra.

'Hello Satendra, by now you would be knowing my name at least...I belong to a business family dealing with the manufacture of cricket goods and gear. Although I am in school in Dehradun, our family belonged to Sialkot, now in Pakistan...we had to run away from there during the partition a few years back. However, thanks to, as I now realise, Subendu's family, we have managed to resettle ourselves here in Meerut. Satendra, you would enjoy this family's company and feel great to associate with them. By the way, how do you know Subendu...since you are in Delhi...?"

Satendra felt blessed to be picked up by this great family without any efforts by him or any of his family members...pure divine destiny...nothing more.

While consumed in his thoughts, he suddenly noticed that Ashok was still looking forward to an answer while Subendu was dragged away by one of his relatives to be introduced to other guests.

'Well...it was like this...this family has an education trust, and I was selected for an engineering scholarship by them...so the reason for my being able to pursue my course at such a prestigious institution without any financial pressures on my family is this great family...as has been in your father's case.'

Ashok was amazed. The Bandhopadhyays, Khannas, and the Rawats...all were settlers in their own way.

The Bandhopadhyays had ventured out from Bengal a long time ago to seek greener pastures and had worked their way up to where they presently were…in a position to support an ecosystem in their adopted region.

The Rawats, and many like them, were venturing out from Garhwal in search of jobs and money to support their families and villages.

The Khannas, and so many from their displaced society, were virtually threatened out of their businesses, homes, and comfort to drift into the uncertainty of a new country…a place foreign to them, having to start from scratch with no support but of the divine.

And the divine, both for the Khannas and Rawats were the Bandhopadhyays…and, thus, was formed the great club of settlers who would continue to support each other to grow themselves… and grow the new nation to a status of respect and affluence.

While Ashok was lost in his thoughts, with the equally lost Satendra, the Band started playing the national anthem. Everyone stood at attention to the rendition of Tagore…another great Indian.

***

The party was in full swing, and so was the bar…and the music and dancing—elegant waltzing and, at times, rock and roll. Trilok, Mulk, and Jai seemed to have hit it off well. They could be seen guzzling down whiskey and gorging on the barbeque as they laughed and talked in good cheer.

At about nine, dinner was announced, and soon the Band was replaced by Shehnai music. Ashok and Satendra were joined by Subendu, who managed to slip out to enjoy some time with his new friends, and discretely share some hidden sips of port which Ashok had smuggled from one of the waiters.

They decided to have a group photograph and keep a copy each for the sake of remembrance as they walked into the future with heady dreams and aspirations...Subendu took up the responsibility of posting a copy to Satendra and hand delivering another to Ashok—a snap that had a long backstory of three journeys and three families...climaxing at this time and space.

The three friends from the three families sat talking into the night, gazing back at how their families had moved from where they once were to where they would be...the good and bad days that they had seen and their dream of living in a more egalitarian, equal and enjoyable country...their India...their Bharat.

Acknowledgement

I inherited my passion for writing from my revered father, whom I used to watch sitting in the garden, basking in the sun, and penning down his stories and travelogues on his notepad, focusing through his half-moons. Or I would hear the 'tip-tap' of his 'Brother Typewriter' incessantly from his study, punctuated only by the space lever taking him back to the starting point of the following line. I used to admire the intense peace and serenity of this activity, which attracted me to reading and writing as well. Even today, he continues to bless me from within.

I started writing articles and essays, and then, one day, the first pages of this book quite late in my life. My mother, wife, and children instilled in me the confidence that I would bring out a winner. However, winner or not, I began enjoying my journey of writing this book right from the beginning.

A young journalist friend of my father, MV Rao, disciplined, goaded, and pushed me to write continuously, especially in my weak moments when interest diminished. He would rebuke me for not completing my daily writing targets when he met me over the weekends when I had the luxury of coming back home.

I continued to write, page after page, covering the years starting from 1935, and the manuscript grew voluminous. My closest friend in life, Puneet Anand, asked me a simple question, 'When are you going to put an end to it? And who is going to read such a thick book from an unknown debutant author?'

To this friend, I owe the book's completion.

As I pen my first acknowledgement, I must not forget the two individuals who took me to the proverbial pond to taste the waters of a published book—Shiv Kunal Verma, a celebrated author, and Pankaj P Singh, a successful publisher and passionate reader. They made me believe in myself and my writing capabilities. Pankaj believed in my book and laboured with vigour and passion to make it see the light of day.

And then…how can I forget the three families whose lives inspired me to weave a narrative around them? These families proved my thinking that history is an aggregate of lives in a geography.

For the privacy of the families concerned, I have decided to keep their identities confidential.

Finally, thanks to all my friends who have had the patience to hear out parts of the manuscript in its formative stages and rendered positive advice and suggestions to make the content more engaging.